A White Coat Is
MY CLOSET

JAKE WELLS

Dreamspinner Press

Published by
Dreamspinner Press
5032 Capital Circle SW
Suite 2, PMB# 279
Tallahassee, FL 32305-7886
USA
http://www.dreamspinnerpress.com/

This is a work of fiction. Names, characters, places, and incidents either are the product of author imagination or are used fictitiously, and any resemblance to actual persons, living or dead, business establishments, events, or locales is entirely coincidental.

A White Coat Is My Closet
© 2013 Jake Wells.

Cover Art
© 2013 Leah Kaye Suttle.
www.leahsuttle.com
Cover content is for illustrative purposes only and any person depicted on the cover is a model.

ISBN: 978-1-62798-256-6
Digital ISBN: 978-1-62798-255-9

Printed in the United States of America
First Edition
October 2013

Completing this book requires me to thank more people than is possible. So for now: to my parents, who have always loved me and to whom I'll be forever indebted; to my friends, who support me unconditionally; to my partner, who completes me; and to my patients, because they make being a doctor worth it. Finally, this book is also dedicated to the L.A. Gay & Lesbian Center's Youth Services division. All royalties from the sale of this book will be donated to Youth Services, because sometimes success in life starts with being given a chance.

Thanks!

CHAPTER 1

THE sound of the beeper ripped through the darkness like a bomb going off next to my ear. I sat bolt upright in bed.

"Delivery room six STAT, Delivery room six STAT." The automated voice cracked an unforgiving, authoritative command.

My feet hit the floor, and I was in motion before I gave it any conscious thought. A STAT call to the delivery room could only mean one thing: a baby was in trouble. Sometimes, even when the monitors attached to the expectant mother gave ominous warnings that something was wrong with the baby, when it was finally born, it could look fine. Other times, the baby's condition at birth could be critical. In those situations, the decisions I made within the first few minutes could mean the difference between a bouncing, healthy newborn and a train wreck. A moment's hesitation or a slight error in judgment and a baby could go from having a bright, promising future to being either dead or brain-damaged.

As I raced down the single flight of stairs, taking them two or three at a time, I acknowledged the knot growing in my stomach. I was in my last year of residency in a top-level pediatric training program, but despite all my experience and having intervened in numerous neonatal emergencies, I was still anxious. I never discounted the magnitude of my responsibility. I wasn't sure I'd ever be able to forgive myself if I thought a mistake I had made resulted in a bad outcome.

I practically sprinted into the central back corridor that connected all the delivery rooms. This area was only accessible to physicians and staff. Each delivery room had two entrances. One entrance was on the outside wall of the delivery room and had a door at least six feet wide, intended for patient use. Hospital beds carrying pregnant women could be easily wheeled through these. On the inside wall of the delivery room was the staff door that opened into the central back corridor. Each of these doors was flanked by a metal sink and cabinets with supplies that had to be immediately accessible. In one sweeping motion, I pulled a scrub cap out of one of the cabinets, secured it over my head, and then tied a surgical mask in place over my nose and mouth.

There was already a flurry of activity when I burst into the delivery room. Several IV bags hung from poles around the head of a woman who lay on an operating table. A quick glance at her expression registered that she was confused and panicked. The anesthesiologist was feverishly drawing up medicines and infusing them into a small tube that disappeared into the middle of the woman's lower back. Apparently, when the team had anticipated an uneventful, normal delivery, he had given her an epidural with the intent of allowing her to experience the birthing process free of pain. Now he was hoping to utilize the same line to administer higher doses of anesthesia and thus allow the obstetrician to safely perform an emergency caesarian. The IV bags had been primed in the event that this was unsuccessful and he was forced to resort to emergency general anesthesia.

I made my way over to the neonatal resuscitation station, knowing this was where my participation would be essential. The station was kind of a platform on wheels. It consisted of a cushioned pad with both a warmer and a bright halogen light overhead. Its back panel housed various switches and gauges. I connected an infant resuscitation mask to an adapter on the end of some sterile tubing and then attached the other end of the tubing to a valve that delivered oxygen. Knowing that getting oxygen to the baby was going to be my first objective, I turned on the valve and made sure there was a strong flow coming through the mask. As I worked, I caught Fern's attention and asked her for a quick briefing. Fern was the charge nurse in obstetrics and pretty much ran the show.

She lifted her index finger in a "just a moment" gesture, then unwrapped a package of surgical instruments and, without touching them, dropped them onto a tray. With practiced precision, they landed next to an empty basin and a couple of sterile drapes. Within the next few seconds, one of the drapes would be used to cover the woman's abdomen and the other hung to provide a barrier between her face and the surgical field. Fern expertly poured an antiseptic scrub into the basin, then stepped back to allow the nurse who was going to be assisting the obstetrician to step into position.

With impressive efficiency, Fern moved to the head of the operating table and leaned over the woman. "Becky," she said. "Everything is going to be all right. I know this is a little disorienting, but we're trying to move quickly so we can deliver your baby as fast as possible. We're almost ready to begin, but before we do, I'll get your husband. He'll be by your side for the whole thing. For now, I just want you to take a few deep breaths and trust that you're in good hands." She ran her fingers softly across Becky's forehead in an attempt to offer a little palpable assurance, then turned her attention to me to give me an abbreviated rundown. She spoke in hushed tones to try to minimize Becky's alarm.

"She was having an uneventful labor when she must have abrupted. There's a lot of vaginal bleeding and the scalp electrode on the baby shows significant bradycardia. The heart rate has already been down for four minutes." Bradycardia was medical terminology for a slow heart rate, and the fact that it had already been down for four minutes wasn't a good sign. Fern glanced over her shoulder at the progress being made in preparing Becky for the surgery.

Dr. Brian Torres, the obstetrician, stealthily pulled on a sterile gown, then pushed his hands into surgical gloves. He barked at the obstetrical resident who had just flown into the room that he would have no time to scrub. "Just throw a gown on and get ready. As soon as I get the go-ahead from Jack that she's numb, I'm going to cut."

The anesthesiologist, Dr. Devin Jack, said, "Give it another thirty seconds, and we should be good to go." Almost without exception, the entire medical staff referred to him as just "Jack."

I cringed. Dr. Torres wasn't particularly known for his diplomacy, and I understood that in this situation brevity was key, but saying "I'm going to cut" within earshot of the patient seemed especially insensitive.

I watched the baby's heart monitor dip even lower, and my anxiety went into overdrive. Fortunately, in the face of huge adrenaline surges, my tendency was to become laser focused. I shut out all the extraneous noise and began a mental run-through of what I anticipated I'd be up against.

A placental abruption meant the placenta tore away from the wall of the uterus before the baby was born. Its attachment to the uterine wall was essential in order for it to transfer oxygen from the mother into the umbilical cord and subsequently to the baby. If it tore away prematurely, the baby would be deprived of essential oxygen. If part of it tore away but some of it remained partially attached, the baby might get limited oxygen, but not in sufficient quantity to sustain life. As soon as an abruption occurred, you entered into a race for life.

I began to assemble all the equipment I anticipated needing so it would be within easy reach. I put the laryngoscope, a device that would allow me to look into the baby's throat and see the vocal cords, on the side of the warming platform. Next to it, I placed what I guessed would be the appropriate-size endotracheal tube. I knew providing the baby with life-saving oxygen would be critical within the next few minutes, and the baby would have to be intubated immediately. I would extend the baby's neck, put the laryngoscope into its mouth, visualize the vocal cords, then pass the endotracheal tube directly into its trachea. With some luck and a prayer, it would happen effortlessly. Was I feeling lucky?

As the frenzy began to reach a crescendo, I saw the big six-foot-wide door open, and a nurse escorted the woman's husband into the room. "Mr. Carson, let me show you where you're going to stand. You're going to be right up here with your wife. We're going to be able to proceed with the surgery using just the epidural for anesthesia. We didn't need to put Becky to sleep. She's awake and alert and will need your encouragement and comfort." The nurse gave his hand a quick squeeze, mustered a smile of confidence, then guided him next to the side of the bed, where only his wife's head emerged from under all the blue surgical drapes.

Mr. Carson had been hurriedly dressed in hospital scrubs identical to those worn by the operating room staff. The surgical cap had been hastily pulled over his head and came too far down his forehead. He repositioned it with a sweep of his hand, revealing more of his face. He was handsome, with strong features. Dark, curly hair stuck out from under the elastic band of the scrub cap. He had matching dark eyes, an olive complexion, and I could appreciate that the cotton scrub shirt covered a muscular torso. When he bent over to kiss his wife's cheek, he disappeared behind the drape that had been hung to cordon off the surgical field.

Mr. Carson was trying to maintain a façade of calm in an attempt to reassure his wife, but when he spoke, his voice faltered a bit. "Honey, you're doing great. The nurses said that it'll be just a few more seconds. I'm right here. I'm sure our little girl will be fine. I love you, Becky. Hang in there, honey. We're going to be fine. All of us, we're going to be fine."

The power of the emotion in these situations always impressed me. The couple obviously loved each other. I was sure their past nine months had been spent in eager anticipation, looking forward to this eventful day, when the culmination of their love and their very seed would come into the world—healthy, pink, perfect. I looked up at the clock. Up until six minutes ago, every indication had been that their dream would come true. Now, their very future was teetering on the edge. The promise of a beautiful baby girl could be supplanted by the tragedy of a fetal demise. Even for me, the gravity of that prospect raised an uncomfortable lump in my throat.

Jack's voice alerting Dr. Torres brought me immediately back into the moment. "Okay, Brian, Becky's anesthesia is adequate to begin. She's ready when you are." Though he continued to prepare drugs to go through Becky's IV, he smiled down at her and winked. "Piece of cake."

Dr. Torres already had his scalpel in hand and had identified the landmarks on the woman's abdomen where he was going to make the incision. Typically, a cesarean was performed under very controlled conditions and the incisions were made delicately, leaving time to carefully control any minor bleeding as it occurred and going through each muscle layer very methodically. This time I knew that Dr. Torres would have his hand into Becky's uterus trying to extract the baby within about ten seconds of making the initial cut.

I held my breath.

Rather than just making a skin incision, Dr. Torres pushed the scalpel blade deep. He quickly tossed it back onto the surgical tray and then thrust both his hands into the cavity he had created. He begin to push the layers of muscle aside, and when he had opened what he hoped would be a hole of adequate size, he gave curt instructions to the resident. "Get a couple retractors in here and hold back the uterine wall." When that had been accomplished, Dr. Torres dove his left hand deeply into the womb. He diverted his eyes to the ceiling, his features fixed with an expression of deep concentration. At this point, trying to see what he was doing would be pointless; his hand had disappeared into a pool of blood and tissue. Instead, he had to rely on feel. His practiced fingers begin to identify landmarks and wrapped them around the baby's leg. He quickly put his other hand into the cavity. He brought the baby's legs together and began to pull. Apparently, he had determined the baby's head was already so far down into the birth canal that trying to turn her would have been a waste of time. Dead or alive, this baby was coming into the world feetfirst.

The next few seconds were a bit of a blur. Dr. Torres pulled what looked like a lifeless, limp, blue body out of the bloody quagmire, clamped the umbilical cord with two forceps an inch apart, then used a pair of surgical scissors to cut between them. In one quick motion, he handed the baby to the resident, who until that moment had had his back to me. The resident pivoted awkwardly on his heel and almost tossed the baby like a hot potato into my waiting arms.

The room then fell immediately silent. All conversation ceased, the rattle of metal equipment being jostled around stopped, and I felt everyone's stare fall directly onto me. It was so quiet I thought I actually heard a little voice in the back of my head whisper, "Do or die." I flew into action.

My stethoscope was already in my ears. I placed it briefly on the baby's chest to confirm there was a heartbeat. The sound I heard was slow and weak, but present. I thrust a suction catheter into the baby's mouth to try to evacuate some of the obvious blood and secretions, then grabbed the neonatal resuscitation mask and placed it over the baby's nose and mouth. I was thankful I had already checked the oxygen flow. By squeezing the little bag, I delivered a series of rapid, oxygen-rich breaths to the baby and was encouraged when I saw her chest rise and fall in response. In one fluid motion, I picked up the laryngoscope in one hand and the endotracheal tube in the other. There was still a lot of crap in the back of the baby's throat, but I could see the vocal cords. The hole between them represented a tiny target, but under the nimble guidance of my fingers, I watched the tube pass smoothly through them.

By this time, Fern was by my side. Without me having to direct her, she was ready with an adapter to put on the end of the endotracheal tube. She connected the adapter to the oxygen line and then began gently squeezing the bag. Relief! At least the baby was now getting oxygen. Whether it made any difference or not was yet to be seen. She was still blue and lifeless.

Having Fern manage the airway freed my hands to continue the resuscitation. The clock was ticking, and the baby was still shocky and had only a weak heartbeat. I knew I would have to be aggressive to optimize her chances. I turned to the nurse standing next to the crash cart. "Pull me up point three milligrams of epinephrine."

She opened the medicine drawer designated for neonates, grabbed a vial, and then filled one of the smallest syringes with a clear liquid. As she did so, she repeated my order to verify accuracy. "Epinephrine, point three milligrams."

I removed the clamp that had been secured to the end of the umbilical cord. The cord had been cut about an inch above the skin of the baby's abdomen. I needed to be able to administer medicine and fluids to the baby quickly. The best way was to utilize one of the vessels from the umbilical cord. They were relatively big, easily accessible, and carried a good blood supply. With a small pair of tweezers, I teased the three vessels contained within the cord apart, identified an artery, then carefully threaded a tube less than half a millimeter in diameter through it. After advancing the tube about two inches, I injected thirty cc's of saline into it, then pushed the epinephrine into it as well.

While Fern continued softly squeezing the bag in rhythmic four-second intervals, another nurse placed tiny little electrodes onto the baby's chest. The monitor indicated that her heart rate was slowly picking up. I again placed my stethoscope on her chest to confirm what I hoped was a sign of improvement. Her heartbeat was indeed a little stronger.

"Now give me thirty cc's of albumin." A syringe appeared in my hand almost before the request escaped my mouth. I slowly pushed it into the tube going into the baby's umbilical cord. Her skin, ever so slowly, started getting pink. The beeps coming from the monitor also sprang to life, orchestrating what sounded like a symphony to announce that the baby's condition was improving.

"Let's follow that with three milliliters of bicarb," I said, apprehensive that the baby had not yet completely turned the corner.

Then, miraculously, the baby started to move. Her movements were tentative at first but soon became more purposeful. Her heart rate climbed to one fifty, and she appeared to be trying to cry around the tube down her throat.

The relief experienced by everyone in attendance was palpable. For the first time since starting the resuscitation, I glanced over my shoulder to look at the parents. Neither of them could see their baby on the warming platform. They were both still locked in a catatonic state. Becky was on her back with her head turned toward me. Her pleading eyes peeked out from under the surgical cap that covered her hair. Her position on the operating table prevented her from moving more than her head and shoulders. One of her arms was secured onto an IV board extending from the side of the gurney. Antibiotics slowly dripped into it.

Her husband, whose name I later learned was Greg, was holding on to her other hand where it appeared from under the surgical drapes. His knuckles were white, and I couldn't help but thinking that if Becky hadn't been so worried about her baby, she would have realized that her hand was uncomfortable in his tight grasp.

Suddenly, all the anticipation and anxiety came to a climax, and Becky emitted a mournful sob. "Why can't I hear my baby crying? Is she dead?" The desperation of her question was heartwrenching. Tears began to cascade down her cheeks, and her chin quivered as she wept. Greg, on the other hand, stood stoically, his expression unwavering. He was obviously trying to prepare himself to hear horrible news and seemed determined to remain strong.

I calibrated my response to make my voice sound intentionally optimistic. "You know, right now I'd have to say this little girl looks pretty darn good. She got off to kind of a rough start, but it appears she's a real fighter and refuses to be kept down. For the time being, I have a tube in her windpipe that's helping her to breathe. It prevents her from being able to cry, but don't worry, she's moving her fists enough to let me know she's not too happy about it. Being angry is a good sign. It means she wants the tube out and intends to breathe on her own."

Both parents froze in suspended animation while they registered what I had just said. Then tears began pouring even more heavily down Becky's face. "Oh thank you, thank you, thank you," she sobbed in a hoarse whisper.

The tension in Greg's face fell as well. The magnitude of the anxiety he'd been suppressing had been so great that, when relief came, it almost overwhelmed him. Its surge must have made him feel as if he'd been struck by a bus. He began sobbing as well. "Are you sure she's going to be okay?" he pleaded; he seemed almost afraid to let himself believe he was really awakening from his nightmare.

"Well, I can't give you a 100 percent guarantee that we're completely out of the woods. I'm still worried that her heart rate was dangerously low for quite a while, but I take a lot of consolation in seeing a baby turn around quickly, and this girl just set a record. She's already looking better. We're going to take her up to the neonatal intensive care unit to monitor her, and we're going to have to run some tests, but I'd put my money on this girl still being Harvard bound."

Dr. Torres, Dr. Jack, the resident, and the entire nursing staff looked as if they wanted to leap into the air and high-five each other. Instead, Dr. Torres peeked over the drape to look at Becky. "You did really well, Becky. This girl's going to make it only because her mother's so strong. Thanks for sticking with me. Now, don't you think that it would be a good idea for me to see about putting you back together? That daughter of yours insisted on making her appearance through a big stage door."

He looked up at the scrub nurse, who I could see smiling under her mask. "You have some suture ready? I have some sewing to do."

I smiled at Becky. "Mrs. Carson, I'll understand if you don't want to get up, but, Mr. Carson, you might want to consider coming over to meet your daughter." Her little fist was now really flailing around. "It would appear she's eager to say hello."

Greg slowing pulled his fingers from his wife's hand. He hesitantly took a step forward, looking like he still didn't trust his legs to support his weight. He stood over the warmer that held his daughter and seemed mesmerized by seeing her. Just moments before, Dr. Torres had pulled a blue, lifeless rag from out of his wife's womb. Now, though, the baby had a tube in her windpipe, a line coming out of her belly button, and electrodes attached to her chest, he looked enchanted by the vibrant, little pink life before him, who was seemingly trying to wrestle herself free from all the restraints.

Not wanting to break the spell that he was enraptured in, I spoke in a hushed whisper. "I'm going to take her upstairs. We'll want to get a chest X-ray and run some other tests. Your wife is going to be, shall we say, tied up for a little while, so if you'd like, you can come upstairs with us. The nurses won't let you stay too long, as they will have a lot to do to get your daughter tucked in, but you can at least see where she's going to be. Then you can come back down to report to Becky."

His tears had begun to subside and he looked jubilant. "I think I'd like that." He turned to his wife. "I'll only be gone a sec, honey." Then, concerned about Becky's own delicate condition, he quickly retracted his intentions. "Or, do you want me to stay here with you?"

She too was jubilant, but exhaustion was catching up with her. Prior to things heading south, she had already been in labor for more than ten hours. The combination of pushing for so long, the stress, and an emergency surgery was rapidly taking its toll. "No, you go up," she encouraged him. "I need to close my eyes for a minute. Just hurry back down to tell me how she's doing. And, honey," she said as she smiled weakly, "be sure to bring me good news."

Encouraged that the baby was doing well and certain she could tolerate it, I disconnected her briefly from the oxygen, picked her up, and carried her quickly over to where Becky could see her. I held the baby to within inches of her mother's cheek. "Let's get a kiss for luck and we're on our way!" Damn! How gay did I sound unintentionally quoting from a Carpenters song?

No matter; no one seemed to notice. Another surge of tears poured from Becky's eyes as she placed a quick, loving kiss on the baby's cheek. She gave me a relieved, appreciative smile. "Thank you, not just for the kiss, but for everything. Thank you."

By this time, Fern had wheeled the transport incubator into the delivery room. I put the baby into it, then attached the endotracheal tube to the portable oxygen canister. Fern resumed squeezing the bag rhythmically. One of the other nurses attached the electrodes to a monitor that was built into the side of the incubator, and another attached an IV line to the tube coming from the baby's umbilical cord. She confirmed that it was infusing at a rate of twenty cc's per hour, then announced that the entire caravan was ready to roll.

"You ready, Dad?" I smiled at Greg. "Your daughter's impatient. Better get used to it!"

He kissed his wife and then followed us out of the room. We took an elevator up one floor then wheeled the incubator into the neonatal intensive care unit. Margo, the charge nurse there, waved us over to a waiting warmer. Fern had called ahead, so the nurses were expecting us. At this point, I was able to step back and enjoy the impressive spectacle as the nurses got to work. They were the epitome of professionalism and efficiency. They had that baby on the warmer and attached to a ventilator before I was able to offer a single directive. *Oh well*, I thought, *this baby is in great hands.*

Meanwhile, Greg wasn't missing a beat. He kept a vigilant eye on everything happening to his daughter. In an attempt to break the tension a little, I asked him, "So, does she have a name?"

He tore his gaze away from the activity occurring on the warmer and appeared to have to think about my question for a minute. "Oh yeah, yeah.

Her name is Sophie. We named her after Becky's grandmother. She's eighty-four but in great health. She's a spunky thing too. Guess we chose the right name. That must be where Sophie gets it from. Her spunk, I mean." The realization seemed to console him. "My daughter's got her great-grandmother's spunk."

He smiled pensively, still reeling from the drama of the delivery. He'd reached up to wipe some of the sweat that had collected on his forehead off when he seemed to realize he was still wearing his scrub cap. "May I take this thing off now?"

"Sure," I said. "You wouldn't want to be confused for anyone other than a new dad. As for me?" I adjusted mine thoughtfully and smiled. "I think I'll keep mine on. Given the number of names on the board downstairs, it looks like I'll probably be making another few trips down to the delivery room before morning."

Greg peeled his scrub cap off and shoved it into the back pocket of the surgical pants he was wearing. In their haste to get him dressed, the nurses had apparently grabbed him a pair of pants that were obviously too big. He'd had to really cinch the drawstring to keep them from falling down.

With the cap off, I was better able to observe his appearance. He was handsome. Kind of rugged-looking. He had a nice smile and a cleft that dimpled the middle of his chin. He wasn't model material but was certainly way above average.

One of the monitors that Sophie was connected to began to sound an alarm. I aborted my review of the guy's features and directed my attention immediately back to his baby. Fortunately, however, the alarm had been triggered as the result of a lead coming loose. Sophie was still rock stable. She didn't appear to have even registered the sudden, shrill beeping.

"Well," I said, "as I told you, we're going to have to run a few more tests. Sophie continues to look great. Why don't you go back down and check on your wife. If you're still awake, you can come back up in a few hours to see how Sophie's progressing. By that time, Dr. Schmidt will have taken over for me. She'll be able to give you a full update and will be the one taking care of Sophie for the next few days."

He looked a little startled. "Why won't you be taking care of her? We really trust you."

I smiled. "I'm working in the cancer wing this month. I was just on call here tonight to help cover. Don't worry, though. Sophie will be in good hands."

His eyes started to well up a little again. "I can't thank you enough. You saved our little angel. We'll be indebted to you forever. Listen!" he said, looking at my name tag. "Dr. Sheldon, I run an automotive shop. I'm gonna leave my card with the nurses. If you need anything, and I mean *anything*, you just give me a call. I know it will be impossible, but I just have to try and find a way to thank you."

I was both humbled and flattered. "Just be a good dad. That will be thanks enough. Now go see how your wife is doing."

He held my gaze for a second, broke it off as he turned for the door, then reconsidered. He spun back around, grabbed me in a tight bear hug, and pounded me gently on my back.

"Thank you, Doc. Really, thank you. You're the best. You'll never know how much this has meant to us."

He relinquished his embrace, gave me another slap on the shoulder for good measure, and then, perhaps fearing that he might once again become emotional, he almost sprinted out of the room.

I turned my attention back to Sophie and began a more thorough exam. A feeling of warmth spread through me. Sometimes being a doctor was a good thing.

CHAPTER 2

THE prospect of going to the gym had about as much appeal as being dragged behind a truck down a gravel road. Naked. I just wasn't into it today. And yet, I knew with my current work schedule, I wouldn't have the energy for working out for at least another month. Being the senior ward resident meant sleep deprivation was going to be my middle name. I could either drag my sorry ass to the gym and at least pretend to work out, or I could surrender to doing what I really felt like doing and sit at home eating ice cream. The only problem with the latter scenario was that my sorry ass would soon become a fat sorry ass, and that just wouldn't be acceptable.

I pushed through the door of the main entrance of the gym and swiped my membership card as I passed the counter. Karen, one of the managers, looked up and gave me a friendly hello. I was one of the privileged few Karen actually liked. I wasn't sure how I had gained that distinction, but I liked her too. She was attractive, but not stunning. Most of her physical appeal was that she was so natural-looking. She wore very little makeup, but her skin was radiant and her hair was shiny. She also had an amazing physique, and it was obvious she took her workouts very seriously.

What I liked most about her, though, was her wit. She was kind of deadpan sarcastic. Many of the gym patrons she dealt with were wannabe actors who were incredibly full of themselves. Part of their pretending to be important was to look down on everyone else. Karen not only saw through their bullshit but called them on it. I remember her telling one guy he should at least put a window in his stomach so that when he had his head shoved up his ass, he could see out. He huffed and puffed, became really indignant, and threatened to cancel his membership. Karen just rolled her eyes, referenced the exit sign over the door with a quick sweep of her hand, and expressed her hope that he'd have a good life. "If you ever get over yourself and decide you want to come to the gym to work out rather than trying to prove you're hot shit, give us a call." That was Karen. She wasn't to be messed with.

I stowed my gym bag in a locker, secured the door with my padlock, then began the ritual of trying to motivate myself. Hopefully, I would run into one of my friends and we could distract each other through the workout thus making the whole process more painless.

Sadly, after making one circuit through the gym, pretending all the while that I was just intent on finding a vacant workout station, I observed no one other than the usual suspects. *Damn*, I thought, *do some of these people live here*? It seemed that no matter what time of day I worked out, some of the same people were always there. Either by amazing coincidence my erratic workout schedule just happened to coincide with theirs, or they spent a hell of a lot of time working out. "Shit," I resentfully whispered under my breath. "Some of these guys need to get a life." Even as I shook my head, however, I had to admit to myself that what I really resented was how restricted my own life was. In my current assignment, it wasn't uncommon to work thirty-six hours at a time.

I sat down at the bench press and tried to motivate myself. I knew I had to begin, because if I stayed motionless for too long, I'd fall asleep. Thirty-six hours! What the hell was up with having to work thirty-six hours? Medical residents must be the only people in the civilized world required to do so.

Every other profession, from garbagemen to hairdressers, had regulations stipulating the number of hours they could work in any given stretch. No argument from me. I mean, if a garbageman was pushed to the point of exhaustion, he might inadvertently mix up the organic trash with the recyclables. Just think of the pandemonium that could result. Beer bottles might be found slipping around with banana peels if they weren't deposited in the appropriate receptacle. Can you imagine that fallout? They'd probably call a presidential press conference to address the consequences.

And if a hairdresser, groggy by pushing into the thirtieth hour of a shift, substituted bleach for cream rinse, he or she might be forced to suffer the consequences of giving a client both a bad hair day and a bad attitude with the simple squeeze of the wrong bottle.

But medical residents, who were in the business of saving lives, were another story. There was really no set limit to the number of hours they could conceivably work. Some senile old physician, who had seniority enough to be in a decision-making position, had suggested there was an advantage to working triple shifts. The rationale was that by doing so, residents gained tremendous hands-on experience and thus enhanced their medical education. Forget the fact that they were frequently so tired they couldn't even think straight—they were being given invaluable exposure to the many subtle ways in which diseases could present themselves. I remembered one senior attending physician quipping that the problem with allowing residents to go home and sleep at night was that they were missing twelve hours of potentially interesting cases. Can you believe the depth of that bullshit?

No one seemed concerned about the mistakes residents could make when sleep deprivation swept them into a state of delirium. And residents, beaten into submission, were minimally concerned that a mistake could cost a patient's life. What they were most concerned about was the inquisition they would have to face the next day. On the morning after an all-night shift, there was always a well-rested attending physician eager to play Monday-morning quarterback and criticize even the most innocuous decisions a resident might have made the night before. The American medical education system: the perfect pecking order!

I thought the bottom line had to do with the hospital finding cheap labor. The institution needed a service, and if a resident ever wanted to practice medicine, they would either provide that service with the grace of a good-hearted humanitarian, or they'd turn their stethoscope in for a position on a paper route.

I looped my fingers around the barbell that had one forty-five pound plate on each side and began the grind. Fifteen reps would be a good warm-up. I tried to stay focused on my technique. I kept my elbows at a ninety-degree angle to my body and brought the bar down to within an inch of my chest, just above my nipple line. I inhaled deeply as the bar dropped and exhaled slowly as I extended my arms. I tried to offer myself some encouragement as I finished the first set. *Just maintain a rhythm, and you'll be done with this before you know it. One set down, four to go!*

Feeling as if my body was already encased in cement, I nonetheless added more weight to the bar.

Unfortunately, when you're tired, your mind begins to sabotage your efforts. *Four more sets? Forget it! Today you can get by with doing only three. Maybe even just two. Take it easy, you deserve the rest. You've been working hard. Don't push your body beyond its limits.* The prospect of quitting the workout completely and just spending the day watching my ass grow bigger became an even less offensive proposition. *What's another couple inches on my waist size? No one will even notice if I wear baggy jeans.* It felt like the devil himself was whispering in my ear.

The inner dialogue consumed so much of my attention that I initially didn't notice the guy working out on the bench next to me. In a split second, however, I was captivated. He was resting between sets. He appeared not to have a care in the world and seemed completely oblivious to anything going on around him. A little white wire wound itself from the iPod attached to his bicep up into his ears, and he seemed totally immersed in the music he was listening to.

Taking my cue from him, I tried to play it cool and pretend I hadn't noticed him. In truth, however, I was taking in the whole picture, hoping that it would be permanently imprinted in my brain. He was about five foot ten and probably weighed a muscular one hundred and eighty-five pounds. He had perfect hair that, despite being messy, framed his face perfectly. He had an olive complexion and a five o'clock shadow that further accentuated his tall, dark, and handsome looks. As he mouthed the lyrics to the song coming through his earbuds, he parted his lips to reveal perfect teeth. His chest was a sculpted mound of muscle that tapered down to a thin waist. He had narrow hips, but his thighs had great definition, and they were capped off by a solid, firm, round butt. Short, curly dark hair covered his legs and also peeked out over the tank top covering his chest. In a word: incredible.

Suddenly, the fatigue I had been feeling just a second before evaporated. Enthusiasm began to course through my body, giving me a renewed surge of energy.

I lay down on the bench and again grabbed the bar above me. Despite having put another ten pounds on each side of the bar, I pumped out another fifteen reps effortlessly. I was winded but felt invigorated. I sat up to rest and tried to inconspicuously divert my gaze over to the bench press next to me. The guy was in the middle of a set. He had two forty-five pound plates on each side of the bar but was pressing two hundred and twenty-five pounds with seemingly minimal effort. I heard him whisper "twelve" under his breath, and then he flipped the barbell back onto the rack. He took a deep breath and then sat up. In doing so, his gaze briefly caught mine. For a microsecond, he held my gaze. A smile flashed quickly across his face, and then he diverted his attention back to his workout.

I was exhilarated. He had smiled. Was that a sign? Was it an invitation that I could casually say "hi"? Maybe even ask for him to spot me on the next set so I could try to push some impressive weight? If he consented to spot me, I could use the opportunity to initiate a conversation. My mind begin racing through my repertoire of clever one-liners. Had to be something subtle, innocuous. Something clever and engaging but not something that could be interpreted as a come-on. An obvious come-on in the gym was not only uncool but gave the impression of being desperate.

My back was to him as I added another forty-five pound plate to one side of the bar, then, feeling a little self-conscious, I stacked on an additional twenty-five. Now each side of the bar would have one hundred and fifteen pounds. I looked at it a little apprehensively. I knew I was capable of lifting it but also had to concede I was tired and not at my physical peak. I mentally calculated the risk. I didn't want to embarrass myself and have the bar come crashing down onto my chest, but if I mustered the courage to impose on him to spot me, the weight on the bar had to be enough to warrant asking for help.

At that moment, feeling a surge of self-confidence, I decided: I would ask him for a spot. If he consented, I'd casually say something like, "You look like you're in pretty good shape. Do you work out here often?" An innocent question, beautifully framing a subtle compliment, which, most importantly, might be the opening to an engaging conversation. I put the lock on the end of the bar, sealed my resolve, and then pasted an appropriate expression of indifference on my face. I didn't want to appear too eager. Rehearsing the request over in my mind, I began to slowly turn. I hoped my tone would be inviting and sincere but not give the impression of being too desperate.

When all systems were a "go," I turned completely around, expecting to catch him sitting on the edge of the bench, resting between sets. My anticipation fizzled. In the interval that I had spent changing the weights and preparing my perfect line, he had moved on. I searched the gym desperately. He had vanished. For a few seconds I began to wonder if maybe, in my sleep-deprived state, I had just imagined him. Was I losing it? Had I fallen asleep on the bench, and was Adonis just a product of my dreams?

I was about to give up when, on the far side of the gym, I saw him doing pull-ups. The stream of relief that swept over me was quickly replaced by a feeling of self-consciousness and anxiety. Striking up a conversation with him sitting next to me would have been easy. It was going to be impossible to walk across the entire gym and try to catch his attention without looking like a stalker.

The magnitude of my dilemma resulted in paralysis. I just stood there, resting one hand on the barbell I had just loaded up with weights, unable to mentally regroup after the unanticipated disappointment. I had bolstered myself up for the prospect of a flat-out rejection, but it hadn't occurred to me he would disappear before I'd even been given the opportunity to speak to him. So much for trying to captivate him with the perfect introduction.

Convincing myself to actually try talking to him had consumed an inordinate amount of energy. When it came to approaching a good-looking guy, I had zero self-confidence. In the hospital, where my intellect was on the line, I was the epitome of self-assuredness. I wasn't cocky, but I knew I was smart and I had pretty good clinical instincts. If a sick kid was my responsibility, I knew I was capable of rising to the occasion. My personal life was another matter entirely.

Despite being relatively good-looking, I was incapable of believing someone who I thought was handsome would ever find me attractive. I had spent so much time in the closet, believing there was something seriously wrong with me, that when I approached someone I thought was attractive, my assumption was that they would immediately see the word "defective" printed across my forehead.

It wasn't that I had lost my self-confidence—it was that I had never had any to begin with. I suspected my low self-esteem had something to do with growing up in a small town with three brothers and with a dad who was a football coach. In that environment, it was more preferable to be dead than to be queer.

I recognized early on that I was different, but I also learned early on that not all differences were acceptable. Both my parents had strong opinions about what it meant to be a boy. My mom was the youngest of four and had three older brothers. She idolized them, thought their very existence epitomized masculinity, and was determined that her four sons would grow up to replicate that ideal. Certainly she was loving, and she enthusiastically showered her affection on all of us. In addition, she was compassionate and encouraging, assuring me that she thought I was capable of anything. Unfortunately, however, the impact of her disapproval, though subtle, was equally powerful.

The way she directed her disapproval toward me might have appeared inconsequential to an impartial observer. For me, though, her critical assessment cut to the very core of my being. It felt like she was psychic. Like she somehow knew I'd never measure up as a real man and was tactfully trying to avert what I was sure she believed would be a disgusting and devastating consequence.

Who would have guessed that for a well-behaved, carefree kid growing up, the opportunities to disappoint my mom could be so numerous?

I was high-spirited and loved to run. I would race through the neighborhood either pretending to fly or trying to outrun the wind. I relished the feeling of exhilaration and happiness and was confident that any neighbors who saw me would be impressed with my unbridled speed. When I caught my mom watching me, I tried to accelerate, certain she would gush over my natural athleticism. Instead, when I went whisking by her, I observed an expression on her face that read disappointment. She called me over and said encouragingly, but with a tone of conviction, that I should lower my hands when I ran. "Boys run with their arms to their sides, not with their hands in the air. That's how girls run." Whether intended or not, the message to me was clear even then. Who I was as a boy was not acceptable. I fell short of the appropriate standard, and I would have to vigilantly modify the image I put forth to the world.

Of course, some of the other messages from my parents were crystal clear, and you would either have had to be blind or retarded to have misinterpreted them.

Dad had innumerable monologues about the essential lessons of manhood, including the importance of playing tackle football, because real men gained obligatory life insight by being knocked on their asses and having to get back up. "Why, if a young man doesn't recognize the importance of this rite of passage into adulthood, then he's simply a sissy and will never amount to anything. Real men prove themselves by being knocked down and by succeeding in getting back up. If a young man doesn't get up when he's knocked down on the football field, he will be incapable of getting up when knocked down by one of life's unexpected challenges." The message? Real men play football. Real men live to knock each other down. If you didn't conform to this adage, you weren't a real man and would never amount to anything in life.

Amidst all of this, I sometimes felt hopeless. I didn't want to play football. I hated the aggression of the game and didn't care about the adrenaline surge I was supposed to feel by being physically dominating. I was athletic and enjoyed sports like volleyball and skiing, but in Echo, California, that wasn't enough. Those sports gave you zero stature as a man. It was okay to play those sports on the side as long you had already earned your testosterone stripes by playing a real man's sport. Combine that experience with locker-room talk and my feelings of inadequacy skyrocketed further.

The locker room was the inner sanctum where your masculinity was really put to the test. There, you were supposed to brag about the sexual conquests you'd had with any number of big-breasted girls and were supposed to infer how impressed they were with the size of your dick and how adept you were at pleasing them with it. At the time, I didn't know that most of what I heard there was 90 percent bullshit; I just shuddered at how overtly disinterested I was in participating. Sure, I threw in the jabs I thought would make me seem like an integral part of the sex-craved fraternity, but it was just an attempt to be included. I put up a façade so as not to be made a social outcast.

In the end, I felt being gay not only signified I was inadequate as a man, but meant I was inferior even as a person. As a consequence, it became my life's mission to conceal who I really was from the world. No one could ever know that beneath the charming, outgoing, confident surface lay a reprehensible secret.

Unfortunately, as I grew into an adult and began to make little inroads into accepting myself, the baggage I carried from childhood didn't instantaneously disappear. I profoundly felt the disparity between coming to an intellectual acceptance of who I was and developing an emotional acceptance of myself. When for the majority of your life you disliked who you were, waking up one morning and trying to tell yourself that you were actually okay had minimal impact on rectifying an abysmal self-image.

Nowhere did the dichotomy that was my life play out more than at work. I wasn't out to anyone at the hospital. Since graduating from medical school, I had begun to develop a tight circle of gay friends, but for me, disclosing my sexuality at work was out of the question. My own insecurities led me to believe that in professional circles, being gay would equate to being inferior, and that was not at all how I wanted to be perceived.

I took my towel and wiped off the bench. Becoming more self-confident would take some time, and in that minute, not even a phenomenal internal pep talk would succeed in getting me to muster enough courage to make the pilgrimage across the gym to say hello to a guy who'd offered no encouragement beyond a two-second smile.

Any enthusiasm I had had for working out leached from my body like water through a sieve. I'd been single this long; who cared about the rest of my life?

I dejectedly made my way back to the locker room. I had to concede that I'd only done two repetitions on the bench press, but the depression I felt, combined with the sleep deprivation, made me feel as if I'd been hit by a truck. The challenge of maintaining my physique would have to be left for another day.

CHAPTER 3

ABOUT eight days after the disheartening gym incident, I had a Friday night off. Though the vast majority of my life was spent in the confines of the hospital, when I did have the opportunity to go out, I was determined to maximize the experience. I typically only had one weekend off a month, so when I did, I began contacting friends of mine days in advance to guarantee maximum debauchery.

Invariably, any foray into West Hollywood involved my best friend Declan. He and I had been friends for more than five years, and we were inseparable. It was unusual for one of us to be seen out not in the company of the other. We were like the dynamic duo. We joked, we laughed, we encouraged one another, we shared insults, but mostly, we had one another's backs. Typically, we would talk to one another on an almost daily basis. We knew intimate details of what was going on in each other's lives, and we were there for each other through good times and bad.

In addition, we shared an amazing group of friends. None of us were in committed relationships, so a night on the town usually meant trying to throw ourselves into the middle of whatever was considered to be epicenter of the gay single scene.

On this particular Saturday night, El Chico Loco had been designated the meeting place of choice. The food was acceptable, the margaritas were strong, and the men were "hot." It offered all the essential ingredients for a fun night out.

I hadn't even pushed through the door of the bar, but despite the volume of the blaring disco music, I could hear Declan's raucous laughter coming from the table occupied by my group of friends. Declan was infamous for his laugh. It was genuine, it was sincere, but mostly it was loud. In recent months I had even shied away from going to movies with him because in the event he found something humorous, I would have to seek refuge from his laugh. Its volume not only drowned out any dialogue coming from the screen, but I swore it could shake the walls of the theater more than its million-dollar Dolby sound system. Sitting next to him could be downright embarrassing and inevitably drew irritated glares from other movie patrons.

Declan, however, caught up in the hilarity of the moment, was oblivious. He'd just continue shoving popcorn in his mouth, ever eager for the next punch line to throw him into another fit of hysterics.

Embarrassment aside, I did appreciate his enthusiasm. He unapologetically approached life with the same zeal he had for comedy. Life was intended to be laughed at. If you don't like it, best to get out of the way.

Mostly, I found his fun-loving spirit to be infectious. On many occasions, I looked forward to getting together with him after a long shift in the hospital just because I knew being with him would lift my mood. Frequently, we'd just hang out together. A typical evening would include hitting the gym together, grabbing a bite to eat, and watching TV. Invariably, Declan's choice for perfect programming was reruns of *The Golden Girls*. Didn't matter that he had the dialogue for most of the episodes memorized, he still laughed uproariously through every line. Same laugh, same volume. Earsplitting. But in the comfort of his living room, his laugh was the elixir that made me smile.

The bar was hopping, and it took a while to navigate through the crowd. When I'd finally made my way to the table, I was greeted by five friendly, enthusiastic faces. Gary pulled the chair they had been saving for me out from under the table and gestured for me to sit down. After licking some salt off the rim of his margarita and taking a healthy sip, he eyed me with an inquisitive glance. "Crowded, huh? Were you looking for us long?"

"You kidding me? I could hear Dec cackling from the parking lot. Just had to follow the sound of him laying that egg!"

The whole group, including Declan, broke into smiles, but Declan was unfazed by my teasing. Without missing a beat, he retorted, "You're just hoping that your ass will see that kind of action. Though, as tight-assed as you are, you'd better hope it's a small egg or"—his grin broadened with anticipation—"that you're nailed by a really tiny rooster."

The group was immediately reduced to sidesplitting laughter. I was pretty broken up too. Shit, I had to admit, Declan was the king of the comebacks. "Okay, Dec, I give up. I guess compared to you, a rooster does have a big dick. You still have to buy me a drink."

That drew another whoop of laughter from our friends, and I caught myself grinning warmly at Declan, a little proud I had rebounded from his teasing and salvaged a parting shot. He could have retaliated again, and we could have fallen into our customary exchange of innocent insults, but instead, he threw his arm around my shoulder, pushed a quick kiss against my cheek, and asked me, "So what are you drinking, asshole?"

"Margarita's good. Rocks, no salt. You really buying?"

"First one's on me. You can buy the next round. It's Friday night— we're gonna be here for a while."

My lightheartedness sank just for an instant. "Just one or two for me. I gotta be home by around ten. I'm on call tomorrow and will have to be up early."

Declan, who was unwavering in his support of me, immediately tried to buffer my disappointment. "No problem. I'll probably be calling it an early night too. Had the week from hell at work. Besides, when you're a real doctor and pulling in the big bucks, all the shit you've had to endure will have seemed worth it." He bumped shoulders with me, lifted his own drink to his mouth, and winked.

I bumped him back, refused to allow myself to become sullen, and quipped, "I already am a real doctor. I just have the privilege of working for slave wages."

His smile brightened, and he seemed determined to keep the mood light. "Slave wages, huh? Didn't know you were into kink. When will we get to meet your master?" He flashed me a cockeyed smile but tried to inflect a tone of absolute sincerity into his voice.

I smiled back. "You wanna meet him, you'd better make my drink a double!"

He gave my shoulder another squeeze, then directed the conversation back to the group. He cast a quick glance in my direction to be sure he had my attention then gestured with his drink toward Alex. "I was laying that egg when you came in because Alex was regaling us with more of his infamous travel stories. No one on the planet could get themselves into more shit traveling than Alex. With the situations he finds himself in, it's a wonder his dick hasn't dropped off."

Alex blushed but offered no argument. "Not my fault my ass has international appeal. It's not like I'm looking to get laid."

That comment almost brought the rest of us to our feet. The shouts from everyone sitting at the table came out in a simultaneous rush. "You don't do anything other than to try to get laid," I said.

Alex just offered a sheepish shrug. "Man's gotta do what a man's gotta do. So much dick, so little time." He wasn't able to duck before the cube of ice John lobbed at him bounced off his forehead.

"Fuck, that hurt." He gave an exaggerated wail and covered his forehead with both hands.

"Head's so fuckin' big, how could I've missed?" John jeered. "Besides, I thought the ice might help to cool you down, seeing how you think you're such hot shit."

Everyone knew the jabs were in jest, and the laughter continued. Fully recovered, Alex tossed a piece of ice at John, intending for it to just fall into his lap. "I do believe that's the voice of jealousy, grasshopper. You just need lessons from someone who knows how to use the force."

"Just because you're wrinkled, green, and have big ears and a little dick doesn't make you Yoda. Besides, the only light saber you own is the pink dildo in your bedside table."

The cumulative laugh again crescendoed and miraculously left Alex momentarily at a loss for words. "It's blue, not pink, and you can borrow it anytime you'd like."

The volume of laughing and talking continued to ebb and flow, and my margarita was put in front of me. I raised my glass in a toast to my friends, all of whom were probably on at least their second drink by then, and toasted, "Here's to the nectar of the gods."

I didn't even have time to swallow before Tyler acknowledged my toast with a question. "Nectar of the gods? Damn, Zack, you drink jizz by the glass?"

A mouthful of perfectly good margarita made with a fine Patron tequila went exploding out of my mouth in an attempt to avoid choking. The whole spectacle brought the table into an even greater fit of hysterics.

Eager to change the subject, I directed my question back to Alex. "So, dude, which travel story were you telling when I walked in? This isn't another rendition of Australia and the blackout, is it?"

Alex went immediately crimson. "Skip it, Zack; that's not a story for mixed company."

His silence, so uncharacteristic of Alex, brought everyone's eyes up in unison, each expression screaming with curiosity, demanding an explanation.

The never bashful Declan took the lead. "So, Alex, sounds like there's something you might want to share with us about your experiences in Australia."

Even the tips of Alex's ears turned pink. He really did have a reputation. Alex was not the best-looking guy in the world, but he exuded self-confidence, and more importantly, was both relentless and had no shame. He could walk up to the best-looking guy in the bar and come on to him. If the response he got was to be told to eat shit and die, rather than crawling away in shame, Alex would be encouraged. "Eating, that's a good thing. Does that mean you'd like to blow this place and go grab a bite with me?" Frequently, I thought the guy Alex was coming on to was so taken aback by Alex's persistence that he'd end up taking Alex home.

The rest of us thought it incredible and might have even been a slight bit jealous, but we were nonetheless kind of stupefied by Alex's success with the "A-list" men. Average-looking at best, he really did have a knack for hooking up with the hotties.

Alex's ears continued to burn, and despite his insistence that he was going to kill me for alluding to what was yet another embarrassing episode in his epic life, he beamed at the prospect of flying solo in the spotlight. It had already been established that he had no shame. Didn't matter if the story might be embarrassing as hell, Alex loved the notoriety and lived to entertain.

He shrugged at me dismissively. "Go ahead, Sheldon. If they wanna hear the story, you tell it." His blush seeped back into his cheeks, and for a second he looked kind of self-conscious. "It wasn't one of my prouder moments, but it will make you guys laugh your asses off. Besides"—his air of cockiness returned—"it was kind of hot!"

"Hot?" I pitched forward in my chair. "It was the most disgusting thing I've ever heard in my life. If it had happened to me, I would have had to shoot everyone in the room just to be sure I left no living witnesses."

The others at the table looked between Alex and me, growing more curious, more expectant, and more impatient. Tyler finally broke the tension. "I don't give a shit which one of you tells the story, but one of you had better start talking or you're both going to get bombarded with a shower of ice."

Alex picked at some of the salt on the rim of his glass with a feigned attitude of indifference. "You tell it, Zack; you tell it better anyway." He sank a little lower in his chair, knowing full well that at the conclusion of the story, he would be without even an ounce of virtue. He shook almost imperceptibly. He'd be embarrassed, yes, but, in his eyes, anyway, he'd be infamous. Worth the price.

"Well." I cleared my throat to ensure I had everyone's attention. "As you all know, our friend here is a world traveler, which for him means there's not a square inch on this entire globe where he hasn't shot a load." Alex sat up a little but slouched quickly when I added, "Though it's mostly the result of him abusing himself with his own hand."

"Sheldon," he protested, "just get on with the story. If we hope to eat sometime within the next five years, the waitress is gonna have to take our orders soon. Skip the commentary. The story is bad enough."

"Anyway," I continued as if I hadn't been interrupted, "shortly after Alex arrived in Sydney, he scored an invitation to a private party." I looked at him with the slightest hint of admiration. "It's beyond me how you succeeded in doing that."

Alex's gaze never strayed from examining the salt on the rim of his glass. "Like I told you, Zack, men find me irresistible; now get to the fucking point already."

"Right. Well, it was about six o'clock in the evening, the party wasn't going to start until around eleven, and Alex was starving. In addition, because jet lag had really kicked in, he knew he was gonna have to take a nap if he wanted any chance of being on his best game for the party. Dilemma. How, in an unfamiliar city, do you find a filling meal and still salvage enough time for meaningful shut-eye? Well, given Alex's infamous travel luck, the solution presented itself in that exact moment in the form of a catering truck that pulled into the beach parking lot. Perfect, he thought. I can grab something, eat it on the walk back to the hotel, and still have plenty of time to sleep and take a shower."

Silence fell over the table as I poured more inflection into my voice to guarantee an entertaining story.

"It took mere seconds for Alex to decide on a burrito grande. He had the foil covering the tortilla peeled back and was biting into it enthusiastically the instant it hit his hands. The whole thing was gone before Alex was within a block of his hotel, and as he walked through the lobby, he could already envision falling unconscious into the comfort of the waiting king-sized bed."

I slowly waved my hand through the air to indicate the passage of time. "Alex awoke at nine thirty. His stomach had a few rumblings but nothing of any consequence, and certainly nothing that would warrant backing out of the party invite. He was showered and out the door by ten forty-five, giving fleeting consideration to maybe grabbing a package of Tums before he thrust the address of the party into the taxi driver's hand. 'Fuck it,' he thought, 'I've never been slowed down by a little indigestion.'"

Already the gang sitting around the table began to nod knowingly. They had a premonition where the story was heading.

"Anyway, by midnight the party was already at maximum velocity, and Alex had scored the attention of one of the hottest guys there. His stomach cramps were more frequent and a little more severe, but Alex was able to ignore them by focusing all his attention on the bulge in 'hot guy's' Levi's. Though, in a situation like this, introductions are superfluous, Alex was surprised to learn that the hot guy in tight Levi's was, in fact, named Levi.

"Levi, who himself was apparently not too bashful, pushed Alex's hand into his crotch, leaned forward, ran his tongue seductively over his ear, then whispered the magic invite: 'This party has a back room; you wanna go check it out with me?'"

The expressions around our table were now mixed. Some were flushed with the image of Levi, and some were already twisting with embarrassment, knowing we hadn't heard the last of the burrito.

"Alex stood, was pulled by Levi through the crowd at the party, and was pushed down an unlit corridor. He put his hand over his own stomach in an attempt to settle its rumblings, but was immediately distracted when Levi pushed him through the single door at the end of the hall. The light was brighter than he'd anticipated, and as a result, he was better able to appreciate all the people having sex around the perimeter of the room. In a word, it was *hot*. New territory even for our experienced traveling friend Alex."

I glanced over at Alex, and rather than detecting any indication of embarrassment, I noted he was completely caught up in the story. It was as if he neither knew the outcome nor that the story involved his own escapade.

I continued. "The tension as well as the passion were both ramped up a notch when Alex felt Levi beginning to unbutton his shirt. Standing behind Alex, Levi pulled Alex's ass hard against his crotch, let his hands slide down his chest, and let the stubble of his beard rub against Alex's cheek. Holding Alex in his powerful grip, Levi was able to pivot Alex's body so Alex was forced to look straight ahead. There, hanging from brackets in the ceiling, was a sling. Levi's breath was warm in Alex's ear. 'You gonna let me have you in that?'

"A cascade of thoughts slammed through Alex's brain. 'This is one of the hottest guys I've ever seen; I've never been in a sling before, but the idea has always been a turn-on. My stomach's been churning for a couple hours, but if the cramps haven't gotten intolerable by now, I'll probably be okay.'

"Sadly, Levi took Alex's hesitation as his unspoken consent to participate, so before Alex knew what was happening, his pants were around his ankles, he was being hoisted into the sling, and Levi was putting a condom over his own massive erection.

"Well, my friends, as a doctor, let me just inform you that though a person might be able to ignore stomach cramps when they're standing upright and clenching their buttcheeks closed, it's impossible to do so when their ass is swinging in a sling and their ankles are bound in stirrups suspended from the ceiling. The second Levi pressed a lubed finger into Alex's pucker, all hell broke loose."

By this time everyone, including Alex, was in hysterics, and like a comedian pushing a crowd into painful fits of laughter, I embellished the story even more.

"It was like a freight train coming out of a tunnel. The burrito grande that had been percolating in Alex's gut for the past five hours required immediate release. Diarrhea shot out of Alex's ass like mud out of a floodgate. Levi looked like he'd taken a swim in a septic tank. Needless to say, the erotic vibe went right down the sewer, and the back room emptied faster than yelling 'fire' in a theater.

"Fortunately, someone took pity on Alex and released him from the sling, or he'd probably still have been hanging there when the hazmat team showed up.

"Needless to say, Alex didn't get any more party invitations in Sydney, and I wouldn't be surprised if stories of his exploits didn't still circulate throughout the entire country of Australia."

The laughter continued for what seemed to be an eternity. The gang was undeniably completely grossed out but was simultaneously convulsing with laughter. Alex laughed harder than any of them. Incredibly, he beamed with pride. It was almost as if he thought his celebrity had ascended to a higher level, and he basked in the recognition. For any of the rest of us, being the central character of the story would have meant complete and utter humiliation. For Alex, it meant that once again, his adventures garnered unsurpassed notoriety and ensured his status as a gay icon.

Gay icon. Unabashed pervert. It was sometimes a fine line, but Alex prided himself on recklessly trying to skirt it.

Declan threw his arm around my shoulder and drew me into an embrace. "You're too much, Zack. You really know how to spin a story."

"Not too difficult when you have Alex to supply the material. I don't have to do anything except sit back and play the part of the narrator."

"Did that really happen to him Down Under?" Declan searched my face for an indication that the story had been a complete fabrication.

"How could I make shit like that up?" I said, trying my best to look offended that he'd challenged the authenticity of my rendition of Alex's adventure. "That shit really happened!" I smiled. "Literally and figuratively."

We were still laughing and exchanging comments about the frustrations we'd each had to endure in our respective workweeks when I looked up and noticed a guy sitting on the far side of the bar.

He looked Asian. Maybe Filipino. Olive skin, dark hair, and a killer smile. He was wearing a collarless shirt that tightly framed an incredibly muscular chest. He had a bottle of beer in front of him, but he only sipped from it occasionally. He seemed more determined to slowly peel the label off the side as he scratched it distractedly with his fingers. He bobbed his head with the music and soundlessly mouthed the lyrics. When he realized he was becoming increasingly animated as he threw himself into the song, he appeared to suddenly become self-conscious. His gyrations instantaneously froze, and he glanced around apprehensively. He looked like he hoped his enthusiasm hadn't become obvious to anyone watching.

Our gazes locked briefly, and he smiled awkwardly. He shrugged like he'd been caught doing something embarrassing, but then winked unapologetically. What the hell, he seemed to say; he'd been having fun.

I tilted my chin in his direction as I discreetly spoke to Declan. "Now that's husband material. Body of death, great smile, and obviously doesn't take himself too seriously."

Declan glanced over his shoulder to see who I was talking about. He immediately picked out the object of my desire based solely on his musculature. He smiled teasingly. "Since when have you become a rice fan. You're usually a bean-only kind of guy."

Declan knew I usually reserved my attraction for Latinos, but I tried nonetheless to appear put out. "Since the menu offered rice with extra muscle, that's when." I jabbed him jokingly in the ribs with my elbow. "Don't stereotype me. I welcome all comers." I lowered my voice an octave and smiled conspiratorially. "As long as they're built, have dark eyes, and don't come too soon."

He elbowed me back. "All comers, huh? When was the last time you went out with a blond guy?"

"Hey!" I responded smugly. "I said I don't discriminate, but I still have standards. I can't help it if it's been scientifically proven that only opposites attract. Would you have me disrupt the laws of nature?"

"Okay, Isaac Newton," he chided me. "Put your money where your mouth is and go talk to him."

My smile quickly faded, and I diverted my gaze. I flushed slightly and tried to play off my discomfort. "No, I'm cool. I didn't come out tonight to crash and burn. I just want to hang out with you guys."

As best friends, Declan and I went out together frequently. On those occasions, when one of us was attracted to someone, we'd frequently goad one another into working up the courage to go talk to them. In an attempt to defuse the disappointment we might feel if our advances were rebuffed, we'd arbitrarily convince ourselves we anticipated rejection.

"Go on," we'd push each other insistently. "Go crash and burn. The sooner you crash, the sooner we can pick up the pieces and continue to enjoy our evening." Even though we fervently hoped for success, we played it off that our intention all along had been to be brushed off. That way, we felt like neither our dignity nor our pride was ever in jeopardy.

We made it a game, but really, it was how we supported one another. We even had an understanding between us that if we'd gone out together, we wouldn't abandon one another. If, by some miracle, one of us happened to hit it off with whomever we approached, our goal was to exchange numbers. We wouldn't relegate the role of wallflower to whoever failed to hook up.

Truth be told, Declan seldom failed. He was good-looking, had an easy manner and a quiet confidence. At the end of the day, that was probably where he had me beaten. He had the confidence I lacked. There was a never a guarantee that when he approached someone they would immediately welcome his advances, but Declan was able to give the impression that they should. Before a word was even spoken, his attitude conveyed that if they declined, they would be the ones missing out. He wasn't cocky, he was just comfortable, and that comfort translated into infectious sex appeal.

That was what I lacked. I gave off a completely different vibe. It wasn't that I came off as desperate, but I'd never been capable of disguising my insecurities. Physically, Declan and I were polar opposites. While Declan had dark features and an olive complexion, I was blond, with lighter skin and hazel eyes. In addition, we were both fairly muscular and outgoing. The real difference was that Declan was confident he could turn heads. Never having really believed in myself, I couldn't imagine that anyone would find me attractive. I too was confident I'd turn heads, but I assumed if I was attracted to someone, they'd turn away.

"Zack," he said as he captured my eyes with his intent expression, "why do you always expect that it's going to be a crash-and-burn? I saw him smile at you. You have nothing to lose. Just go say hi. The rest of us aren't going anywhere. If he blows you off, come on back, and we'll continue laughing the night away. If he seems interested, give him your number and come back anyway. Either way, we're gonna have fun tonight. It doesn't matter how he responds. If he's cool, it's a bonus." He shrugged in the guy's direction. "There are empty barstools on both sides of him, so he looks to be alone. Pull your thumb out of your ass and go say hello." He bumped my shoulder again, intending to give me an encouraging shove.

I brightened. Why the hell not. Everything Declan had just said rang true. Despite his bolstering my confidence, however, I couldn't walk away without giving myself an escape clause. "All right, I'll go see if I can buy him another beer. But in case I crash and burn, you'd better have your fire extinguisher ready."

He gave me another shove. "Don't be defeatist."

As casually as I could, I walked over to the bar and stood next to the guy. I didn't acknowledge him initially and instead tried to get the bartender's attention. When the bartender circled over to me, I asked for another margarita.

"Margarita, rocks, no salt, please." Then I turned and gave the guy what I hoped was a winning smile. "Looks like you've pretty much succeeded in getting the label peeled off that one. Can I buy you another?"

He looked up at me, smiled appreciatively, but quickly diverted his gaze back to his bottle. "No, thanks. I'm good. One's my limit tonight. Thanks anyway, though."

Encouraged that his smile had at least been genuine and he didn't give the impression of being perturbed, I decided not to be put off by him declining my offer and mustered the courage to talk to him.

"Did that bottle do something to piss you off? You about have it stripped to the glass." Even as the question escaped my mouth, I regretted sounding like a complete idiot. What the fuck was I even talking about?

With a hint of embarrassment, he acknowledged the little shreds of paper around the base of his bottle. "No, the beer was okay; guess my fingers just need to be kept busy." He pushed the confetti into a neat little pile. "I was just listening to the music. I guess I wasn't even aware I was doing it. Oh well." He smiled briefly and brought the beer up to his lips to take another sip. "It will make it easier to recycle."

His comment carried a hint of humor, but after he said it, rather than looking at me, he stared out over the bar and continued to focus his attention on the beat of the music.

Discomfort began to surge through my body like ants racing up an anthill. Suddenly, I didn't know where to direct my gaze or what to do with my hands. I was still waiting for my margarita, so I couldn't just crawl back to my friends. I shifted my weight from one foot to the other and tried to act as if I hadn't noticed his indifference. "I'm Zack, by the way." I extended my hand.

He looked a little confused. In fact, by my estimation, he was embarrassed by the fact that I was being so pathetic and insistently trying to get his attention.

He shook my hand just before the bartender put my drink in front of me. "Gabriel," he said curtly. "Nice to meet you." I was reaching into my pocket to retrieve my wallet to pay for my drink when he pushed himself off his barstool and began making preparations to walk away.

For some reason, sensing that he was almost desperate to get away from me made me a little angry. Shit. It wasn't as if I'd tried to molest him. I'd just offered to buy him a drink and tried to start up a little conversation. My irritation suddenly overshadowed my insecurity, and as I pushed a couple of bills onto the bar, I interrupted his retreat.

"No sense in giving up your seat." I pushed as much nonchalance and confidence into my voice as I could. "I'm headed back to my friends anyway." I lifted my margarita in a mock toast, trying to give the impression that I had decided his existence on this earth couldn't have been any more insignificant to me. "Have a good evening. Enjoy the music. And," I said as I pushed off the bar, "go easy on pillaging those beer bottles. They're a protected species."

I turned away before offering him an opportunity to respond. I didn't want my joke to be mistaken as an attempt to further promote conversation. I walked back to my group of friends and to an overtly expectant Declan.

"Well?" he asked enthusiastically. "Did you get his number?"

"Hardly," I answered glumly. "I got little more than an invitation to drop dead."

"Really?" he continued a little disbelievingly. "Was he a dick?"

"No," I continued, still feeling a little dejected. "Not a dick, just not interested. Add my most recent attempt to fly to the growing list of aviation fatalities. Guess I'd better start wearing an inflammable suit when I go out. The crash isn't so bad, I just hate the burn." I gave him a weak smile as I lifted my margarita and took a generous gulp. "Here's to 'Go Greyhound.' I'm thinking about giving up flying all together."

He again threw his arm around my shoulder and gave me another encouraging squeeze. "His loss, dude. Forget it." He smiled broadly. "Going out is like fishing. Sometimes you catch a few." His smile widened. "Some you have to throw back. And sometimes"—he was now beaming and holding up his drink like a trophy—"you don't catch shit. Point is, just to concentrate on enjoying the fishing trip."

"Easy for you to say, oh master fisherman. I've never known you not to land anything less than ten inches." Now it was my turn to grin. "And we're not talking tuna."

He looked across the bar as he slapped me on the back. "Hey, look over there." He motioned with his chin. "The guy you were talking to has his arms wrapped around another dude, and it doesn't look like it's because they're brothers. No wonder he didn't talk to you, Zack," he said, looking at me earnestly, "he's got a boyfriend."

I glanced over my shoulder and confirmed his impression. Gabriel and the other guy were lost in one another's eyes. It was obvious they had something going on.

"Terrific." I stared into my drink. "Nothing like throwing yourself to the wolves when the prize isn't even available. No big deal. He probably wouldn't have liked me anyway."

"Zack." Declan grabbed my chin gently and forced me to look at him. "Why do you go there? Why do you always get down on yourself? The guy has a boyfriend. He probably would have blown you off if you'd been a *GQ* model with a degree in rocket science who worked for NASA. It's not about you. He's taken."

To be sure his admonishment was getting through, Declan held my gaze and spoke with even more conviction. "You're too tough on yourself. You only concentrate on the rejections. You never give yourself credit for all the guys who have been interested in you. Worse, you're completely oblivious to all the guys you yourself aren't attracted to."

So as to emphasize his point, he directed me to look over my shoulder to the other side of the bar. "Without being obvious, look at that Hispanic guy sitting with his friends at the table in the corner. Next to the banana plant. He hasn't been able to take his eyes off you since the moment you walked in, and he's good-looking to boot. Trouble is, he doesn't work out, so because he lacks a rack of solid muscle, he has no prayer of catching your attention." Declan looked at me even more intently. "Does that mean he should go home and cry in his porridge? Or should he keep looking until he finds someone who thinks skinny guys are hot?"

Though I understood the point Declan was trying to make and appreciated his support, I couldn't help but to poke a little fun at the intensity of his lecture. "Does he really eat porridge?" I asked while trying to look appropriately confused.

It took Declan a second to register that I was being facetious, but when he did, he whacked me on the back of the head. "You know what I mean, Zack. You're your own worst enemy. You either bring most of your disappointments on yourself or you blow them way out of proportion."

CHAPTER 4

As I made my way down the stairs from the locker room at the gym to the cement pool patio, I noticed that the pool was pretty crowded. All the lanes had at least one swimmer, and most of them had two. *Great. Just what I needed: an opportunity to give someone a piggyback ride.* Though I was in damned good shape, I wasn't a strong swimmer. Invariably, when I had to share a lane with someone, they would overtake me, and I would either have to allow them to pass or end up having them swim over me. On crowded days, it seemed I spent more time trying to avoid the faster swimmers than I did swimming.

My motivation for getting into the pool was that I had aspirations of participating in a mini triathlon. Though I was excited about the prospect and had the best of intentions, the swimming part of the competition was definitely going to kick my ass. I was a natural runner and could bike with the best of them, but swimming? My goal was just to survive. Some guys would enter the pool and their stroke was effortless. They would glide through the water like a knife slicing soft butter. They'd barely make a ripple. Watching them reminded me of seeing a shark's fin cutting through waveless surf. Theirs was a sharp contrast to my style. As smooth as I tried to be, to an observer it probably appeared as if I were drowning or that I was trying desperately not to be sucked to the pool floor by a giant vacuum. No wonder I swam slowly and fatigued quickly. For me, it was more a battle for my life than it was a sport.

My friend Gary had once suggested that I should be filmed swimming so a network could use the footage on a *Jerry Lewis* telethon. He was confident if an audience were to see my antics in the water, the viewers would be persuaded to donate money to help the handicapped. As I lowered myself into the pool and adjusted my swimming goggles, I reminded myself that next time I had dinner with Gary, I would mix some extra-strength chocolate ex-lax into his dessert. Asshole wouldn't think he was so funny if he shit himself in public.

My goals were to concentrate on my breathing and on my stroke. When I watched more experienced swimmers, I noticed that they only breathed every third stroke. For me, it required significant concentration, and I invariably felt that with the exertion of swimming, I had to hold my breath for longer than I was capable. It was almost impossible for me to take three strokes without taking a breath. Then, by the time I rolled my head out of the water to breathe, I ended up releasing an explosive gasp and felt forced to try to take two or three deep successive breaths while my mouth was still above the surface of the water. I felt pretty certain that to an impartial observer, the whole performance looked more like a near drowning incident than a display of athleticism.

For me, it was an accomplishment to swim three consecutive laps without having to stop and rest. It was absurd. Swimming a mere three laps had me standing at the end of the pool gasping as if I'd just sprinted five miles. Pathetic! How would I ever succeed in finishing the mile swim required in the mini triathlon if I couldn't swim more than three laps? I envisioned them having to drag the bottom of the lake for my body.

If nothing else, I was persistent. I refused to be discouraged by my uninspiring aquatic skills, and eventually I succeeded in completing my goal of twenty laps. Miraculously, I even pushed myself to swim four laps at a time without resting. I felt a sense of accomplishment for not having given up prematurely, but I was definitely beat. When I finished, I was so winded from the effort that even climbing the ladder out of the pool was a challenge. I tried to console myself by repeating over and over in my head that practice would result in impressive improvement. Or alternatively, as I ran my towel over my chest, practice would secure me a spot in the Special Olympics. "Damn Gary for planting that picture in my head."

It was a sunny weekend day, so in addition to the pool being crowded, most of the patio lounge chairs were also occupied by guys sunbathing. I circled through the throngs of lazy sun worshippers, hoping to find a vacant lounge. The exertion of my water escapades left me eager to lie down and soak up some rays. Finally, I saw someone getting up on the far side of the pool, and I navigated quickly through the maze of chairs, hoping no one standing closer would snag it.

Thankfully, I had no other immediate competition for the empty chair, and I succeeded in walking over to it and covering it with my beach towel. I sat down lazily and reached into my backpack. I pulled my sunglasses out, put them on, and then proceeded with my sunbathing preparations. Once my eyes were shielded with the dark lenses, I could look at all the golden bodies on display without fear of being detected. I squeezed some suntan lotion into my palm and began to rub it over my arm as I carefully surveyed the crowd. *Let's see, is there anyone on today's poolside menu who looks particularly delicious?*

My initial preview was generally disappointing. A guy a couple chairs down from me was wearing a bright-yellow thong, but I wasn't sure what kind of attention he was hoping to attract because his stomach was so big it pretty much engulfed his cock. I thought the point of wearing a thong was to display your jewels to the world. It had never occurred to me it could be substituted for a sausage tie. On him, the thong was reduced to little more than a flash of yellow that disappeared between his rolls of fat. Maybe he was hoping a chubby chaser would wander down to the pool craving a hookup with Oscar Mayer. I shook my head in disbelief. What was he thinking?

Well, I thought as I tried to recover from the visual assault, *after seeing that, the view has to get better.* As was usually the case on sunny days, the gym patio served as a display case for some prime meat. I recognized a few of the guys reclining casually on the chairs from the cover of *Men's Fitness* magazine. I had to chuckle. Physically, they epitomized the essence of masculinity—strong and muscular, with chiseled abs and sharp features. Ironically, however, for many of them it was all a ruse. They could only pull off being testosterone poster boys until you heard them speak. They'd open their mouths and a purse would fall out. How many straight men who pored over the pages of the magazine, desperate to pick up workout tips, would shudder at the realization that the guys they were idolizing were in fact big old queens? Though I myself was envious of their bodies, I had to laugh at the irony.

I let my gaze continue to wander around the poolside spectacle. There really were quite a number of good-looking guys, but many of them were sitting in groups. Even if I had the courage, there was just no inconspicuous way to walk up to a tight group of good-looking men and try to break into the conversation. I mean, I suppose you could pretend to be taking a survey and approach them about participating, but for that kind of charade, you'd better come prepared with a clipboard and some questionnaires.

I chuckled, embarrassed at even considering the scenario, but spent more time than I'd ever admit letting my brain work out some of the details of implementing such a ploy. Once the object of my desire had been identified, I would boldly grab my clipboard and break confidently into his group. I'd promise that participants in the survey would be eligible to win a big-screen TV, and then I'd single out the guy I was attracted to and proceed to ask him to reveal his favorite movie, what he looked for in a perfect date, and his telephone number. *Oh*, I thought mournfully, *were only I to have the balls, my personal life would be significantly more scandalous and eventful.*

The sun began to lull me into a state of blissful relaxation, and even my daydreams began to slowly disappear into the shadows of my consciousness. I felt like I was floating, fading in and out of even a partial awareness of what was going on around me. I was so out of it that I barely noticed when the guy sitting right next to me evacuated his chair and someone new took his place. It wasn't until I heard an iPod slide off the chair and clatter onto the cement that I even fully opened my eyes.

When I did, I was shocked. Standing next to me, adjusting a towel over his chair, was the good-looking guy I had seen in the gym a week or two before. I recognized him immediately. His hair was wet from having just gotten out of the pool, but when he gave it a quick shake, it fell perfectly into place. He looked more clean-shaven than he had the first time I'd seen him, and his skin was flawless: olive colored, slightly flushed from exercise, radiant. Shirtless, his body was even more impressive than I'd initially imagined. He had an unbelievably sculpted chest, washboard abs, and a mat of softly curled black hair lightly covering both. A tight waist tucked into the drawstring of form-fitting Speedos and a pair of incredibly muscled legs sprung from beneath. As I drank in the essence of his amazing physique, I had to steady my breathing. I didn't want to embarrass myself by hyperventilating.

I vacillated over saying anything. I mean, it wasn't as if his sitting next to me represented an invitation to strike up conversation. His intention might have been to just relax in silence and enjoy a little solitude. On the other hand, he had just shown up. It might appear rude not to even acknowledge him. I silently chastised myself. *Zack, when are you gonna grow a pair. He's standing right next to you. What do you have to lose by saying hello? Opportunity might only knock once. You never know if you'll get a second knock… or chance… or what the fuck ever. Just say something.*

I repositioned in my chair, giving the impression of only trying to get more comfortable and then, as noncommittally as possible, casually asked, "How was the water?"

He glanced briefly in my direction, seeming confused about whether I was directing the question to him. When he realized I was looking at him, he smiled and offered a single word response: "Good." Then, after appearing to deliberate whether to continue, he added, "I saw you swimming earlier." A thick accent accentuated his words, and a kidding smile spread across his face. "My neighbor's three-year-old son has a pair of water wings. You might consider investing in a pair."

Forgetting my nervousness, I burst out with a laugh. "Hey," I said, pretending to be insulted, "I happen to be an incredible swimmer. In fact, it's seldom that I even enter a pool without someone approaching me about the possibility of being a lifeguard."

His eyes danced mischievously and his smile broadened. "Listen, I don't even know you, so I certainly don't intend to hurt your feelings, but I think that you might have misunderstood their question. I suspect they were actually asking you if they should call a lifeguard. Anyone watching you swim fears for your life."

My heart soared. He had a sense of humor. "Oh, now I get it." I tried to inject a little remorse into my voice. "That explains why a life preserver always seems to be randomly tossed into my lane shortly after I start swimming. I thought it was just a coincidental training exercise." I sat up enthusiastically and faced him. "Where are you from, anyway?"

At that instant, the joking expression faded quickly from his face and his answer was curt. "Why do you ask? Do you think I have an accent?"

I was startled by the abrupt change in his demeanor and immediately tried to compensate for unintentionally offending him. "Man, I'm sorry. Yeah, I noticed you have an accent, but I think it's great. Your voice sounds like music. I lived in Brazil for a few years and learned to speak Portuguese while I was down there. I never lost my American accent. People said it was part of my charm." I slowed down. I didn't want to appear to gush. "Your accent," I said apologetically, "is part of your charm."

He continued to look a little offended, and rather than being warm, his expression was now dubious. "I'm from Italy." He went about organizing his things, then put his earbuds into his ears, giving the unmistakable indication that the conversation was over.

I was crestfallen. I didn't know what I had said to offend him, but his ethnicity was obviously a sensitive issue for him. I pushed myself back onto my chair. I felt immediately despondent. I really hadn't meant to insult him and was sorry he had misinterpreted my intentions. I would like to have tried to make amends, but he was clearly not receptive to more conversation.

I tried to console myself and initiated an internal pep talk. *Let it go. You'd be justified in beating yourself up if you'd purposefully been a dick, but you were just trying to be friendly. Give yourself a break.*

Though I didn't understand why the guy had suddenly become put out, I knew I'd completely blown my chances of even shooting the breeze with him. I sank back into my chair and exhaled a sigh of defeat. Without really giving it any consideration, I absentmindedly whispered, "Hope your iPod still works."

"What?" He turned slightly toward me and pulled one of his earpieces out.

I was kind of surprised because I didn't think I had actually vocalized my thought.

I looked at him more intently than perhaps I would have liked but answered very unemotionally, "I was just saying that I hoped your iPod still worked. It made a pretty loud crash when it fell onto the cement."

"It's okay." He lay back against his chair and closed his eyes, but didn't attempt to reinsert the earpiece. He was quiet for a few more seconds, then offered, "I've dropped it a million times. Damn thing just refuses to break." He went quiet for so long I figured he'd just answered me to be polite, but then, out of the blue, he asked, "What kind of music do you like to listen to?"

I tried to contain my euphoria. He'd asked me a question. Granted, there was no enthusiasm in his tone, and he might not have cared whether I answered, but at least he was taking the initiative.

I couldn't help to be a little guarded, however. Once bitten, beware. I didn't want to risk saying something that would cause him to withdraw again. Then I found myself getting irritated at my own caution. Why was I so worried about being careful? It wasn't like I had been overtly obnoxious before. I had just asked an innocent question. Inquiring about where someone was from wasn't like reaching into their pants.

My brain was already a train wreck of conflicting thoughts, and no more than fifty words had thus far been exchanged between us. I made the decision to relax. Despite thinking he was drop-dead gorgeous, second-guessing myself in an attempt to impress him would only result in making me look like an idiot. Nothing to be lost by being honest.

"You're going to think my taste in music is totally lame," I said with a sincere chuckle.

He glanced over in my direction and seemed to be genuinely curious. "Try me."

"It sounds so clichéd. I like classic disco, and I like songs by Streisand, Celine and"—throwing one more in for good measure—"Bette Midler." I smiled. "So, it's either the soundtrack from a pride parade or a gay piano bar. Take your pick."

Now it was his turn to laugh. "Add Judy Garland to your list, and I'll paint a pink triangle on your forehead."

"Hey," I protested, "they're icons! I bet you were singing their songs from your mother's knee when you were a child in Italy."

I froze for a second. Damn if I hadn't again referenced his country of origin. If it was a sensitive subject, I was persisting in poking at it with a stick.

This time however, it didn't seem to faze him. His smile remained steadfast on his face and he began to conjecture. "Let me guess, Whitney Houston has a dozen entries on your playlist."

"Who doesn't love Whitney? Don't you wanna dance with somebody who loves you?"

He continued to smile. "As long as it's just one moment in time." He rolled to his side and looked directly at me. "So, you're a diva. What else do you do for fun?"

I wrinkled my brow. "I'm not the only one who knows all of Whitney's greatest hits. You're probably president of her fan club." I fell back against my chair and lazily pulled up one knee. "What do I do for fun?" I repeated his question rhetorically. "Well, I'm kind of a sports enthusiast. I jog, I bike, and I like to hike and rollerblade. Also, I used to snow ski a lot. In fact, I used to ski professionally. And"—I paused for dramatic effect—"I'm a hell of a swimmer." I barely got the last words out before I started laughing. "I really am thinking about applying for a job as a lifeguard."

He laughed too, then said, "I guess some pool somewhere is going to see an increased body count."

I looked at him seriously. "Does that mean you think I should withdraw my application to be on the US men's Olympic swimming team?"

"No, don't withdraw it." He continued to smile. "They probably need a towel boy."

"Hmmm." I thought contemplatively. "I can think of worse things than working in the Olympic locker room. Where do I apply?"

He huffed. "I knew the minute I saw you that you were a pervert."

I just smiled more broadly. "May I offer you a towel?" After a minute, I said, "Seriously, I also like to read. Murder mysteries are my favorite. I'm a pretty fair cook, and as soon as I live someplace with a yard, I'm gonna get a dog." I smiled again. "It sounds like a list from a personal ad, doesn't it? I give up. Your turn. Other than obviously staying in great shape," I said as I appraised his body again briefly, "what do you do for fun?"

He flopped back on his chair. "Everything I do is fun. I'm Italian. Life is a party."

I was confused. Suddenly his heritage was no longer a dangerous topic. I decided not to press my luck. "That's not fair. You have to at least give me a partial list. You can't default by saying 'everything.' That's cheating."

He pushed his glasses up to the top of his head captivating me with his amber eyes and offered me a cocky grin. "It's not cheating if I make the rules."

Looking at him made it difficult to concentrate, but I was determined to hold my ground. I replied with unequivocal certainty, "Italian rules are invalid here. We're governed by the international playbook. If you don't list at least three things you do for fun, you automatically forfeit, and the medal goes to the American." I smiled at him expectantly.

He tried to look indignant for a minute, then returned my smile. "I tease blonds, I'm a swimming judge, and,"—he lay back and pulled his sunglasses back down—"I'm a professional sun worshipper. Is that three?" He assumed a pose of utter relaxation.

"Yeah, that's three," I said with joking defiance. "But I'm still going to contest your answer to the judges. I'm betting you'll get points off for being too vague."

"Okay." He shrugged. "I tease American blonds." He rolled his head slightly in my direction. "Is that specific enough for you?"

"It will still be a violation of the rules unless the blond American gets to know your official name." It had occurred to me that I could turn our innocent little exchange to my advantage. What better way to learn his name? I teased to be a little more coercive. "Come on, gold medal is on the line. Will the Italian go for the glory or go down in flames?"

He was undeterred. "I can sit here without saying another word and still take silver. That's enough glory for me. You can keep the gold, and I'll even throw in the flames as a bonus." He rolled back to a more comfortable position and sighed contentedly, as if his triumph had been effortless.

I had to admire his stubbornness. He sure wasn't going to allow himself to be backed into a corner not of his choosing. Not wanting to jeopardize the light mood, I resisted pushing him to divulge any more information about himself. I, too, let my head fall against my chair and pretended my teasing had never had an ulterior motive.

"Too bad," I said. "Crowd had their money on the Italian. Never figured the blond would capture the gold." I was quiet for a minute, then felt compelled to throw out one last try.

"Zack." I said. "His name was Zack."

Taken a little off guard, the guy turned back toward me. He looked genuinely baffled. "Whose name was Zack?"

"The guy who took home the gold. His name was Zack." I couldn't help but smile. "Same as mine."

He shook his head, and though his face offered an expression of impatience, his voice was warm. "Silver went to Sergio. Nice to meet you, Zack."

CHAPTER 5

ONCE the ice between us had been broken, conversation became much more fluid. Initially, we both exhibited a fair amount of restraint and avoided asking questions that could be construed as being too personal. Slowly, however, we became more comfortable with one another, and as a result were less guarded. Our dialogue became more spontaneous, my feelings of self-consciousness evaporated, and we spent the next hour laughing, joking, and slowly getting to know one another.

"So," I said hesitantly, watching him out of the corner of my eye to gauge any indication of discomfort, "how long have you lived in the United States?"

He answered without hesitation and as casually as if I'd ask him for directions to the corner store replied, "About seven years."

"Really?" I said. "What brought you west? No, wait. Don't tell me. You had dreams of becoming a big star in Hollywood." I initially suppressed a grin—I was confident he would interpret my question as being a joke—but I became a little anxious when I considered that wanting to break into acting might very well have been his motivation for coming here. His looks certainly qualified him as a tall, dark, handsome leading man. As far as I knew, he might actually have been either a successful actor or an actor wannabe.

I continued to smile but realized I was holding my breath to disguise my anxiety. Things between us had been going well, and I didn't want to inadvertently fuck things up by insulting him. Actors had a tendency to take their craft very seriously.

If he'd considered even for a second that my question had potentially been offensive, it didn't register in his expression. He launched into his response without a second thought. "No, I came here without a specific plan. My youngest sister, Lala, had moved here a year earlier. I was still living in Rome, and I was looking for a change. She told me that Los Angeles was great and that I would love it here. If you want to know the truth, I think that she was actually a little homesick and would have said anything to convince me to come join her. I arrived without a plan and was unable to speak much English." He eyed me a little defensively. "I speak English a lot better now, but guess I do still have a slight accent." He emphasized the word "slight," though he smiled in acknowledgement that his accent was in fact still pretty thick. "That was seven years ago." He rolled onto his back and relaxed as if he was fatigued from having narrated an entire biographical documentary. "The rest is history."

I smiled too. I was smitten. In the time we'd spent together, he had proven himself to be charming, humorous, and warm. He undoubtedly had an edge, but I was learning it usually only revealed itself when he felt threatened or ill at ease. He used his defensiveness as a shield to deflect discomfort. Beneath a confident, cocky exterior, I was beginning to believe there lay a genuinely nice guy. Or maybe I was choosing to believe that because I was developing a crush on him.

"Man! Coming here under those circumstances took incredible courage. You're, like, an Italian superhero." I grinned to assure him I was being facetious. "No, really, it did take balls. To leave your native environment and move to a country where you didn't speak the language and without the guarantee of a job. You must have been scared shitless in the beginning."

He let the corners of his mouth creep up as if he was reminiscing. "Well, it's not like I was going it alone. When I first arrived, I stayed with my sister. Her English had become pretty fluent by then, and she helped me land a job pretty quickly." He smiled fully. "You're making it sound as if I traveled over here on a banana boat and was forced to live on the streets."

"You're Italian. I know you didn't come over on a banana boat." I grinned like I was going to clarify what I knew would have been the more likely scenario. "It was probably in a pizza box." He threw his rubber sandal at my head but couldn't stifle a soft chuckle.

"So what did you do?" I asked curiously. Though Sergio was playing it down, it seemed apparent, to me, anyway, that he had somehow managed to succeed despite a fair amount of adversity.

"What do you mean, what did I do?" He looked at me as if he expected my question to have some hidden element of complexity.

"For work? What kind of job were you able to get without being able to speak English?"

"Oh." He relaxed with the realization that my intention hadn't been to extract some deep-seeded personal information. "I started working in an Italian restaurant. Lala—my sister's name is Laura but we call her Lala—was pretty well connected in the Italian community, so when I arrived, helping me to find a job wasn't too difficult. As a matter of fact, because I had waited tables before, it was easy. The trouble was not speaking English. I had to start as a busboy, and everyone assumed I was Mexican. Pissed me off." He sneered when he looked at me. "Do I look Mexican?"

"No." I tried to keep a serious expression. "With your accent and dark features, I would have guessed that you were Swedish." I grinned. "Who cares if they thought you were Mexican? How long did it take you to work your way up? How long before you became a waiter?"

His tone gave the unmistakable impression that I had again touched on a sensitive subject. "There's a big difference between Mexicans and Italians." Then, apparently deciding not to make it an issue, he continued. "I bussed tables for about six months, then became a waiter. I worked at the same restaurant for about a year, then was recruited to the restaurant where I'm working now. I still wait tables but am also the floor manager." His voice definitely resonated with a tone of pride. "Osvaldo's on La Cienega. Have you been there?"

"Wow," I said, conveying to him that I was genuinely impressed. "That's one of the nicest Italian restaurants in town. I've never eaten there." I smiled at him, giving the impression that what I was about to say was also intended as a compliment. "Too rich for my wallet."

He seemed pleased by the recognition. "You'll have to come by sometime. I'll treat." Then, realizing that the invitation might have seemed too forward and not wanting me to assume he was already suggesting a bona fide date, he quickly retreated. "I'll throw a scoop of gelato in your direction. We make it ourselves. I'll even go so far as to let you choose the flavor."

"Cool, I'll hold you to that." Then, to let him know I recognized an attempt to backtrack when I saw it, I continued teasing. "A scoop of gelato." I smiled enthusiastically. "Sounds like an excellent first date." I continued to hold his gaze, looking for any indication that my comment had made him squirm. It wasn't a direct proposition, but the intent was none too subtle. Make no mistake: I was hoping for a first date.

His expression, however, remained completely neutral. He looked neither uncomfortable nor eager. In fact, he lay back down as if any inference had been lost on him completely.

I was disappointed. I had been hoping for a sign. Was he interested? I knew his English wasn't perfect, but I also knew that he wasn't naïve. He had probably understood my hint perfectly and had decided to just play it cool.

I arbitrarily decided not to let my disappointment leave me disheartened, though. It was pretty obvious we had been enjoying each other's company, so I convinced myself to stay in the moment. Why let expectations sabotage a good thing? If nothing progressed beyond the next five minutes, at least I would remember having had a fun afternoon.

I too assumed a more comfortable posture on my lounge chair. "Okay, Mr. Silver Medalist, because I am such a gracious winner, I'm going to give you a second chance in a rematch." I figured we were comfortable enough with one another that there was now no risk in asking more questions to try to get to know him better. "What gives your life meaning other than working out in the gym and waiting tables?" He looked confused when I glanced over at him, so I clarified. "What else do you do for fun?"

He was quiet for a minute, and I began to fear that I had again allowed myself to skate out on to thin ice. He was a difficult read. I never knew when he was going to interpret something I asked as being too intrusive. I forced myself to relax. We were just having a conversation. He didn't have to volunteer his blood type. He could be as vague as he wished.

I waited casually, as if I wasn't aware of his prolonged silence. Though, if he didn't answer, I wasn't sure how I would redirect the conversation. It would be hard to choose a safer topic than what he did for fun.

When he did answer, his voice was soft, but its tone was filled with an unmistakable resolve. "I'm an artist." He looked at me to affirm that I hadn't reacted negatively to the disclosure, then elaborated. "At least I want to be."

"That's amazing," I said with genuine enthusiasm. I had always been envious of people who had artistic ability, and even had I not been attracted to Sergio, I would have been impressed. "What kind of medium do you work in?"

Above his dark glasses I could appreciate that he had furrowed his brow. "Medium?" he asked.

"Yeah, do you paint, do you sculpt, do you draw? What kind of artist are you?"

"Oh." He relaxed when he understood my question. "I paint. Well," he said, his smile betraying a slight embarrassment, "at least I try to."

"Oh, come on," I chided, "I bet you're being modest. Has any of your work ever been displayed?"

"Only in some small galleries," he conceded almost apologetically. "Nothing big." Then, with either a renewed sense of pride or with a little bit of bravado, he interjected, "Yet!"

"That's so cool." My enthusiasm negated the promise I had made to myself not to be too forward. "I would love to see some of your work."

He seemed to appreciate my sincerity. Rather than acting as if he thought my response was an attempt to manipulate him, he seemed genuinely pleased. He smiled, idly scratched the hair in the cleft of his impressively muscular chest, then answered, "Maybe we can make that happen one day."

Giving the impression that he sensed we had connected on more than a superficial level, Sergio ran his eyes over me appreciatively. Almost as if he were seeing me for the first time, he burst into an enthusiastic line of questioning. "Okay, Zack. Italian, pizza box, waiter, artist...." He smirked at me teasingly. "... and swimming judge. That's me. Tell me something about you. What kind of work do you do?"

Surprisingly, I hesitated. Certainly I was proud of being a doctor. In fact, it was one of the few things about myself that I was proud of. It was just that in the past, when guys learned what I did, I felt that they came to one of two immediate conclusions: I was either boring or I was rich. I didn't want Sergio to assume I was boring, and as a resident, I damned well wasn't rich.

As I considered my options, I tried to buy myself some time by replying noncommittally, "I work in a hospital."

He smiled, as if he realized I was purposefully dodging the question. "Do you sweep the floor, or are you a nurse?"

So much for being vague. I let my gaze float over the pool, acting as if I'd inadvertently forgotten to disclose only a small detail. "No, I'm a doctor." I paused for a second, but then quickly interjected, "Actually, I'm in my last year of residency." I didn't sound defensive. I guess my immediate clarification was an attempt to dispel any expectations that I might be rich. I looked at him guardedly and tried to gauge if he had concluded that if I was a doctor and not wealthy, I therefore must be boring. *Damn*, I thought. *Could I, just once, assume that someone might actually have a positive first impression of me?*

Unbelievably, his face brightened immediately. "Wow, good-looking *and* a doctor. That's not something you see every day." He gave me a cockeyed grin. "I might even pretend to be sick just for the benefit of an exam." He gave me an almost imperceptible wink.

For reasons I couldn't fully explain, I was dumbstruck. I would never have dreamed that his reaction would be both affirming and flirtatious. Whenever I was talking to a guy as good-looking as Sergio, before the first words were even spoken, I began building myself up for rejection. It was as if I could feel myself being sucked back into my adolescence and being swallowed by all the insecurities I had ever felt.

I was sure that as a subconscious attempt to protect my feelings, I had preemptively begun to write "defective" across my own forehead so I wouldn't be hurt if Sergio read it. I had indoctrinated myself to believe that anticipating rejection made dealing with it more tolerable. Years of conditioning made it implausible to think, even to hope, that my interest in him would be reciprocated.

When he responded so positively, it became impossible for me to suppress my smile. "Hmm, for you we might even be able to work out a private house call." I smiled broader. "That's usually a service provided only to my celebrity clients, but for you I think I'd be willing to make an exception. And," I said as I pushed my sunglasses down so he could see my eyes, "the exam would come with a satisfaction guarantee."

He laughed and shook his head gently. "I'll keep that in mind." Then, just to prevent me from building immediate expectations, he smiled and flexed his bicep. "Fortunately for me, right now I'm feeling pretty damned healthy."

I was sure my expression registered how impressed I was with his physique, and now, if he was trying to retract what had been a subtle come-on, I wasn't going to be discouraged. Also, because I sensed we really had begun to hit it off, I replied, "Yeah, but you might still benefit from an exam to officially certify that impression." I winked. "You never know what might turn up."

With seemingly no effort, his expression went from teasing to an intensity that took my breath away. "If something turns up, I'd better find myself in good hands." Apparently, the come-on hadn't been accidental.

I swallowed, felt a blush creep into my cheeks, but held his gaze and tried to answer with the same intensity. "Like I said—satisfaction guaranteed."

We stared at each other for a brief instant, then both started to laugh. He pitched himself back against his chair, then asked with genuine interest, "What kind of doctor are you, anyway?" Then he turned and looked at me a little skeptically. "You're not one of those who works on dead people, are you?"

I laughed. "What? Would that make you less enthused about me examining you? All you have to do is lie still."

The creepy expression that crossed his face was so funny it made me laugh harder. "Come on man, it's kinky. My bedroom is a walk-in freezer. Don't knock it until you've tried it." I continued to wail in hysterics but then, not wanting to carry the joke too far and have him run screaming away from the pool, I finally admitted I was teasing. "No, really, I'm a pediatrician. So don't worry, you're safe with me. In fact, you fall a little out of my age range, so you couldn't be my patient anyway." I paused. "Though the offer for a complete exam still stands. It would just have to be done after hours." I continued to grin.

He smiled too. "I'll let you know when I'm ready to make an appointment. In the meantime, why pediatrics? What made you choose that?"

As much as I had been enjoying the teasing, I was pleased he seemed to genuinely want to know more about me. I sat back, and my voice took on a more serious tone. "It just seemed like a natural choice. I love medicine. Love feeling like I'm helping people. It's just that I get a lot more satisfaction out of working with kids. They're innocent, they're resilient, and"—I looked at Sergio intently—"they're never really sick through any fault of their own. I mean, it wasn't very gratifying to take care of adults who were in liver failure because they had spent their whole lives drinking. Besides," I said with a smile, "when a kid throws up on you it can be kind of cute. When an adult throws up on you, it's always gross."

He looked a little taken aback. "I can't imagine throw up ever being anything other than gross."

"Guess you kind of develop a stomach for it. There are days when a little vomit is the least of your problems." I laughed, enjoying the easiness of our conversation.

I was relaxed, and as I sat there, I became contemplative. "Why pediatrics?" It was something I was frequently asked, but I usually just offered my standard response without giving it any real thought. Something about being asked by Sergio, however, necessitated a more intensive examination of my motives. I began to elaborate, as much to clarify my own thoughts as to give Sergio a more insightful explanation.

"I guess by nature I'm kind of nurturing." I blushed a little but was determined to answer sincerely, even if that meant being made to look ridiculously sentimental. "I like the intellectual challenge of medicine, but by taking care of kids, I'm free to love my patients too. Children were put on this planet to be loved. You can't look at a child without feeling something. I get the best of both worlds. My job requires me to use my brain, but I have the freedom to lead with my heart."

When I finished, I felt too embarrassed to look directly at him. "Does that sound really sappy?"

When he didn't immediately answer, I felt even more self-conscious. Maybe I had freaked him out with my Mother Teresa sermon. When I finally did get the courage to look at him however, I caught him staring at me intently. Rather than being put off, it seemed my honesty had made a profound impression on him. He held my gaze for a moment, smiled approvingly, then gave a nod. "Sounds like you've found your calling. That's cool." He lay back and tilted his face toward the sun. "Really cool."

When I lay back, I reached to fish my watch out of my backpack. "Man, it's almost five o'clock. We've been talking for three hours already. I have to get moving. I'm supposed to meet some friends for dinner at six."

I hesitated. I clearly didn't want to leave and would have preferred to continue talking to Sergio but wouldn't have felt right bailing on my friends. I felt immediately uncomfortable. Three hours of talking, and I suddenly couldn't make my tongue work. *What's the protocol here? Do I ask him if he wants to get together sometime? Do I ask him for his telephone number? Do I write my phone number down, hand it to him, and hope for the best?*

In an attempt to disguise my discomfort, I began desperately searching through my backpack as if looking for something of vital importance. Then, realizing I could only seek refuge in it for so long, I pulled my T-shirt and shorts out. The obvious progression would have been to begin putting them on, but I felt paralyzed. In protest, my body refused to move until my brain came to some sort of conclusion as to what to next say to Sergio. Feeling defeated, I just looked at him.

He seemed to be entertained by my exaggerated flurry of activity and just lay there smiling at me. Then, seeming to take pity on my nervousness, he came to my rescue. "You know, Zack...." He even managed to look a little embarrassed himself. "It might be fun to get together again sometime. Can I give you my number?"

Somehow, I managed to calm the adrenaline coursing through my body. I looked back at him and offered an apologetic smile. "That would be easier than me having to set up a vigil outside of Osvaldo's hoping to accidentally run into you."

We both laughed.

CHAPTER 6

THE next day at work was like an exposé on contradictions. On one hand, I was floating, feeling like the afternoon I had spent with Sergio was like having been given a free pass to spend a few hours in heaven. On the other hand, it was torture. How should I proceed? Should I call him that evening? Tell him how much I enjoyed meeting him? Or was this one of those situations wherein I was obligated to follow the three-day rule: when you met someone and exchanged numbers, you should wait three days before calling them so as not to give them the impression of being too desperate.

Those were but the beginning of the contradictions. Any memory of him lightened my mood, and I caught myself smiling even at staff who I ordinarily thought were incredibly obnoxious. The downside, however, was that the day dragged. I kept looking at my watch and tried to convince myself that when I got home, there would be a message from him waiting for me on my answering machine. In fact, I had to resist the urge not to check my messages every fifteen minutes because I knew that, in the event he hadn't called, dealing with the disappointment would consume so much mental energy I would be prevented from working effectively.

Shit! I felt like a fourteen-year-old girl struggling with her first crush. If I didn't keep myself in check, I was going to start to menstruate and break out in acne. I sighed at my own ridiculousness, and as I pushed myself away from the nurse's station, I subliminally chided myself. *Get a grip or get a tampon.*

I began to review the list of the patients on my service and groaned with the acknowledgment of how much work I had yet to do. At that moment, Peggy, another resident from my year, walked over and offhandedly said, "Hey, Zack, the ER just called. They've got an admission for you downstairs."

I cast a glance up at the clock above the nurse's station and then fixed my gaze on Peggy. She was the designated resident on call that night. It was two minutes before four. The official policy was that any patient requiring admission before four would go to the daytime admitting team, and any patient requiring admission after four would go to the night call team. I cast another dejected look down at my list of patients, and in as conciliatory tone as possible, said, "You know, Peggy, it's two minutes—correction: it's one minute before four. I still have a shitload of work to do. Could you just go ahead and take the admission?"

She looked at me as if I was speaking Greek. "The admission request was received before four; rule is that it goes to you."

I felt my ears flush. Peggy was such a bitch. Any of my other colleagues would have taken the patient without question. We all worked hard and understood the concept of protecting one another's free time. The on-call team was going to have to work all night anyway. One admission more or one admission less at that time of afternoon wasn't going to be a deal breaker. But a four o'clock admission assigned to the day team could delay being able to leave the hospital by two hours or more. And, because of the amount of work I had yet to finish, I knew I had another three hours ahead of me regardless.

My voice tightened. "The rule doesn't apply to when the request is received; the rule applies to when the kid hits the floor. If you get a call at six fifty-nine tomorrow morning, or one minute before you're supposed to sign out to me, about a kid coming from Santa Barbara, do you think you should be expected to wait the four hours it will take for the kid to arrive because the rule says that the request was received on your shift?"

Peggy flung her hair over her shoulder dismissively and smiled condescendingly, "Hell no, but in this case," she said, her smile oozing sarcasm, "the kid's already here. Just waiting for you down in the ER." She turned and began to walk away to indicate definitively that the discussion was over, but hazarded a parting comment over her shoulder. "Let me know when you're ready to sign out. I'll be in the resident's lounge."

Not even the memory of spending an incredible afternoon with Sergio did anything to squelch my anger. My blood pressure skyrocketed so quickly I thought I was going to have a stroke. The only thing that prevented me from telling her to go fuck herself was that technically, with an emphasis on the word "technically," she was right. The fact remained, however, that had it been anyone else, it would have been a no-brainer. The conversation would have been more along the lines of, "Zack, I'm going to run down and see the kid in the ER. When I get back, let me know what else I can do to get you out of here." The sacred expectation that trumped any rule was that we had one another's back. Peggy was the exception. She only had her own back. And for that reason, most of us could barely tolerate her.

I looked up at the charge nurse, who had overheard most of our exchange. She was shaking her head in disbelief. She mouthed the words "Prima donna" and rolled her eyes. Her reaction made me laugh. Another recruit into the "Everyone Knows Peggy's A Bitch" club. I smiled at her broadly and, with a feigned inflection of forced enthusiasm, said, "An amazing opportunity to impact the life of yet another sick and suffering child. I think I'll skip on down to the ER."

When I got down to the ER, I was directed to a room where I found a four-year-old with asthma. He was cute, had initially been pretty cooperative, but now was apprehensive about wearing the mask the respiratory therapist was trying to put over his mouth and nose. The mask appeared to be belching steam. It was connected to a compressor, and the mist escaping from it was actually medicine intended to improve his breathing. The respiratory therapist, who was apparently more accustomed to working with adults than with children, was getting frustrated and just kept repeating the same instructions to the little boy over and over.

When I entered the room, I heard him trying to maintain a sense of calm but detected the irritation in his voice. "I said, all you have to do is put this on and take deep breaths. It won't hurt. Come on. You have to do it. It will make you feel better."

The child's eyes widened in fear. He was sitting on his mother's lap, and he tried to press himself more forcefully into her chest. He had blond, closely cropped hair, big blue eyes, and rosy red cheeks. I wasn't sure if his cheeks were naturally that color or if they were redder from breathing hard.

I pulled the chart out of the door, read the patient's name, then directed my comment to the therapist. "I'll take it from here." He handed me the mask and grunted an unintelligible response, either out of irritation or out of relief that I'd rescued him from having to deal with an uncooperative four-year-old.

I rolled a stool over, nodded to his mom to ensure that she knew we were forming a team, then sat down so I'd be at eye level with the little boy. "Is your name Logan?" I asked.

He nodded but didn't answer. Instead he just eyed me apprehensively.

I smiled. "Did I see you ride in on the fire truck parked outside?"

He looked at me and his eyes displayed an expression of complete bewilderment. He remained transfixed but curious. I continued, "Yeah, I saw a big red fire engine parked right outside, and I thought that I saw you climbing down off of it. Some of the other firemen were telling me that their friend Logan had done a great job helping them put out the fire. Wasn't that you?"

If possible, his eyes became even larger, and though he still didn't speak, he began shaking his head.

"Hmmm." I tried to look confused. "You look an awful lot like a fireman to me. If they need help putting out a fire, do you think that maybe you could lend a hand?"

Now, with his interest piqued, he whispered, "Yes," and nodded. It wasn't loud but it was enthusiastic.

"Okay, I know they could use your help, but before you can get on the fire truck, you have to pass the fireman test. See this mask?" I held up the mask and realized as I looked at it that most of the medicine had been expelled uselessly into the air. I'd have to add more before I could give an adequate treatment. Nonetheless, I looked intently at Logan. "All the fireman have to prove to me that they can use one of these masks. Haven't you seen pictures of firemen going near a fire? All of them are wearing a mask. It protects them from the hot air. If you want to become an official fireman, you have to take the mask test."

I held the mask up again and shrugged indifferently. "You want to give it a try? Or should I see if I can find another little boy to help the firemen?"

Suddenly, he leaned forward with eager determination. "I'll try. I can pass the test."

"You sure? I mean, they said they were looking for a guy named Logan, but if you don't want to do it, I'm sure there's another little boy around here somewhere who would love to become a fireman."

"No, I can do it." Now he was reaching for the mask.

I helped secure the strap around his head and watched him as if I was evaluating a critical test. "Wow! You're doing great. You already look like a fireman. Let me see you take some deep breaths."

He beamed with pride and took a few deep inhalations without even modest hesitation. Such a concerted effort would ensure the medicine had optimal benefit. "You're doing great, Logan. The firemen are going to be really happy that they'll be able to add you to their team. Let me ask you something. Do you think you and your mom can stay here one or two days so you can do some more of the fireman training classes? It looks like you're on your way to becoming one of the best."

Logan turned to his mom and began pleading through the mask, "Can we, Mom? Can we stay here so I can learn some more fireman things?"

"Well," his mom said, trying to appear as if she was hesitating, "I suppose so. If you promise to do all the tests, I guess we can stay a day or two." She smiled at both of us.

I grinned at her warmly, and though I continued to direct my comments to her, I returned my gaze to Logan. "I'll need to take a more complete history and will still have to examine your son, but I hope that we'll have him as good as new within a couple days."

I then ran my hands through Logan's short hair and spoke to him teasingly. "Well, before you can become a fireman, I have to look you over head to toe. Are you ready?"

I had to push him gently back onto his mother's lap to prevent him from leaping into the air. What a transition. From trepidatious four-year-old to enthusiastic participant in little more than four minutes. If he could recover from his asthma attack at the same impressive rate, we'd have him home in no time.

I completed my exam and filled out both the paperwork and admission orders as expeditiously as possible. I was still irritated with Peggy for being such a bitch but had kind of enjoyed having been able to meet Logan. With any luck, I'd be able to complete the rest of my work and still be ready to sign out by seven. If Peggy thought I would expend even minimal effort to make her night on call go more smoothly, she was sorely mistaken.

I went through the list of all my patients and even went back and reexamined some of them. Most were doing well, and I didn't anticipate any major changes in their conditions overnight. I pulled a few of their charts to ensure I had reviewed all the recent labs, and then, satisfied I had fulfilled all my obligations, I sighed in preparation of paging Peggy to let her know I was ready to sign out for the evening.

I went into the residents' office and punched her pager number into the phone. She didn't call back for a full eight minutes. I was ready to page her again when the phone finally rang. "Hey, Peggy." My voice was completely without warmth but wasn't overtly hostile. "I'm ready to get out of here. Should be an easy sign-out. Are you ready?"

Forget a lack of warmth: Peggy response's came back to me like water dripping off a glacier. "I'm in the middle of eating. I should be up there in about twenty minutes. You can sign out then."

For the second time that day, I had to choke back the desire to tell her to go fuck herself. Instead, as calmly as was humanly possible, I responded, "Look, though I know this makes no difference to you, I would actually like to go home and have the opportunity to get something to eat myself. I've been here more than thirteen hours and have to be back in little over ten. Where are you? I'll bring the sign-out to you. I'll talk to you while you're eating. Shouldn't require that you even stop chewing."

She knew she really had no argument, so she begrudgingly replied that she was in the cafeteria.

"Fine," I said shortly, "I'll see you in two."

When I got to the cafeteria, I found her sitting alone at one of the back tables. A group of interns was sitting a few tables over, and a couple of them smiled and waved when they saw me come in. *Figures*, I thought. *Not even the intern working with Peggy for the night can tolerate being with her more than is absolutely necessary. If she wasn't such a pain in the ass, she wouldn't have to eat most of her meals alone.*

I smiled as I walked past the interns and joked facetiously with them, "You guys really have time to eat? Man, when I was an intern, we had to walk to the hospital in three feet of snow. We had no shoes, and if we wanted to eat, we had to scrape scraps off the patients' abandoned trays. You guys have it so easy."

I had to duck to miss being hit by a dinner roll that came soaring past my head, but it was accompanied by good-natured laughing. "Yeah, Zack," one of them shouted lightheartedly, "haven't you heard the song? It never rains in Southern California, and it sure as hell doesn't snow. If you had to walk through three feet of snow, it was because someone was trying to save patient lives by dropping your ass in Antarctica."

I laughed too. "Yeah? Well, apparently it didn't work. I succeeded in finding my way back, am here now, and am determined to make your lives miserable, so eat up. I've got a list of scut a mile long to keep you all from getting any sleep tonight."

Scut was a word that went down in infamy with interns. It referred to all the tedious, disagreeable chores that had to be done to keep a hospital running. Since shit rolled downhill, those jobs were usually delegated to the interns. Some scut was unavoidable. I was relatively popular with the interns because I was pretty conscientious about dividing it up equally with them. My philosophy was that the sooner the work got done, the sooner we could all relax, so even as a senior resident, I ended up doing as much scut as they did. Peggy was another story. Her attitude was that she had done her share of scut as an intern, so now, as a rite of passage, it was someone else's job. Thus, she was sitting alone and I was dodging flying dinner rolls.

Without so much as a greeting, I sat down next to Peggy and pulled the list of patients out of my pocket. "Everyone is pretty stable and shouldn't give you any difficulty tonight." I went over each name one by one, briefly discussed each child's diagnosis, and reviewed their condition with her. I concluded my fifteen-minute summary by saying, "Baby Martin's fever spiked a couple hours ago, so I ordered another CBC. If her white count is going up, you might consider changing her antibiotics to get broader coverage. I thought I'd probably switch from clindamycin to vanco."

She eyed me disapprovingly. "Have you checked on it yet?"

For a second, I didn't understand the context of her question. "Checked on what?"

"The CBC," she answered snidely.

"First of all," I answered impatiently, "I ordered it not more than thirty minutes ago, so it probably hasn't even been drawn yet. Secondly, Peggy, let me explain a concept that may be unfamiliar to you. The point of sign-outs is not for me to stay around all night to ensure that you don't have any work to do. The point of sign-outs is to make you aware of the things that are still pending to give you the opportunity to follow up on them. I know that under the current system, you might actually have to do something tonight, and I apologize. But that's the point of having a night call team. Sending me down to the ER to admit that kid at one minute before four was already a huge dump. Maybe within the letter of the law, but a huge dump nonetheless, and you know it. Now, why don't you pop a few Imodium? They might control your dumping tendency by slowing your bowels down for a few seconds and thus allow me time to finish signing out to you."

She glared at me but offered no rebuttal. "I've heard enough. Go home."

"Thanks," I replied, but my voice didn't offer even a hint of gratitude. "I'll see you in the morning." I almost knocked the chair over as I stood up. I wanted to leave quickly, before she had the opportunity to ask for any additional clarification. I thought she'd start nitpicking me for the sole purpose of keeping me captive.

When I got to my apartment, the light on the answering machine in my bedroom was flashing. My heart almost leapt out of my chest. I practically tripped as I launched myself across my bedroom and over to the blinking machine. My hand was shaking as I pushed the play button, and I unsuccessfully cautioned myself not to build up any high expectations. I held my breath as the automated voice announced in staccato beats, "You have one new message and four old messages. First new message: Mr. Sheldon, this is the West Valley Insurance Agency. You may be paying too much for car insurance. Please give our offices a call and ask to speak to one of our friendly sales representatives about…."

I didn't even listen to the end of the message. I almost broke my finger stabbing the delete button. I even cursed the answering machine for its blatant betrayal. The nerve of it to even record a damn solicitation when I was waiting to hear from Sergio. It was infuriating.

I drew a few breaths and calmed myself. I even felt a twinge of embarrassment for having allowed myself to feel such huge disappointment. *No big deal that he didn't call. He's probably busy. All I know for sure is that I had a good time talking to him. I'm powerless to influence whatever impression he might have had of me.* My mind raced with every cliché I had ever read in any self-help book. *Your only alternative is to continue to lead your life as well as you can. Give up trying to control variables over which you have no control. If he's not interested, better to know before you become even more emotionally invested.*

I caught myself in the middle of my own mental therapy session and released an almost pathetic chuckle. Shaking my head, I began consoling the empty room. "Could you forego doom and gloom long enough to at least take off your shoes? You said good-bye to him little more than twenty-four hours ago. Quit acting as if you've just been dumped. Jesus, within the confines of your own head and within a matter of mere seconds, you've created and destroyed an entire relationship that in reality hasn't even begun yet. It's a little too early to enter into the obligatory period of mourning."

I jumped into the shower and was relieved that I actually did succeed in putting Sergio out of my head. I let the hot water pour over my shoulders and felt the day's tension slowly seep out of my body. I even succeeded in pushing away thoughts of Peggy. I was sure she had already begun plotting how to guarantee tomorrow would be hell for me, but screw it; I refused to worry about it.

I closed my eyes, braced my hands against the wall next to the showerhead, and stood motionless for what seemed like an eternity. Then I grabbed the bar of soap and begin running it slowly over my body, concentrating only on the sensation of my own wet fingers against my skin. As I passed my soapy hand over my dick, I briefly considered getting myself off, but dispelled the inclination because I knew any fantasizing would bring memories of Sergio flooding back into my head, and the mental torture of second-guessing myself would immediately resume. Instead, I tried to imagine myself on a white sandy beach, enjoying a relaxing vacation, relieved of any responsibilities related to the hospital.

When the hot water began to run out, I rapidly rinsed off any remaining soap and grabbed my towel. Having successfully washed away most of my aggravation, my attention was drawn to my loud stomach rumblings. *Damn*, I thought. *I haven't eaten anything since the turkey burger at lunch more than nine hours ago. No wonder I'm starving. It's already past nine o'clock.*

I pulled on a pair of gym shorts, grabbed a raggedy tank top, pushed my arms through it, and tugged it on as I headed into the kitchen. I consider eating some of the leftover pasta in the refrigerator but was hesitant to consume so many carbs right before bed. I tried to limit most of my carbohydrate consumption to around workouts so the calories would be burned off. I'd never have the definition I wanted in my abdominals if I indulged in carb-loading as a bedtime ritual. Instead, I grabbed a can of tuna from the cabinet, some low-fat vinaigrette salad dressing, and a single slice of multigrain bread. A healthy tuna sandwich would have to do for dinner tonight. Besides, I was exhausted.

I was so focused on my hunger and so intent on my sandwich preparation that I was startled by the sound of the phone ringing. I grabbed it without really considering who might be calling. I pushed the talk button and cradled the phone under my chin to keep my hands free to spread the tuna over the freshly toasted piece of bread. "Hello." Apparently, even the tone of my voice sounded distracted.

"Uh, hi. May I speak to Zack, please?" Not even the uncertainly in his voice disguised his accent. Sergio was calling. I was so surprised, the phone tumbled off my shoulder, and I had to throw both the knife and the piece of bread I was holding onto a plate to grab it before it hit the kitchen counter.

Trying desperately to recover, and in an attempt to not sound like an idiot after I interrupted the phone's free fall, I paused a few seconds before replying, "Hey Sergio. It's Zack. How are you? I was hoping to hear from you." The last sentence came tumbling out before I could engage my filter. I wrinkled my forehead, closed my eyes, and reminded myself not to sound like I'd been obsessing about him all day.

Sergio's response sounded animated and musical. To my surprise, his tone actually suggested he was happy I had picked up the phone. "I was looking forward to talking to you too, Zack. This is the first opportunity I've had to call. I'm at work, and it's been crazy busy." He sounded irritated, though just briefly. "Some of my customers have been a real pain in the ass. But," he said, his voice lightening again, "I was calling to see how you were and to ask if maybe you wanted to get together this weekend."

I had to adjust the phone in my hands because I was concerned he could hear my heart pounding through it. I felt momentarily light-headed so took a few deep breaths to prevent my answer from betraying my excitement. There was nothing on the planet that I'd rather do. "Yeah, that would be great. I'm on call on Sunday, so I'll have to be in the hospital by 7:00 a.m. I'm off all day Saturday, though. What did you have in mind? Will Saturday work for you?"

I gritted my teeth, praying for what I hoped would be an affirmative response. "That works," he said happily. "I have the closing shift Saturday night, so I don't have to be at the restaurant until five in the afternoon. We could hook up in the morning. What do you think?"

My brain raced with any one of a million acceptances, but again, I tried to modulate my enthusiasm so he wouldn't suspect that were it possible, I would have climbed through the phone that very instant.

"Saturday morning would be great. What would you like to do?" I silently congratulated myself for sounding appropriately interested but not ridiculously excited.

"Do you have a bike? Maybe we could meet for breakfast then go for a bike ride. We could put my backseat down, throw the bikes into the back of the car, then head down to the beach. What do you think?"

"Excellent." I was no longer worried about trying to contain my enthusiasm. The plan sounded like a blast. "What time do you want to hook up?"

"Well, I'm going to need time to clean up before work, so I should be back no later than three thirty. If we want to make a day of it, we should get an early start. Can I pick you up at eight?"

I couldn't believe what I was hearing. Make a day of it? He wanted to spend the whole day with me? Again, an answer escaped my lips before my brain engaged, but at least it was accompanied by a lighthearted chuckle. "You can pick me up now."

There was a brief silence and a confused question followed. "Now?"

I continued to laugh. "I was just kidding. Saturday is good. I just don't want to have to work another four days before being able to see you again." I realized I was blushing and was relieved that Sergio couldn't see me. Trying to temper my response, I followed quickly with, "I love bicycling on the beach on a sunny day."

"Great." I could swear that Sergio's enthusiasm was equivalent to mine and smiled even more broadly when I thought I heard him catch himself when he replied, "It's set, then. It will be our first—" His voice caught. "Our first bike ride together."

I was sure he had intended to say date, and ordinarily I would have been concerned that his hesitation to do so indicated a reticence about going out with me. Then I shook my head and forced myself to admit that not even my abysmally low and twisted self-esteem could draw that conclusion. The man had just voluntarily suggested that we spend the whole day together.

Instead I smiled into the phone and said, "Yeah, our first bike ride together. If I didn't know better, I'd even say it was a date."

Refusing to take the bait, Sergio just responded, "Okay, I'll pick you up at eight. Listen, I have to get back to work. Let's try to talk again this week." Before I could reply, the cadence of his voice picked up. "Wait, wait, wait. I don't even know where I'm going. What's your address?"

I was still beaming as I basked in the prospect of "Let's talk again this week." However, in an attempt to return the conversation to a low-key exchange, and not wanting to scare him off with my eagerness, I opted for a casual response. "Have a pencil handy?"

His comeback was light with soft laughter. "I'm a waiter; I have a pocketful of them."

I laughed too. "Okay, it's 8753 Fourth Street. Near where Fourth Street runs into San Vicente. It's a duplex. We're on the second floor."

There was only a brief silence before an only slightly suspicious question followed. "Who's 'we'?"

What he was asking took a second to register, then I replied with a joking hint of surprise, "I have roommates. But you're not extending the invitation to them too, are you?"

"No," he answered. I couldn't tell if he was relieved or embarrassed about having asked for clarification. Either way, when he continued, he maintained the same good-natured tone. "The invitation is personal. I've got the address. I'll be there at eight. We'll talk before then, when I have more time. Oh, and Zack?" I could imagine him curling his lips slightly upward. "I'm looking forward to it too."

"All right, Sergio." I leaned against the counter, held the phone against my ear, and hugged my arms into my chest. I knew I sounded soft, warm, and content. "We'll talk. Have a good night at work. Saturday will be great." Before I hung up, I couldn't resist adding, "You made my day."

He laughed. "That's what I do. Good night, Zack."

CHAPTER 7

THE craziness of my work schedule had prevented Declan and me from seeing much of each other, so we decided to meet for dinner when I got out of the hospital the next day. The restaurant he had chosen was in the heart of Santa Monica, on the south side of Wilshire. It wasn't difficult to get to the actual location, but parking was a bitch and, because both of us were on a budget, neither was willing to spring the requisite seven dollars to valet. We ended up finding a free parking space on an obscure side street and walked about four blocks back to where the soft light of a neon sign designated which of the three glass doors was the entrance.

When we entered, we were greeted warmly by the hostess. She was an exotic-looking Thai woman with striking features. High cheekbones accentuated almond skin, dark eyes, and a beautiful smile that was welcoming though not flirtatious. She was petite but shapely, and her tight dress flattered the curves of what appeared to be an athletic and toned body. She escorted us to one of the tables and encouraged us to sit down. The table was so small it looked incapable of accommodating two people who intended to eat more than a single wonton, so it took some effort to maneuver into place. She laid the menus onto the placemats and then graciously informed us that our server would be over shortly. Her sinewy figure was so svelte it appeared she floated back to the hostess counter rather than walking.

I smiled at Declan as we unfolded our napkins. We both seemed to be thinking the same thing as we watched her walk away. "Sexy!" I noted. "And it all comes together for her without the slightest effort. Kind of reminds you of me, huh? If you're nice to me tonight and pick up the tab, I might even be willing to give you lessons."

The corners of Declan's mouth turned up to reveal what really was a handsome smile. As he hung his sweatshirt over the back of his chair, he retorted, "The only lesson I could possibly learn from you would be on the art of attracting trolls." He chuckled at his own joke as he tried to make himself comfortable on the narrow seat. Encouraged by the laugh I unintentionally allowed to escape, he continued. "You did have to write a dissertation to get into medical school didn't you? What was the title? 'Sleeping With Trolls: the Precautions and Perils. An Exposé of My Life!'"

In an attempt to interrupt what I thought for sure would become one of Declan's stand-up monologues, and despite the fact that he invariably made me laugh, I quickly interjected, "Hey, I can't help it if trolls think I'm irresistible. Besides, you're the one who makes the mistake of sleeping with them."

An expression of feigned indignation crossed his face. "There was just that one guy. Give me a break. The club was dark. In that mysterious blue haze, you thought he was pretty hot too."

"Yeah, but at least I have the sense to drag a potential trick outside and look them over under a streetlight before I take them home."

"But!" He averted his gaze and his grin became a little sheepish. "It was just that once, and in my defense, I had been doing a little drinking."

Now I was the one hesitant to let the subject drop. I was having fun watching Declan squirm. "Poor guy. He thought that you sleeping with him meant the two of you were engaged. Didn't he end up calling you five times a day for about a month after that?"

Declan tried to look noble. "Don't remind me. That's what I get for trying to let him down easy. I end up with a stalker who thinks if he's persistent enough, we'll end up registering at Pottery Barn."

Truth be told, the guy hadn't really been bad-looking. It was just that he had seen Declan from afar on a bunch of occasions and had developed a crush on him. When they ended up finally meeting and actually going home together, the guy thought his feelings for Declan were completely reciprocated. He'd immediately envisioned a future of wedded bliss. The whole episode had occurred more than a year before, but it still made for prime teasing material.

"Don't sweat it," I said. "In the sequel to my dissertation, I intend to devote a chapter exclusively to you."

"Don't flatter yourself," Declan taunted. "You couldn't even sell a copy of the first edition to your parents."

"Thank God for that. Like you'd want your parents reading about your bedroom exploits."

"Speaking about the next chapter in your book, you still haven't told me about the guy you met at the pool. He must be something, because when you first mentioned meeting him, you had such a sickening sweet smile on your face, I figured you'd given yourself an enema with honey." He sat back and grinned, ever proud of his uncanny ability to come up with witty one-liners.

"Hmm. I wondered what your secret was. A high colonic with honey. No wonder you attract bears." Satisfied that I had succeeded in turning the joke back on him, I continued despite being certain I was wearing a shit-eating grin. "Funny you should ask. A few days ago I might have told you that I'd probably never hear from him, but he actually called last night. We're going to spend the day together Saturday. We'll meet for breakfast and then go for a bike ride on the beach." My smile threatened to consume my whole face. "To say I can't wait would be an understatement. I've got to say, Dec, it's been a long time since I've been this excited about a date."

"How cool is that, Zack! Well, come on. Spill the beans. What does he look like, what does he do, where does he live? Give me the whole scoop and spare no sordid detail."

"What does he look like? That's easy. One word: incredible. Probably five ten, around a hundred eighty-five pounds, body of death, hair the color of polished walnut, olive complexion, killer smile, and eyes that make you feel like you're looking into a golden sunset." Realizing that I sounded like a love-struck teenage girl, I tried to dampen my enthusiasm. "Did I mention that he was good-looking?" I was a little embarrassed about my overexuberant gushing, but I continued nonetheless. I was enjoying having the opportunity to tell Declan about the guy who had consumed my every waking thought for the past three days. "He's Italian. And I mean *really* Italian. He grew up in Rome and has only been here about seven years. His English is excellent, but you should hear his accent. It rolls off his tongue like a fine wine. He could be telling you you had shit for brains and it would still sound like he's trying to seduce you. Totally mesmerizing. He works as a waiter at Osvaldo's, that high-end Italian restaurant on La Cienega, but he has aspirations of being an artist. I guess he's maybe a couple years older than me. Maybe twenty-nine or thirty." I realized I had been speaking without taking a breath, so, feeling a flush creep into my cheeks, I slowed down and tried to ask as casually as possible, "Does that cover the essentials?"

Declan just leaned back in his chair and smiled. He stared at me for a few seconds, then, in a tone exuding smug satisfaction, said, "If I didn't know better, I'd say you've already developed quite a crush. Just remember, I hold the top spot for the privilege of being maid of honor."

I wadded my napkin into a ball and threw it at him. "Maid of honor? You'll be lucky to be a valet. Besides," I said, trying not to let my voice reveal my apprehensions, "even if I admit to having a teensy crush, we're getting ahead of ourselves. After our bike ride, he might never want to see me again."

Now it was Declan's turn to lean forward. "Okay, Zack. We won't get ahead of ourselves, but you've got to promise not to start with the self-put-downs. Even if this guy is God's answer to greatness, he's still lucky to have scored a date with you. I refuse to sit back and listen to you go off into one of your self-loathing sermons. I'm not saying you're perfect." He rolled his eyes but smiled to indicate that he was joking. "In fact, we both know you're far from it. But this whole package here"—he waved his hand up and down my body—"is a pretty darn good one. Brains, brawn, and a heart of gold. You've got to learn to stop selling yourself short."

I smiled. I really did appreciate Declan's support. "You're just saying that because you're president of my fan club and don't want to get demoted."

"I'm saying it because it's true. Besides, being in your fan club sucks. Other than free drugs, there are absolutely no perks, and the membership dues are killing me. Who can afford a buck fifty a year for the privilege of being your friend?" He threw my napkin back at me.

As usual, the time I spent with Declan was easy. In the five years we'd known one another, our friendship had become solid. We knew most of one another's secrets, depended on one another for support, and reveled in the opportunities just to laugh.

I REMEMBERED the day I met Declan like it was yesterday and marveled at the fact that our introduction proved to be an unexpected twist of luck. At the time, I hadn't dared to whisper to even a single soul that I was gay. Desperate to talk to someone about my inner turmoil, and with the fervent hope that I might meet someone to whom I would be attracted, I answered a personal ad in one of the local throwaway newspapers. I pored through all the various descriptions, then finally worked up the courage to answer one of the ads.

The "Men for Men" section of the personals had a specifically assigned telephone number, and each ad was associated with an individual extension. It cost two dollars per minute to respond to an ad, and the fee would appear directly on your phone bill. You dialed the number and were prompted to enter the appropriate extension. Then you'd hear a voice recording from the guy who placed the ad offering a more detailed description of himself. Upon hearing his message, you were encouraged to record a confidential response that should include your contact information. Only after you were completely enamored with the prospect of finding the love of your life did you hear the disclaimer informing you that the newspaper's sponsor made absolutely no guarantee as to the authenticity of the client's statement.

With trembling hands, I willed myself to dial. I listened to the guy's enthusiastic outgoing message and description of himself, and then, with my intestines in a knot of anxiety, I began to record my response. Despite knowing I was being charged per minute, I felt compelled to rerecord my message multiple times because during the first two attempts my voice cracked like a testosterone-deficient teenager.

By the third attempt, though I was still convinced I must have sounded like a lovesick, mentally deficient, knife-wielding Freddy Krueger, I hung up before I gave myself permission to delete my response. Too late. The die was cast. He'd either call me back or make efforts to get a restraining order.

Two days later, Miles, the guy who had placed the ad, finally called me. As testimony to my insecurity, the anxiety of waiting for him to respond had caused me to lose two pounds. We spoke on the phone for about twenty minutes. At some point during our conversation, I relaxed enough to actually breathe normally, and we ended up sharing a fair number of laughs. Because I was still really cautious about disclosing too much personal information, I answered many of his questions with kind of vague generalities. The vibe he got from me, however, must have been mostly positive, because by the time we concluded our conversation, we were both eager to actually meet in person. We decided to hook up at a coffee shop the very next evening.

In order to be able to recognize one another when we met on our blind date, we described to one another what we would be wearing and then hung up.

I went to bed shortly thereafter but didn't sleep a wink the entire night. I was too excited about the prospect of going on my first ever date with a guy. I wasn't sure which contributed more to my insomnia, my eagerness, or my erection.

When I walked into the coffee shop the next day and recognized the blue polo shirt Miles promised to be wearing, I was immediately crestfallen. Physically, he wasn't at all what he'd described himself to be. He had some definition, but rather than being muscular, he was actually a little flabby. As superficial as it sounded, I knew in an instant that I'd never be attracted to him, and had I not been so eager to talk to someone who was also gay, I might not have summoned the courage to even say "Hi."

As it turned out, though, Miles really was very friendly and engaging. He made me laugh easily, and I found myself relaxing. In fact, shortly after our introduction he volunteered, "Look Zack, I can see by your reaction that you're probably not as into me as I'd like you to be, but if you're willing, I still think it would be cool to be friends. You up for it?"

My simultaneous relief and joy might have been palpable. I had no desire to see him naked, but I was also desperate to have a gay friend, and I genuinely liked Miles. In fact, I was probably more relaxed around him because I *wasn't* attracted to him. Had I been, I'm sure I would have continued to be a bundle of insecure nerves.

The more we talked to one another, the more we laughed and the more relaxed I became. I ended up telling him how insecure I felt, how I had never actually dated another guy, and why, given that I was going into pediatrics, I felt it was so imperative that I remain in the closet. He was unbelievably encouraging, assured me that I was most definitely a good catch and was emphatic that if we were going to hang out together, I should accompany him and a couple of his friends to the gay beach down in Laguna on the upcoming weekend.

I enthusiastically accepted his invitation.

The following Saturday, I drove to Miles's house early in the morning, was introduced to his two friends, and the four of us piled into his car and hit the road. Halfway through the two-hour drive, we pulled in to a grocery store to stock the ice chest with beverages and snacks. It felt both energizing and empowering to be visiting with three men and not feel like I had to be vigilantly guarded about everything I said. Riding with them, I didn't have to hide the fact that I was gay. In his car, being gay was the norm, not the exception. More importantly, when I was with them, I was not made to feel like my sexual orientation was a shameful state of being. The experience was so liberating I felt almost giddy.

I asked a lot of questions about how they had each come out and about the men they had previously dated. I also wanted to know if their bosses knew they were gay and how that information had affected their employment. Thinking about that day made me smile. Those three guys, who were essentially almost complete strangers, appreciated how new I was to the whole scene and immediately took me under their wings like mother hens. They were determined that I would have a good day and feel comfortable and accepted.

We parked the car in a neighborhood about a quarter mile above the entrance to the beach and began walking down the hill. To get to the beach, which couldn't be seen from the road, we had to descend a long flight of stairs. The second we arrived at the bottom of the stairs, I was struck by feeling like I had died and gone to heaven. It appeared that every square foot of the sand was covered by good-looking men clad in sexy swimwear. Everywhere I looked I saw men swimming, lounging on towels, talking to one another while standing in the waves that lapped gently against the sand, or playing smash ball just at the water's edge.

Miles and his friends must have anticipated my reaction, because they commented on how much my jaw had dropped. Miles jokingly bumped my arm with his shoulder and asked, "See anything you like?"

I turned to look at him but couldn't bring myself to either speak or close my mouth. My expression said it all: *Oh my God!*

The gay beach in Laguna was apparently famous for attracting men from all over the county on sunny weekends. It was almost more than I could process. Wall-to-wall *Hunk of Delicious.* Never in my wildest dreams had I imagined such a place could exist—a virtual army of good-looking gay men who didn't appear to be thinking about anything other than having a good time. For a brief instant I feared maybe I would stand out as being an obvious "newbie," but I was so caught up in the sheer euphoria of the moment that, surprisingly, I was able to squelch my anxiety.

It took a little maneuvering, but we were soon able to commandeer a respectable place on the sand to lay out our towels, and then I ran for the water. The next hour was spent neck-deep in the waves, ecstatically trying to body surf. Amazingly, many of the guys I ended up swimming next to were exceptionally friendly. After a few introductions, one of them invited me to play smash ball.

I had never played before, but after a few misdirected swings I found I picked the game up pretty quickly, and within fifteen minutes I actually looked like I knew what I was doing. When the guy who invited me to play ended up tiring, he asked a friend of his to substitute in for him… and handed his paddle to Declan. That was the moment our friendship began. We shook hands and were pretty much inseparable from then on. It was one of the best days of my life.

DECLAN and I both became quiet as we studied the menu. I made my selection quickly and looked around while Declan was deciding. The interior of the restaurant looked pretty cool but probably fell short of completely attaining the LA-chic look it was aiming for. The colors were understated, and the furniture was modern with clean lines. The tabletops were made of thick clear glass and each hosted a vase with an arrangement of fresh flowers. In an attempt to add an impressive final touch to the table setting, the utensils were carefully wrapped in a linen napkin, making them appear to be integrated into an origami sculpture. Truthfully, however, as was the case in many trendy restaurants, the tables were too close together to create real comfort. In an attempt to accommodate as many patrons as possible, customers were made to feel as if they were eating on top of one another. Two adult men sitting across from one another ended up competing for legroom under a table that would have been better suited for dollhouse furniture.

Fortunately, the restaurant was sparsely crowded, and the tables on either side of us were empty. There were four people sitting at a table in the far corner, two couples at separate tables next to the wall behind us, and one couple at a table along the side wall. Because the guy at the side wall table was facing the woman, and because their table was in an area of the restaurant that was a little wider, it put him in my line of vision when I looked in their direction.

I thought, *Funny, he looks kind of familiar. I wonder if I know him from somewhere.*

I didn't have too long to ponder his identity, however, as Declan had closed his menu and the waiter was standing next to our table asking if we had made a decision or if we needed more time. I ordered the pork noodle bowl, and Declan selected different types of sushi. I wanted to opt for a glass of wine, but I had been on call the night before and knew that even a single glass of wine would put me under the table. Declan was more bold and requested a beer.

After the waiter walked away, I found myself being unable to resist teasing him. "Beer and raw fish? Geez, Dec, if I didn't know better, I'd think you'd gone straight! What's next? Are we going to leave here and go toss around the pigskin? Or maybe shoot some hoops?"

Declan laughed. "Don't be intimidated by my masculinity, Zack. Just because your entire CD collection consists of Streisand and Cher doesn't mean that the rest of us have to conform to a stereotype."

"Right! This coming from the straight-acting dude who practices synchronized swimming in the privacy of his own bathtub. Wearing a swimming cap, no less!"

Even if the insults we threw at each other were stupid, they succeeded in helping us to unwind. We casually munched on shrimp chips and became consumed in conversation, trying to determine which of us had had the shittiest week. Declan taught junior high, so even his best days were an exercise in riot control.

The waiter delivered the beer, and before it had even come to rest on the table Declan scooped it up and took a satisfying gulp. Apparently his last period, eighth grade science, had been particularly harrowing. He took four more swallows before he was able to continue his story.

"So, there I was, in the middle of what I'm sure was a captivating lecture on photosynthesis, when someone in the back of the room lets out a huge fart." He rolled his eyes. "My inclination was to try to ignore it, but the sound was immediately followed by bursts of laughter, pointed accusations, and protests of denial. It was friggin' chaos," he continued. "Everyone was either laughing hysterically or making exaggerated retching noises and threatening to throw up."

As Declan's story became more animated, he flung a little dipping sauce from his chip onto the cuff of his shirt. He wiped it off with the finger of his other hand, then licked his finger in what he apparently hoped would be perceived as just inconspicuously scratching his upper lip. Smooth. He at least got points for trying to maintain the façade of polite etiquette.

"Anyway," he continued, "any hope of restoring order was lost when Johnny Grimes shouted out that this guy Carlos Mena was responsible. That only served to piss Carlos off, at which point he turned around and said that such a rank smell could only come from Karen's ass. Karen is Johnny's girlfriend and sits right next to him. This, of course, resulted in Johnny jumping up, angry as hell, and threatening to kick Carlos's ass for talking shit about Karen. I had to grab Johnny when Carlos suggested it was Karen's ass that had started the whole thing and the next time she felt the need to fart, she should just plant it on Johnny's face." Declan took another long swallow of beer. "They don't pay me enough to be a referee."

By this time, I was the one rocking with laughter. Suddenly, my day didn't seem all that intolerable. I could just imagine Declan trying to intervene in a science minirumble. "Man," I said. "Maybe you can apply for hazard pay. If they give it to cops, they should give it to teachers who have to police fart demonstrations."

"Funny," he said. "Let's see if you get any sympathy from me next time the shit hits the fan in your job and you just happen to be standing in front of it." Declan tried to look indignant but couldn't quite pull it off. By the time our food arrived, he'd ordered another beer, and thoughts of Johnny and Carlos dissipated into a distant memory. Now, spicy tuna on sticky rice consumed all of his attention.

I took advantage of his silence to begin telling him about some of my patients. Declan was inherently compassionate, and stories about the kids that I took care of always made a genuine impression on him. His brown eyes became soulfully attentive as I begin talking about a five-year-old who had been admitted for evaluation of a neuroblastoma.

"What's a neuroblastoma?" he asked, his concern genuine.

"A neuroblastoma is a tumor that develops from neural tissue. It's the most common extracranial solid tumor in children." Declan looked immediately bewildered. I put down my fork in order to more fully explain a complex condition in a manner that could be easily understood. "Extracranial means something occurring outside of the skull. And when a cancer is described as being a solid tumor, the intention is to differentiate it from a malignancy that occurs in the blood. Take leukemia, for example. It's a kind of cancer, but rather than being a tumor, it occurs in the blood."

It struck me that I sounded more like a professor than a peer, but Declan nodded, confirming that he understood. I paused, aware that the details of medical conditions weren't on the list of the top-ten dinner table conversations, but his attention was unwavering. He was clearly interested in knowing more and already seemed vested in the well-being of the kid. In addition, I felt a little subliminal pride. Who would have guessed I had enough medical knowledge to give an extemporaneous lecture on pediatric cancer?

"So, is he going to make it?" Declan asked.

"Hard to say at this point. It's not a great prognosis." After I had finished my noodle bowl, I pushed my chair back and extended by legs to the side of the table to try to relieve the cramp in my hamstring. Having my legs crammed under the trendy table for the duration of the entire dinner was the recipe for a killer muscle spasm. By repositioning, I was directly facing the guy at the table by the wall. Dark curly hair, dimpled chin; why did he look so familiar? I was pretty sure I hadn't met him in a bar. I briefly recounted the teasing I had just extolled on Declan about the mistake of taking someone home who you met in the dark. If you spend the night with a guy between the sheets and with the lights off, you might never recognized him again. I chuckled to myself. *I'm pretty sure I didn't sleep with him.*

Having been only momentarily distracted by trying to determine the guy's identity, I continued my story. "Christopher, the little boy, is stage four, which means that the cancer has already spread to other areas of his body. First he'll undergo chemo to try to shrink the tumor, then they'll operate on him to try to remove it. After he recovers from that surgery, he'll have to have more chemo in preparation for his bone marrow transplant. It's gonna be a tough road. A lot of kids don't even survive the initial rounds of chemo."

Christopher's prognosis left Declan looking a little dejected. "That sucks. Do they know what causes something like that in a five-year-old?"

"The cause of neuroblastoma is unknown; environmental exposures have not been shown to be causative. There might be some kind of genetic predisposition, but that hasn't been clearly determined either. There are reports of multiple cases within families, but mostly it just seems random.

Either way, it always sucks. Especially when the cancer is already stage four at the time it's discovered."

"Should his doctors have suspected it sooner?" Declan asked defensively. He fell naturally into the role of child advocate.

"In this case, I don't think so. Christopher didn't have any symptoms until about a week ago, when his mom noticed that he had become disinterested in playing. He was usually bouncing off the walls, and then one day, without explanation, he was instead opting to just sit quietly with a book. Really, there were no obvious symptoms. When his listlessness went on for a couple days, his mom became concerned. When she brought him to the emergency room, she was almost apologetic. She said that though it was probably just her imagination, her intuition was telling her something was wrong. The parents are pretty broken up about the whole thing."

"That's probably the biggest understatement in the world." Declan became pensive as he pushed the last of his sticky rice around his plate with his chopsticks.

I too was lost in thought. I was just staring off into space, contemplating how much the family had yet to go through and considering the injustice of it all. The kid was super cute. Dark hair, dark eyes, captivating bright smile. The day his parents brought him into the hospital to be admitted, he had insisted on wearing his Superman costume. He'd raced around the nurses' station with his arms extended and his cape flapping behind him. I remember asking him if he could teach me to fly. He'd looked a little bewildered by my question but nodded.

I was pulled from my delirium by a caustic, accusatory outburst. "What the fuck are you looking at?"

It took me a minute to realize that the question was coming from the guy seated at the side table, and that it was directed at me.

I froze. Bewildered as to why he had singled me out and uncertain of what I had done to provoke such an explosive interrogation, I looked over my shoulder, suspicious that his anger was actually intended for someone else and I had just unfortunately wound up in the cross fire. Regrettably, I discovered otherwise. There was no one behind me. The couple that had been there before had already left, and the only remaining couple was as shocked as we were. They looked between me and the hotheaded guy, obviously self-conscious. They did their best to turn their attention back to their dinners and started talking to one other in almost inaudible hushed tones.

I returned my disoriented focus to side-table guy. His face was visibly flushed with anger. His wife cast an embarrassed, almost apologetic glance in my direction, then reached across their table and delicately touched her husband's hand. I heard her whisper in a soft plea, "Just let it go, it's no big deal."

Her request seemed to infuriate him even more. "No, no.... I'm not gonna let it go. Goddamn faggots. Think they can impose themselves on anyone." He turned his attention back to me. "Hey! I asked you a question: What the fuck are you looking at?"

My head whirled. I hadn't been intentionally looking at anything. I had been lost in thought, trying to make sense of how a wonderful little five-year-old could be struck by such an awful illness. I was confused, embarrassed, and tongue-tied. Declan looked equally shocked. He had dropped his chopsticks onto his plate and darted his gaze between me and my inquisitor. I suspected we had identical expressions: a combination of "deer in the headlights" and "what the fuck is happening?"

When I finally found my voice, the only thing to escape was a weak, perplexed, "Excuse me?"

"Shit." He snorted his defiant retort. "Don't you speak English? I wanna know what the fuck you think you're looking at." His wife continued to implore him to keep his voice down and tried to sound a little more insistent that he just ignore us.

Slowly, I began to regain my composure and my brain began to form a more coherent stream of thought. As the element of surprise started to dissipate, it was replaced by an undercurrent of anger.

When I did answer, my words were carefully chosen and my voice carried an imposed measure of calm. "I assure you, I wasn't looking at anything. Initially, I thought you looked familiar, but I haven't been able to remember from where I might know you. Really, I'm just trying to enjoy a quiet dinner with my friend."

Interpreting my response as being dismissive, he became even angrier. "Quiet dinner? Right! I don't know where you faggots get off thinking you have the right to flaunt your perverted life style in public, but it gives me a pain in the ass. And I resent the fact that you've spent your whole night looking at me. Keep your goddamn eyes in your own fucking head."

The situation was really heating up. "Perverted life style?" Declan echoed, and I had to insist he sit back down. Despite the fact that he was a pretty easygoing guy, when he was provoked, he wouldn't hesitate to come out swinging. Also, Declan could bench press 245 without breaking a sweat and, having been raised in the Midwest, he was well accustomed to using his fists when homophobes decided to entertain themselves by tormenting him.

By this time, his wife's pleas had also reached the volume of normal conversation. She was visibly trying to restrain her husband. But he wasn't to be dissuaded, and his hateful rhetoric continued. Directed at her for the time being, but intended for our provocation.

"I think that they have the right idea in Uganda. Fags should just be put to death. No questions asked. Not only is that a surefire way to cleanse the gene pool, but it brings the world back to the natural order God intended."

Declan had yet to enter into the fray, but I was sure that the guy's last comment would send him into a ballistic tirade for retribution. Though I put my hand across the table to prevent Declan from getting up, I was simultaneously struck by my subconscious ambivalence about stopping him. Part of me was enthused about the prospect of both of us beating the shit out of the guy. Fortunately, however, the higher functioning parts of my brain realized that a public brawl could put my medical license in jeopardy.

In that exact moment, the adrenaline surge pounding through my brain produced a miracle of clear thinking. From out of the blue, I remembered where I recognized the guy from. I was suddenly overcome with a renewed sense of calm. The effect must have been impressive, because Declan, whose face was contorted with anger, also seemed to relax when he saw my expression. Almost telepathically, he picked up on the understanding that this conflict was going be resolved and it would be resolved in our favor. Without prompting, he sat back down and let the tension flow out of his taut muscles.

I took a few moments to compose myself, then turned to face the guy. He must have interpreted my calm demeanor as a concession of defeat, because his expression resonated smug satisfaction. He probably felt he had succeeded in putting us in our place.

When I did speak, my voice was clear and authoritative. I ignored the guy and instead addressed my comments to his wife. "I apologize if you were made to feel uncomfortable this evening. It took me a while to remember why your husband looked familiar to me. I believe that your daughter, Sophie Carson, was born at Mount Zion Hospital five or six months ago. You had an emergency cesarean, and Sophie was admitted to the neonatal intensive care unit. I'm Dr. Sheldon. I'm the pediatrician who was in the delivery room. I saved her life."

In that instant, you could have heard a pin drop. I stared at Mr. Carson. Whereas seconds before his face had been flushed with anger, it now went completely pale. The blood ran out of it like air escaping a balloon. He slumped in his chair and his lips started opening and closing without emitting any sound. His wife looked horrified. She glanced disappointedly at her husband then looked at me. I stood, pulled my jacket off the back of the chair, and reached for my car keys. I noticed that the couple behind us was now silent. I knew they had overheard the entire exchange, and though they were holding their utensils over their plates, neither of them was eating. They were just looking at me. They seemed to be embarrassed but also somehow emboldened. I think, even as spectators, they were feeling my vindication.

I understood why Becky Carson would not have recognized me. My interaction with her and been brief. I had only spoken to her when we were in the delivery room, and at the time, she had been completely consumed with worry about Sophie. In addition, our entire conversation occurred while she was on the operating-room table. Not an optimal scenario to make a lasting impression. Not only had she been held down by monitors and IV tubing, but she was completely stressed and disoriented.

But I had spent more time with Greg Carson. He had accompanied me when Sophie was transported up to the NICU. Not only had we spoken at length, but at the time, his gratitude toward me had been overwhelming. He had all but wept in my arms. Looking back on it, though, I understood why he might not have immediately recognized me sitting across from him in the restaurant. During our encounter at the hospital, I'd never removed my scrub cap. Dressed in standard-issue scrubs, with my hair covered by the cap, I was anonymous. Now dressed like a civilian and out of the context of the hospital, it was no wonder he hadn't recognized me.

I remembered him, though. His eyes were the giveaway. I remembered them. I remembered how his sorrowful, pain-stricken eyes had become jubilant when I'd declared with great confidence that his daughter was going to live. I now remembered the intensity of the situation like it was yesterday: pulling Sophie narrowly from the jaws of death—the tears, the heartfelt appreciation, and the declaration that he'd be forever indebted to me.

I looked at Declan, who himself was kind of reeling in amazement. "You ready to get out of here?" I asked, "It's a little stuffy in here."

"Yeah," he replied, a smile spreading across his face. "Way stuffy!" Then, not being able to resist he said, "Ignorance can be really stifling."

As we headed for the door, Mrs. Carson stood up and grabbed my arm. She was tearful. "Dr. Sheldon, I would like to apologize for my husband's behavior."

I looked at her and then glanced at her husband. He was just staring blindly into his plate. His arms were resting limply on the table, supporting him just enough to prevent him from falling into his green tea ice cream. The blood still hadn't returned to his cheeks, and he had the expression of a man who had just witnessed a fatal car accident.

"You don't need to apologize for him," I said, trying to force a little warmth into my tone. I turned and had begun to follow Declan to the exit when I had an afterthought. I reversed my direction and faced her again.

"I just hope you teach that precious little daughter of yours better. She's a miracle and shouldn't have to grow up in a world made ugly by bigots."

I left without even hazarding a parting glance at Mr. Carson. I figured he had enough problems. Not only was I sure he was going to have to endure his wife's profound embarrassment and disappointment, but I suspected he had some more deeply seated issues that, in the future, might become more difficult to fully conceal.

CHAPTER 8

THE next four days couldn't have dragged by any more slowly if you had captured time in a bottle and encased it in lead. While I was working, if I was specifically involved in caring for patients, I was able to remain focused, but otherwise I was completely distracted. I found myself glancing at my watch every fifteen minutes, willing the day to be over. I had been on call that Wednesday night, and though it hadn't been particularly busy, I still hadn't been able to take advantage of any opportunities to sleep. Usually, if there was a lull between admissions, I would return to the call room and fall asleep within seconds. I would savor those little interludes to try to partially recuperate from an otherwise grueling shift. That night, however, it was useless. The minute my head hit the pillow I would begin thinking about the upcoming weekend, and my mind would race with anticipation. The prospect of spending the day with Sergio affected my body more than a triple shot of espresso.

No matter how you sliced it, though, I had to get through one more day of work, so as best I could, I tried to push thoughts of Sergio out of my mind. I looked at my watch. This would probably be as good a time as any to grab a bite to eat. I shook my head to focus and headed toward the cafeteria, where I knew a number of the other residents would already be congregated.

As was usually the case, I had just sat down at a table on the outdoor patio to join some of my colleagues for lunch when my beeper vibrated. "Shit," I whispered under my breath as I peeled the despicable little black mechanism off my belt to read the number. It was as if it was programmed to go off the minute my ass hit the seat of a chair to relax for a few seconds. If I recognized the number, I would sometimes opt to put off calling back for five or ten minutes so I could consume half my meal before responding to the pending crisis. One time, I returned a page only to discover that the call had originated from medical records department and it was some secretary insisting a bunch of charts required my immediate signature. Hell with them; I wasn't going to provoke indigestion for the sake of completely bullshit paperwork. This time, however, I was directed to call the hospital page operator and the numbers on the readout were followed by 911, indicating that it was an emergency.

"Damn, guys," I said apologetically, though everyone picked up on the irritation in my voice. "It's a STAT page. I gotta go answer this. Don't let anyone steal my plate. I'm gonna try to be right back."

My friends teased me but were sympathetic. "Better you than me," Beth said. "I'm eating for two and can't afford to miss a meal." She smiled warmly while pulling her plate closer to the edge of the table. Because she was in her third trimester of pregnancy, her ample stomach still put her a foot away from the breast of chicken she was trying unsuccessfully to cut. "Though, by the looks of things"—she paused a second to grit her teeth—"you're not missing anything. This crap is made of rubber."

I couldn't help but find her endearing. She was wicked smart, a good team player, and a hard worker. I loved being on the same service as her. I was not, of course, going to give her the satisfaction of knowing how much I admired her. "At least I didn't get myself knocked up to get out of doing any of the tough rotations."

She grinned at my dig only because she knew I was kidding—the respect we had for one another was mutual. "Child, if you could have been knocked up, you would have beaten me to the punch a long time ago. It's just that your ass is too damn ugly to get any attention from anyone." She stopped cutting long enough to flick her knife in my direction. "Now, speaking of ugly asses, you'd better get yours moving, answer that page, and let the rest of us eat in peace."

The fact that her flippant remark caused a chorus of laughter from the rest of the table brought her overwhelming satisfaction. She really was a hoot, and I laughed too. Had she known that I was gay, she might have thought twice about broadcasting the action status of my ass, but at least with regard to my sexuality, she couldn't have been more clueless. As a matter of fact, on a few occasions she had intimated that were she not already married, she would have wanted to cozy up to me on a cold night on call. When the innocent flirtation had occurred between us, I tried my best to look appropriately disappointed and had even tried to throw out the subtle inference that I, too, had spent time imagining the possibilities. I pasted on my patented sad-puppy-dog eyes and telepathically conveyed to her that I understood the injustice of it all. "To have the delicate petals of an exotic flower just within my grasp but, alas, still out of reach." Thank God I had an excuse. Those petals… not my cup of tea.

She put her fork down and pushed her hair out of her eyes. The grin she threw my way was triumphant, but her expression radiated real warmth. "Don't worry, if you don't get back before we finish, I'll wrap something up and save it for you. I have to keep you healthy so when I do finally have this baby, you'll be able to pick up all of my shifts while I'm on maternity leave."

"Yeah," I teased in retaliation, "and I hope that when have your baby you'll end up needing a huge episiotomy!"

"Ouch," she said with a grimace, "now you're fighting dirty." She waved her knife more menacingly. "If I do end up with an episiotomy, it will be because you willed it to happen, and I'll have no choice but to hunt you down and perform a similar procedure on you. Hope it's been your life's dream to sing soprano."

"Okay, you win." I walked away from the table with my hands protectively shielding my groin. "My wish for you is that you pass that baby like a bar of soap. Now, protect my plate."

I went into the corridor just off the main entrance of the cafeteria and picked up the in-house phone. "This is Dr. Sheldon. I was paged."

"Yes, Dr. Sheldon. You're needed in the Emergency Room. Three-year-old. Auto versus peds. Trauma room three."

"Auto versus peds" was the verbal shorthand to signify that a pedestrian had been hit by a car.

"Do you know the condition of the child?" I inquired.

Her answer was terse but not antagonistic. "I don't have that information, Doctor, but they requested that you come STAT."

"Thanks, on my way."

As was always the case when I was called to an emergency, my mind went into overdrive generating the list of the possible complications I might be required to manage. A three-year-old hit by a car. I felt a brief surge of panic. The possibilities were limitless. The only certainty was that when a kid was hit by a car, the car always won.

I willed my legs to push myself a little faster without breaking into an overt run. Running through the hospital was bad form. It usually only succeeded in making visitors feel really anxious and seldom improved the outcome for a patient.

I knew because the child was the victim of a trauma, the trauma team would be in charge and, I had been called just to lend my expertise as it applied specifically to a three-year-old. I approved of the policy. All the trauma surgeons were extremely competent, but at the end of the day, they were most experienced in treating adults. Fortunately, the medical establishment had come to appreciate that children weren't just miniature adults and had the potential of having unique complications. Having a pediatrician involved in the treatment of an injured child from the outset was more optimal for the patient.

As usual, the emergency room was a flurry of activity best described as controlled chaos. The trauma rooms were situated closest to the ambulance entrance, so I had to navigate my way to the far side of the building. The radiology technician was just maneuvering the portable X-ray machine out of the door of room three when I arrived. "Have fun," he said with sullen sarcasm, "Dr. Klein is in rare form."

Dr. Klein was infamous in the hospital. He was revered for being an exceptional surgeon but had the reputation of being arrogant and condescending. Were you ever to need emergency surgery, you'd hope he was available to operate, but you'd have an equally high sense of dread about the prospect of having to work with him. He was a perfectionist and would ridicule anyone whose job performance didn't meet his standards. Unfortunately, on any given day, his expectations were arbitrary, and he seemed to derive a perverse sense of pleasure out of harassing his subordinates under any circumstances. He had recently kicked a surgical resident out of the operating room because the guy, frustrated that nothing he had done thus far had met with approval, had finally responded defiantly to Dr. Klein with a question: "So, do you want this suture to be cut too long or too short?"

Dr. Klein was barking orders at everyone as I approached the bedside.

Knowing Dr. Klein wouldn't acknowledge my presence, I asked the surgical chief resident to give me a brief summary about the child's condition.

The resident actually seemed relieved to see me, probably because he was optimistic that having another doctor in attendance would deflect some of Dr. Klein's criticism off him. In the medical hierarchy, he was confident a pediatrician fell beneath a surgeon. With me in the mix, he was probably hoping I would become the new target.

The resident's name was Victor Maldonado, and having followed a number of patients with him, I knew he was a pretty good guy. Clinically, he was smart. He worked to take good care of his patients, and for me, of equal importance was the fact that he respected me as a colleague. He hadn't, at least as of yet, developed that surgical air of superiority.

Victor started his brief but concise summary. "I don't know all the details, but this kid apparently got hit by a car when he was running through a parking lot. The car was reported to only have been going about ten miles per hour, which is why the kid's still alive. Because he has a lot of contusions and abrasions over the left side of his head, we suspect a brain injury, so Klein is eager to get him into the CT scanner. Trouble is, his IV just infiltrated, so we don't currently have access, and his blood pressure is a little unstable. Given the rest of the bruising over his body, he may have sustained other internal injuries too." Victor glanced up at the clock on the wall above the bed and said, "He arrived about five minutes ago, and Klein insisted on being the one to intubate him. You're now up to speed. Welcome to Disneyland. Enjoy the ride."

Apparently, the paramedics had started an IV in the field, but it was no longer working. At that instant, a male nurse pulled a needle out of the kid's arm after what was apparently his second unsuccessful attempt at starting a new one. His failure brought Dr. Klein into an immediate rage.

He yelled into the nurse's face, "Get the hell away from my patient before you mutilate his limbs any further." The nurse recoiled backward in demoralized embarrassment. Under Dr. Klein's scrutiny, performing even a simple task raised the level of difficulty exponentially and significantly lowered the likelihood for success.

Dr. Klein's stare bored unforgivingly into the nurse. He whispered under his breath, but loud enough to be heard, "Why do we have to hire incompetent faggots?"

I bristled from the comment. Not only did it make me feel infinitely sorry for the nurse, but it resulted in making me feel immediately self-conscious. Dr. Klein was inarguably a homophobic bigot, but I was apprehensive that his attitude was pretty pervasive in the hospital. Hearing such slurs accentuated my fear that I would be ostracized by my peers were they to ever know the truth about my sexual orientation. The internal struggle I had wrestled with for years came surging to the surface. On one hand, I was infuriated by his comment. On the other, knowing such sentiments existed in our society inevitably pushed me further into the closet.

Though the taste of my emotion was acidic in the back of my throat, challenging the inappropriateness of his remarks would have to be a battle for another day. For now, I had to swallow my feelings of both inadequacy and outrage and focus on the patient.

Dr. Klein steadied his glare onto Victor. "Can you get a line into this kid? Or am I gonna have to do a cut-down?"

Given the circumstances, with only one nurse having tried to start an IV twice, a cut-down would have been a little extreme. It was a procedure where an incision was made through the skin so the veins could be fully visualized, and then a catheter was threaded directly into one of them.

Victor paled ever so slightly, but he stepped forward confidently. "I'll get it." He reached for a tourniquet, wrapped it around the child's left bicep, and looked anxiously up and down his arm, looking for a vein that would successfully welcome a needle. I could see a bead of sweat appear on Victor's forehead when, after careful examination, he failed to identify anything he could predictably hit.

I could tell Dr. Klein had observed the same thing and that he was suppressing an urge to release another brutal barrage of criticisms.

As casually as I could, I reached past Victor and released the tourniquet. Victor snapped his head up furiously, but before he could level me with an indignant objection, I humbly suggested that I take a quick look.

Knowing Dr. Klein continued to critique the entire interaction, the offended expression on Victor's face was unwavering. I knew, however, that rather than being irritated, Victor was actually relieved that he'd been made exempt from trying. If I was unsuccessful, it would be apparent to Dr. Klein that I was responsible for the failure. Victor, at least temporarily, was absolved from potential humiliation.

I drew a breath to calm myself, trying to quell the fear that I'd just kicked an angry hornet's nest and at any second would have my ass handed to me. I took the catheter out of Victor's hand and whispered to him without looking up, "You be my tourniquet. Put your hand around the kid's calf and give it a gentle squeeze."

I carefully ran my finger down a line just behind the child's anklebone. I couldn't see anything, but I knew where his saphenous vein ran and thought I could feel it as I softly palpated with the tip of my finger. Very slowly, I slipped the needle of the catheter into the skin where I predicted the vein would be. Miraculously, I was reward with a flash of blood. I threaded the catheter carefully into the vein and secured it with a piece of tape. I then confirmed the placement was good by flushing it with some saline. Finally, I connected the catheter to the IV tubing.

"We've got a line." I tried to sound clinically objective rather than triumphant. *Friggin' A*, I silently congratulated myself. *I nailed it right under Klein's pissed-off eyes.*

The kid's condition, however, left no time to bask in the glory. While the nurses went about inserting a urinary catheter into the child and attaching the IV line to a pump, I resolved to quickly examine him myself.

The readout on the monitor indicated that his blood pressure was still dangerously low. While the respiratory therapist squeezed air into his lungs, I listened to his chest with my stethoscope. I was concerned that I couldn't hear good breath sounds on the left.

"Okay," Dr. Klein barked over the noise emanating from around the table. "Let's get him to the CT scanner."

I stiffened and my heart raced with anxiousness. I didn't think the child was stable enough to be moved, but the prospect of contradicting Dr. Klein made my blood run cold. He was a god. He was infallible.

I reassessed the numbers on the blood pressure monitor and listened with more intensity through my stethoscope. I was concerned that his pressure had dropped a few more points from a couple of minutes before, but who was I to second-guess a directive given by the head trauma surgeon?

Dr. Klein became more impatient. "Get those portable monitors connected so we can roll. Pretend you know what you're doing, people, and quit moving around like a bunch of damn amateurs. For Christ's sake, I want this kid to still be alive tomorrow."

Everyone started moving with an increased sense of urgency. No one wanted to fall victim to another one of the infamous Klein tongue-lashings.

Unexpectedly, I heard my tentative voice rising shakily above the uproar. "Dr. Klein, I'm afraid the child is too unstable to take to radiology yet. I don't hear good breath sounds through his left chest, and his blood pressure appears to be dropping."

Dr. Klein's irritation was almost paralyzing. "Dr. Sheldon, thank you so much for your astute observation. You bet your ass the patient is unstable. He's got a goddamned head injury that we have to identify before we can fix. How much of our time do you intend to waste before we can proceed with saving his life?"

His entire persona radiated intimidation. I immediately regretted interjecting, but now that I had gone out on a limb, my concerns would have seemed doubly irrelevant if I retreated from defending them. Incapable of injecting any confidence into my voice, I nonetheless proceeded. "I concur that the patient probably has a head injury, but that doesn't explain the reduced breath sounds, and if his instability is the singular result of trauma to his brain, wouldn't you expect his blood pressure to be elevated?"

Dr. Klein's cheeks reddened with anger. "You concur? You concur?" The sarcasm cascaded from his mouth like hot lava from a volcano. "Dr. Sheldon, I can't tell you how ecstatic I am that you concur with my assessment, but frankly, I could give a rat's ass whether you concur or not. I'm in charge of this patient, and my job is to ensure that your negligence doesn't kill him. Now, I'm impressed you succeeded in getting a line into him, and I guarantee you that I'll recommend you for a good job on the phlebotomy team. The fact remains, however, that the responsibility of managing his care falls on the shoulders of a real doctor, so unless you have any other extenuating objections, get the hell out of the way."

His reprimand was strident and demeaning, but even as it concluded, he was reaching for his stethoscope to listen to the patient's chest. As belittling of me as he'd been, my concerns must have at least registered. Undoubtedly he was rechecking the child only to confirm that he'd been justified in dismissing me completely.

I held my breath expectantly, certain that his examination of the little boy would bring only a brief respite before an even more humiliating critique of my clinical abilities. Standing frozen in place, I was surprised when I observed his expression transforming from one of complete exasperation to one of confusion. He seemed incapable of interpreting the sounds he was hearing.

He had no sooner pulled his stethoscope out of his ears before the radiology technician returned with a copy of the chest X-ray. Without preamble, the technician slapped it up on the viewing box and, without directing his comment to anyone in particular, said, "Looks like the kid has a developing tension pneumothorax on the left. Must have broken some ribs on that side."

In that split second, it was almost impossible to contain my jubilance. I had been right. As we had been futzing around with placing lines and securing the monitors, the child had been bleeding internally into his chest. As the blood accumulated, it had been both compressing his left lung and putting pressure on his heart. As a consequence, his heart was beating less efficiently, his blood pressure was dropping, and his left lung was being prevented from inflating completely. My concerns had been right on the money.

Dr. Klein cast only a confirmatory glance at the chest X-ray, then, without pause, he began to again bark orders. "Hand me a scalpel." Without additional ceremony, he poked a hole through the skin in a space between two of the child's ribs and inserted the chest tube. Bright red blood gushed through the tube and soaked the floor between his feet. By the time the force of the stream began to subside, more than a pint of blood had flowed out of the tube. The child's blood pressure rebounded immediately, his color improved significantly, and the respiratory therapist indicated that he was meeting much less resistance bagging oxygen into his lungs.

"Okay," Dr. Klein screamed though with a little less vibrato, "now get him the hell into the scanner." His look at me was little more than cursory. He made no apology. Nor did he conclude he'd been wrong. In fact, I was surprised when he actually whispered a staccato, "Good call, Sheldon."

From Dr. Klein, that was pretty much the ultimate compliment, and it resulted in a wave of shock and admiration from everyone else in attendance. Miracle of miracles, David had slayed Goliath.

In my mind, I began trying to reconcile my own schizophrenia. I was reasonably confident that though Dr. Klein was incensed about having been challenged, he'd respected that my suspicions had been accurate. I suddenly felt like an insecure kid striving to obtain an indifferent parent's approval. I was elated that I had perhaps won an even modest amount of admiration from him, but I still thought he was a complete dick. Why was his opinion of me so important?

Begrudgingly, I had to acknowledge to myself that in many respects, I still was an insecure kid. Being gay, I had felt for many years that there was something grievously wrong with me. How could anyone feel confident in who they were if they felt that the majority of their character was flawed? Of course I wanted Dr. Klein's approval. He was confident, respected, and was indisputably admired for being a superior member of the old boys club. No one questioned either his sexual orientation or his masculinity. I had spent my life seeking validation from men like him. I guess I felt if he respected me, I could respect myself.

I grimaced as I followed the little boy's gurney toward the radiology suite. I dejectedly thought, *How fucked up was that?*

It didn't take long for the child to be moved onto the platform of the CT scanner. The platform slid back or forth over a track that moved between the lenses of the actual machine. Once the little boy was secured to the platform bed, his whole body could be scanned without having to again disturb him. He would just glide in and out.

I was most apprehensive about the possibility of a significant brain injury because it looked as if his head had sustained the brunt of the impact. From within the observation room, we all stared anxiously at the computer monitor as the initial images begin to appear on the screen. One by one, individual pictures of descending parts of his brain popped up on the monitor, and when all of them were determined to be completely normal, the entire group released a collective sigh of relief.

We had gotten over the biggest hurdle. Though we were still concerned about serious injuries to other parts of his body, ruling out an obvious brain injury significantly increased the probability of him making what we hoped would be a complete recovery.

As the scan continued, we became increasingly optimistic. He had several broken ribs, but all his internal organs looked okay. His liver didn't seem to have sustained any damage, and neither had his spleen or kidneys. The urine collecting from the catheter had no apparent blood in it, and once the chest tube and been placed, his vital signs remained remarkably stable. He did have a broken left wrist, but nothing that would require surgery. A simple cast would undoubtedly result in complete healing within a few weeks, tops. In fact, it didn't appear he'd have to go to the operating room at all.

"Good enough, team." Dr. Klein's voice sounded upbeat but still lacked any warmth. "Let's get him up to the pediatric intensive care unit. We'll keep him sedated while we monitor him overnight, but by tomorrow we should be able to start letting him wake up. Looks as if the kid caught a lucky break."

At that point a soft voice rose from the back of the crowd. The social worker, Sheila Olson, had made her way in to join the medical team. She now seemed to feel she could safely ask her question. "Dr. Klein," she said hesitantly, "up until this point no one has spoken to the family. When might one of you be prepared to do so? They're very anxious to get some information."

He responded in his typical fashion—gruff and indifferent. "I have to get back to check on some of the more critical patients." He pivoted his head in my direction. "Sheldon, you go talk to the family. Until now, you're the only one who's contributed anything positive anyway. Might as well follow this through to the end. Page me when the kid's tucked in and you get the initial labs back. I don't want any more fuckups."

He picked his lab coat up, threw it over his shoulder, and without another word, walked out.

Silence followed his departure from the room, and everyone looked at one another uneasily. Well, that had been a quick end to a mood that had had a glimmer of being celebratory. I mean, given his rocky start, it looked like the kid might very well be okay after all. In an attempt to break the tension, I cleared my throat. "Something tells me I still top the list of people Klein thinks are fuckups, but let's get moving regardless." My comment was met with repressed laughter. I moved over to talk to the social worker.

"Do we know any more about what happened? And has this kid got a name?"

Sheila began telling me the story. Her tone was compassionate and caring. "The child's name is David. The family is visiting from out of town. They were here for a wedding. In fact, the child was hit in the parking lot of the church. Apparently, Dad thought the boy was with Mom, and Mom thought he was with Dad. Obviously, in the confusion and excitement, they lost track of him. The rehearsal dinner had just concluded, and Dad was walking out to get the car. David saw him from the steps of the banquet hall and raced to catch up. His dad thought he might have been afraid of being left behind."

As Sheila continued the story, her voice became more heavily laden with emotion. She knew that David's panic had been needless. Though he might have temporarily escaped his parents' supervision, they would never have left without him.

"He darted out into the parking lot just as the bride's father was pulling his car around to the entrance to transfer the gifts. Apparently, the lot is poorly lit, and I get the impression that the guy driving didn't see the little boy at all. He wasn't going very fast but didn't realize David was even in his path before he heard the thud and felt the impact. The accident was witnessed by a bunch of people. Everyone is pretty broken up about it. In fact, I think that by now, the entire wedding party and all the guests have shown up here. There are so many people that security has had to cordon them off in the side corridor. The waiting room isn't big enough to accommodate everyone."

I grinned despite the seriousness of the situation. "I'm glad I'll be able to give them some good news. You wanna walk me over there and make the introductions?"

"Be glad to." Now her smile began to brighten. "If we cut through the back corridor, we'll run right into them without having to go through the waiting room. Let's head out." She consulted her notes. "Their last name is McGregor. Mom's name is Christine and Dad's name is Kevin. The bride is Kevin's future sister-in-law. She's marrying his brother. The bride's father, the guy who was driving, was just cleared himself by the ER doctors. He was so upset by the accident he had a panic attack and thought he was having a heart attack." She shook her head in disbelief. "This family has had a busy night."

"Well," I said, trying to keep it light without sounding irreverent, "if the couple's relationship survives this drama and they still succeed in pulling off the wedding, I suppose it will survive anything."

I could hear the rumble of low voices as I rounded the corner. Everyone had been speaking in hushed whispers, but the minute they saw me, silence fell over them so suddenly it seemed as if all the air in the room had been instantaneously sucked out with a vacuum. No fewer than fifty pairs of eyes locked immediately on to me, and no one breathed.

It was surreal. I still had another twenty-five feet of empty corridor between me and where the family stood motionless. It would have been uncomfortable to start talking across such a significant distance, so I just kept walking. It was like something from the movies. The silence was tomblike. The only noise was the sound of my footsteps echoing off the walls. I'm sure that to the grief-stricken family members, it sounded like a death march.

I got to within a few feet of the parents, but before I could offer them a prelude to the good news concerning their son's condition, David's mom, Christine, choked out an almost inaudible whisper. "Is my son dead?"

The very effort of asking the question seemed to have consumed the last remnants of strength from her legs, and she could no longer hold herself up. She collapsed backward into her own father's arms.

"No, he's not dead." I wanted to continue to sound clinically objective but couldn't refrain from disguising the elation in my voice. "In fact, with the exception of a few broken ribs, he's looking pretty darn good. We're very optimistic that he will be fine."

Of course, my intention was to offer a more complete summary of his overall condition, but before I could utter a single additional word, the entire crowd released a collective gasp and any further meaningful discussion was drowned out by the sounds of grateful sobbing.

A huddle formed with David's mom and dad squeezed in the middle. The words were mostly unintelligible, but the meaning was clear: The nightmare was over. Their son was alive.

Sheila and I stood back, enjoying the opportunity to observe such a raw demonstration of relief and joy. We were both keenly aware that more frequently than not, the outcome was much less fortunate.

Christine and Kevin eventually extricated themselves from the arms of the group, tried unsuccessfully to wipe the tears from their eyes, then asked me to fill them in on the finer details of David's condition.

They were eager to see him but understood our plan to keep him sedated through the night. As soon as he was settled in the intensive care unit, however, Sheila would escort them up, and they could sit by his bedside.

I suspected he wouldn't be out of either of their sights for many months to come.

At moments like this, I felt overwhelming satisfaction in my decision to become a doctor. Gay or not, it felt pretty damned good.

I walked over to the phone to page Beth. I hoped she had stayed true to her word and saved me something to eat.

CHAPTER 9

SATURDAY morning, I went so far as to agonize over what to wear. We were biking, for God's sake. I wanted to look casual, as if I hadn't given even the slightest consideration into what I threw on, but I also wanted to look good. Finally, I chose a tank top tight enough to flatter my musculature but also allow for comfortable movement and a pair of khaki shorts. In addition, I spent way too much time combing my hair. It was hard to succeed in striking a balance between the "just rolled out of bed" look and the "man, I like your hair" look without having to experiment with three different gels. So much for spontaneity.

At about five minutes after eight, I heard a horn give a quick honk. I grabbed the fanny pack that carried my wallet, keys, and a tube of sunscreen and bolted for the door. I had already taken my bike out of the storage area and locked it to the bottom of the stair railing that led up to the front door. I put on my sunglasses as I stepped onto the front porch, and then I locked the door and turned to wave at Sergio. I felt my heart flip in my chest when I looked down at him.

He had popped the hatchback of his car and was leaning against its side window with his foot braced against the curb. He had his arms folded across his chest, and he was smiling up at me. He, too, was wearing a tank top, and his golden shoulders were a sharp contrast to the navy-blue material. His muscular chest looked like a mountain range surging out from under a cloud-filled sky, and his biceps gave the appearance of being boulders on his impressively defined arms. Most mesmerizing, however, was his smile. A Broadway marquee couldn't have shone more brightly. I was glad I could distract myself with having to retrieve my bike, or I might have just stood there and stared.

I secured the lock to the bike's crossbar and wheeled it down the sidewalk. Sergio pushed off the car and opened the passenger door. "You lift your bike into the back, and I'll reach over and guide the wheel in from the front seat. Hand it to me butt first. Both bikes should fit if we turn your handlebars sideways once it's all the way in." Before he bent into the opened door, he added, "It's a beautiful day. You want to ride from Temescal Canyon all the way to beyond the harbor?"

"Sounds perfect. Is there somewhere in particular that you'd like to eat?" I lifted my bike and began to carefully navigate the back wheel into the small space between his bike and the upholstery on the inside ceiling panel. The bike pedal had barely even neared the doorframe before Sergio yelled in an angry voice, "Zack, watch the toe clip on the pedal. I don't want the fabric on the roof to get torn."

The hostility of his tone startled me. It was a tight squeeze into the back of the car, but the pedal hadn't even gotten close to the roof when he yelled. I froze for a second but then withdrew the entire bike and set it down on the pavement. Sure, I was infatuated with Sergio, but I still didn't want to get yelled at. In fact, getting yelled at was something I had a huge aversion to. It felt so belittling and condescending. Maybe I was overly sensitive, and maybe I did have compromised self-esteem, but I refused to be yelled at by anyone.

I looked at Sergio and was surprised to find that the fire that had been in his eyes not two seconds before, seemingly stoked by irritation, had been completely extinguished, and he was smiling expectantly at me. "Come on, if you have any intention of being able to keep up with me biking, you're going to have to eat to build your strength. Let's get the bike loaded."

I was still reeling from having been yelled at, and in response, my body had shut down. It felt like it was going to take monumental effort to even move much less to lift the bike. Additionally, I was confused by the fact that looking at him, you'd never guess he'd even raised his voice. The moment had passed. He was calm and apparently eager to get going.

I lowered my gaze and spoke more to the ground than to him. "Maybe this wasn't such a good idea."

He extracted his head from the car and walked over to look at me. Now it was his turn to be confused. "What do you mean? You want to ride somewhere other than the beach?" He tried to catch my gaze.

I slowly looked up and answered. His outburst had so affected me, I was thankful my voice didn't waver. Sometimes, when I was feeling the simultaneous combination of embarrassment and anger, my voice would start to quiver, almost like I was trying to hold back tears. "I guarantee I wouldn't have ripped your interior, Sergio. You didn't have to yell."

The expression of confusion that spread across his face seemed genuine. "What do you mean, Zack? I wasn't yelling."

Now, though my anger didn't really escalate, it overwhelmed any residual feelings of embarrassment. My voice strengthened as I challenged him. "Of course you yelled, Sergio. You screamed at me to be more careful of the roof." Then, in hopes of exonerating myself from the implied accusation that I had been careless, I let my gaze drop back down to the pavement and said a little more softly, "It wasn't necessary. I was fully intending to be careful."

Rather than going on the defensive, Sergio reached out and gently grabbed my shoulders between his hands. "Listen, Zack." He took one of his hands off my shoulder and gently lifted my chin so I had to look at him. "I'm Italian. We don't even know when we're screaming. It's just part of our regular conversation. Just wait until you meet my sister. Then you'll hear screaming. You'd think we hated each other if you judged our conversation by the volume." He began to offer an apologetic grin. "Sorry." His smile broadened. "We're expressive! If it makes you feel any better, it's how we talk to family. Don't worry; you'll know if I'm really angry." He gave my chin a slight squeeze, then pushed my shoulder to give me a friendly nudge. "Now, are we going bike riding or not?"

"Yeah." I felt a smile creeping across my face and a slight blush. "We're going. I guess I'm just not used to it. Next time, give me a warning if I'm walking anywhere near a landmine."

He leaned into me and gave me a quick kiss on the forehead. As he leaned back, he winked. "I told you, I'm Italian. We come without warnings." He offered me another grin, then returned to help navigate my bike into his car. "Now can we get going? You'll really see grumpy if my stomach is left empty for too long."

I was so taken aback by his spontaneous gesture of affection that I could do little more than stand there smiling like an idiot. I had to shake myself in response to his prodding to once more engage in the task of loading my bike. I couldn't help myself from at least getting in an innocent dig. "You sure you trust me to do this? If you'd like, I can wrap my bike in bubble wrap first."

I heard his answer through the back of the car. "If you don't move your ass, we won't even need the bikes. Remember, I have to be to work at five. It's already a quarter after eight. That gives us less than nine hours. At the rate you're moving, we won't even have the car loaded by then."

"Okay, okay. Grab the wheel. But be careful this time. I don't want your interior fabric to scratch my bike."

Because he had taken his sunglasses off to lean into the car, I could see him roll his eyes. "I knew I should have suggested we go roller blading. How long would it take you to throw your skates in the backseat?"

I smiled. "Not long. But they give my feet blisters. You'd have to carry me back."

"Maybe it would be better if we just went to a matinee. I'm going to starve to death before we even pull away from the curb."

Between the two of us, the bike slid into the back of his car pretty effortlessly, and I carefully pushed the hatchback closed. He withdrew from the passenger seat door, put his sunglasses back on, and stepped aside to create room for me to get into the car. As he held the door open, he waved his hand like a chauffeur gesturing to an important client. "Breakfast awaits, sir."

I dropped into the seat, laughing. "Hope you don't expect a tip."

"Of course not." He paused a beat. "It will be easier if I just let you buy my breakfast." He shut the door and began walking around the car before I could answer.

When he slid into the driver's seat beside me, he was still smiling, but his tone was more serious. "All right. Where are we going to eat? And did I mention that I was hungry?"

"I'll eat anything." Then, as if to avoid any additional misunderstandings, I offered a single clarification: "Except sushi. I don't do sushi." I looked at him and tried to sound serious when I asked, "You didn't want sushi for breakfast, did you? Is sushi the Italian breakfast of champions?"

The context of the joke was lost on him, and he just wrinkled his nose. "I'd prefer eggs and pancakes. You want to go to the Morning Grind? It's early enough that we shouldn't have to wait for a table."

"Perfect." I pulled my glasses back over my eyes and looked straight ahead. "Drive, my good man. There's a bike path requiring my presence." I tried to give my best impression of a business executive, but the impersonation was ruined when I started to laugh. It was pretty lame anyway.

They still had a fair number of empty tables on the patio at the Morning Grind, and we were escorted immediately over to one close to the fountain. A fine mist emanated from the water flowing off the fountain's edge, so though the table was in the sun, the temperature was pleasant. The hostess dropped menus in front of us and offered a parting smile as she informed us that our waiter would be over to take our orders shortly.

I reveled in anticipation of the day. Delicious breakfast, perfect weather, an afternoon of biking… and the entire time spent with Sergio. I couldn't imagine a better prospect.

I picked up the menu and began to contemplate the choices. After not more than a minute, without shifting my eyes from the considerable number of options, I absentmindedly asked, "What sounds good to you?"

I glanced up and was a little startled that rather than having picked up the menu, Sergio was just looking at me, smiling. He turned his lips up in an even bigger grin. "Such intensity. Is that a menu or are you studying quantum physics? I'd settled on eggs and pancakes before we'd even loaded the bikes."

I shrugged and returned my attention to the menu. "Okay, so now I know you're a 'back to the basics' kind of guy. I'm more a 'variety is the spice of life' type." I didn't look up but couldn't suppress a grin.

His chuckle carried across the table. "We'll see which one of us ends up being the most predictable."

"Really?" I looked at him over the top of the menu and gave him an inquisitive smile. "Care to make a prediction?"

He scoffed teasingly. "Between the two of us? You're definitely going to be the most predictable." He then relaxed into his chair. "But don't take my word for it. Let's just see how the day plays out."

I laughed as I set the menu down. "You're probably right. But," I said as I looked at him expectantly, "I'm going to have the egg scramble tossed with pasta. Did you predict that? Pasta; it more likely should have been your choice."

He held his palms up defensively. "No, the thing is, I would have predicted you would succumb to stereotypes. And," he said, smiling smugly, "it would appear that I'm right."

"Okay, Mr. All American Breakfast. I cry uncle. I'm predictable, you're spontaneous."

His grin transformed immediately into a look of confusion. "What does that have to do with calling me your uncle?"

"Your uncle? No, I'm sorry." I shook my head and smiled apologetically. "That's slang. When someone cries uncle it means they give up. Your English is so good I sometimes forget it's your second language and you're not familiar with all our slang."

Rather than being offended, he grinned, his smile spreading quickly across his face. "Yeah, this American slang thing sometimes gets me into trouble. One of my customers became a little apprehensive the other day when I told her that our minestrone soup had everything *under* the kitchen sink. She looked like she was afraid I was going to feed her Drano."

I laughed. "Who would guess that one of the ingredients in Osvaldo's secret recipe included Comet?"

The waitress swept over to our table and introduced herself. "Hey, you guys. Welcome to the Morning Grind. I'm Jennifer. Can I bring you something to drink?"

"Hi, Jennifer. Sorry you have to work. A beautiful Saturday morning should be anything but a grind." I smiled, hoping she'd appreciate a little humor, then said, "I think we're ready to order."

"What'll it be?" She took her pad out of her smock pocket and touched her pen to it expectantly.

I looked across the table and grinned. "Go ahead, Sergio. You decided yesterday."

Rather than looking at me, he looked up at Jennifer and offered a hugely flirtatious smile. "You can ignore him. He's just grumpy because thus far this morning, he hasn't been right about anything. I'll have two eggs over easy with bacon and a short stack of pancakes. Also, I'd like a small glass of fresh-squeezed orange juice." He handed her the menu, nodded in my direction, then shook his head disapprovingly while silently mouthing the word, "Grumpy."

I too handed her the menu. "I'm in an excellent mood, Jennifer. He's just sore because his spontaneity score dropped this morning. I'd like the egg scramble with pasta and a cup of coffee. Thanks." I looked at Sergio and tried to look victorious.

Jennifer was completely unfazed as she tucked her pad back into her pocket. "Got it. Breakfast for two grumps, neither of whom can suppress their shit-eating grins. If I didn't know better, I'd say you were both about ready to burst with happiness." Then she smiled. "Don't worry, we have two Miss Congeniality crowns—one for each of you." She winked as she walked away from the table.

I tried to look disgruntled. "See what you did? You blew our cover. Now she thinks we're gay." I sat back, huffed, but then let my smile creep up. "She probably even thinks we're on a date."

Sergio raised a quizzical brow. "Don't worry, when she gets back, I'll set her straight."

I laughed. "I suspect she's already straight. We're the ones she thinks are gay."

He rolled his eyes. "Then you can wear the crown. Maybe it can substitute for a bike helmet."

"Hey, she said they had two. We'll both have to wear one. We'll be mistaken for brothers. Or sisters," I said with a grin.

He looked up and held my gaze for a second. "Would that be better than being mistaken for lovers?" He let the question hang in the air.

I casually reached for my water and answered flatly, plainly wanting my answer to have two interpretations. "That might not be such a bad mistake." I held his eyes and smiled around the glass as I begin to take a sip from it.

His confidence unflappable, he just smirked and said, "We'll see after a day bicycling together if this was a mistake or not."

I tried to match his confidence. "Only one way to find out." I raised my water glass in a toast. "We're at breakfast. So far so good." Then I grinned. "I'm the one who's predictable, and I predict that not only will this not have been a mistake, but it will have been a good thing."

He smiled too. "I said you were predictable, not psychic." Then he reached for his water to mimic my toast. "But for what it's worth, here's to an accurate prediction."

I lifted my glass again and clicked it against his. "Doctor by day, psychic hotline by night. And, just so you know," I said, grinning, "I'm never wrong."

"Really? Never wrong?" He set his glass down, and his eyes sparkled with amusement. "We shouldn't be wasting our time biking. We should be playing the lottery."

I did my best to look offended. "The accuracy of my predictions is limited to issues of the heart. I don't waste my talents on monetary gain."

He looked disappointed. "In that case, keep your predictions a secret. I don't want anyone predicting my heart attack. I'd rather it be a surprise."

I frowned at him and acted like his skepticism was misdirected. "Oh ye of little faith. You may doubt my predictions now, but I guarantee that by the end of the day, you'll be admitting this was the best day you've ever had." I paused. "Well, maybe not the best day, but a pretty damn good one."

Not long after, Jennifer returned with our breakfasts. The food was great, the coffee was strong, and the conversation between us was easy. We continued to get to know one another, the mutual teasing was enjoyable, and we laughed a lot.

When the bill came, we both reached for our wallets, and rather than have any uncomfortable discussion about who was going to pay or how we were going to split it, we each just laid a twenty onto the tray. When Jennifer returned with our change, I calculated a little over a 20 percent tip, then divided the remainder between us. Sergio casually looked down at the tray as if he was completely disinterested, but I was sure he was evaluating the amount I had left. Because his livelihood depended on tips, I knew it was important to him that we leave Jennifer a generous amount. He gave a quick nod, offered me a satisfied smile, then stood and dropped his napkin on his empty plate. "You ready to ride?"

"Right behind you." I stood up too. "Shall we swing into a 7-Eleven on the way to grab a couple bottles of water? Looks like it's going to be a warm one." I gave his shoulder an affectionate shove. "Wouldn't want dehydration to prevent you from being able to keep up with me."

His smile radiated both amusement and confidence. "As usual, I'm way ahead of you. In more ways than one. Firstly, I threw four bottles of water into an ice chest that's under the seat. Secondly, not only is it going to be warm today, but the ocean views should be beautiful. Sadly for you, however, most of that will be lost on you. You're going to be seeing little more than my back wheel and the sight of my ass as you struggle to keep up with me."

Rather than giving him the satisfaction of looking as if I intended to react to the unspoken challenge, I just smiled and said, "You're right about one thing, then; if my only view is that of your ass, it will definitely be beautiful."

I walked by him, avoided direct eye contact, and clenched my teeth to suppress a laugh. He stood there, unmoving, with his mouth slightly open. He was at least temporarily at a loss for a quick comeback.

I glanced over my shoulder. "You coming?"

He smiled as he too began to amble toward the door. "Guess I'd better. I have the car keys."

Rather than parking in the beach lot, where we would have had to pay, we parked on the side of the road about a half mile up Temescal Canyon. Getting down to the beach would be a breeze as we would have to do little more than coast. Getting back up to the car after an entire day of riding, however, was probably going to be a different story. The street presented a pretty steep incline. *Oh well,* I thought. *It will be a great glute workout. Give them a good burn.*

Once we made it down to the bike path, we were indeed welcomed by a gorgeous day. There were only a few fluffy white clouds floating through an otherwise beautiful blue sky. The waves crashed gently against the rocks at the edge of the beach, and the sun reflected off the white sand. There were a few other bikers, but the path was unusually uncrowded, and from Temescal almost down to the Santa Monica pier, we were mostly able to ride side by side.

We pedaled at a pretty good clip, but even with the exertion, we could still talk to one another. I learned more about his family and what his life had been like growing up in Rome.

"There are five of us. I have two older sisters, an older brother, and my younger sister Lala, the one who lives here. I was the troublemaker. I never really did anything bad; I was just always creating mischief. In Rome, there are a lot of street policeman, and the one who worked on our block knew me by name. Our home was near the Trevi Fountain, and even on hot days, it was forbidden for children to get into the water. Legend has it that if you throw a coin into the fountain, you will one day return to Rome. So, of course, during the day, tourists throw hundreds of coins into the fountain." Sergio grinned. "Some must believe valuable coins result in a faster return, because by day's end, there were always quite a few silver dollars collecting on the bottom of the fountain." The more he talked about his childhood adventures, the more animated he became, and he begin to peddle faster as he spoke. "It seemed a waste for that money to be lost on the promise of some tourist trying to return to Rome when it could be better spent on the certainty of buying us ice cream, so my friends and I made it our mission to try to sneak around the guard and scoop out as many coins as possible. That poor guard must have worn out fifteen pairs of shoes chasing me down the street after some of my more successful diving missions. On the bright side, the owner of the gelato shop loved me. I was his best customer, and he always had plenty of change."

I found myself laughing too. In addition to finding the story of his childhood antics entertaining, I was amused by the enthusiastic narration of his story. It was evident he had warm memories of his childhood and that his carefree, unencumbered, impetuous spirit had existed since the early days of his youth. I might have been a little envious. I had no delusions about having been a perfect child, but I would have been hard-pressed to knowingly defy authority. Even as a child it was important to me that I be perceived as being a people pleaser. I didn't want to be thought of as a troublemaker. Even on a beautiful day, peddling aimlessly down an incredible bike path on a picture-perfect beach, I had to shake my head at the absurdity. It occurred to me that even as a child, I'd known something about me was different. Something about me that might one day be considered shameful. So even as a child, I overcompensated. I worked to be well behaved, to play by the rules. Carrying a shameful secret meant trying to put up a façade of perfection.

I thought about my realization for a minute but decided to put it behind me. The day was too perfect to get bogged down in introspection. Besides, despite my feelings of inadequacy, my childhood had been mostly consumed by life-affirming experiences. I'd been athletic, I'd been smart, and though not the class clown, many of my friends had sought my company when they wanted to laugh.

Feeling exhilarated by the ride, by the warm breeze rushing past my face, and by the excitement of being in Sergio's company, I felt inspired to share recollections of some of my own adrenaline-drenched moments of childhood.

"Well, I never had to run from the police, but I did have to outrun an avalanche once." I looked at him to be sure he looked appropriately impressed, then continued.

I had told my larger than life story so many times I could have recited it backward, and every time I told it I embellished it a little more. The truth? Though it was a real avalanche and it could have knocked me down, when it happened, I was skiing far enough beneath it that even if it had reached me, I probably wouldn't have been buried beneath more than about eight inches of snow. Excluding that information, however, made for a better story.

"Yeah, my dad started me on skis when I was about three, and this must have happened when I was about thirteen or so. Having grown up on skis, even as a young kid I was a pretty good skier. It was late in the afternoon, and though it had snowed the entire night before, it had been relatively warm that day, so the snow was getting soft. I was determined to get one more run in before the lift closed, so as my other friends headed toward the lodge, my friend Torin and I raced down the hill to get into the lift line one last time before they roped its entrance off."

Sergio peddled more slowly and steered his bike closer to mine so he could hear me over the wind. He nodded to indicate he'd understood the progression of the story, so I continued.

"Anyway, when we got off the lift at the top of the slope, I needed to adjust my boot buckle, so I stopped on the top edge, took my gloves off, and reached down to tighten the one that had become unfastened. Torin was impatient, so he signaled to me that he was headed down and dropped over the lip. When my ankle felt appropriately secure in my boot, I too skied over to the edge of the lip and looked down the mountain. We had been the last ones allowed onto the lift, so except for a few slower skiers, who were still creeping their way down close to the bottom, Torin was the only other skier on the hill, and in the time it had taken me to fix my buckle, he was already a couple hundred feet below. I took a deep breath and for a couple minutes relished the idea that when I pushed off the top, I would literally have the whole mountain to myself. The feeling was intoxicating. It wasn't just that the steep slope represented a challenging descent, it was knowing the contest would be just between me and Mother

Nature. Like I was pitting my ability against the elements and there were no other contenders."

I smiled over at Sergio, hoping my rendition of the experience was building suspense. "When I pushed over the edge, I was aware that a jet was flying overhead but paid it little attention. I wanted to make a good impression. I knew people who were down on the lodge deck were aware the hill was closing and would be looking up to watch the last skiers make their way down. I was essentially going to get to be a one-man show and wanted it to be spectacular. I pushed off and tried to ski vertically down the fall line. My legs worked like pistons, checking into the slope to control my speed, and I silently complimented myself for what I was sure was flawless technique. When I was about a couple hundred feet down the hill, I was shaken by a sonic boom. In itself, the sound wasn't too alarming and was something almost anticipated when a jet crossed an empty horizon. What I hadn't anticipated, however, was the loud cracking sound that followed in sequence. The vibrations from the sonic boom had broken a shelf of softening snow off the cornice above me, and when I looked over my shoulder, I saw it cascading down the hill at what appeared to be at the speed of sound. In that instant, my only thought was, 'To hell with the one-man show, now I'm fucked!'"

Sergio glided over to the side of the bike path and came to a stop. He stood and straddled the cross bar of his bicycle, then took his water bottle out of his waist pack. He signaled me with a nod of his chin to stop next to him, put the spout of the water bottle to his lips, and tilted his head back to take a long satisfying gulp. After he swallowed he looked at me expectantly. "So, given that you obviously lived to be able to take this bike ride with me, what happened?" He smiled, and for a brief second I completely forgot what I was even talking about.

"Well, I really had no choice but to bend over and grab my ankles."

He almost choked on the water he had just squeezed into his mouth and began to laugh as he sputtered, "You did what?"

"Well, I didn't actually grab my ankles, but I did drop into a tuck, press my body as closely into my legs as I could, and point my skis straight down the hill. If the avalanche was approaching at the speed of sound, I had to haul ass at the speed of sound squared." His confused expression registered that he didn't get the analogy, so I clarified. "I had to ski faster than the friggin' wall of snow cascading down the mountain, threatening to bury my ass.

"The main face of the mountain I was skiing down converged into a valley framed on each side by mountains with gentler slopes. As the bulk of the accumulating snow from the avalanche began to funnel into the valley, I used my momentum to turn up one of the side slopes. I was going fast enough that I was able to ascend about fifty feet, then hid behind a tree. Most of the avalanche went tumbling by me then came to a stop some two hundred yards beyond. The people on the deck had heard the avalanche come crashing down and so were looking up the slope. They had seen my terrifying race and broke out in applause when they saw me successfully evade being swept into the icy jaws of death. It's a rare individual who dares to challenge Mother Nature and wins." I pumped my fist and grinned. Of course, though the intention of the story was to try to impress Sergio, I didn't want to be taken too seriously. My encore was giving what I hoped appeared to be a humble shrug. "I should be on a Wheaties box."

I laughed, grabbed the water bottle out of his hand, and squeezed some water into my mouth. "Hey," he good-naturedly complained, "I brought you your own water."

I winked. "Don't know why, but I'm sure your water tastes better." I tossed the bottle in the air so he could easily catch it. "Besides, narrowly escaping death works up a big thirst. I'm saving mine for later." Before he could either answer or squirt water in my face, I pushed off the path and began peddling.

Within seconds, he passed me, gave me little more than a sideway glance, and said, as if he was talking to himself, "That story explains a lot."

I peddled a little faster to catch up. "What does it explain?"

He looked at me, pushed his sunglasses down his nose so I could see the humor in his eyes, then, as I watched a smile spread across his face, he answered, "Explains why you have an icicle stuck up your ass." He accelerated and swerved in front of me so I was forced to follow him.

"It's essential," I yelled into the wind. "When you have an ass as hot as mine, the icicle serves as an equalizer." He flashed a crooked grin over his shoulder, then stood up on the pedals to exaggerate the undulation of his own butt muscles.

"This is what a real hot ass looks like. I suggest you study it carefully, because it will be a cold day in hell before you ever catch it." With that, he sat back down, tucked his head closer to his handlebars, and for the next hundred yards maintained an Olympic-record-setting pace. I only caught up to him when he stuck his legs out spread-eagled over the crossbar of his bike and began to coast.

I was winded when I caught up to him but was more flushed from laughing than I was from exertion. "You didn't have to slow down. I was getting ready to pass you."

"Dream on." He waited a beat, then offered a grin that was the slightest bit seductive. "Besides, maybe I wanted you to catch me."

I smiled too. "Careful. If I catch you, I might not let you go."

We rode side by side for the next few minutes, neither of us breaking the silence, just offering the other bashful, contented smiles, enjoying the warmth of the day and the enjoyment of one another's company. Then he offered a confident nod and said, "Let's try to at least make it to the other side of the marina before we turn around."

"Cool. I won't leave your side." I tried to maintain a neutral expression, as if my comment related only to our bike ride and could have no other interpretation.

He looked at me intently. "Good. Should be a perfect day, then." His gaze held mine for a few seconds, then he offered an innocent shrug. "I mean, there's not a cloud in the sky."

Easy conversation continued between us as we made our way down the beach. "Okay, so you're aware that my parents produced an army of kids. How about you? Do you have brothers and sisters?" He grinned. "Or were your parents so traumatized by having you that they were afraid to have any more?"

"No," I said, laughing, "I'm one of four boys. I'm number two. My parents had their first child, achieved perfection on their second, and then continued to try to replicate their success. They gave up after two more attempts. Though they're all right guys, my three brothers have never measured up to my greatness." I tried to maintain a serious expression but ended up breaking into hoots of laughter as the last comment fell out of my mouth.

"Wow." Sergio succeeded in looking totally unimpressed. "If you're perfection, American couples must set the bar really low." Behind his dark glasses, I could see him raise an eyebrow to indicate he was joking. "Are you guys close? Do you see your brothers very often?" he asked.

"Since I'm the only one of the four who lives in Southern California, we don't see that much of each other. But we're close. Growing up, my parents were big on family activities, so we spent a lot of time together. Some days were spent playing around, other days were spent working. Because we were all good skiers, when the Sheldon clan hit the slopes together, it was an impressive spectacle. Though we were frequently able to spend winter days skiing with our friends, there were also days when Mom and Dad insisted we ski together as a family. Invariably, we grumbled and complained that we'd rather be with our friends, but I've got to say, we actually had a lot of fun together. There was a lot of teasing, a lot of laughing, and generally, warm camaraderie."

I felt genuine warmth spread through me as I reminisced about my childhood. Despite feeling much of my inadequacy was grounded in my upbringing, I had to concede I also had a lot of really great memories. It made for a funny dichotomy. On one hand, I felt like I never measured up in my parents' eyes. On the other, I was indisputably confident I was truly loved.

Because Sergio seemed to be honestly interested in getting to know me better, I kept talking.

"It wasn't always all about having fun, though. Both my parents were determined to instill in us a strong work ethic. Sometimes, the family event consisted of forcing us to perform slave labor. Had my parents not worked right beside us, doing the same things, I'm sure we could have reported them to child protective services." Sergio didn't look like he was completely following, so I felt compelled to provide an example.

"You know, I grew up in a small town in the mountains. Winters would get really cold, and we heated our house exclusively with a fireplace and a woodstove. In order to ensure that we were warm through the entire winter, we had to spend a number of weekends during the spring and summer filling the garage with firewood. This consisted of driving our truck way up into the hills, felling a dead tree, cutting it up, splitting it into pieces small enough to be lifted into the truck, then hauling it back home and unloading it. Only trees that were already dead could be cut down. Sometimes, the dead trees were hundreds of feet away from where we parked the truck. Getting the wood from where the tree was cut down back to the truck took a herculean effort. If the logs were small enough, we could sometimes roll them to the truck and split them there. Frequently however, the circumference of the dead tree was so immense that even cut, the logs were too heavy to move. At those times, the logs had to be split wherever the tree had fallen and then carried back to the truck. Either way, it was a shitload of work. We couldn't complain, though, because Mom and Dad worked shoulder to shoulder with us. Actually, they probably worked harder than we did."

Fearing my long-winded story would drive Sergio to such an extreme degree of boredom he would opt to peddle his bike head-on into the crashing waves, I brought it to a quick conclusion. "I've got to hand it to my parents, though; they taught me the value of hard work. I'm sure it was their influence that enabled me to successfully get through medical school."

I looked over at Sergio, expecting him to be only half listening, but instead, he seemed to be paying full attention.

"Sounds like, all and all, it was a good way to grow up. And," he said as he gave me a cockeyed grin, "if their influence resulted in you becoming a doctor, it couldn't have been all bad." Then he asked, "How are things now? Are you still close to your parents? They must be really proud." He smiled. "Or at least happy that their ass-kicking paid off."

"Yeah, we're close. I talk to them at least once a week. They not only like hearing about the kids I take care of, they like to feel as if they're being kept in the loop. They want to make sure I'm happy. You know, typical parent stuff."

"Sounds really good. So they're cool with you being gay?"

CHAPTER 10

SERGIO probably sensed a subtle change in me the minute he asked the question, because I was sure my posture involuntarily stiffened a little. I looked out over the ocean as if I was distracted by something. I realized I was ill-prepared to answer his question and that, at face value, my answer would seem to be a contradiction in itself. In one respect, I was super close to my parents. I sought their counsel, I respected their advice, I depended on them for love and encouragement, and I enjoyed feeling that in many respects, in addition to being my parents, they were also my friends. I shared all aspects of my life with them. All aspects except one: the little detail of my being gay. It wasn't like I lied to them—I just steered away from the topic and when asked, provided only vague, noncommittal information. They assumed the demands of my residency program precluded me from dating much, and I encouraged that impression. It prevented me from having to answer many questions. When asked, I just offhandedly remarked that I'd spent the weekend with friends or that I'd just hung out. I'd have died at the prospect of volunteering that I'd spent the past few weeks agonizing about going out on a date with Sergio and feeling consumed with worry that I'd fail to make a favorable impression on him.

In order to wipe the sweat from his forehead, Sergio had hung his sunglasses over the neckline of his tank top, and I caught him looking at me. His expression was intense. I wasn't sure I really wanted to have this conversation with him, but I felt as if his gaze had locked onto my very soul. It somehow seemed he would be able to detect even the slightest degree of insincerity.

I shrugged as if my response was inconsequential, then answered in what was unfortunately a less than confident tone, "I haven't really told them yet."

I started to peddle, trying to give the impression that the conversation had come to a natural breaking point and no additional discussion was even remotely necessary, but Sergio quickly caught up with me.

"Zack!" I didn't immediately turn. "Zack," he called with significantly more determination. When I looked at him, his voice softened. "What do you mean you haven't told them?"

"I just haven't told them. Look, it's really no big deal. It's just never come up." I averted my gaze. I knew I was failing at making the topic seem somehow irrelevant, but at the moment, hiding behind the illusion of being obtuse seemed infinitely easier than trying to explain myself. I offered him my patented smile of feigned confidence and then said, "Really, it's no big deal." I willed my body to give off a carefree "all's right with the world" vibe and again began peddling. But I looked over my shoulder, I saw that Sergio had stopped moving and pulled his bike off the path onto a sidewalk that led up to one of the parking lots.

As the bike path was empty where we were, I easily turned around and rode back toward him. When I was close enough to be heard, I called into the wind, "You ready for another water break already?"

He smiled slightly, but his eyes held a cool seriousness. "No, not a water break. I'm taking a quick bullshit break."

For an instant, I was genuinely confused. "A bullshit break?"

"Yeah," he said. "That's what you're dishing out right now, isn't it? Bullshit? Look, Zack, I don't want to be a hardass, but I thought the whole point of this day was that we'd spend it getting to know one another. If there's something you don't want to tell me, just say so. But it bums me out to see you trying to lie to me. We hardly know each other. A bunch of topics are probably off-limits. But I want honesty. Just tell me you're uncomfortable and that you don't want to talk about something. Hell, you can even tell me to fuck off. That would at least be honest." He gave me a cockeyed grin. "But if we're going to start our first date off on the right foot, let's make it real. Whatever we're gonna build," he said as he raised one eyebrow playfully, "if we're gonna build, let's start by at least being honest with one another."

I studied him for a while and was drawn to his sincerity. His eyes were bold and unapologetic but also warm and caring. I felt alternately embarrassed and ecstatic. Sergio had expressed a sentiment I deeply respected. When challenged, I was the first to advocate for integrity, both professionally and personally. And yet, in a number of ways, when I was uncomfortable, mostly as it related to being gay, I was content to hide behind a lie. Without intending to do so, Sergio had touched something deep down. He was talking about honesty in our conversation, but I was thinking about honesty in my life.

I still felt a little hesitant, however. I appreciated both his sincerity and his aversion to dishonesty, but I was struggling with where that line should actually be drawn. I mean, shit, I didn't want to put all my cards on the table all at once. Besides, in addition to finding him incredibly attractive, I was beginning to see he was a genuinely high-quality guy. If I allowed him to peek too far beneath the surface of who I was, he might get the impression I had serious psyche issues.

He looked at me expectantly, waiting for any kind of response. My brain felt like it was caught in a tug-of-war. I had never been confident. If he knew how vulnerable I sometimes felt, would he quickly try to disentangle himself from a loser? I tried to carefully weigh all my options, but in the end, it appeared that there was only one. Somehow, I suddenly felt determined that at this point in my life, any movement, no matter how small, had to be in a forward direction. If there was going to be a second date with Sergio, I didn't want to worry about having to continue to hide.

Sergio allowed the silence between us to stretch out. He waited patiently for me to respond, but he kept his gaze trained on mine. When I still didn't answer, I suspected he felt he could read the truth in my expression. "It's your call, Zack," he said. "If you don't wanna talk about it, I'm cool. But rather than just trying to blow me off, I want you to make the call. I'm good either way." Then, for a brief second, he let his gaze sweep over the endless ocean. "But if you are intent on just trying to blow me off, there's not much point in our riding together any farther." His gaze came back to mine with an even deeper intensity.

I was nervous. I hadn't intended for the conversation to become so serious. Still feeling a little apprehensive, I was nonetheless inspired by his directness. I did want to feel more confident. I did want to feel more proud. I was tired of continuously trying to hide what I thought were my deficiencies. I returned his stare. "Sergio, I can't predict what's going to happen between us. Who knows if we're going to end up being compatible with one another. Hell, by next week, we might decide we can't stand each other. I can, however, say one thing with certainty. If you're looking for honesty, I'll never intentionally blow you off." Then, in an attempt to lighten the moment, I said, "Intentionally blow you? Maybe. Blow you off? Never!"

He held my gaze a little longer, then his expression softened. He rolled his eyes slightly. "Let's keep our clothes on at least long enough to finish our ride." He pulled his bike back onto the path and balanced his foot on the pedal, readying himself to push off. He looked at me over his shoulder. "We real?"

"Guaranteed." I knew, based on what he had said before, that he was really asking for an assurance that I intended to have whatever developed between us be based on truthfulness. I smiled and pushed off to ride next to him. "Does this mean we can get naked when we finish our ride?" I looked at him and raised a single eyebrow. I was thankful the joking provided a brief interlude, but I was also aware of his question, still hanging there. Ignoring my internal discomfort, I decided Sergio was worth putting my feelings of vulnerability on the line.

I took a deep breath and kept my eyes directly on the path ahead of me as I started my explanation. "I really do want to tell them. It's ridiculous to exclude them from such a big part of my life. I guess the thing that prevents me from doing so is my fear that they'll be disappointed in me—"

Sergio looked over at me and interrupted. His voice was both sincere and nonjudgmental. "Zack, I don't want you to feel you have to talk about something you don't want to. I was serious when I said a lot of things are probably still off the table. My intention wasn't to push you into talking about something you're uncomfortable with; my intention was to make you understand I want you to be honest with me. And...." He paused. "You can honestly say you'd just as soon not talk about it."

I was surprised at how comfortable I felt talking to Sergio. For reasons I didn't even begin to understand, I felt safe. For a minute, I worried it might be my dick doing the thinking. Maybe I subconsciously wanted to feel safe with him to justify my overwhelming attraction to him. I quickly dismissed that possibility, however. Though I definitely thought he was hot, the connection I was beginning to feel with him was way more than just physical.

"No, I'm good." I smiled over at him. "In fact, it might be helpful to talk about it. But only on one condition." I smiled bigger. "Well, two conditions actually. First, you tell me if I start boring you to death, and second, you promise not to let anything I tell you make you think I'm a complete loser."

He smiled. "Both those conditions have already been met. Look, Zack, I enjoy spending time with you, and if I thought you were a loser, we wouldn't be together on this damn bike path now." His grin broadened. "I have a pretty good sense for people, and you're solid. I wouldn't care about the honesty thing if it wasn't important to me that I really get to know you." He tried to make his expression look serious. "So, tell me about your mommy issues."

I tried to kick his back wheel but only succeeded in losing my balance. When I was confident I wouldn't go careening into the sand, I begin to try to pull my thoughts together. "They're probably both mommy and daddy issues." I thought for a minute. "You know, when I stop to think about it, I'm not really sure what I'm afraid of. I'm secure in knowing that they love me, and I'm certain finding out I'm gay wouldn't jeopardize their feelings for me in the least." I tried to bring my apprehensions into better focus. "I guess what I really do fear, however, is the likelihood of disappointing them." I tried to elaborate to help Sergio better understand.

"Without getting into great depth about all my psychoses, I think realizing I was gay as a child resulted in me feeling a tremendous sense of shame. Being gay was just totally inconsistent with who I thought I should be. I was a strong, confident, capable guy. I was the son of a football coach, the nephew of a war hero. I couldn't be gay. I'd been taught it was not only an abomination against God but that it was unnatural. I thought it meant being weak and…" I struggled to think of an appropriate adjective. "… that it meant being defective."

I felt a little embarrassed about the intensity of my confession, but kept talking before I felt too self-conscious to continue. "I guess I felt like being gay meant I was worthless. So, probably in an attempt to compensate, I worked really hard. I worked to be well liked, I worked to be good at sports, but mostly I worked to be successful. I needed to establish myself as a leader; I had to maintain good grades, and I had to win multiple achievement awards."

I peddled without looking over at Sergio. "Fortunately, many of my efforts paid off. I'm not sure they succeeded in making me feel better about myself for being gay, but they did succeed in earning me a lot of positive attention. People were impressed by me. Some were even inspired by my accomplishments. Indeed"—my voice became a little softer—"I became the kind of guy anyone would be proud to call their son."

My voice was little more than a whisper, but Sergio was still able to hear me. "That's why I can't tell them. If they knew the truth, I don't think they would love me less, I just think they would be less proud." A few tears welled up in my eyes, but they were hidden behind my glasses. "And I'm not sure I could take that, Sergio. I've worked my whole life to be someone they could be proud of. It would kill me to feel like I had disappointed them."

Sergio's attention was unwavering. He listened intently to each word, then began to consider the total meaning of what I had said. As he thought it through, he became more and more agitated. It was almost as if each of my individual words was a stick of dynamite being dropped closer and closer to an open flame. When one exploded, the whole pile blew up.

"That's fucking ridiculous, Zack." His cheeks were flushed and he was visibly angry. "How could they not be proud of you? You're amazing." He looked briefly self-conscious, like he hadn't intended to be so overtly flattering, but then continued his rant. "I mean, I don't know you that well, but look at what you've accomplished. You were top of your class in med school, you're saving children's lives in the hospital, and you're not bad-looking, to boot. You don't have anyone to apologize to, least of all your parents."

I was surprised at the ferocity of his response. Sergio wore his feelings on his sleeve, and they were never difficult to interpret. If he was angry, his temper could escalate in less than a second. He had gone from being serene bicycle companion, pontificating on the importance of honesty in a relationship, to a fierce grizzly bear protecting its cub. Initially, the intensity of his reaction was a little disconcerting, but it occurred to me that this was just another example of his Italian volatility, a minor earthquake on the emotional Richter scale. It would take some getting used to.

As embarrassed as I was about talking to him about my relationship with my parents, I smiled at how resolutely he had come to my defense. In fact, seeing him so obviously wound up made me want to calm him. The conversation had taken an interesting turn. I had been the one to share one of my big insecurities, but he was the one all riled up.

"Don't misunderstand me, Sergio. I do think they're proud of me. What I said is that I don't want them to be disappointed in me." As I tried to explain, I even found myself becoming confused. "I mean, I've worked hard to make them proud of who I am. In fact, I've worked hard to make them proud of everything I've done. But how can they be proud of the fact that I'm gay? That's asking a lot. I mean, shit, I can't even say *I'm* proud of being gay. Of course they'll be disappointed. What alternative is there? They'd have to be."

Sergio again stopped peddling and motioned for me to do the same. He pulled his bike over to the side of the bike path, and I stopped next to him. We stood side by side, looking at each other. For a while, all we could hear was the gentle lapping of the waves against the sand. His appearance had again been transformed. The agitation that had animated his features just moments before was now completely gone. Instead, he was the epitome of calm.

His voice was quiet, not accusatory. In fact, it was caring and supportive. "So, it's not so much that they'll be disappointed in you as it is that you're disappointed in yourself." He let his statement percolate through my mind for a second and then continued. "I mean, think about it, Zack. Let's say you were aware that your parents always aspired for you to be a plastic surgeon, and you ended up choosing pediatrics instead because you loved it. If that had been the case, you would have anticipated their disappointment when you decided to become a pediatrician. In fact, their indifference about pediatrics might even have resulted in you thinking longer and harder about your choice. I doubt, however, that their opinion would ultimately have caused you to change careers. You would have been aware that they were going to be disappointed, but feeling confident in the decision you'd made, their disappointment wouldn't have devastated you. I suspect you would feel strongly that you were making the best choice for your own life and would hope that with time, they'd eventually see it the same way."

His brown-eyed gaze bored directly into mine. He didn't shift for even a second. When I became uncomfortable with the intensity of his stare and tried to look away, I was aware that his gaze followed me. When he did speak, his voice came out even more softly. "So, the question here is, who are you really trying to protect? Are you protecting them from the truth? Or are you protecting yourself from having to face it?"

I looked out over the endless expanse of the ocean. I felt stymied. Certainly, Sergio had succeeded in stabbing into the heart of the problem, but it wasn't that simple. Deep down, I really did feel ashamed. I would have loved nothing more than to be able to say I was proud of being gay, but I knew that was a lie. The best I could do was to say that for many years, I had been trying to accept it. I had been trying desperately to convince myself that fundamentally, it was just an integral part of who I was. As I matured, it had become more apparent to me that I could no sooner dismiss my sexual orientation than I could decide to ignore my right arm. But there was a significant difference: I hadn't spent my whole life being told there was something wrong with my right arm. That it was defective. That it was something to feel vehemently ashamed of.

I looked back at Sergio. I was sure he could detect the subtle pleading in my question when I asked, "If you've always felt ashamed, how do you make yourself feel proud?"

Sergio immediately opened his mouth to answer but then paused. I think he realized the answer was more confounding than he anticipated. "How do you make yourself feel proud?" It was almost as if the predicament I was facing was foreign to him. He had always been proud. It wasn't something he'd decided be, it was just who he was: confident and unapologetic.

Sergio was aware that now I was the one staring at him, and it was his turn to feel a little uncomfortable. He pushed his bike back and forth and concentrated on how the wheel crackled against the grains of sand that had blown across the bike path. I wondered if he felt pressured to reveal some great secret to me. The secret to being proud, the secret to being comfortable. In that instant, I suspect he thought the situation was a little ironic. I mean, here the presumably accomplished physician was asking the Italian waiter, who'd been in this country for little more than seven years, what it meant to feel proud.

When he did begin to speak, his voice was halting. "Look, Zack, I'm not perfect. In fact, I don't even pretend to be." He gave me another crooked grin. "Bet you're not surprised by that." He continued in a more serious tone. "I've done a lot of things in my life for which I'm not particularly proud. In fact, I've done some things I'm downright ashamed of. But—and this is an important but—I'm not ashamed of who I am." He paused, apparently trying to think of words that would better illustrate what he was trying to say.

"Let's take an example." He thought for a second, then threw out the first example that came to mind. "You're blond and you have green eyes. That's just who you are. You might have wanted to be born with dark eyes, but by some fluke of nature, your eyes ended up being green. A genetic catastrophe of sorts. I'd wager a million dollars, however, that despite the fact that their color is not your preference, you're not ashamed of having green eyes. Maybe the first step toward feeling proud is simply to decide to stop feeling ashamed. At least with regard to those things about yourself that you can't change. Or..." He again let a smile spread across his face. "... you can wimp out and get brown contacts." He cocked his head at me as if struck by a realization, and his expression again became more serious. "In the end, though, you'd still have green eyes. You could do a million things to hide it, but behind the contacts, your true eye color would remain unchanged."

I reflected for a second on what he had said: *The first step toward feeling proud is simply to decide to stop feeling ashamed.* I ran the statement through my brain again. On the surface, it was overly simplistic. But as I continued to think about it, I realized its meaning was incredibly profound. I had long since reconciled myself to the fact that being gay hadn't been a choice. I knew beyond any reasonable doubt that I had been born that way. In fact, every day, more and more scientific research was pointing to the genetic origin of an individual's sexual orientation. So, if I had no choice about being gay, and if it was indeed an inherent part of who I was, why feel ashamed?

I began to smile. The burden I had been carrying on my shoulders hadn't gone away, but I had to admit, it felt damn lighter. I reached toward him, grabbed him in a headlock, and pulled him toward me. I gave him a playful squeeze, but before I released him, I quickly kissed the top of his head. "You should give up waiting tables and think about becoming a therapist."

"Couldn't possibly work. One of my clients would eventually piss me off, and I'd end up telling them to fuck off. I'm not sure anyone would be willing to pay me for giving them that advice."

I laughed. "Yeah, but that's the exact advice some people need to hear."

We pushed our bikes back into the middle of the path and resumed peddling. The feelings our conversation had stirred up reverberated in my head. *Decide to stop feeling ashamed.* Easier said than done. Sometimes my shame felt so deeply engrained, it didn't even require conscious thought. It was just there. Wired into me. Influencing every emotion that entered my brain.

I lifted my head up and let the sun wash across my face. As painful as it was, I also felt kind of energized. What the hell! What better time than now to start feeling better about who I was. The old psyche could use some renovating.

Sergio looked at me without slowing. "You okay?"

"Yeah, I'm good. Just not sure I'm happy about revealing to you how crazy I am the first time we're out together."

"To begin with, this isn't the first time we've spent time together. We talked to each other by the pool for more than three hours the other day." He smiled. "Secondly, I knew you were crazy even then."

"Damn." I laughed. "And to think I was trying to be on my best behavior. Well, guess there's no point in hiding now. You wanna come by my place to see the bodies buried under the floorboards?"

"I said I knew you were crazy, not psychotic. Now you're scaring me." He laughed, then looked at me out of the corner of his eye. "How many bodies are we talking about, anyway?"

"Not more than two or three." I allowed for an appropriately dramatic pause then clarified, "Americans, that is. There've got to be a couple dozen Italians, though." I leered at him and tried to pull off a convincing crazed expression. "They're my favorite flavor."

He maintained a façade of seriousness. "My mother warned me about guys like you. If you offer me a piece of candy, I'm gonna run like hell."

"Come on, Sergio. Your mom would be delighted—I said Italians were my favorite flavor. As a matter of fact, I'm getting kind of hungry."

"Creepy."

I laughed some more.

In order to get around the marina, we had to bike down Washington Boulevard, so on the way back we decided to stop in one of the convenience stores to grab a snack.

Sergio dismounted his bike and walked it over to a column that supported the awning over the storefront. He leaned his bike against it, then, hearing my approach, took my bike from me and balanced it against his, facing the opposite direction. He unwound a cable from around his seat, used it to secure our bikes together, and then clamped a padlock on its ends. "We won't be in here long, but this isn't the greatest neighborhood. No sense making our bikes easy targets."

Sweat glistened off his forehead, and he pushed his damp hair back by running his fingers over his head. He smiled and pushed me in front of him. "You're not slowing down, are you?"

"Me? Man, I'm just getting warmed up. I figured if we only take a short break, then kick the pace up a notch, we can make Santa Barbara by sundown." I paused briefly, then tried to look appropriately disappointed. "Oh, that's right. You have to work tonight. Any excuse to wimp out." Anticipating what was coming, I leaned into him so he could push me again with a little more force.

"The only way you'd make Santa Barbara is if I carried you on my shoulders."

"Sounds to me like you're volunteering. Let's do it. I'm looking forward to riding you." This time, I laughed and ran ahead to avoid being shoved. In doing so, I noticed that my hamstrings were a little tight. Though I had been doing a lot of cardio, it had been a while since I had been on my bike. "Man, I guess I'm using some muscles I haven't used in a while." I smiled over my shoulder. "Still feels like the bike seat is riding up my ass."

"That's probably the icicle I was telling you about."

We separated to wander through the store, looking for something to take the edge off our hunger and provide us with a little energy for the ride back. I had picked up another bottle of water and was considering grabbing one of the freshly baked cookies displayed on the counter when I saw Sergio coming back with an apple in his hand.

"Damn. Now you're going to make me feel guilty. That cookie had my name all over it."

"Go for it. Then the cookie will have its name all over you. Forget about having six-pack, abs. I'll just call you 'cookie gut.'"

When I had initially seen him with the apple, I'd thought about getting a piece of fruit instead of the cookie, but now I was unwilling to give him the satisfaction. "That's the advantage to having the metabolism of a finely tuned Ferrari; you can eat as many cookies as you want and still maintain a six-pack." I picked up a chocolate chip cookie and dangled it in front of him.

"Is that the truth? So, why are you still carrying that liter bottle around under your shirt?"

"You're an ass. And an eight-pack is the equivalent of a liter." I put my money on the counter and took a satisfying bite. "Besides, a little sugar might sweeten your disposition. Want a taste?" I thrust the cookie under his nose.

"No, thanks. You enjoy it. My body is a temple, and I won't have it polluted with sugar. Besides, in case you haven't noticed, I'm naturally sweet. No artificial substitutes for me." When he brought the apple up to his mouth, he intentionally flexed his bicep. Rolling my eyes only seemed to encourage him, and he proceeded to raise his arms up and flex both his biceps. "Mountain grown for better flavor."

"You've been watching too many American coffee commercials, and besides, being born in Rome doesn't make you mountain grown. But...." I paused. "Keep that arm up there a second longer, and I'll taste it for myself. I'll let you know if it's a good brew."

He smiled. "Imported directly from Italy. The world's finest grind."

I gave the cashier enough money to pay for both our purchases. "This one's on me." I looked at Sergio and smiled. "It's not every day I get to feast on international cuisine."

He tried to look indignant. "Who said anything about a feast? You just get the sample!"

I had devoured my cookie before he'd even taken the second bite of his apple, so I took his key and went to unlock the bikes while he finished it.

When the wire cable was again secured around his bike seat and he had thrown his apple core into the garbage, we pushed our bikes into the street, mounted them, and started the ride back. As the day wore on, it had gotten a little warmer, and we now had the wind blowing in our faces. Pedaling required a little more exertion, and we kept the conversation light.

I was ecstatic as I thought about how much I was enjoying spending time with Sergio. He was insightful, communicative, and really funny. As an added bonus, he seemed to get my sense of humor, and when I teased him, he was never short of a quick comeback. In fact, with the exception of our intense conversation regarding coming out to my parents, we had spent the majority of the day laughing.

CHAPTER 11

BY THE time we had peddled back up the hill to where the car was parked and had gotten the bikes loaded without incident, it was already almost three o'clock. Sergio looked at his watch and wrinkled his brow with concern. "I hope we don't hit much traffic. It's going to be a little tight to get back, drop you off, and still have time to get home and shower before I have to be at work by five. I probably should have thought about bringing my work clothes with me in case we ended up running short on time." He shrugged. "Oh well. No sense worrying about it now. Worst-case scenario, I skip the shower." He smiled. "I can't smell that bad. I'll just put a little oregano in my underwear. Customers will just think they're picking up a spicy aroma from the kitchen."

I tried to look suspicious. "Careful, there. I'm not sure I'm thrilled about you giving customers an excuse to push their faces into your crotch. When we get to my house, you jump out, and I'll spray you down with the garden hose. If you drive back to your house with the windows down, you'll be dry by the time you get there. You can skip the shower, still make it to work on time, and save the oregano for the house pizza, not your own sausage." I smiled triumphantly, then, for good measure, added, "Problem solved."

He looked at me skeptically out of the corner of his eye. "Better if we just hope for no traffic. There's no way you're coming at me with a garden hose. Though," he said, keeping his stare straight ahead as he pulled into the street, "had the invitation been for you to help me shower, I might have been willing to be late for work."

My mouth dropped open. "Let me submit another proposal! I demand a do-over. I had no idea showering with you was even a possibility. Give me one more chance. Did I mention I would even provide lavender-scented soap?" I was anguishing over the lost opportunity.

"Sorry." He grinned. "All applications are final. I suggest that in the future you lead with your strengths. Never give your competition the edge. When the stakes are this high, it's winner take all."

"Wait!" I slapped the dash as he drove. "I want to speak to one of the judges. I demand a retrial. The rules were never explained to me and...." I slowed my rant and looked at Sergio coolly. "I wasn't even aware this was a competition. Who am I up against? Someone else you planning on jumping into the shower with?" I smiled ruefully.

He gave me another sideways grin. "It's always a competition, Zack." He paused. Despite the fact that we both knew the entire conversation was nothing more than a joke, he seemed to be enjoying seeing me squirm. His smile broadened. "You can relax, though. You don't have to get your panties in a bunch." He was obviously proud of his successful use of trendy slang. "Your position as the top contender on my list is still secure."

I slumped back against the seat. "I'll only feel better when I'm certain I'm the only contender." I pulled my glasses back down over my eyes. "Now, when we get to my house, I'll have no alternative but to drag you, even if it's kicking and screaming, into my shower. Then you can just throw the list away. You'll have no need for any of the other names on it." I refused to look over at him and instead crossed my arms over my chest. I couldn't however, prevent the small quiver of a grin from creeping across my lips. "Desperate times call for desperate measures." I turned my head slowly toward him. "And I'll do everything within my power to prevent you from feeling desperate."

"As much as I genuinely appreciate your generosity, don't worry yourself too much. In a pinch, I'm actually able to shower by myself. In fact, I've been doing it for years." He punched my arm. "But stay close; you never know when I'll be looking for a volunteer to help."

"When that day comes, and for the record, you might as well know I'm hoping it comes soon, I can say to you without hesitation, 'I'm your man.'" I smiled. "I would offer to provide you with *my* list of references, but that would make me sound like a slut."

"That's okay. I'm not interested in what anyone else thinks of you. I prefer to be my own judge." He looked at me and shook his head confidently. "And just so you know, so far so good. And I'm a pretty good judge."

"I'm relieved. Flattered... but relieved. 'Cause as of this moment, there's no other judge in the entire world I'm even remotely interested in trying to impress. Now, when do I get to get my hands on the trophy?" I reached across the middle divider and pulled him into a hug.

"Hey, at least wait until I get you home. If we're in an accident, the trophy will be little more than damaged goods."

The rest of the drive home passed with easy conversation. It was still early enough in the afternoon that returning beach traffic was light, and we made it back to my house with time to spare.

Sergio helped me to unload my bike out of the back of his car and then stood on the sidewalk appearing only slightly ill at ease. He looked at his watch and said, grinning, "I can still shower and make it to work on time without having to break any traffic laws. This means that rather than oregano, I'll be able to use real deodorant."

"Excellent. I wouldn't want a speeding ticket to put a damper on what was otherwise a perfect day." I let my gaze drop to my hands. I gripped my bicycle handlebars and absentmindedly kicked my tire. I looked up, as if inspired by an idea, but truthfully I just wasn't ready to say good-bye. It really had been a perfect day. "You wanna come up really quick? I could give you the grand tour and at least offer you something to drink. You've got to be a little thirsty. I mean, you must have really exhausted yourself trying to keep up with me."

Rather than even acknowledging the facetious challenge, he instead answered, "Yeah, I've got a little time. A glass of ice water would be good."

"Excellent. Come on up. That's one of the great things about this place; we've got a faucet with an unending supply of water."

I carried my bike over my shoulder as we climbed the steps to our upstairs balcony, then I secured it to one of the rails with my lock. Then I reached into my fanny pack to retrieve my keys and proceeded to unlock the door. I paused before pushing it open and said, "The décor is a little lacking, but it has all the comforts of home." I stepped aside to allow Sergio to walk through the door in front of me.

Actually, for an apartment occupied by two medical residents and a medical student, the place was really quite tasteful. We lived on the second floor of a two-story duplex, and because it was Spanish style, we had adopted a southwest theme. The walls were white stucco, and the living room, dining room, and kitchen were all separated by spacious arches. We had painted the arches a warm turquoise to match one of the colors woven into the throw pillows tucked in the corners of the couch. The furniture in the living room was overstuffed and comfortable. One wall was dominated by a large fireplace. Its mantle was painted the same turquoise as the arches and covered by framed pictures, vases, and other architecturally interesting pieces. The coffee table in the middle of the room was large and rustic. It was built of weathered gray wood and doubled as a footrest. Leaning against one of the walls was an old-fashioned country ladder built out of gray wood that matched the coffee table. It was surrounded by potted plants and large earth-tone ceramic urns. It provided a beautiful focal point for the room. The walls were covered by framed prints that also complemented the theme. Some were of desert canyons; one was a painting of an old abandoned adobe mission.

Sergio smiled at me as he walked through. "Not bad. I'm impressed. My guess would have been that, as a doctor, you were artistically challenged. But this place is really nice."

"What do you mean you thought that I'd be artistically challenged? I'm more like the Michelangelo of modern medicine. My genius extends well beyond the walls of the hospital. The world is my canvas." I paused long enough to strike a thoughtful pose and then started laughing. I pushed him toward the kitchen, then clarified, "Actually, I'm better with a roller than I am with a paintbrush."

Sergio leaned against the counter as I reached up into the cupboard to grab a couple of glasses. As I filled them with ice, he gazed around the kitchen. It was long and narrow. On one end was a small breakfast nook partially separated from the rest of the kitchen by a decorative archway. In it was a small wooden table with wrought-iron legs, surrounded by four chairs. The cushions on the chairs were covered with a southwest print, and because both exterior walls had big windows, the nook was bright and welcoming. The rest of the kitchen was dated but functional. The counters were made of heavy four-inch cream-colored ceramic tile separated by half-inch light-gray grout. The cabinets were an antique off-white, the walls celery green, and the appliances black enamel. Nothing about it screamed gourmet, but it served our purposes nicely.

Once I'd filled the glasses with water from the Arrowhead dispenser in the corner, I handed one to Sergio, then clicked its edge with my glass. "Here's to a perfect first date." I grinned. "Or, if you'd prefer a little less pressure, here's to a perfect bike ride." I raised my glass in a toast and then took a satisfying swallow.

Sergio looked at me intently for a second before lifting his glass to his mouth. He took a quick drink, then set his glass on the counter next to the sink. In an instant, he grabbed my glass out of my hand, set it next to his, and wrapped his arms around me. He pushed against me until my back was pressed against the counter, then whispered in a deeply resonating voice, "I'd say you were right the first time. It was a perfect date." I felt his lips, still cold from the ice water, press against mine without hesitation. I let my head fall back and melted into the kiss. It was like I'd been swept off my feet, toppled by a wave cresting on the beach of a tropical island. He gently pushed his tongue between my teeth, and I felt it dance against mine. Rockets went off in my head and brought time to a standstill. In that moment, all that existed was the sensation of Sergio against me. I couldn't think, could barely breathe, and certainly couldn't stand. If Sergio hadn't been supporting me, I would have collapsed onto the floor. He traced his hand up my back to rest against my head. As the kiss intensified, he pulled me against him with hungry passion. I had a hard time convincing myself it was real. From the moment I had seen Sergio in the gym those many weeks ago, I had fantasized about holding him in my arms. Maybe I was still just dreaming.

When the kiss broke, he pulled his head back without releasing his grip on me. His smile was brilliant, and his eyes radiated like burning embers. They held my gaze with an intensity that continued to make my head swim. When he finally spoke, his deep voice coupled with his rich Italian accent sounded like music being played from a distant mountain. "Well, Doctor, we've unfortunately run out of time. Do you think it would be possible for me to make another appointment?"

I gave him another quick kiss, then rested my head on his shoulder as I pulled him back against me. "If it means getting to spend more time with you, I'll have my nurse clear my entire schedule." I released a soft chuckle. "Except for Wednesdays. Doctors golf on Wednesdays." I lifted my head and looked at him. "I don't suppose you could teach me to golf?"

He looked up at the ceiling and acted as if he was considering my question. He answered in a very thoughtful tone, but he didn't succeed in suppressing a smile. "Well, I can at least teach you how to grip a club."

I started laughing as well. "Fair enough. But seeing as how I'm a beginner, I'll depend on you to also bring a couple of balls." I raised an eyebrow. "Think you'll be up for that?"

"Definitely." He lowered his voice another octave, then repeated himself. "Definitely." He caught my gaze for another second, offered a reassuring nod, gave me another quick kiss, and then pushed back. He began walking toward the front door. "But if I don't get to work, I'll be unemployed." He smiled over his shoulder. "I can't afford to instruct golf full time."

I walked him back down to his car. He opened the driver's door and leaned against it. He brushed his fingers down my arm. "It was a great day, Zack. Thanks." He shifted to sit down and put the keys in the ignition. "Call me. We'll schedule that first golf lesson."

He rolled down the window as I pushed the door closed.

"Excellent," I said. "I suspect that with your instruction, I'll be ready for the pro circuit within a month."

He smiled and began to pull away from the curb. "Going pro is going to require having a perfect stroke." He smiled more seductively. "We'll work on it. Call me, Zack. See ya."

As he drove away, I yelled loud enough for him to hear, "You can bet on it."

CHAPTER 12

I WATCHED Sergio's car round the corner before I turned to head back up to my apartment. I felt like I was floating. I wasn't even sure my feet touched the stairs before I again found myself walking through the front door. I couldn't remember ever having had a better day. A part of me felt like I should have been embarrassed about discussing my shame. Surprisingly, however, I didn't feel as self-conscious as I might have anticipated. Though I worried about having come across as being a little pathetic, the conversation had actually ended up being helpful. Expressing some of the apprehensions I had about my own identity had helped me see some of my issues more objectively. It helped me to better understand how I had accumulated some of my emotional baggage, and as a result, made me feel genuinely optimistic that I might succeed in unloading some of it. In addition, Sergio hadn't seemed the least bit put off by it. Instead, he had been incredibly supportive. He hadn't made me feel like disclosing such personal information made me appear weak. In fact, he'd defended me and encouraged me to appreciate my strengths. And that kiss. Oh my God! My head was so high in the clouds I felt dizzy. It must have been oxygen deprivation.

I knew I was on call the next day and as a consequence would be captive in the hospital for the subsequent thirty-six hours, so I spent the duration of the afternoon and evening getting myself organized. I had to get some groceries, do a couple loads of laundry, and think about getting something to eat. I usually felt like doing such mundane chores was an exercise in drudgery, but after having spent the day with Sergio, I felt completely energized.

I went into my room, peeled off my tank top, shucked my shorts and threw them into the laundry basket, and grabbed a clean T-shirt and pair of Levi's. Once I was dressed, I dumped the laundry basket onto the floor, separated the whites from colors, collected all the whites into my arms, and headed for the washing machine. As soon as the machine started filling with water and I had poured liquid laundry detergent into it, I added bleach to the dispenser. Estimating that the load would take about forty minutes to compete, I grabbed my wallet and headed for the store. After having spent the day mesmerized by Sergio's impressive muscular definition, I was inspired to make some healthy selections.

Because the Ralphs was a convenient two blocks from my house, I decided to go there despite the fact that navigating through the parking lot was a nightmare. Fortunately, when I drove into the lot, a car was leaving a space immediately next to the exit booth. Apparently, whatever good luck token I had drawn that morning hadn't yet expired. I was parked, out of my car, and pushing a shopping cart through the store no more than five minutes after I had left my house.

I went directly to the produce section and grabbed an assortment of fruits and vegetables. I had to keep my enthusiasm in check, however, because I had a tendency to buy too much, especially when I was hungry. Invariably, I would haul a bunch of bags of groceries home only to get consumed by busy shifts at work. Then, when I got home from the hospital, I was usually too tired to even consider food preparation, and all my purchases would end up wilting in the refrigerator. It was a wasteful, and expensive, cycle.

Bearing the "quick and convenient" concept in mind, I navigated over to the section that contained refrigerated, already prepared fresh food. I grabbed a package of low-fat turkey meatloaf and another of precooked chicken breast. Chicken was always a dependable standby. I could either eat it with brown rice or could just throw it over some fresh spinach to make a salad. Finally, I grabbed a package of pasta and a bottle of sauce for those evenings when I craved carbohydrates, then headed over to the toiletries aisle.

Fearing I might be running low and not wanting to risk forgetting something, I grabbed a bottle of shampoo, a tube of toothpaste, and a new stick of deodorant. I chuckled as I threw the deodorant into the cart, wondering if instead I should swing through the spice aisle and pick up a jar of oregano. I didn't really think it could legitimately serve as a substitute, but under the right circumstances, it might contribute to pulling off an awesome joke.

I was just coming to the end of the aisle and figured I had about found everything I needed when I looked up and saw a row of personal lubricants. For some reason, just seeing them brought me to a halt. Memories of Sergio's body pressed up against mine just an hour before came catapulting into my head. It was suddenly as if his masculine smell, a combination of soap, sweat, and aftershave, came wafting into my nose. My entire body responded as if I had swallowed a bottle of Viagra. There, standing in the middle of the grocery store with no provocation other than a memory, my dick suddenly threatened to rip right through my Levi's. Blushing, I looked up and down the aisle. I was relieved to see I was still alone, but I still felt like a teenager caught masturbating. Giving it little more than a second's consideration, I reached up and grabbed one that advertised itself as being extra sensitive. The day had been near perfect; no reason not to keep dreaming. *Hope springs eternal.*

By the time I got home, finished my laundry, made something to eat, and reviewed some notes for a presentation I had to make the next day, it was almost ten thirty and I was beat. I jumped into the shower, then headed for bed. My last conscious thought was of a bright smile, golden-tan skin, amber eyes, and a thick Italian accent. I slept like I was under general anesthesia.

When I dragged my ass out of bed at five thirty the next morning, I still had a smile on my face. Sergio's parting comment was still ringing in my ears: *Call me, Zack.* Pure music.

Though I had showered before climbing into bed no more than six hours earlier, I nonetheless again threw myself under its spray. I just couldn't start my day without a shower. It was an integral part of the morning routine and necessary to wake up. By the time I finished, the coffee, which I'd set on a timer to start brewing five minutes before my alarm went off, was ready. A cup of coffee and a quick bowl of instant oatmeal, and I was out the door. I lived three short blocks from the hospital, so it was no more than a brisk ten-minute walk.

I pushed through the double doors that lead onto the pediatric ward at six fifteen. A near record—from under the covers to ready to work in forty-five minutes flat. Such an accomplishment should be recognized with a medal. I walked up to the nursing station. Diane McClure, also a senior resident, had been on call the night before. She looked a little haggard as she leaned on the counter. We were in the same year, and in addition to having grown to really respect her, she had become a good friend. She was smart, caring, had good clinical instincts, and was a hard worker. Being her peer, I was grateful that she was mindful of not leaving any loose ends hanging before she signed out. Some of our other colleagues had the reputation of being "dumpers." They dragged their asses during their shifts, neglected to do much of the less desirable work, and then unapologetically handed it off, defending their negligence as having been "too busy." Too busy, my ass! How about fucking lazy? None of us relished working thirty-six-hour shifts, but damn it, that didn't excuse dumping. If it happened on your shift, goddamn deal with it. If you thought you'd get through a rotation and never be shit on, you should have signed up to be a florist, not a physician.

"I don't even have to ask how your night was. I can read it in your face."

She offered me a tired smile. "Do I really look that bad? So much for my plan to leave work and go cruise men in the automotive section of Walmart. That's usually where I really score."

"Hey," I teased. "Don't sell yourself short. I'm sure you can still hook up with a grease monkey. Though, in this case, he might be a real monkey." I bumped her shoulder with mine. "Anything I can do this morning to help get you out of here? Most of the kids on my service have been pretty stable, so my head should be way above water." I smiled. "Why don't you give me sign-outs, and then I'm here to serve. Hit me with your best shot."

"Thanks, Zack. Don't think I wouldn't be willing to take you up on your offer, but I think I have most of the loose ends pretty well wrapped up. We had a fair number of admissions, but none of the kids were too sick. Let me bring you up to speed on all the patients, then why don't you go in and say hi to Christopher, your little guy with the newly diagnosed neuroblastoma. He had a rough night last night. The side effects from the chemo are kickin' his ass. He's been asking when you were coming back since about two in the morning. I had to promise him he would be your first stop."

"I hate hearing he's not doing well. I'm starting to really love that kid. What's been going on?"

"The nausea and vomiting have been wicked, and despite having bumped up his acyclovir dosage, the cold sores in his mouth continue to be really painful. Poor little guy. He's trying to be brave, but this must be so bewildering. One day you're outside climbing trees, and the next day you're in the hospital being given medicine that makes you feel like shit and causes your hair to fall out. When you're five, it's gotta to feel like someone's idea of an ugly joke."

As she was talking, I pulled Christopher's chart and looked at his medicine profile. "I'll have the nurse give him more Zofran now. Hopefully that will calm his nausea some. It shouldn't take me more than about an hour to check on my other patients. I'll save him for last and see if I can cheer him up a little."

"Okay, but I'm warning you, he's pretty glum. You're really gonna have to work your magic."

"Hey." I smiled though not as confidently as I would have liked. "Why do you think they call me the Amazing Dr. Magic?"

Diane rolled her eyes. "Because you can perform finger puppets with both thumbs up your ass?" She smirked.

"Finger puppets nothing. I can pull a rabbit out of there!" I realized that in my haste to respond with a clever joke, I had spouted off before really thinking it through. I stopped abruptly. I wrinkled my brow and whispered a soft, almost apologetic follow-up. "Okay, that was a little gross. But I guarantee no animals are ever hurt while performing any of my tricks."

I smiled weakly but inwardly chastised myself. I was close to confiding to Diane that I was gay, but I didn't want the conversation to occur in the middle of a busy morning, and I certainly didn't want the disclosure to come out in the form of an anal-sex joke. We had been doing this dance with each other since we were interns together. The intensity of our jobs often pushed us into situations where we found ourselves feeling particularly vulnerable. Invariably, during such times, a lot of intimate information ended up being exchanged. I'd come close to telling her that I was gay, but I always ended up holding back. Partly, my personal shit prevented me from being able to make the disclosure. But the pervasive homophobic attitude in the hospital was also a deterrent. You didn't have to spend more than five minutes in the same room with Dr. Klein for it to become abundantly obvious that, in the medical hierarchy, gays were ranked somewhere just below the bottom dwellers. In addition to being scorned, they were pond scum. I was hugely apprehensive that coming out would not only jeopardize my reputation, but my future opportunities as well.

I playfully whacked Diane's shoulder with Christopher's chart and attempted a partial recovery. "And, contrary to PETA's accusations, I don't trick with either rabbits or gerbils."

I pushed off the counter and started down the corridor to begin my work, knowing that I had left Diane standing behind me shaking her head in bewilderment. She had to figure I was either a genius or I should be committed. Probably the latter.

An hour and a half later, I had reviewed the labs on all of my patients and had been into their rooms to give them cursory exams. I would follow each of them up more thoroughly later in the afternoon. I preferred to see them when they were more awake and when I could better determine if the therapeutic interventions we had implemented were indeed helping. The purpose of morning rounds was principally to ensure there had been no worrisome changes overnight and to verify the plan for the day with my interns. Later in the morning, all the patients on our service would have to be presented to the attending physician in charge. The attendings ultimately had the final say on management decisions and were charged with making sure our plan of care was appropriate. Fortunately, I had earned their confidence, and though I continued to be carefully supervised, they felt secure in giving me a lot of autonomy.

I wanted to make two stops before visiting Christopher. The first was to the inpatient pharmacy. I knocked on the door and was relieved to see my friend Bonnie through the thick security glass. She was my favorite pediatric pharmacist. In addition to being friendly and approachable, when it came to drugs and dosages, she was a walking textbook. I had never asked her a question she couldn't answer off the top of her head. She pressed a button, the lock on the door buzzed, and I was able to pull it open.

"Hey, Bonnie! What's shaking?"

"Hey. Zack. I'm good. But you can skip the buttering-up part. If you're down here this early in the morning, it's a pretty good bet that this isn't a social visit. What can I do for you?"

"Oh, Bonnie. You're so cynical. What's makes you so sure I didn't come down specifically to just wish you a good morning?"

She braced both hands on the stainless steel counter in front of her and gave me a deadpan expression. "Because I wasn't born yesterday."

She brightened with a slight smile but turned to look up at the shelf above her. She began to methodically pull down specific vials in an array of different colors and covered with labels cautioning extreme care. When she continued her reply, her voice maintained a clipped, efficient tone. "I've got gallons of chemo to constitute this morning, so if you just came down to say good morning, let me return the courtesy." She turned to face me and offered a forced, brief, but exuberant smile. "Good morning." She returned her focus to the counter in front of her. "Now get out."

"Well, since I'm here, there is maybe one small favor."

"I knew this was coming." She didn't look up, and after conferring with the computer that sat in front of her, she began to arrange the vials in a specified order. "It had better be small."

"Christopher, our five-year-old with neuroblastoma, is really suffering with the mouth sores. Can we whip him up some of our special concoction? If I coax him through it, I think I can get him to swish it in his mouth and spit."

Bonnie immediately pulled her attention away from the computer and looked at me. "Of course, Zack. Why didn't you say so in the first place? You can reserve your charms for when you're trying to hit me up for some Advil to help your own hangover. As for Christopher, it's whatever he needs. You've gotta watch him, though. I don't want him to swallow this."

In pediatrics, one of the recipes to reduce the pain from blisters in the mouth was a combination of three medicines. You mixed 2 percent viscous lidocaine with Benadryl and Maalox. Lidocaine was a topical anesthetic and, at least temporarily, could really relieve the almost excruciating pain from oral cold sores. The Maalox did little more than to thicken the solution, give it a palatable flavor, and make it sticky enough to adhere to the problem areas. The Benadryl aided in reducing inflammation.

The problem was that the concoction couldn't be swallowed. If a five-year-old swallowed it, their gagging mechanism could be numbed and put them at risk of choking. It was effective and was easily used in older children. However, in younger kids, it could be a little tricky. They really didn't get the concept of swishing something around their mouth to coat the painful areas but then spit it out without swallowing.

I would have to figure out a way to coach Christopher through it. I was determined to help make him feel more comfortable without using so much morphine that he'd spend his day in a medically induced delirium.

After Bonnie completed the mixing, I thanked her profusely for always being willing to help me out in a pinch, then left the pharmacy and headed for the cafeteria. Hoping to avoid the midmorning breakfast rush, I went around back and entered the main food preparation area through the door reserved for kitchen staff. Ora, one of the shift managers, looked up when she heard me walking through the maze of counters and shelves.

"Dr. Sheldon. What are you doing? You're not supposed to be back here. You know this area is for kitchen employees only." Ora was a robust black women. Her skin was the color of polished ebony, and her face was etched by permanent laugh lines. She had worked in food services at the hospital for more than thirty-five years, so I frequently teased her that her labor had been the foundation on which the cafeteria was built. Even her sharp reprimand couldn't belie her warm, caring smile.

"I know, Ora. I'm sorry. But I need a quick favor, and I knew I could count on you to help me lift the spirits of a sad and sick five-year-old."

Her expression immediately reflected her concern. She walked closer to me so she could speak in a loud whisper. "Whatever you need, Dr. Zack. You just tell me. I've seen you with those sick kids up there and think you're wonderful. If one of them needs something, you just tell me what it is. If I can get it for you, it's as good as in your hands."

She looked at me earnestly. Ora had a heart of gold. I loved it when she called me Dr. Zack. She was old school, and though incredibly friendly with patients and staff alike, she rarely compromised hospital formality. The fact that she would call me Dr. Zack implied that in addition to respecting me as a physician, she also regarded me as a friend. I had huge regard for her too. Through her years working there, she had seen thousands of residents come and go and appreciated those she thought had made a difference. I was flattered to be included in the circle of the ones she thought highly of.

"You happen to have some sherbet hiding around here anywhere? This little guy is going through chemo and has some nasty mouth sores. I figure he might be willing to taste strawberry sherbet, and the cold sensation will help relieve some of his pain." I smiled and nudged her shoulder. "When it came to finding someone who knew where the dessert was hidden, I knew I should start with you."

"Child!" A deep southern accent rolled off her lips like thick maple syrup. "You came to the right person. I have me three or four flavors right here in the deep freeze." She opened the door of the walk-in freezer and ambled way into the back. "Here, take one of each. Let him choose whichever one he wants. Bless his little heart." She stacked four cartons into my arms and then shooed me on my way. "He wants anything else, you just come to me. Need be, I'll make him something special. Now, go on. You're gonna get us both in trouble for being back here." She closed the freezer door but called to me before I had gotten more than a few feet away.

"And Dr. Zack. Give him a hug for me and tell him I have him in my prayers. God bless you both." She waved and picked up the clipboard and checklist she had been working on before I had interrupted her.

I went up to Christopher's room and knocked lightly before pushing the door open. He lay in bed and looked at me from under heavy lids. His pillowcase was covered with hair. The chemo was causing it to fall out, and he had reached the stage where it was coming out in handfuls. Ordinarily we would have just shaved his head, but he'd resisted, so there was nothing to be accomplished by forcing the matter. Might as well let him retain whatever independence he could. I saw no point in making an issue over something that had little clinical relevance. Save the arguments for the things that mattered.

"Hey, my man, I heard you weren't feeling so hot. What's going on?

I nodded at his mom as I walked in. If possible, she looked even more tired than Christopher. Her eyes were bloodshot from crying. She cried frequently, almost to the point of becoming dehydrated, but never allowed Christopher to see her. With him, she tried to always appear upbeat and sympathetic. I'd seen it before. His cancer was slowly killing her. But for him, she put up a convincing charade. She tried to offer me a welcoming smile and sound enthusiastic. "Hey, Dr. Zack. Christopher, look who showed up. Dr. Zack is here to visit you."

I walked over to sit next to him on the bed. In order to get as close to him as possible, I had to dislodge Yogi, his beloved teddy bear, from under his right arm and tuck him securely under his other arm. I pulled the sheet up over both of them and traced my finger over Christopher's forehead. He hadn't spoken thus far. I looked at him and smiled as warmly as possible. "So? Tell me what's up, champ. Maybe I can help."

He could barely speak through swollen, cracked lips. "My mouth hurts."

Thinking quickly and remembering that on the day of admission he had been wearing a Superman costume, I looked into his eyes and asked inquisitively, "Really? That's rough. I'm not sure I'm strong enough to fix big pain, but I thought for sure Superman would have been able to help. What did he say to you while he was in here? Didn't the Superman medicine that he gave you help the pain to go away?"

My question succeeded in at least getting a little life to come back into his eyes. He opened them more widely, and I was able to appreciate the smallest hint of a sparkle. But it was still difficult for Christopher to talk. "I didn't see Superman."

"You didn't? Really? He was here not too long ago. I spoke to him just before he flew out the window. He said he had come to visit you. You must still have been asleep, and he decided not to wake you." I nodded as if coming to a sudden understanding. "That must be why he left this Superman medicine with me. He was going to give it to you, but you were asleep. He said that it was super strong and that it was what he used when his mouth was sore." I looked at Christopher as earnestly as possible. "He said that a long time ago this really bad guy named Atomic Skull tricked him and had gotten him to swallow kryptonite. You know what kryptonite is, don't you?" Christopher nodded. "It's a powerful poison and is the only thing on the planet that can hurt Superman. Superman's mouth must have been really sore when he swallowed the kryptonite." I paused but continued looking at Christopher and stroking his forehead. "Anyway, this genius scientist"—now I was really improvising—"from Superman's planet Krypton saw that he was suffering and invented a medicine to try to save him. It's red, just like Superman's cape. Superman left some here for you. You want to try it? If it's powerful enough for Superman, it's bound to help you. And after all, Superman flew all the way from New York to bring it to you. He was there fighting Lex Luthor but heard you needed some help, so flew right over. Bet he's sorry you were sleeping. I'm sure he wanted to give you the medicine himself." I never imagined that there would ever be a professional benefit to having been a DC comic enthusiast. "So, what do you say?"

Christopher looked at me a little warily, but he nodded and in a soft, gravelly voice answered, "I'll try it."

"Great, I think that that will make Superman *super* happy. Let me go get it for you." I stood up and started walking out of the room, then turned around as if remembering something. "There's just one thing, though. You can't swallow it."

Both Christopher and his mom's faces registered confusion.

"Well," I started to explain thoughtfully, "you have to remember that this medicine was invented for Superman, and he's a lot bigger than you. Swallowing it would be too much for someone your size. Superman said because you were just five, all you had to do was swirl it around in your mouth, then spit it out. You think you can do that?"

Christopher still sounded gravelly, but had the slightest hint of a smile on his face. "You mean I don't even have to swallow? Usually the nurse makes me swallow, and I don't like medicine."

"Just swish and spit. Think you can do that?" He nodded; maybe not gleefully, but with more optimism than I had seen in him for a while.

"Excellent. I'm going to try to get a message to Superman so he'll know you woke up and you're going to try the medicine. That will make him really happy." I looked at my watch. "He left here five minutes ago, so he's probably already back in New York. He's stronger than a locomotive, can leap tall buildings in a single bound, and he flies at the speed of sound. Guess he arrived back there in less than a minute. He's pretty darn fast." I smiled and walked out to the nurses' station, where I had left the concoction sitting on the counter. Though Diane wasn't quite sure what I was talking about, I lifted the medicine up as if making a toast and nodded in the direction of Christopher's room. "Let's hope the Superman ploy works!"

I also picked up a basin for Christopher to spit into and the bag that contained the four cartons of sherbet. With any luck, the concoction would quickly alleviate a lot of his pain, the Zofran he'd been given a couple hours before would leave him feeling less nauseous, and he could enjoy his preferred flavor of sherbet.

When I got back into his room, Christopher's mother already had him sitting up in bed. I swirled the medicine around in the clear bottle. "See, it's red, just like Superman's cape. I suppose the genius scientist from Krypton wanted to make it a color that could overpower kryptonite." I pulled my attention away from the swirling contents of the bottle and looked at Christopher with a perplexed expression. "I don't remember. Do you know what color kryptonite is, champ?"

Christopher nodded authoritatively. "It's green and it glows in the dark."

"Wow, you really are a kryptonite expert. Well, Superman guaranteed me that this would work. You ready to give it a try?"

Christopher nodded again. "Remember," I said, "you just take a big mouthful, swish it all around, then spit it into the basin. In fact, when you have the medicine in your mouth, I'm going to count to ten slowly. You keep swirling it around with your tongue until I reach ten. When I say ten, you give me a Superman-size spit." I smiled encouragingly. "Got it?" He gave me another nod. "Let's do it. If the Atomic Skull couldn't beat Superman, nothing is going to beat you."

I held the bottle up to Christopher's lips and tilted it until he had taken a big mouthful. "Okay, start the swishing but don't swallow. One, two, three...." I watched him carefully and was delighted to see that though he pushed out his cheeks as the solution washed around in his mouth, I saw no indication that he was swallowing. If he were to swallow, his Adam's apple would bob up and down. "Eight, nine, ten! Okay, give me a Superman spit." I held the basin under Christopher's mouth, and he forcefully spit the solution into it. I gently dabbed the drizzle that ran down his chin with a Kleenex.

I knew the lidocaine became effective almost as soon as it touched the blisters, so I looked at Christopher expectantly. "What do you say, champ? Is it a little better?"

He moved his tongue around in his mouth very cautiously, but his expression registered approval. "It still hurts, but not as much." He moved his tongue some more, tentatively but with less hesitation. "It's a little better."

"Excellent. I knew Superman would come through for you. I think he's hoping you will one day be his helper. Can I tell Superman that when you're all well you'd be willing to help him fight bad guys?"

Christopher's nod was much more enthusiastic. I replied, "Super! Superman is going to be super happy." I nodded with each "super" for emphasis. "Let's give it one more try, then I've got a treat for you."

We went through the process one more time, and after Christopher had successfully spit the solution into the basin for a second time, I reached into the bag I was carrying and pulled out the cartons of sherbet. "Superman told me that if you did a good job with his medicine, you could have a treat. Look what he left for you. Four flavors of his favorite sherbet! Which one do you want?"

Christopher immediately looked a little dejected. "Eating hurts my mouth."

"Hey," I said, acting as if his hesitation was now patently silly. "That was before you swished Superman's red medicine. Superman told me that after he swallowed the kryptonite and before he took the medicine, he couldn't even swallow water. Then, after he took the medicine he was able to chew through bricks. If he could eat bricks, I'm sure you can taste a tiny spoonful of sherbet. It's soft and cold." While I was talking, I had taken the lid off the container of strawberry and run a spoon across the surface of the sherbet. A red ribbon curled onto the surface of the spoon. I held it in front of Christopher's face. "Superman will be disappointed if you don't at least give it a try." I lifted the spoon a little closer to his lips to try to coax him. "Come on. Just one small taste. Then I can give Superman a good report."

Christopher leaned forward, but just before drawing the spoon carefully into his mouth, he looked at me and said, "Superman doesn't eat bricks." He let the sherbet melt slowly on his tongue, then smiled. It was the first real smile I'd seen since entering his room. "That tastes good."

My smile threatened to overcome my face. "Superman thought you'd like it."

I spent the next ten minutes spooning strawberry sherbet into Christopher's mouth while I told him as many stories about Superman's adventures as I could remember. Hell, I even made a few of them up. When my beeper went off, I handed the carton to his mom and assured him that I'd be back to check on him.

His mom mouthed an appreciative, heartfelt, "Thank you," as I got up to leave. I had almost made it to the door when I turned back around to offer Christopher a little more encouragement. "Superman is going to be really happy his medicine helped you, and he said that next time he came to town, he was going to bring Yogi a cape. He said something about needing a superhero teddy bear to help him catch bad guys. Looks like you and Yogi are going to be his team."

Even through cracked, sore lips, Christopher's smile was radiant. As I walked out, I made a mental note to find something that could serve as a teddy-bear-sized red cape. I had to be sure Superman made good on his promise to Yogi.

CHAPTER 13

MERCIFULLY, the rest of the shift was mostly uneventful. I checked on Christopher a couple times throughout the afternoon. It could hardly be said that his spirits were soaring, but at least he appeared to enjoy moments of happiness, and his overall discomfort seemed significantly reduced. I had gone to the cabinet in the play-therapy office and absconded with a couple of Superman DVDs. I had even had time to sit on Christopher's bed and watch a fifteen-minute episode with him. I tucked Yogi under my arm and Christopher leaned against both of us. In the episode we watched, Bizzaro had hatched a dastardly plan to try to crush Superman in an earthquake. Christopher and I agreed that plan was doomed for failure even at its inception. Everyone knew that, even if buried under tons and tons of dirt, Superman merely had to spin around like a supersonic drill and he could bore himself through solid rock and ultimately to safety. The villains always underestimated his super strength.

Before the DVD had even ended, Christopher was snoring quietly beside me and his mom was curled up asleep in the chair next to us. I carefully extracted my arm from underneath both Yogi and Christopher, tucked Yogi in securely next to him, and snuck out silently. They could both benefit from some much-needed sleep.

Sundays were historically the quietest day of the week. There were no scheduled admissions, and except when something couldn't logistically otherwise occur, there were no elective procedures. Our team admitted three patients from the emergency room through the night, but none of the children were seriously complicated, so their management was relatively routine. Danny, my current intern, and I were each able to sleep for about four hours ourselves. An enviable accomplishment.

Making rounds the next morning was also relatively painless. The attending assigned for the week was Dr. Perkins. She was young, smart, and rather than try to intimidate, actually liked to teach. She hoped her involvement with house staff would actually contribute to them becoming better doctors, not just bully them into submission. Also, she had a great sense of humor and tended not to take herself too seriously. Her approach on rounds was to encourage us to think through both the diagnostic and patient-management process. She illustrated potential pitfalls by relating examples of mistakes she had made in the past. I was sure she exaggerated the magnitude of her errors, but the process succeeded in making her seem more human and, as a consequence, infinitely more approachable. We never hesitated to discuss anything with her—clinical impressions, questions about patient management, uncertainties related to formulating a definitive plan of care. Nothing was off-limits. Rounds with her were instructive and entertaining. The perfect combination.

My work was done by two o'clock in the afternoon, and I was ready to sign out. Though I had been working for more than thirty hours, because I had gotten four hours sleep, I actually felt relatively refreshed. I could even imagine being able to go to the gym to work out before the fatigue I knew I would eventually feel caught up with me. Regrettably, however, getting out the door meant having to talk to Peggy. Once again, she followed me in the call rotation and was scheduled to be on call that night. Despite having completed everything I was required to do and even having double-checked some last-minute details, I knew Peggy would resent seeing me leave. Any of my other colleagues would have given me a high-five and congratulated me on being able to salvage a couple hours of daylight, but not Peggy. Her perspective was that if she was miserable, everyone else should be too. I tried to buck myself up for what I knew would be the ensuing confrontation.

Rather than paging her and giving her an opportunity to create reasons that would prevent me from leaving, I decided to just surprise her. No sense in giving her a heads-up. Given a warning of merely a few seconds, her diabolic mind could pull shit out of thin air that would not only require my immediate attention but could be amplified into four more hours of work. Sadly, she was that mean-spirited.

I strolled over to the nurses' station just as Connie was disappearing into the med room. As a charge nurse, Connie was one of the best—hard-working, levelheaded, conscientious, energetic, and organized. Also, she had an exuberant laugh that in most situations was an integral part of any conversation you had with her. Working with Connie not only contributed to making the shift tolerable, invariably, it succeeded in making it a pleasure.

I rapped on the door and caught her attention through the glass. When she opened it, I was greeted by an ear-to-ear grin. "Sorry, Doc. There's no point in even begging. I refuse to give you any more Vicodin." She was laughing before she had even completed the sentence. There was something to be said for enjoying your own sense of humor.

"Damn," I said between clenched teeth, shaking a frustrated fist. "I knew it was a mistake to choose you as my sponsor. With my supply from the med room cut off, I'll have no choice but to sell my body on the streets to support my drug habit." I plastered my most seductive smile across my face. "So, what do you say, lady? Twenty dollars will buy you a good time in the linen closet." I let my eyebrows dance across my forehead.

Connie let out such a boisterous laugh she had to immediately bring her finger to her lips to shush herself. "Dr. Sheldon, you're going to get us both in trouble. The only time I've had fun in the linen closet was when me and four of the other nurses joined Weight Watchers. That's where I hid my Snickers bar." She laughed again although significantly more quietly.

"So?" She looked at me, her eyes still gleaming. "What can I do for you?"

"Actually, I was hoping you would know where Peggy is. My work is done, so I'm ready to sign out. It will be the first time I've seen the sun on a weekday since I started this rotation."

Trying to hold a neutral expression and maintain a tone void of cynicism, she raised a conspiratorial brow. "And you're going to sign out? Now? To Peggy?"

I continued to smile, and I too injected as innocent a tone as possible into my response. Both of us were biting our tongues. Our joint inclination would have been to acknowledge that neither of us had ever observed the bitch to willingly do anyone a favor. But that would have been indelicate. Instead, I nodded and answered. "I'm sure the good Dr. Wang will be delighted to extend me the courtesy of taking my sign-out now. After all, it's a consideration she insists the rest of us give her after she's been on call." My smile broadened. "And that's whether she's completed her work or not."

Connie just stood with her hand on the door of the med room and shook her chin. We both knew we were laying it on thick. "It's refreshing to see someone willing to give her the benefit of the doubt. A lot of people might prematurely conclude that Dr. Wang is selfish and unreasonable. How benevolent of you to endeavor to emphasize her more positive personal attributes." She suppressed a smile. "As difficult as they may be to appreciate." The smile crept farther up her cheeks. "Or even see!" She started to back through the still open door. "I think she told me she was going to be in the residents' office."

"Thanks, Connie. Wish me luck." I started to walk away but called over my shoulder before she again disappeared into the med room, "And if you change your mind about the linen closet, just let me know. I could use that twenty for lunch money."

She waved her hand at me dismissively. "You can put that money toward your sexual-harassment defense. Or better, use it to stock the linen closet with more Snickers bars." She again broke into a grin. "There's nothing you could do to satisfy me that couldn't be done with chocolate."

I could still hear her laughing through the closed door.

Peggy looked up at me with an almost disdainful glare the minute I walked into the office. Refusing to be intimidated by her coolness, I pulled my sign-out sheet out of my pocket and launched into my monologue before she had an opportunity to object. "Hey, Peggy. Thanks to having had a relatively quiet night and already having ensured that the work on all my patients is done, I'm ready to sign out. I won't impose on you too long. This shouldn't take more than a minute."

Before she answered, she looked at her watch cynically. "It's only a little after two."

Trying to avoid being baited into an argument, I replied, "Pretty fortunate, huh? Given that all my team's work is completed, I was confident you would want to give me the opportunity to get out and enjoy what's left of the day. Don't think for a minute that I don't appreciate your consideration." I expended my best effort in trying to smile warmly.

"Cut the crap, Zack. It's so patronizing. Sign-outs are at four. What if we get an admission? I will be unavailable to cover for you."

My smile immediately disappeared. "First of all, there's nothing to cover. I prefaced this discussion by saying that all my work was done. Secondly, as of now, there aren't any admissions pending. Thirdly, even if you were to get an admission and something unforeseen occurred with one of my patients, I'm sure you are capable of running interference. It's called multitasking, and it's one of the prerequisite skills for being a physician. Now, I'll stop being patronizing if you stop being such a hardass. You want to take my sign-outs? Or should I page the residency director, explain the situation, and get his permission to leave?"

Peggy looked at me like she'd swallowed a lemon. "Relax, Zack. I'll take the sign-out." She smirked condescendingly. "You can be such a girl."

I could feel my ears burn red hot. It was just like her to wield a low blow. She probably assumed I was gay and relished the opportunity to interject a vicious little dig. It took all my restraint to contain my anger.

"Fine, Peggy. I'm a girl, but you're a bitch. Fortunately, we won't have to be littermates much longer. Let's just get through this."

It took less than ten minutes to summarize the condition of each of my patients. Because they were all pretty stable, none would require that Peggy even stick her head into any of their rooms. I concluded by telling her about Christopher. "He had a relatively good day today, and his pain has been pretty well controlled. Unfortunately, he starts another round of chemo tomorrow. His nurse will start hydrating him tonight at 8:00 p.m. The chemo will hang at two in the morning. They'll premedicate him with Benadryl and Zofran to try to prevent the nausea he historically feels as it's infusing. I hope he does okay. He's a brave little guy."

Even Peggy, who typically gave the impression of having a heart of stone, seemed genuinely moved. She shook her head, and her expression actually revealed a hint of sympathy. "I hope he does well too."

I put the computer printout with all the relevant patient information in front of her and bolted for the door. I didn't want to give her an opportunity to create a reason to prevent me from leaving. "Okay, Peggy, see you tomorrow." Then, in the interest of demonstrating my willingness to take the high road, I said, "If you have a quiet night, I'll do everything I can to get you out early tomorrow." I didn't even turn around to hear a reply.

When I got home, the message light on my answering machine was blinking. I hit the play button and began peeling off my scrubs to change into my gym clothes. I had my shirt pulled halfway over my head when Sergio's voice came wafting out of the speaker. With my eyes covered by fabric and with my arms twisted in the sleeves, I almost lost my balance.

"Hey, Dr. Zachary, it's Sergio." I heard a soft chuckle. "The guy from Saturday's bike ride. Just calling to see if you survived your long day of work and to ask what you're doing this weekend. If you're not busy, I thought that I'd introduce you to some authentic Italian food. I'm cooking. If you're going to be free, give me a call. Talk to you soon."

By the time I succeeded in getting my shirt off, I was breathless. Less from the effort, more from having heard Sergio's voice. *If you're free, give me a call!* Hell, I'd crawl a mile on my hands and knees over broken glass to accept the invitation. Fortunately, I was going to be off the entire weekend. Our call schedule required us to be on call every fourth night, so we each only had one full weekend off a month. I had been on call Sunday and anticipated being on call again Thursday. Even if I had a horrifically busy night on call Thursday, I was still guaranteed to be able to leave sometime Friday afternoon, and I wasn't scheduled to return to the hospital until early Monday morning. I was ecstatic.

I finished changing into my workout clothes, threw a clean towel into my gym bag, grabbed a water bottle from the refrigerator, and sprinted for the door. Sleep deprivation be damned. I was so energized I felt like I could leap tall buildings in a single bound. *Eat your heart out, Superman. Zack got invited on a second date. Now who's the man of steel?*

I waited until I had gotten home from the gym and had finished showering before I nervously pushed Sergio's number into the phone. Once again, the prospect of talking to him had reduced me to a jittery high school girl. My mind flashed briefly to Peggy's snide comment. Bitch. Maybe, however, she wasn't too far from the truth. I unconsciously ran my hand over my chest to confirm that I wasn't developing breasts.

The phone rang four times, then his answering machine picked up. Because it was after five, I suspected he was already at work. I was disappointed but also a little relieved. After having spent such a great day with him, I wasn't sure why I suddenly found myself tongue-tied. It must have been that damn amazing kiss. Three days later, it still left me speechless. I was so consumed in the fantasy of having his lips pressed against mine I paid no attention to his outgoing message. Only the abrupt sound of the beep signaling me to begin speaking brought me back to reality. Having given no consideration to what I intended to say, I just began blathering like an idiot. "Hey, Sergio. It's Zack. Yeah, I seem to have a vague recollection of having taken a bike ride on Saturday. Was it with you? Just kidding. Actually, I've thought of little else." No sooner had the comment escaped my lips than I felt my cheeks flush. Had I really just said that? Way too much information. Trying to salvage a modicum of dignity, I continued in what I hoped would be a tone of indifference. "Dinner this weekend sounds great, especially if authentic Italian food is on the menu. I'll bring the wine. Will look forward to talking to you before then to confirm the address and time." My voice softened. "Thanks, man. Second time in less than a week that you've made my day." The last comment escaped my mouth before I could successfully engage my filter, but I couldn't help giving him a small hint as to how amazing I thought he was. I was a romantic at heart.

The next few days in the hospital were relatively quiet. Peggy only got two admissions the night she was on call, so, as promised, I worked to get her out early. I figured she'd be less inclined to give me shit in the future if she too was able to reap the benefits of a slow shift.

Christopher tolerated his infusion of chemo as well as could be expected. I succeeded in keeping his discomfort under pretty good control, but he was still really wiped out. It was difficult to get him interested in playing, even if the bribes included superheroes and ice cream. As testimony to his sweetness, however, even though he felt beat-up and exhausted, his friendly personality endured. Not even being hit by a proverbial truck prevented him from trying to smile and say thank you. That kid was really worming his way under my skin. When my workload allowed, I tried to spend as much time with him as possible, though much of it was with him falling asleep in the crook of my arm as I read the adventures of Superman to him.

When I signed out Friday late afternoon, I was damn near giddy. I had gotten very little sleep the night before, but my spirits soared nonetheless. It was still relatively warm outside, so there was still some daylight yet to be enjoyed, and from the moment I said good-bye, I didn't have to step foot back in the hospital for another sixty-two hours. The prospect was monumentally thrilling. Best of all was the anticipation of spending time with Sergio. Apparently, Osvaldo's had been booked for a private party Saturday night, and Sergio had opted out of working. Therefore, he had designated Saturday as the night he would make me dinner. He had called me while he was working a few times during the week. Though we hadn't been able to have extended conversations, they were enough to keep me almost jittery with excitement. Our last conversation concluded with him giving me his address and instructions to arrive hungry. I congratulated myself for hanging up without asking him to clarify if he meant I should arrive hungry for food or just hungry for him. Despite having a big appetite, presented with those two options, I probably would have opted to skip the meal entirely.

My enthusiasm must have been obvious, because even some of my colleagues commented as I was completing sign-outs.

Diane observed me inquisitively and asked, "So, Zack, if your smile gets any bigger, I might feel obliged to treat you for facial seizures. What gives? That life-size inflatable doll you ordered finally going to arrive this weekend? Should I ask the pharmacy to send up that industrial-size jar of K-Y so you don't return to work chafed on Monday?" She smiled sweetly at me and acted as if she'd just made the most sincere, benevolent offer on earth.

I couldn't help but chuckle a little but didn't want to allow her the satisfaction of thinking she was funny. I replied with the same sincere tone and sympathetic smile. "Gee, Diane, that's so gracious of you to offer, but I wouldn't think of leaving with your jar of K-Y. You might find yourself with a little down time *while having to be here working*, and I wouldn't want to be responsible for you having to experience any, shall we say, *friction*." The emphasis on the fact that she was going to be left working was intended, but I had to elaborate to get in one more good-natured jab. "I saw the cucumber you hid in the residents' room for your night on call. It appears to have slightly rough skin. We all know you're a tender little thing and that the cucumber is intended for a purpose other than just a healthy midnight snack. You'd find yourself in a painful predicament without the benefit of the lube." My grin broadened. "And just so you know, we've made some significant technological advances." I attempted to make the tone of my voice more serious, like I was imparting the details of a cutting-edge scientific discovery. "There are now devices that come with batteries. Multiple speeds for more satisfaction." Between my elation at the prospect of being free for the weekend, sleep deprivation, and the mutual teasing I was sharing with Diane, I was laughing pretty uproariously by the time I concluded my last jibe. "Save a vegetable: switch to Black & Decker." The interns witnessing our exchange were now laughing as well.

Though Diane was also now smiling, she made a stoic attempt to appear unfazed by my teasing. "Really? Technological advances? Sounds like your ass is speaking from experience."

"Ouch, Diane." I tried to look offended but turned the joke around as quickly as possible. "A speaking ass? How did we sink down to that area of the anatomy? I had no idea you intended to point the cucumber in that direction, but whatever floats your boat." I smiled as I picked my bag up off the table. "You have a good weekend, and I'll expect a full report on Monday. If that cucumber ends up getting julienned, I will only be able to assume you had a fair amount of free time on your hands."

"Give the cucumber a rest, Zack. If there is one hidden in the call room, it's because you snuck it in there. Maybe that's why you're so happy—you had a call night full of organic ecstasy. Remind me to wear gloves when I dispose of it. It will have to be thrown away with the hazardous waste."

Now the whole room was laughing. "Careful, Diane. That cucumber might one day represent the foreplay to producing our love child."

"A little green love child. Just what I always wanted. If it has your ears, he will look just like a miniature Yoda."

Just before the door closed, I squeezed in one more reply. "But on the bright side, he'll know how to use the force."

I got home, changed quickly into running shorts, and bolted for my car. It was already five thirty, so I had little over an hour of adequate daylight. Just enough time for an invigorating run. If I took side streets, I figured I could be at the base of Runyon Canyon within thirty minutes, so I would still have plenty of time to get to the top and back down before it got too dark. Given its popularity, the trails in Runyon Canyon were hiked frequently, so the ground was worn smooth and was free of obstacles. Even in fading light, it was pretty safe to run there. Besides, the incline made for a challenging workout, and the opportunity to be outside was infinitely better than having to settle for running on the treadmill in a crowded gym.

I was so enthused about seeing Sergio the next day that even getting caught in traffic at the corner of Crescent Heights and Melrose did little to sour my mood. Hell with it; I'd run in the dark if I had to. The adrenaline from my excitement alone would get me to the top of the mountain with minimal effort, and besides, I was determined to start looking my best. No way would I allow love handles to even think about colonizing a little homestead on my sides. I was on a determined track for a true six-pack.

The run was invigorating, and when I arrived back home I found my roommate Christian busily making dinner. His boyfriend Brent was also there. They had only been dating about two months, so although the relationship was relatively new, they seemed genuinely happy about having found each other. When I walked into the kitchen, I wasn't surprised to find them both wearing almost identical shit-eating grins.

Christian was the first to speak. "Hey, Zack. What's up? We were just about to eat dinner but made plenty. You want to join us?"

"And horn in on your date? I wouldn't think of it. First of all, I wouldn't dream of being a third wheel, and secondly, I couldn't forgive myself if I were to be responsible for interrupting this ancient mating ritual."

Brent chimed in before Christian could answer. "Don't sweat it, Zack. We made way more food than we can eat by ourselves, and besides, I guarantee we're gonna mate later whether you eat with us or not." He gave Christian a salacious smile.

We all laughed. "Okay, let me clarify: I don't want to be a voyeur should you guys get yourselves all worked up and decide to mate right here on top of the dinner table."

"Wow, sounds hot, Zack." Brent reached for Christian's hand. "What do you say, babe? Isn't it your turn to cover me in spaghetti sauce?"

Christian grinned. "No, we used spaghetti sauce last time. Tonight we were going to use the caramel sauce and marshmallows." He leaned over and kissed Brent gently on the lips. "Just wait until you see where I intend to put the cherry."

"Okay, guys," I bellowed. "Too much information. I'm going to have to stick needles in my eyes to rid my brain of that visual. Keep your dicks in your pants long enough for me to make a salad. I'll be out of your way in a second. Then, at least spread plastic before either the spaghetti, the caramel, or the marshmallows begin to fly. I don't want to have to clean body fluids or refrigerator contents off the upholstery."

Christian and Brent slowly released hands and broke the warm stare they'd been sharing. Christian said, "Seriously, Zack, eat with us. Or at least share some of our salad. It's already made, and I feel like I haven't seen you in over a week. Besides, we both want to be brought up to date as to what's going on with your new Italian stallion." He grinned. "Anything scandalous to report?"

Being hungry and actually too tired to take the initiative to make my own salad, I accepted the invitation and pulled out a chair to sit down. "Well, nothing involving caramel sauce, if that's what you're asking. But," I said as I took the napkin that Christian handed me and unfolded it onto my lap, "we do have a date tomorrow night. He's making me dinner."

In reality, it felt good to share my enthusiasm about Sergio with someone. As roommates, Christian and I were close, but our call schedules prevented us from seeing much of each other. He was a resident in internal medicine, and though he wasn't on call as frequently as I was, his hours were brutal as well. In addition, in order to spend more time with Brent, he occasionally went from the hospital directly to Brent's apartment, so on those days, our only communication was through notes posted on the refrigerator.

Christian brought the rest of the food to the table and sat down next to Brent. They locked hands again briefly, but then, in order to allow Brent to pick up his utensils, Christian dropped his hand to Brent's thigh.

I watched their interchange and reflected on how much better my living situation had become. During my internship, I had had roommates as well. They were graduate students from other departments within the medical center, but they were both straight, and I wasn't out to them. That year had been agonizing. I was working horrific hours, was invariably made to feel incompetent in my first rotations at the hospital, and never felt like I could completely relax when I came home. I recognized that much of my misery was self-imposed, but at the time I felt powerless to change it. I hadn't really been fearful that my roommates would have thought less of me had they known I was gay, it just felt too risky. We moved in some of the same professional circles, and I didn't want them disclosing personal information about me to people who I wouldn't want to have it. In addition, my parents occasionally came down to visit, and I didn't want my roommates volunteering tidbits about my private life that I was disinclined to willingly share. As a consequence, my whole living situation felt extremely claustrophobic.

During my last year of medical school, I had begun venturing out. That was when I had met Declan and our amazing friendship had blossomed. When we first met on the beach, there was initially an attraction between us, but because Declan had just ended a six-month relationship a few days before, he had zero inclination to start dating again. By the time he had recovered from the breakup, the foundation for a wonderful friendship had already been laid, so neither of us looked back. We became best friends, and the friendship continued not only to endure but to represent the rock in our lives that we both frequently leaned on for support. Romantic interests would come and go, but we'd found stability in one another.

During my first few years of residency, though I had precious little free time, I would on occasion venture out into West Hollywood. Mostly it would be with Declan and other friends of ours. Back then, when I would actually hook up, I would have to awkwardly explain why going back to my place was impossible: "I have straight roommates." "They don't know about me." "Blah, blah, blah, blah, blah, blah." Even to my ears it sounded tedious and juvenile. As untenable as it was, however, my life with straight roommates was my reality, and there seemed to be few alternatives. I mostly remembered it feeling oppressive and depressing.

That was why, in my last year of residency, moving in with Christian and Jeff had been so liberating. They were both friends of mine, they were both gay, and we were all immersed in the medical education system. No one could better understand the tribulations of our lives better than one another. We were sympathetic to the challenges we were all having to endure, understood the grueling time commitment being residents required, and supported one another in the quest for the perfect guy. Or at least supported one another in the quest for mind-blowing sex. Now, if I was fortunate enough to hook up, the only caution I would have to offer my date was "Keep your voice down, I have roommates." Or to give the impression of being less uptight I would sometimes tease to impart the same message. "Because I have roommates, I'm going to have to try to be quieter. I'm so good in bed that I sometimes scream my own name." I hadn't said that recently, though. It was a good icebreaker, but it set up some unrealistic expectations. Lots of pressure to take someone to bed and have them anticipating a Cirque du Soleil performance.

Now, though my life continued to be inordinately busy, coming home was a pleasure. Rather than feeling like an outcast, home was a welcoming sanctuary where I was free to be myself and supported by caring friends. The feeling was more liberating than could be described. As compared to my previous living situations, it felt as if I'd been paroled from jail.

Christian and Brent and I ate, teased, shared some of the frustrations we had recently been feeling, and regaled one another with stories of our mutual friends' dating catastrophes. They also pressed me for more details about Sergio. I couldn't help making it obvious that I was pretty smitten, but I nonetheless tried to maintain a low profile. In reality, Sergio and I had only recently begun dating, and it was way too early to predict if the relationship had potential. The fact that I already felt head over heels was sometimes just an omen that I was destined to suffer a monumental disappointment. So, though I sat there talking to them about Sergio and expending a huge effort to keep my expectations in check, I was sure my enthusiasm was seeping out all over the place.

After I finished dinner, I washed my plate and began reaching for the cookware to clean up. Christian, however, refused my offer to help. "Go to bed. We've got this covered. You were on call last night, and you need to rest up for your big date tomorrow. Besides," he said, smiling, "Brent and I were going to fill the sink with bubbles, get naked, and have our own little soap and suds party." Brent carried his plate over to the sink, wrapped his arms around Christian, and broke out into a huge grin.

"Someone is going to be squeaky clean, though I can't say I can guarantee the condition of the dishes."

I laughed and rolled my eyes. "Thanks for dinner, guys. The meal was great. But given your intended festivities, I might never eat off those plates again. From here on out, it will be disposable paper products for me. The vision of one of you using your hairy ass as a sponge is downright revolting."

Christian just laughed harder. "Wait until you see what I intend to use as a bottle brush."

"Good night," I shouted. "If I hear any more, I'm gonna have horrible nightmares and will develop such a dish phobia I'll become anorexic."

I disappeared into my room and closed the door. Laughter and thoughts of Sergio engulfed my mind in the mere seconds it took me to fall asleep.

CHAPTER 14

I HAD written Sergio's address on a little piece of paper and had it clutched between my fingers as I slowly navigated down South Manhattan Place. It was a street a few blocks west of Western Avenue, and he said that he lived between Third Street and Sixth. I compared the numbers on the buildings to the number written on the paper. I had to be getting close. He'd instructed me to leave my car in the red zone with the flashers on. Once I'd parked, I should run up to the intercom at the main entrance and enter his apartment code, then he would open the security gate to the subterranean parking lot. He said the two spaces clearly designated for guest parking were almost always empty, and I should park in one of them. Easy enough.

When I identified his building ahead on the right, I swung into the red zone flanked by driveways on either side. I checked my reflection in the rearview mirror, then jumped out to alert Sergio that I had arrived by punching his code into the intercom. I reminded myself that I should run the brush through my hair one last time after I had parked in the lot. We hadn't seen each other for a week, and I wanted to make a good impression. Sergio said he would take the elevator down into the lot to meet me. Apparently, the elevator could only be accessed by using a tenant's key. I laughed. Maximum security.

The gate swung open. I drove from street level down into the garage and located the empty spaces in the back without difficulty. Again, I looked in the mirror, ran the brush through my hair, and gave my collar a tug to straighten the creases. I stared at my reflection and practiced an unassuming smile. Maybe not Brad Pitt but certainly not Chicken Little either. The bike ride from the week before had left me with a slight tan, my hair had cooperated, and the shirt I had chosen complemented my eyes. *Fuck it. This is as good as it is going to get.*

As I was getting out of my car, the elevator door opened. I silently congratulated myself on the timing. I wouldn't have wanted Sergio to catch me preening.

I grabbed the bottle of wine out of the passenger's seat, slammed the door shut, then looked up to see Sergio approaching. The second our eyes met, my breath was taken away. Knowing I would see him did little to buffer my reaction. I was overwhelmed by how incredible he looked: dark hair, olive skin, captivating eyes, radiant smile, confident stride, emanating an aura of sex appeal seldom achieved even in Calvin Klein underwear ads. I tried to surreptitiously lean my hand against the car door handle but was really reaching for it to hold myself up. It took a behemoth effort to speak and have my voice come out as more than a soft whisper.

"Hey, Sergio. You make one fine-looking chef. Heck with dinner—I might just want to spend all night in the kitchen."

In a few strides, he was standing within arm's reach of me. He still hadn't spoken. He stood quietly in front of me, his smile getting increasingly warm, and he ran his thumb across my cheek. When he did speak, his voice was gentle and teasing. "Oh yeah, you're gonna eat. I have to introduce you to what real Italian food tastes like." He continued to stroke my cheek and let his fingers creep behind my neck to pull me forward. "We might, however, have to discuss dessert. I suddenly find myself craving something a little more American." He leaned forward and took my mouth in his.

The kiss was rich, seductive, and quick. No sooner had I wrapped my arms around him and gotten the wine bottle pressed into his back than he drew back and smiled. "Welcome to my home." He smiled self-consciously. "Or, at least welcome to my garage. Come on up. I've got some things on the stove that I don't want to burn." He let his hand slide down my back, but in doing so, he caught my hand in his and started pulling me toward the elevator. "I'm on the third floor. It's perfect because the building is only three stories high. No one above me, so no heavy footsteps clomping across my ceiling."

As we neared the elevator, he dropped my hand to pull his keys out of his pocket. I was able to stand back and look at him while he was scrutinizing the ring to select the appropriate key. He was wearing a long-sleeved cotton shirt, meticulously pressed but unbuttoned far enough to offer an unobstructed glimpse of his muscular chest. Underneath the shirt I could see a gold chain with a matching gold crucifix. His jeans were designer but casual, and he wore leather shoes without socks. The entire ensemble screamed "stylish European," and I suspected that he had pulled it together with little consideration. I, on the other hand, had again agonized over what to wear. I always found opening my closet to be a depressing endeavor. My wardrobe consisted either of hospital clothes or gym attire. I thought it was completely void of anything that could fall into the "dress to impress" category. I reminded myself with a sigh that not only was it time to go shopping, but I'd better bring along a consultant. I might have been gay, but I somehow had missed out on that shopping gene.

We exited the elevator and stepped onto an outdoor corridor with a railing overlooking the complex courtyard. The door to his condo was at the very end, so he had a corner unit. We walked side by side until we reached the door, then he stepped back and motioned me forward. "Go on in. The door's unlocked."

I reached for the knob and pushed the door open. Before I even crossed the threshold I was struck with the impression that I had stumbled into a beautifully decorated Italian villa. Soft music filled the air, amazing smells overwhelmed my senses, and my gaze was drawn to beautifully situated furniture and walls covered with incredible paintings.

I sensed Sergio was observing my reaction, but I couldn't disguise how impressed I was with the room's beauty. "Wow, this is amazing."

I walked in and swept my gaze over the room. One of the first things to stand out was the fact that the main wall was painted two different colors, separated by a diagonal line that stretched from the floor of one corner to the ceiling of the other. The lower half was painted a light seafoam green, and the upper half was a soft peach. Had someone tried to describe the wall to me, I probably would have envisioned something aesthetically unattractive, but overall, the effect was both elegant and appealing. In addition, almost the entire wall was covered by beautifully framed paintings. Individually, each was spectacular, but when seen collectively, the wall became a collage of color. The furniture was equally impressive. Each piece looked comfortable, was beautifully crafted, and fit perfectly in the decorative scheme. Finally, each of the objects that covered the coffee tables and shelves against the wall added wonderful artistic touches.

I walked slowly into the room and admired each of the paintings. "These are fantastic. You've apparently been collecting them for a long time and either have an inside scoop where to shop, or you've robbed some pretty high-end galleries." I stood back and admired one that I especially liked. "This one is particularly unique." I turned and offered him a genuinely approving smile. "They're beautiful."

Sergio smiled as well, but I detected a subtle blush creep across his cheeks. "While it's true I've been collecting them a long time, I haven't had to do any shopping. They're originals. I painted them. I told you when I met you at the pool that I liked to pretend that I was an artist."

My mouth dropped open, and I turned back to stare at the paintings incredulously. "These are amazing, Sergio. When you told me you one day hoped to be a painter, I had no idea you were so talented. These paintings really are incredible." I looked back at him. "The color, depth, and detail on these canvases blow my mind. These are more than professional—they're friggin' masterpieces."

I recognized that my compliments were a little effusive, but they were honest. Sure, I would have wanted Sergio to feel flattered, but in this case, none of my comments were the least bit embellished. I genuinely thought his paintings were fantastic.

Sergio walked over to me and swept me into a warm embrace. "You're probably exaggerating a ton, but I appreciate the compliment. One of these days I hope my work will hang somewhere other than on the walls of my condo." He kept one arm around my shoulder, turned to survey his paintings with a critical eye, and then turned back to me. "I'm proud of some of them, but others are a little amateurish." He held my gaze. "But I'm happy you like them." He bent forward and kissed me again. This kiss was unhurried, and I was quickly lost in its intensity. When he drew back he was smiling. "I'd better take that bottle of wine out of your hands before I kiss you again. One slip and you might accidently break it over my head."

I blushed and handed the bottle over to him so he could read the label. "Chianti. The guy in the wine store assured me it was a good one. Figured I couldn't lose by bringing a good bottle of Chianti to a home-cooked Italian meal. Might not score any points for originality, but I hope to maintain solid standing in the Roman-tradition category."

Sergio took the bottle and motioned me into the kitchen. "Come in here while I finish cooking. Everything is almost ready." He opened one of the drawers, reached in, and pulled out a corkscrew. "You want to open this? Or would the job be better left to the hands of a professional?"

I grabbed both the bottle of wine and the corkscrew from him and tried my best to look indignant. "Hey, I might have neglected to mention that I supported myself through undergrad by waiting tables. I might not wear the apron anymore, but I work diligently to maintain my skills. I've been known to drink a whole bottle of wine by myself just to prove that I can still open it like an expert." He knew I was joking, and I laughed as I cut the foil away from the top of the bottle. "Now I'm under a lot of pressure not to break the cork."

"If you can't open a bottle of wine without breaking the cork, I'm definitely changing doctors. There's no way I'd trust you with a scalpel if you can't handle a corkscrew."

"First of all, we already discussed this. You're a little out of my age range. Secondly, because I'm a pediatrician and not a surgeon, they refuse to allow me to operate, so you don't have to worry. No one trusts me with a scalpel."

Sergio walked over to the oven, opened it wide enough to peek over the door, then nodded. "Go ahead and pour the wine. Wine glasses are on the table. After these cool a bit, we'll start with appetizers."

I had been so intent on admiring Sergio's paintings I had paid little attention to the dining area. The table was beautifully set with a white linen tablecloth, colorful Italian ceramic plates, and fresh-cut flowers in shades that complemented the dishes perfectly. "Wow," I exclaimed. "You went all out. This table looks like it's been set for royalty."

Sergio laughed. "No, just a couple of queens."

Ironically, the pun put me at ease. I appreciated that Sergio could poke fun at himself and at his sexual orientation. He really was completely comfortable with himself. Of course, calling oneself a queen when you reeked of masculinity was probably pretty easy. Had it been my joke, I would have immediately become so self-conscious that anyone I was speaking to would immediately assume I was girlish. Would I ever succeed in stifling the inner voice in my head that maintained a perpetual derogatory critique?

I intentionally shook my head to quiet the internal dialogue. I refused to let any insecurities ruin the promise of an incredible evening. "What are we having? It smells delicious."

"Ah, I hope you're hungry. It's a traditional five-course Italian meal." He smiled over at me. "With a few of my own personal twists. I had to improvise a little, because I wanted you to taste some of my favorites. We'll start with asparagus wrapped in crispy prosciutto, followed by a serving of homemade fagioli soup. I used my grandmother's recipe to make the soup." He tried to look humble, but it was obvious he was bursting with pride. "Then, even though it deviates a little from a traditional third course, because I made my own crust, you'll get to sample a few slices of pizza. I made a small pizza rustica with Sicilian sausage." Even as he was speaking, he again opened the oven and pulled out a piping hot bubbling pizza. He smiled over his shoulder at me as he transferred it from a thin baking sheet to the surface of a large wooden cutting board to cool.

"Then, in keeping with a more authentic fourth course, we'll have a serving of pasta." He lifted the lid off a pot on the stove to confirm that the water had reached a rolling boil. "Though I won't cook the pasta until just before we're ready to eat it. It has to be fresh or it doesn't taste as good." He moved around the kitchen, stirring some pots and lowering the flames under others. When he'd assured himself the cooking process was proceeding according to plan, he again focused his attention on me. "Our main course will be veal scaloppini in a portobello mushroom sauce." The smile crept back across his face. "It's a family favorite, and I haven't eaten it since the last time I visited Rome. As for dessert? Never let it be said that I'm not a man of my word." He crossed the kitchen, opened the door of the freezer, pulled about a plan white container, and slowly opened the lid. "Homemade gelato." He beamed. "Our vendor came by the restaurant yesterday and gave me a carton of pistachio. Now, in addition to making good on my promise to you, we have the perfect finale to what I hope will be a great dinner."

I was so overwhelmed I didn't trust my mouth to speak. Instead, I crossed the kitchen and kissed Sergio passionately on the lips. I really was touched. I couldn't believe he would go to such tremendous lengths for no reason other than to please me. My mind was having trouble connecting the pieces. Sergio could have his pick of almost anyone. Given his physique, model good looks, and sexy accent, he would be a prize catch on even the most exclusive list. Why was he wasting his time with me?

168 | JAKE WELLS

I threw myself more deeply into the kiss, as much because I enjoyed it as to prove to myself that I really was in Sergio's arms and to push the negative voices out of my head. For whatever reason, I was there. An incredible dinner was waiting, Sergio was holding me possessively, and the night had the potential for being damn near perfect. If I woke up the next day to find that the whole experience had just been one big cosmic hoax, so be it. For now, I would live in the moment, and frankly, it was hard to imagine that either time or eternity could ever provide a better one.

When we broke the kiss, Sergio looked at me happily. "I take it that means you approve of the menu?"

Just seeing his warm smile focused directly on me succeeded in pushing the majority of my insecurities right out of my head. "Oh yeah, I approve." I planted one additional quick kiss on his lips, then leaned back to look at him. "But I have a confession to make. At the risk of sounding like I'm coming on too strong, I'm being perfectly honest when I say that, if it meant being able to share it with you, I would have been content with Chinese takeout." I lifted my hands to cradle his head and make him look me directly in the eye. "But authentic Italian is way better." I smiled warmly and pulled him forward so our foreheads touched. "Way better. In fact, I feel guilty that you're spoiling me."

He laughed and turned back to the stove. "You better taste it before you accuse me of spoiling you. If it's awful, you'll be begging for Chinese takeout."

I walked up behind him and wrapped my arms around his waist as he pushed a spoon around in the pasta sauce. "I'll take my chances. It smells delicious. Just the aroma is making me light-headed." I kissed the side of his neck and chuckled. "Or maybe it's you that makes me feel that way."

"Or, more likely," he said, laughing, "you're light-headed from hunger. Sit down." He guided me over to my chair. "Dinner is ready." He took the napkin off my plate, unfolded it, and laid it on my lap. "This is more than just a meal; it's an experience. Your only job is to enjoy. I'll handle the rest."

"My only job is to enjoy? I think the spoiling has already begun."

He put the asparagus down in front of me. It was beautifully plated. A couple sprigs of parsley tucked carefully under the ends of the asparagus supported a wedge of lemon, and the smell of warm prosciutto came wafting through the air. I gasped softly. "Wow, if I didn't know better, I'd say you did this professionally." I smiled up at him and gave his hand a gentle squeeze before he circled to the other side of the table. "Presentation, presentation. If it tastes as good as it looks, I'd say you've found yourself a winner."

Sergio sat down across from me. He tried to sound modest but looked genuinely pleased. "This is just to whet your appetite. A little something to prepare your stomach for the avalanche of food to follow." He raised his glass of wine in a toast. "Bon appétit."

I lifted my glass as well. "Bon appétit. Thank you for inviting me and for going above and beyond in preparing such an incredible meal." We touched the edges of our glasses together, and I smiled. "And here's to our second date. May there be many more." I lifted my glass a little higher. "God save the queens."

Sergio had to pull his glass quickly away from his mouth to prevent himself from spitting wine across the table as he started to laugh. "This might be our last date if you make me choke to death." He smiled at me warmly and again lifted his glass in the air. "Definitely. To more dates." He winked, then took a sip. He held the wine in his mouth briefly before swallowing, then studied it swirling around in his glass. "The wine-store guy gave you a solid recommendation. This is a good Chianti."

I heard a soft crunch as I cut through the prosciutto and into the asparagus. I lifted the fork to my mouth, slid the bite of food in, and chewed appreciatively. "Delicious. I could make a meal just of this. Is there anything in the world that doesn't taste better with bacon?"

"Right! I've heard of some people pairing it with chocolate."

"Okay, let me ask another question: Is there anything in this world that doesn't taste better with chocolate?" I smiled and shrugged, as if stating the obvious. "Two of the best flavors on the planet. It just stands to reason that they'd taste good together."

"I'm not sure that's always the case. I can think of a few things I like by themselves but that would offend each other if served on the same plate."

"Like what, for example?"

"I don't know." Sergio swirled the wine around in his glass contemplatively. "Like, for example…." He shifted his focus away from his glass and looked at me. "Like Italians and Americans. They're unlikely to make a palatable combination." He chuckled softly.

I smiled too. "I beg to differ. Sometimes combining ethnicities produces amazing results. Almost like the sum of the two parts is greater than the whole." I began to bring my glass of wine toward my mouth. I wanted to hide my smile. "Take us, for example. I can say with certainty that when I'm with you, parts of me get bigger." I took a quick sip to try to stifle my laugh.

Sergio held my gaze without wavering. "We might have to put the theory to a test later this evening."

The meal was extraordinary, each subsequent course better than the previous. The fagioli soup was incredible, and because it came from his grandmother's recipe, it prompted more stories about his youth in Italy. We laughed easily, and though our childhoods had been vastly different, we found we actually had a lot in common. We compared notes on our relationships with our siblings and were empathetic to one another about how it felt to be a middle child.

In addition, Sergio discussed what it was like being gay in a conservative Catholic country and why it felt liberating for him to come to the United States. His contention was that though culturally Italians were a warm, accepting, and tolerant people, being gay wasn't well accepted socially. Religious sentiments still heavily influenced societal thinking, so being gay was generally considered to be taboo. It was common knowledge that men could have sex with each other in secret, but in order to maintain social status, it was important that they be married to women. You could be gay, and you could discreetly have sex with men; you just couldn't live with your partner.

Even as a young man, this situation had caused Sergio significant conflict. It wasn't that he'd felt compelled to flaunt his sexuality in other peoples' faces, he'd just had a strong personality. He'd refused to alter who he was in order to fulfill someone else's expectations of who he should be. I admired his strength of character.

The pasta and the veal were also delicious. So good, in fact, that I pretty much exceeded my capacity. By the time I took my last bite of veal, I could hardly move. I was certain if someone even looked at me wrong, my stomach would revolt and the entire five-course meal would surge forth like the launch of the space shuttle. I pushed my chair back, stretched my legs, and gently rubbed my stomach. "How could you let me eat so much? This is torture. It was too good. I'm suffering, here. Now I know what a beached whale feels like. They probably purposefully throw themselves onto the sand to do penance for eating too much veal scaloppini." I looked up at Sergio and smiled but continued to rub my stomach. "Until this moment, I didn't even realize whales ate veal scaloppini." I closed my eyes again and moaned.

Sergio just laughed. "I'll take your pain as the ultimate compliment. Does this mean that you want to hold off a few minutes before dessert?"

Startled by the question, my eyes flew open, only to find Sergio smiling at me. I relaxed and scooted down in the chair a little farther to rest my head against its back. I closed my eyes and locked my fingers protectively over my stomach. "Two minutes, then I'll be ready to devour half that carton of gelato." I opened one eye and looked at him. I let a hint of a smile creep across my face. "Better make that five minutes. A couple pints of pistachio will require a little more room than I can currently accommodate."

He laughed again and gently slapped my thigh. "That's okay. We aren't in any hurry. Let's go relax in the living room. You'll be more comfortable. I'll make some cappuccino to have with our dessert."

I rolled out of the chair, stood on shaky legs, and began to navigate toward the living room. I swore I had gained five pounds. Just walking the short distance seemed akin to trying to push a huge shipping barge through a narrow channel. "Better make mine decaf. If I drink regular this late in the evening, I'll be up all night."

Sergio looked at me with a seductive smile. "That's the idea." He winked, but fortunately he turned his head before he could see me blush. To my great embarrassment, not all the blood went into my cheeks. The majority of it went directly to my groin. Now, closing the distance between me and the couch became even more of a challenge.

I sat down and leaned against the soft, welcoming cushions. No sooner had I settled in than another moan escaped my lips. "Ah! Better! It's like sitting on a cloud. Now I know what heaven must feel like." I watched Sergio again busying himself in the kitchen. "If you need any help in there, just holler. I can be over in no less than thirty minutes." Sergio's smile from across the room encouraged me to continue. "You know, if your intention was to take advantage of me, you didn't have to incapacitate me first. I would have come along willingly. Stuffing me with food to prevent me from being able to move was unnecessary. I had no intention of trying to run."

"Hey. No one forced you to have two helpings of pasta. That was your choice. Don't they feed you at the hospital? You either really liked my cooking, or you haven't eaten in a week."

I laughed. "Yeah, they feed us. But, compared to what I just finished, I'm not even sure what they serve us is real food. You really outdid yourself." My smile broadened. "At least in the cooking department. In the eating department, I'm clearly the champion." I paused and let my head fall back onto the cushion. "And now I'm hating you for it."

He ceased his cappuccino preparation and came over and sat next to me on the couch. "Don't be a hater." He smiled. "I don't intend to attack you until you've fully recovered." He laughed as he pulled me toward him so I was leaning against his chest. He began to massage my shoulders. "Assuming you can recover within, say, the next half hour. Any longer than that and I refuse to be held responsible for what I might do to you."

I smiled without opening my eyes. "Man, you keep those fingers moving and my recovery time will be reduced to about four seconds. Not sure why, but in your arms, even having a full stomach is an aphrodisiac."

He kissed the top of my head and continued to knead my shoulders with his strong fingers. "You just relax. We have all the time in the world. We're not in the hospital. There's nowhere you need to be, nothing you have to be doing. Talk to me. You said you had a tough week. What's going on?"

I felt myself melting into his caresses. "A lot of the same old, same old. Sick kids, difficult parents, demanding attendings." I was quiet for a minute. "There is this one kid, though. He's really special." I quickly clarified, "Don't get me wrong. I went into pediatrics because I pretty much love all kids, but this one has really gotten to me. He has a really aggressive cancer, and every minute of his hospital admission has been an uphill climb. Right now, he's having to endure really kick-ass chemo. The intent is to shrink his tumor to a smaller size so it can be surgically removed. Then, about the time he begins to recover from that operation, the fun really begins. He has to go through even more potent chemo in anticipation of a bone marrow transplant."

I opened my eyes and looked back at Sergio. His expression was caring and sympathetic. I dropped my hand so I could gently stroke his leg as I continued sharing my impressions of Christopher. "There's something about him, though. He's only five, but he's an old soul. He rarely complains, tries to remain upbeat, and is actually appreciative, even though 90 percent of the things we do to him contribute to his misery. He's amazing. I'm not even sure he fully realizes how serious his situation is, but he has a way better attitude than almost any adult would have in similar circumstances." As I thought about Christopher, a smile crept across my face. "The kid loves superheroes. I was telling my friend Declan that on the day Christopher was admitted, he was wearing a Superman costume. He flew around the nurses' station. He won my heart the minute he consented to teach me to fly. I can't explain it. I'm drawn to that kid. He's courageous and loving—qualities admired in the best of mankind."

Sergio worked his hands from my shoulders to my neck. When he didn't interrupt, I kept talking. "I'd love for you to be able to meet him. Three minutes in the same room with him, and you feel like your life has been forever changed." I let out a soft chuckle. "He even made Peggy Wang smile, and that's pretty damned impossible. When my workload allows it, I spend as much time with him as possible. Well," I said, laughing a little more, "with him and Yogi." I again looked back and tried to catch Sergio's gaze. "Yogi is his teddy bear. He and Christopher are inseparable." When Sergio shook his head and smiled to indicate that he understood the importance to the relationship, I continued. "So, Christopher and Yogi and I do puzzles, watch superhero movies, or color in coloring books. I tell myself I'm doing all this for his benefit, but truthfully, I think spending time with Christopher makes me a better person. Sometimes I think I'm getting more out of it than he is."

Sergio dropped his hands to around my waist and hugged me fiercely. "I wouldn't bet on it, Zack. Somehow, I suspect a lot of the kid's courage comes from knowing you care. Your caring is genuine, heartfelt, and powerful. Kids sense that. I guarantee you that you're making a tremendous impact on him simply by being who you are." Sergio hugged me tighter and placed a soft kiss against my neck. "He's got a smart doctor and a loving guy taking care of him. That combination has to improve his condition." He kissed me again. "I know it improves mine." I felt his lips form a smile against my skin.

I laughed softly. "You're looking for a smart doctor?"

He stopped massaging my neck and gently whacked my head. "Yeah, that's it. I'm so transparent. I needed to meet someone with access to a prescription pad." He laughed softly and let his hands again drop to my shoulders. "For me, the doctor part is a bonus. As for you being a loving guy? Why do you think I've tried to seduce you with my cooking?"

I started laughing too. "Haven't we now come full circle? What do I have to say to convince you that you could have seduced me with a package of ramen noodles?

"You're that easy?"

"I didn't say I was easy. I just love chop suey." I turned my body so I could rest my cheek against his chest. "As long as it's prepared by a good-looking Italian artist."

He ran his hand through my hair. "Well, I'm glad to hear you at least have high standards."

He gently pushed me forward so he could stand up. "You sit tight. I'm gonna scoop up a small portion of gelato for us and finish making the cappuccino." He must have seen me grimace at the prospect of putting any more food into my stomach, because he laughed and slapped my leg. "I said a small portion, and besides, everyone knows that gelato aids in digestion. In this case, eating dessert will actually make you feel better. Just lie down here and relax." He fluffed one of the cushions and propped it against the arm of the couch. "Besides, you don't have to be hungry for at least another five minutes. It's going to take that long to prepare. By that time, you'll be ready to have an entire second meal."

I just groaned in response. I closed my eyes until my curiosity was piqued by hearing a strange sound emanating from the kitchen. I opened my eyes to investigate what Sergio was doing. I was astonished to discover that he had what appeared to be a professional-grade espresso maker and he was swirling a small metal pitcher under the steamer to heat the milk. The steamer sounded like a low-pitched train whistle blowing in the distance. Inexplicably, the prospect of hot cappuccino and homemade gelato awakened my taste buds and made me feel suddenly capable of incredible feats of power eating.

I sat up on the couch and spoke loud enough for him to hear me over the sound of steamer. "That's quite a machine. Did you steal it from the restaurant?"

He smiled over his shoulder. "A good friend of mine is part owner of an Italian restaurant on Melrose. He knows a distributor who imports espresso machines from Italy. My friend pulled some strings and was able to get this one for me wholesale. It's the small size, for domestic use."

"You could have fooled me. With all those buttons and gauges, it looks more like the inside of a cockpit. You sure you know how to drive that thing?"

He nodded smugly. "Better than a fighter pilot. We'll see if you have any doubts about my flying ability after you taste this." By this time he was tilting the metal pitcher and pouring steamed milk over the espresso he had already made. Just as he was completing the pour, I saw him shake the pitcher gently. Then he put two cups, along with the bowls of gelato, on a tray and carried them over to where I was sitting.

Sure enough. When I looked into the cups, I saw that the foam from the steamed milk formed the pattern of a perfect leaf. I looked up and smiled. "I was going to ask if you had any sweetener to stir into it, but it seems a shame to ruin the beautiful presentation."

"The best part of the presentation is your enjoyment." He lifted the lid off a bowl of sugar cubes. "One lump or two?" His smile was both captivating and seductive.

"Just one lump." I smiled as I reached for the spoon to stir it into my cappuccino. "Why do you think I've eaten so little this evening? I'm watching my waistline." My grin broadened. "Or more accurately, why do you think I had to loosen my belt already? Two lumps and I'd have to take my pants off entirely."

Sergio didn't even respond initially. He just lifted the lid that covered the sugar cubes, grabbed one on the end of the spoon, and held it out in front of me. "If that's the case, I'll have to insist on two. Those pants are coming off sooner or later anyway." He held my gaze as if his suggestion was intended only to be helpful. His mouth worked its way into a smile, however, when, before waiting for my response, he just dropped another cube into my cup. "It's a little strong. The cappuccino and the evening will go down smoother with one more lump." When he finished stirring mine, he lifted his cup to his lips, then asked innocently as he smiled around the rim, "What? I only want you to enjoy"—he took a sip before he finished the sentence—"the cappuccino."

I lifted my cup to take a sip and imitated his serious tone. "If you're really that concerned about my enjoyment," I said before I swallowed innocently, "you would already have taken your pants off."

Sergio just laughed. "I apologize. It was an oversight. My guests' comforts always come first."

I was consumed by a gentle warmth. The evening really had been perfect. We'd talked, we'd laughed, and we'd shared. In addition, the gelato was delicious and the cappuccino provided a marvelous finale to an exceptional dinner. When we had finished, we sat quietly on the couch. I was nestled comfortably under Sergio's arm. He had dimmed the lights and lit a few candles. The colors on his paintings were softly illuminated by the candlelight.

I sank deeper into his embrace and admired the artwork. "I love the one of the clown. His expression is so sorrowful. It's not just his makeup. You can see it in his eyes. And yet, the colors around him are so vibrant. The effect creates quite a contrast. It's powerful."

He too studied the painting. His expression became reflective. "I was going through a challenging period when I painted that. I suppose the clown's face is representative of my struggles. His eyes reflect my uncertainty and pain." He hugged me tighter. "But even during the worst of it, I somehow knew I'd get through. Without realizing it at the time, I think I chose the surrounding bright colors to signify my underlying optimism. It's like the colors were beacons signaling the happiness waiting in my future. It's funny—during that period of my life, painting was a distraction for me. It was an escape. Kind of ironic that the actual process of painting that damn clown ended up providing me with encouragement." He continued to stare at the clown's face as if lost in a memory.

I lifted the arm wrapped around my shoulder and pulled it more tightly against my chest. "Well, I'm no critic, but I think it's amazing." I kissed the skin of his wrist.

"I'm glad you like it." Sergio laughed and kissed the top of my head gently. "Every artist needs a following. Now you've been promoted to president of my fan club."

Out of nowhere, my stomach lurched. Sadly, it wasn't unusual. The most innocuous comment could provoke my insecurities, and they would surge forth as if released from the depths of hell. Sergio wasn't belittling me. Far from it. In fact, he couldn't have been more gracious and admiring. He wasn't responsible for making me feeling insecure. My insecurities came from decades of rigorously cultivated self-doubt, and they would rear their ugly heads without provocation or reason. Even more regrettably, expressing them invariably made people feel defensive.

Historically, many a wonderful evening had been sabotaged by my spewing unpleasantries rooted in feeling insecure about myself.

"Sergio, I don't even want to think about how many admirers you have in your fan club. Forget your paintings; your eyes alone could generate a 'members only' list that half of West Hollywood would sell their souls to be included on. Just thinking about it makes me want to go back and climb underneath my rock. I'm having trouble believing you even want me here."

Sergio drew back and looked at me with an expression of genuine confusion. "What do you mean you can't believe I want you here? You know I was joking about having a fan club. There is no list, and even if there was, it wouldn't matter. What matters is that I invited you here because I wanted you here. Leave any other hang-ups at the door. And for the record, I'm pretty sure I didn't pull you out from under a rock." The anger that I had seen flare a few times before began to reveal itself again. "And what does that say about me? Do you think I choose the people I want to spend time with by turning over rocks?"

He pushed me forward so he could get up. When he was angry, his hands became even more animated and his eyes sparked with emotion. He stood directly in front of me and stared me down.

"What's your game, Zack? You show up here, we have a great evening, you give me the impression that we've genuinely clicked, and then you say something that implies I'm nothing more than a player. You think the only reason you're here is to enable me to put another notch in my bedpost? Is that it? If that's what you think, I can assure you, you can wipe that idea right out of your head. I'm not that desperate." He began to pace as he spoke, the cadence of his speech increasing and the volume getting louder. "Why do you think I went through the effort of making dinner? It didn't occur to you that I thought you were a quality guy who I wanted to get to know better? You think my only goal here is to check your name off a list?" He turned and again stared at me. "A list that, by the way, exists only in your head. It doesn't exist in mine." He looked like he intended to say more, but he subsequently fell silent. He just left his gaze locked on mine, his jaw clenched, waiting for me to respond.

I, on the other hand, had fallen into a daze. I had no idea why I couldn't have just kept my mouth shut. Seconds before, I had been enjoying one of the most amazing nights of my life. Sergio really was everything I was looking for in a guy: personable, funny, compassionate, insightful, and incredibly good-looking. The last thing I had intended by my comment was to offend him. Even sitting there, incredibly self-conscious under his angry stare, I was absolutely dumbfounded as to why the comment had come pouring out of my mouth. Most certainly, it had been motivated by panic. As enamored as I was with Sergio, being in his company also made me feel extraordinarily inadequate. He was good-looking, confident, and exuded sexuality from every pore—all qualities I felt I was completely lacking. Any self-esteem I had evolved from my confidence in my intellect. Not an attribute to apologize for but certainly not a huge allure for enticing a hunky guy into the bedroom. My inability to see myself as a reasonable catch also prevented me from accepting that a guy like Sergio would have even a modicum of pleasure in being with me. The byproduct of my insecurity? Open mouth and say something to deflect my feelings and ruthlessly obliterate the enjoyment of the moment.

I looked back at Sergio's intense expression, but any attempt to form coherent words was impossible. I folded my hands across my lap and stared at them intently as if by contemplating them, the secrets of self-realization would magically be revealed. I racked my brain for an explanation that would justify the inappropriateness of my comment, but none came.

The volume of the silence became deafening. I felt like if I didn't break it, I would be consumed by it. My whole world, all my insecurities, seemed to cascade into the spotlight of that single moment, but I was aware only of the tear that ran slowly down my cheek. How could I make Sergio understand that he'd done nothing wrong? It was simply that I was broken.

When a more eloquent explanation couldn't be found, I looked up at him through tear-filled eyes and choked out an emotion-filled apology that was little more than a whisper. "I'm sorry. I'm an idiot."

In another amazing transformation, Sergio's demeanor immediately softened. Again, his anger seemed to dissipate instantaneously, and he sat down next to me and pulled me into his arms. "You can say that again. Where do those ridiculous comments come from anyway? Do you carry a bag of self-put-downs around on your shoulder? Can't you just leave it at home for one night and enjoy the evening? Doesn't carrying it around ever become a burden?"

The relief I felt crashed over me like a wave. As stupid as my comment had been, it apparently hadn't caused Sergio to conclude that I truly was defective. I was too embarrassed to look directly at him. "I don't know what possesses me to say things like that." I wiped my eyes with the back of my hand. "I told you I was an idiot. I guess now I'm trying to prove it to you." I looked at him out of the corner of my eye and forced a smile. "Did I succeed? Is it unanimous? Should you just call 911 and have me admitted to the psych unit? There must be a special ward for people who see what they want dangled in front of them and rather than grabbing it, they kick it over the cliff." I turned my palms toward the ceiling and looked up, as if searching for an answer. "When will the craziness stop?" I put my elbows on my knees and cradled my head in my hands. "You must think I'm a complete loser."

Sergio again reached out and pulled me against him. "Would you quit trying to tell me what I think of you? I'm thirty-two years old and have lived independently since I was eighteen. I haven't needed someone to tell me what I should think for a long time, and I'm not about to let you start telling me now. The only one in this room who thinks you're a loser is you." He hugged me tighter. "I'm not exactly sure how you came to that conclusion, but I, for one, am pretty damned sure you're wrong." He gently grabbed my chin and turned my head so I was forced to look him in the eye. "And for the record, I've never been known to be wrong about these things. So," he said before he kissed me on the cheek, "if you're absolutely sure this pity party of yours is over, can we continue our wonderful evening?"

He stood up and reached for my hand. "Ideally, in the bedroom. Unless you'd prefer to eat more dessert."

I stood and pulled him into a deep kiss. "I was kind of hoping *you* were the dessert."

Sergio smiled. "I knew that, given enough time, you'd come up with an idea I agreed with."

He pulled me toward the bedroom.

CHAPTER 15

MONDAY morning I was still floating on a cloud. With the exception of my brief psychotic break, the evening with Sergio had been sensational. When he pulled me into the bedroom, I was greeted by the most romantic welcome imaginable. Soft music filled the room, and it was illuminated by antique wrought-iron candelabras on either side of the bed. Each held three pillar candles. The bedspread was folded neatly on the foot of the bed, and the mattress was covered in soft ivory sheets. We kissed, embraced, and slowly undressed each other. Just prior to pushing me down onto the bed, Sergio stood naked in front of me. I reached out, let my hand slide slowly down his chest, and just looked at him. Had I been able to make a wish, I would have wanted time to stand still in just that second. I felt like I had died and gone to heaven. Handsome, sexy, understanding, gentle, and, in that moment, inexplicably mine. The night was a torrent of passion.

When we finally did sleep, I felt like I had been put into a medically induced coma. I lay on my side with Sergio pressed firmly against my back, his arm wrapped around my chest to pull me tightly into him. I was exhausted. In Sergio's hands, I had been inspired to reach sexual heights I'd never before even thought imaginable. It felt like I'd participated in a climax marathon, but the exertion was indescribably satisfying. Mostly, however, I felt content. Like, perhaps for the first time I could remember, being in his arms, I felt like I really belonged. The feeling was simultaneously calming and intoxicating.

We had slept until late in the morning, had one more raucous toss in the hay, then jumped into the shower to get Sergio out the door in time. He was scheduled for a double shift that day. On Sunday, the restaurant served a special brunch. He was supposed to be floor manager for the brunch, then stay to work as headwaiter for the dinner shift. I suspected because we hadn't officially fallen asleep until almost four in the morning, despite sleeping in, he still would be tired. I had volunteered to stay and wash the dishes from the night before, but Sergio rebuffed my offer. "You are my guest. There's no way I'd relegate you to the cleanup detail. What kind of host would that make me? I'm Italian. When you extend a dinner invitation to someone, the guest isn't expected to pay for his meal by being placed on kitchen detail. The very concept is appalling."

I had tried to argue. "I wasn't your guest, I was your date. There's a difference, and it's the least I can do. The dinner was incredible, and I will feel guilty knowing that after coming home from working a double shift, you'll walk into a dirty kitchen. It would be my pleasure."

Sergio responded by pushing me toward the door. "Don't test me. Mention it once more, and the next time I invite you to dinner you'll get a Pop-Tart on a paper plate. That will spare either of us any cleanup."

I laughed but didn't offer any additional protests. Before I opened the door, I turned and reached out with both arms to grab Sergio by the shoulders. "Make mine a chocolate Pop-Tart." I smiled but then looked at him a little more seriously. "At the risk of sounding too corny, I just wanted to tell you that last night may well have been one of the best of my life." I coughed. "Okay, not only corny but so sickeningly sweet you might require a shot of insulin."

It was obvious Sergio didn't get the joke, but I moved on without trying to clarify. "Forget it. I'm just trying to say I had an incredibly great time, and I hope to be able to see you again soon." I pulled him closer and leaned in to kiss him. "There's a strong possibility you could become habit-forming."

Sergio responded to the kiss with passion and enthusiasm. When it broke, he was smiling at me. "I'm not the only one who might end up being a hard habit to break. You've got 'addiction' written all over you." He smiled warmly. "Doesn't that break some medical code of ethics? Promoting addiction?"

"Not if you're a healthy addiction. I'm in the same category as regular exercise, a high-fiber diet, and polyunsaturated fats. I'm actually good for you." I leaned in for another kiss and whispered, "At least, I *want* to be good for you."

After Sergio pulled away, he opened the door and gave me a gentle push. "You're on the right track. Unless, of course, I end up getting fired because you make me late for work. Then you get added to the list of potential health hazards."

I was almost out the door when I felt Sergio grab my shoulder. "Zack, I had a great time too. Call me tomorrow from the hospital. We'll get together soon." He pressed a quick kiss against my cheek, then gave me another gentle push. "Now get out of here."

Recalling the evening so warmed my heart that even reading down the long list of patients who had been admitted over the weekend did little to squelch my incredibly good mood. Diane came and sat down next to me, looking bleary-eyed from the long night working. I smiled up at her. "Hey, sweet thing. Looks like you had the weekend from hell. What did you do? Admit every child in the city? How many patients do we have on this list? Looks like no fewer than fifteen new names." I reached over and brushed the hair off her forehead. "I'm sorry. Guess I have to assume that the cucumber was left untouched."

She was too exhausted to counter with her usual clever reply. "Yeah. Must have been a full moon or something. Cory admitted ten kids on Saturday, and I admitted twelve yesterday, six of whom came in after midnight. I couldn't catch a break last night. I feel like I've been chewed up and spit out."

I smiled warmly at her. "Sorry, honey. You look more like you've been chewed up, swallowed, and passed out the other end." I threw my arm around her and pulled her into a quick hug. "Don't worry. I'm rested and ready to go. Let's see what I can do to help you get out of here. We'll have you back to your gorgeous self in no time." I ran down the list of new admissions. "Give me a quick rundown on these kids, then tell me which still have loose ends to be tied up. I'll be your wingman."

Diane looked at me suspiciously. "If I didn't know better, I'd say you were the one who spent the entire weekend in the company of the cucumber. What gives?"

I looked back at her but was unsuccessful in turning my smile into a frown. Even so, I avoided her question. "Is that the thanks I get? Do you want to get out of here or not? The sooner we run this list, the sooner you're home. Now let's get cracking." I gave her a little shove.

She seemed a little reluctant to let me off the hook, but her exhaustion, coupled with knowing how much work was yet to be done, deterred her from interrogating me further. "Okay, let's get started. Some of these kids are actually pretty sick."

It took forty minutes just for her to fully describe the condition of each of the patients to me. Some had only been on the floor a couple of hours, so many of them had yet to have their blood drawn, and a couple were still waiting for X-rays to be taken. "Tell you what," I said. "I'll take a quick run down to Radiology and look at the X-rays that are already completed. Sounds like it's important to know if the kid in"—I scrolled down the list of patients—"room twenty-four has pneumonia or if his shortness of breath is singularly the result of a severe asthma attack. While I'm gone, you compile a list of all the work that still has to be done." I smiled. "We'll divide and conquer."

I got up to start down the hall but hesitated. "What's going on with Christopher?"

Diane looked down at the scribbles on her list of patients. "Tomorrow is his big day. They're going to take him to the operating room to try to remove his primary tumor. Apparently, Surgery is a little nervous. He had another MRI on Saturday. The tumor is situated extremely close to his spinal cord and encroaches on both his left adrenal gland and part of his left kidney. They're afraid excision is going to be tricky. They're not sure how much of it they'll be able to remove, nor do they know if they'll be able to save the kidney. For his part, Christopher, as usual, seems to be going with the flow. His parents, however, are a mess. Knowing this operation might result in partial paralysis and anticipating that he still has to endure a bone-marrow transplant has them worried sick. I don't think his mom has eaten anything all weekend."

The news knocked the wind out of my sails. "Okay, as soon as we get on top of things, I'll go see him." I shook my head dejectedly. "Even if I succeed in cheering him up, I don't know what I'm gonna say to his parents. The whole situation absolutely sucks. No way to sugarcoat that."

"You can say that again. Makes me question whether I'll ever want to have children. Having to watch them suffer would be a living nightmare."

I tried to lighten the mood. "Duh! Having you as a mom would be a nightmare." Then, recognizing the sincerity of her worry, I walked over and hugged her. "Come on, Diane. You're gonna be a great mom, and remember, Christopher's condition is, like, one in a million. You can't let the prospect of bad things happening prevent you from living your life. I mean, come on. If you really thought about it, the statistical likelihood of being in a car accident could theoretically prevent you from ever driving on the freeway. You can either live your life locked in your house, worrying about all the bad things that could potentially happen, or you can get in your car and head for the beach. Not only is a wonderful day at the beach a better alternative than worrying, there's never a guarantee. You could choose to stay locked in your house only to have it swallowed by an earthquake." I gave her a tighter squeeze. "We only have one life. We can't be afraid to live it. Take reasonable precautions, and don't be stupid, but forge ahead." I pulled back and looked at her. "Life is only an invitation to dance—getting out on the dance floor is our decision." I pushed more hair away from her face. "So come on. Let's get you out of here. Any real dancing occurs outside of the hospital, and I want you to save a dance for me."

A hint of a smile crept back across her face. "Just my luck. Partnered with Fred Astaire."

"Yeah? Doesn't that make you the envy of the hospital? To be able to work with someone who is devilishly good-looking, light on his feet, and wicked smart? Come on. It's a Hollywood movie in the making. It's impossible to write stuff this good."

Diane smiled, and I saw a glimmer of her wit returning. "Being light in your loafers doesn't make you a dancer. Now get out of here and try not to trip on your way down the stairs."

I knew she was baiting me, but I just casually waved over my shoulder and discreetly flipped her the bird. I heard her laughing softly behind me.

The whole way down to Radiology, I contemplated Christopher's condition. I didn't think they were going to operate on him until next week. They must have felt it necessary to move up the date. Hopefully, their decision wasn't an indication that the cancer was continuing to spread despite the chemo.

Once in the radiology department, I found it difficult to thoroughly evaluate the X-rays in front of me because I was mentally distracted. It was impossible to concentrate on anything other than Christopher. I knew from the minute he hit the door that he had a guarded prognosis, but I wasn't prepared for him to already be getting discouraging news. Rather than waiting for the elevator, I took the stairs two at a time back up to the fourth floor. I wanted to get going on my morning's work so I could spend some time being brought up to speed about what was going on with him.

The morning truly was a grind. A lot of the patients admitted over the weekend really were pretty sick, and for some, the diagnosis wasn't immediately obvious. Formulating a treatment plan for them required careful assessment of their labs and prolonged discussion with subspecialists whom we had consulted for help with their management. I devoted my whole day to putting out fires. Patients we believed were stable experienced unanticipated setbacks, and a few of the kids we knew were sick failed to demonstrate the improvements we expected. Everything was so hurried that I barely remembered my feet touching the ground. I seemed to run from one crisis to the next. Had I not, in those brief seconds of downtime, been able to draw on memories of having spent much of the weekend with Sergio, I almost certainly would have gone crazy.

Despite my diligent efforts, I wasn't able to spring Diane free until late in the afternoon. We were both just too harried to even take a break, much less allow her to leave early. By four, however, enough of the fires had been put out that, though I still hadn't completed all my work, I felt sufficiently caught up to take over her responsibilities.

I found her sitting at the nurses' station dejectedly going over her list of patients. I snuck up behind her and pulled it out of her hands. "Go home. You've saved enough lives for one day."

She tried to snatch the list back out of my hands. "Come on, Zack, I still have a bunch of things I need to check."

I kept the list out of her reach. "And none of them are things I can't do for you. Look. Have you even eaten anything today? You've been on your feet now for more than thirty-three hours. Enough. I'm pretty much caught up with all my essential work, and given all the conversations I've participated in today, I'm familiar enough with all the patients that you can go without even having to sign out. Just tell me which labs still have to be checked on." I shoved her list into my back pocket and began to gently massage her shoulders. "Besides, you'll be back here in less than fifteen hours. I think I can hold down the fort until then. Don't tell me you've begun to doubt Fred Astaire's ability to multitask. I dance, I sing, and I do differential calculus in my head. Don't think for a minute that I'm not capable of singlehandedly taking care of twenty sick children." I smiled and laughed softly. "Well, you can doubt it, but that shouldn't prevent you from going home. Besides, by tomorrow morning you'll be back to bail me out, and you're a way better dancer than Ginger Rogers. No way, this late in the game, is our Oscar in jeopardy. We've got it in the bag."

My ministrations on her shoulders began to relax her, and for a second I thought Diane had fallen asleep. When she spoke, it came out in a voice ridden with fatigue. "Okay, you win. I'm out of here. I'm fried. At this stage, trying to think is little more than an exercise in futility anyway. You just have to do me one more favor."

"What's that?"

"Help me out of this chair. Now that I've come to a complete standstill, I'm not sure I can get up."

I pulled her to her feet and gently pushed her down the corridor. "Go home, get something to eat, take a hot bath, and go right to bed." As I watched her walk, I realized she was a little unsteady on her feet. "On second thought, better make that a quick shower. I don't want you drowning in the tub."

"Don't worry. I'll only stay under long enough to ensure that I remain unconscious for a day or two. I could use a few days off."

"At the risk of sounding selfish, I'll kill you if you drown. No way I'm gonna try to hold this place together flying solo. Astaire's best performances were dancing as a duo. Don't even think of abandoning me."

Diane waved over her shoulder without turning around. "If I'm not here by six thirty tomorrow morning, call 911. I'll bring you a cappuccino."

Her comment stopped me in my tracks and prompted a huge smile to cross my face. "Better be sure it's a good one. When it comes to cappuccino, I've recently been kind of spoiled."

She turned briefly, gave me a confused glance, then shrugged and continued walking without saying anything. She was clearly too tired to try to read anything into my parting comment.

As soon as she had disappeared down the corridor, I returned to the nurses' station and pulled the list of patients out of my pocket. In the margin, I made a list of the tasks still to be completed. As none of them were critical, I decided to try to locate Christopher's oncologist before I went to visit him. In the event his parents asked me any questions, I wanted to be sure I clearly understood his current clinical status as well the rationale for pushing up the day of his surgery.

Dr. Herbert was in her office with the door open, but I still knocked gently before entering. "Hey, Dr. H., you have a second?"

She looked up from her computer screen and motioned me in. "Sure, Zack, just trying to complete the paperwork for a grant application. I could use a break. Have a seat." She pointed to a pair of the chairs on the other side of her desk but quickly stood when she realized they were piled with stacks of journals. "Damn, hold on one second." She started toward the piles, then, with a frustrated expression, just waved her hand in defeat. "Tell you what; just push those onto the floor. With this grant proposal due next week, all my good intentions of organizing them have flown right out the window. As a matter of fact, if I were more of a realist, I'd tell you to just drop that stack in the garbage can. Those are the more obscure journals; I probably won't have a chance to read them anyway."

I picked the whole pile up, held it briefly over the garbage can, then smiled, shook my head, and stacked them neatly on the corner of her credenza. "I'd love to help you out here. Really, I would. But if I were the one to throw them away, then I would be responsible. I couldn't live with myself if my impulsiveness resulted in you failing to see some innovative new therapy that could change the course of cancer treatment as we know it." I laughed and sat down on the seat of the chair I had just cleared.

"Curses. Now I'll feel even more guilty if I don't read them." She started chuckling softly. "All right for you, Zack. You had your chance to do the right thing. Just don't blame me if for some unknown reason you're dropped from the program. I hear McDonald's is hiring. I'll put in a good word for you. They're always looking for people to staff their drive-up window."

She returned to her chair, sat down, and folded her hands on the desk in front of her. "After the day I've had, it feels good to laugh. Now, what can I do for you?"

"I came down to ask about Christopher. What's going on with him? I didn't think he was going to surgery until next week. Why was his operation moved up? I guess I'm just feeling a little out of the loop and was hoping you could bring me up to speed."

Dr. Herbert's features immediately softened, and she looked genuinely shaken. "Christopher isn't progressing nearly as well as we had hoped. Despite aggressive chemotherapy, there is little evidence his tumor is responding, and on his recent MRI, the metastases in his liver appear unchanged. At this juncture, the size of the primary tumor in his abdomen is forcing our hand. It has begun to compress both his spine and his left kidney. His kidney is being compromised, and the upcoming chemo is going to be even more difficult to tolerate. We're hoping that by removing the tumor now, we'll be able to preserve adequate kidney function for as long as possible. There are no great alternatives. He's got an awful disease."

As I listened to her explanation, I felt my stomach tighten. The blood rushed out of my head and I felt dizzy. The only thing I could think of was how embarrassing it would be to pass out in front of her. I leaned forward with my elbows on my knees and rested my head in my hands. I hoped I was giving the impression of just looking pensive, but truthfully, I was trying not to throw up. I took a few deep breaths and mercifully was able to steady my breathing. I willed my eyes to focus. "Sounds like the prognosis is worse than we originally assumed."

"A stage-four neuroblastoma never carries a great prognosis, but we had hoped he would respond more favorably to this new chemotherapy regimen. Remember our conversation when he was initially diagnosed? I told you the three aspects of his condition that were particularly worrisome were the tumor size, the presence of metastases in his liver and lymph nodes, and that the genetic markers from the biopsy showed it was a particularly aggressive cancer. We knew from the get-go that it would be an uphill climb. We were just hoping to be able to make that climb without any mishaps. Unfortunately, the results of the MRI indicate we've taken a bit of a stumble." She was speaking very analytically, but I recognized the emotion in her voice. "We have by no means given up. We've just decided to treat fire with fire; we're going to deal with an aggressive disease more aggressively. In addition, if push comes to shove, I'm not above using my secret weapon." She smiled weakly. "I'll keep my fingers crossed." She shrugged almost imperceptibly. "A little superstition couldn't hurt, and never underestimate the power of positive thinking."

I shook my head dejectedly. "I've got to say, that categorically sucks." I looked up quickly and immediately apologized. "Sorry, Dr. H. I didn't intend to be disrespectful."

"That's okay, Zack. I couldn't have said it better myself. The important thing is to support Christopher and his family as much as possible. This situation is more than any family should have to endure.

Medical technology makes important advances every day. The trouble is that it sometimes doesn't make them as fast as we need them." She began to organize the papers on her desk. "We can't get discouraged, though. There are children alive today who ten years ago we would have held little hope for." She sat up straighter and her voice became more resolute. "Day by day, case by case, child by child, we press onward. And ten years from now, when we look back at where we currently are, struggling against seemingly impossible odds, we pray we'll have had more successes than losses." She looked at me intently. "And I believe we will." She waved her hand around the room. "If I didn't believe that, I'd just pack all this up and head home."

I stared at the floor in front of me. "I believe that too." My voice was not nearly as confident as I would have liked. I glanced up to see that her gaze had never left me. "I mean, I kind of have to. Working to become a pediatrician would be senseless if I didn't truly believe my efforts would ultimately result in making a positive difference in children's lives. It's just that I never imagined that process could be so difficult. Though my contributions as a resident are insignificant, I'm nonetheless participating in the evolution of medical science. And as a participant, I experience it." I brought my hands to my chest. "I feel the victories and the failures. It's just that in this case, a failure means having to watch a precious little kid die." I stared back down at the floor. "It just sometimes makes me wonder if participating is really worth it."

Dr. Herbert stood up, walked around her desk, and knelt down in front of me. She gently laid one of her hands over mine. "We all wonder sometimes. But just imagine. Imagine a day in the future when a little boy like Christopher flies into the hospital wearing an identical red cape." She smiled warmly. "Imagine that he too has a serious malignancy. And imagine that, because of our caring and perseverance, he's eventually able to fly home—healthy and disease-free." Her voice took on a bit of a lilt. "Ready to once again bring dastardly villains to justice. On that day, you will know it was worth it."

I looked up into her caring and compassionate eyes. "Any tricks as to how to get from today to that day in the future without totally combusting?"

She patted my hand once more and stood. "Absolutely, Zack. Never quit caring. You have to remind yourself that Christopher was sick when he came to us. His disease is not our fault. If he dies…." Her voice became more solemn. "And I'm still not saying that's a certainty. But if he dies, he will die in the care of someone who has grown to love him. Under those circumstances, even if his death is inevitable, it's easier. Easier for him and his family." She dropped a hand to my shoulder. "That's still a success, Zack. Not nearly as sweet, but a success nonetheless." She walked back around her desk. "Appreciate the power of caring. That's the trick, Zack. That's what will get you through the day. And sometimes," she said as she looked at me over her shoulder, "it's all we've got."

I stood up and began making my way toward the door. "Thanks, Dr. H. I really appreciate your time." Before clearing the threshold, I turned back and smiled at her. "And may I go on record right now as saying that I think you should get a raise? I'm not sure how much they're paying you, but whatever it is, you deserve more. Being a good oncologist? Five grand a month. Being an awesome person? Priceless." I waved at her as I left. "I'll put it in a memo, and I'll take it right to the top. You'll be living the *vida loca* within a week."

I heard her call after me. "Forget the *vida loca.* Just tell them I need new tires on my Toyota."

I slowly made my way back to the pediatric ward. Though I understood the importance of going to check on Christopher, I genuinely felt like I'd had the wind kicked out of me. I wasn't sure how I would be able to appear in his room and manage to look upbeat. I sat down in front of the computer at the desk behind the nurses' station in order to review his recent labs. As despondent as I felt, I still had to ensure there were no irregularities that would jeopardize his being able to go to the operating room. I scanned down the columns of values. I saw a number of significant abnormalities but most were the expected consequence of the chemotherapy. I did, however, notice that his potassium was trending dangerously low and made changes to his IV fluids to correct it. That done, I dragged myself out of the chair and headed toward his room. The burden of my concern for him felt like a six-ton weight teetering precariously on my shoulders; threatening any second to crush me like a bug.

I was standing just outside the door of his room when I remembered something. Weeks before, I had asked Juan, the supervisor in charge of ordering supplies, if he could put in a requisition for a child-size Superman hospital gown. One day on call, I had gone to the charge nurse's office to speak with her. While I was waiting, I happened to see a hospital supply magazine sitting on a stack of charts. I was thumbing through it when I came upon the picture of the gown and immediately decided it would be perfect to boost Christopher's spirits. I tore the page out and presented it to the supervisor the next day. He said we had an account with the vendor and he would see what he could do. Before I knocked on Christopher's door, I did an about-face and headed to the supervisor's office. I was certain Christopher would be a little less apprehensive about his surgery if he went into the operating room as Superman.

I approached Juan's office and saw him sitting at his desk, so I rapped the side of the door as I walked in. "Hey, Juan! Has the Ferrari I ordered come in yet?"

Juan looked up and smiled. "Yeah, it came in, but there was a small glitch. It was delivered to my garage by mistake." His smile broadened. "I've been intending to try to get it to you, but every time I begin the trip over to your house, I get disoriented driving up the coast with the top down. I end up having to just drive back home. Sorry, I'll have it to you in no less than three months or whenever the insurance premium is due. Whichever comes first."

"Really? You get disoriented driving up Pacific Coast Highway on the way to my house? I can see where that could be a problem, given that Pacific Coast Highway is no fewer than ten miles away and I live just three blocks from here. Before you return the car to me, better get the navigation system checked out. Better yet, why don't you just send the whole thing back? Who wants a $400,000 car if it can't even get you where you need to go?"

"I was thinking the same thing. Besides, the administration is getting so picky. Questioning every million-dollar purchase from the discretionary fund like it's not going to improve patient care. Very irritating!" He stapled a stack of papers together. "Now that we've settled that issue, is there anything else I can help you with?"

"Please. Listen, I know it's not your top priority, but were you able to make any headway on ordering that Superman gown? The kid who I wanted it for is not doing great and is scheduled for surgery tomorrow. If you were able to get it, this would probably be the best time to give it to him."

"That's right. I'd forgotten about that. Let me check." He turned his attention to the computer screen. "After I spoke to you, I did include it in my next order. There were a bunch of things the hospital needed from that vendor, so one more gown was an easy addition. Let me check." He clicked a few more buttons on the keyboard, and a copy of the invoice appeared on the monitor. "Yep. It's recorded as having coming in. Should be down in Central Supply. Item number 15-748-VM. I'll call down and have someone pull it for you. If you wait five minutes before walking down, it should be waiting for you."

"Thanks a lot, Juan." I smiled. "I don't care what everyone else says about you, you are a damn nice guy." I headed out of the room. "I owe you."

His laughter carried across his desk. "Wait! What is everyone else saying? Someone says something unflattering about me, you let me know. See if they get to ride in the Ferrari!"

A few minutes later, with the package from Central Supply tucked securely under my arm, I slowly opened the door to Christopher's room. He lay in bed watching television, but his eyes weren't focused on the screen. Yogi was peeking out from under the sheet next to him. His parents were sitting in chairs on the other side of his bed. They both looked like they'd been to hell and back. Their faces were gaunt, their clothes were wrinkled, and his dad's hair was in complete disarray. His mom, for her part, had at least combed her hair and had applied some makeup, but it did little to conceal the fatigue and worry on her face. Christopher slowly turned his head away from the screen and looked at me when he heard me approach.

I tried to push some animation into my voice. "Hey, champ. I missed seeing you over the weekend. Did you and Yogi catch any bad guys while I was away?" I saw a subtle flicker in his eyes, but it endured for less than a second. His eyes were significantly more yellow than they had been just a few days ago, and his reaction to seeing me failed to reach his lips. He couldn't muster even the slightest smile.

I nodded to his parents, then went over to sit down next to Christopher on the edge of his bed. I pulled the bedspread up and tucked him and Yogi tightly under it, then I ran my fingers across his forehead. "I hear you're going to have a big day tomorrow. What do you two have planned?"

His voice was soft and defeated. "They're going to give me an operation tomorrow, but I don't want it." His eyes brightened but almost imperceptibly. "Would you tell them, Dr. Zack? Would you tell them I don't want them to give me an operation?" He looked pleadingly at me, probably hoping to have found an ally. My lip quivered slightly, but I was able to maintain a smile. I looked over at his parents, but they avoided my eyes. This was a conversation they themselves had probably already had with Christopher no fewer than one hundred times. Despite having racked my brain, I hadn't come up with an explanation that would result in Christopher feeling anything other than dread about the pending surgery.

I looked back at Christopher and tried to look confident. "Look, champ. I know you're scared, but you're forgetting—you're the man of steel. A little operation will barely slow you down. If bullets bounce off your chest, I doubt you'll even feel something as small as an operation."

Christopher looked soulfully into my eyes, his expression wiser than should ever be seen on the face of a five-year-old. "Yeah, but I'm not really Superman. I'm just a little boy."

I leaned into him and hugged him. "Yes, but remember, there was a period, a long, long time ago when Superman was just a little boy too. And if he were going to have an operation, he would also have been scared. He wasn't grown up enough to understand that when you're made of steel, even if you're just a little boy, you can't get hurt." I pulled back so I could look at him. "That's what I came in to remind you. Even though you're just a little boy, you're still made of steel and you're invincible. You'll fly through tomorrow's operation. No problem. In fact," I said as I lifted the gown off the foot of the bed, "the real Superman left you this to wear tomorrow. Now everyone who sees you will know how strong you are, and most importantly, you'll remember yourself."

Christopher's eyes brightened unmistakably when he saw me hold up the gown. "Did Superman really leave that for me?"

I looked back at him as if his question was ludicrous. "Of course. He was going to give you a suit just like the one he wears, but he knew all little boys in the hospital have to wear a gown. So he made this one especially for you. It's made like every other hospital gown except"—I pointed to the insignia on the front—"it's got Superman's special 'S' and is red and blue. Who, besides Superman, would have a special hospital gown? They don't sell these things, you know. Bet you've never seen anyone else wearing one." I looked at him inquiringly. "Have you?" Christopher shook his head. "See, I knew it. This is the only one on the planet. Superman left it specifically for you." I looked at Christopher intently. "He wanted to remind you that you're made of steel and you'll do just fine tomorrow." I ran my fingers across Christopher's head. All his hair had long since fallen out because of the chemo. His head was as smooth as a bowling ball. "You don't doubt Superman, do you?"

Christopher shook his head again. I couldn't guarantee he was fully convinced, but his expression looked significantly more confident than it had before. I spoke softly but with great certainty. "And remember, I'll be with you the whole time."

His eyes widened. "You will?"

"Of course. You're my main man. You didn't think I'd let you go in there alone, did you?"

Christopher looked extremely relieved. "Can Yogi come to?"

"Absolutely. The three of us are a team. Nothing is going to break us up."

I punched him gently on the chin, then drew my hand back with my palm up. "Now give me five." He gave my hand a weak slap. "I've got some more work to do, but I'll be back to check on you. In the meantime, I want you to change into your new gown. People gotta know who they're dealing with. You might not be the man of steel, but you're the boy of steel, for sure."

As I stood, I looked over again at his parents. They still looked like they had been hit by a truck, but were visibly less tense. Christopher's father walked over and shook my hand. "Thanks, Dr. Sheldon. This has been a long haul. We appreciate having you in our corner. You're great with Christopher. All the doctors have been exceptional, but we're not sure how we would have made it this far without you."

"It's been my pleasure. Christopher is a great kid. I'm pretty sure he inspires me way more than I inspire him." I punched his dad softly on the arm. "He must have good parents. Doesn't work any other way." I smiled, but my voice was still thick with emotion. "I'll see you guys later tonight. Big day tomorrow."

As I walked out of the room, Dr. Herbert's words rang in my ear. *Being under the care of someone who loves him makes a difference.* It still didn't feel like a success, but I hoped I was nonetheless making a difference. Christopher so deserved a break.

I was able to finish the rest of my work pretty efficiently and double-checked to make sure the things that Diane had been unable to complete were wrapped up as well. I knew she was depending on me, and I didn't want to risk disappointing her. One of the foundations of our relationship was trust. It was important that we both believed we had the other's back and when one of us was exhausted, we could depend on the other to complete our unfinished work with the same commitment to doing a good job.

I pulled the list of patients out of my pocket to look it over one last time. As I checked the final item off as being completed, I reflected on our relationship. Though we worked almost exclusively as colleagues and seldom saw one another outside of the hospital, I realized what an important part of my life Diane had become. For a brief instant, I felt a tinge of embarrassment. It seemed almost ridiculous that we had become such good friends, and yet I continued to feel disinclined to tell her about Sergio. I was coming to the point in my life when still being closeted didn't even make sense to me.

In that moment, however, rather than wrestling with the question, I did what I was accustomed to doing: I pushed it out of my head and justified doing so by rationalizing that there was still work to be done. It wasn't the most mature solution, but at least it was productive.

I received a page to go down to the emergency room, and by the time I completed evaluating the child and getting her admitted, it was late. I quietly stuck my head into Christopher's room and saw him sleeping peacefully. The Superman emblem was clearly visible on the gown that covered his chest. His mom was stretched out on the foldout bed in the corner of the room, staring at the pages of a book. A small handheld light illuminated the print, but I was pretty sure she wasn't reading. Instead, she was using the words to distract her from having to think.

I walked over to the edge of the bed and adjusted one of Christopher's pillows. After assuring myself that he was comfortable, I whispered quietly to his mom. "Can I get you anything? You should try to get some sleep too. You both have a big day tomorrow."

She shrugged, looking disheartened. "I don't think I've slept since we've been here." She stood up and went over to the other side of Christopher's bed. She ran her hand lovingly over his soft scalp. "Besides, I like to watch him sleep. He's so peaceful when he's sleeping. It's the only time he gets a break from the procedures, the worry, and the pain." She stroked his head without looking up. "It's not good, is it, Dr. Sheldon?"

My voice caught in my throat. Involuntarily, I dropped my hand to gently cradle Christopher's fingers. "Truthfully, it's more serious than we would have liked, but that doesn't mean we're not still in this fight. You've got a whole team behind you, and this isn't the first time they've come up against something serious. Dr. Herbert is a brilliant oncologist, and she still believes we're in this fight to win. We're optimistic that one day we'll look back on this as having only been a setback." I continued to lightly rub his fingers in the palm of my hand. "This isn't where we'd like to be, but this is where we find ourselves, and we all believe Christopher is too precious to give any less than our very best. Even if that means fighting an uphill battle."

When I looked up, I saw tears pouring down her face. "I'm willing to fight to the ends of the earth," she said. "I just wish he didn't have to."

"You're his mom. It's your job to worry. But don't underestimate how tough this guy is." I tried to smile encouragingly. "After all, he's the man of steel."

She wiped the tears with the back of her hand. "I'm trying to see things that way, but when I look into this bed, all I see is my little boy, innocent and in danger." A flood of tears escaped her eyes. "I'm his mom! My job is not just to worry; my job is to protect him." She was now sobbing uncontrollably. Her voice came out in a choked whisper. "And I can't, I can't protect him. What kind of mother can't protect her precious son?"

I released Christopher's hand, walked to the other side of the bed, and drew her into my arms. "Of course you're protecting him. You've never left his side. No one could be a better mother than you have been. That's what makes cancer such a horrible disease. It can get past impenetrable barriers. When it attacks, no one is safe from its devastation." I pulled her more tightly into my embrace. "You can doubt anything you want. You can doubt us, you can doubt modern medicine, you can even doubt God himself, but what you can't doubt is yourself. There is nothing that you could have done to protect him from this." I pushed her away and held her shoulders so she had to look at me. "You have to believe that. If being an incredibly loving, nurturing mother could prevent illness, Christopher would be the healthiest child on the planet. No one is powerful enough to protect someone they love from cancer. You certainly can't expect yourself to accomplish something impossible."

She slowly began to compose herself. She reached for the box of Kleenex on the bedside table, wiped the tears off her cheeks, and then began to blot her eyes. "Thanks, Dr. Sheldon. I'm so sorry. I usually do a better job keeping a stiff upper lip. It's just that I've been feeling so overwhelmed lately. Every day I keep hoping for even the slightest bit of good news, but every day things just keep getting worse." She looked down at Christopher sleeping in the bed. "He seems to be getting closer and closer to the edge, and I worry that if he gets much closer, I won't be able to pull him back."

"Please don't apologize to me. I can't think of anything scarier than feeling like you're unable to prevent your child from falling. Feeling powerless is one of the worst feelings imaginable. You have to remember, though, you're not in this alone. Our part is to do everything humanly and medically possible to succeed in beating this. Your part is to hold his hand every step of the way. It's not a guarantee that he'll maintain sure footing, but with you by his side, he'll feel like he can. And that's what's most important. Being in danger is not particularly frightening to a child if he feels like he's protected. Try not to dwell on what you're incapable of doing and focus instead on what you are doing. You're loving him, you're encouraging him, and you're making him feel safe despite the fact that the danger he's facing is truly overwhelming. You do that, and I'll give you a guarantee." I again wrapped my arm around her shoulder. "As a mom, you're doing everything possible. I'd much prefer to be able to guarantee a cure, but I can't. What I can guarantee, however, is that you've never failed him. Not even for a second. I know that given what we're facing tomorrow, that's little consolation, but, really, to him it's everything."

Her tears began to dry, and she brought the Kleenex up to her face to wipe her nose. "I guess I have no choice. If that's all we've got, then I have to take it." She again looked at Christopher. "It just seems so little. I wish I could take this all away from him." She turned back toward me and said in an almost inaudible whisper, "I wish it were me."

"That's yet another indication that there's nothing you wouldn't do for him; another example of how you love him unconditionally. Really," I said, squeezing her shoulder a little tighter, "you're just proving my original point. If the power of love could have prevented him from getting cancer, he would never have suffered so much as a sneeze. I don't expect you to see this now, but he really is lucky to have you."

She was quiet for a minute, then, without looking at me, she said softly, "We can't thank you enough. You've been great with him. He'll do things for you that he won't do for anyone else." A subtle panic suddenly worked its way into her voice. "Are you really going to be with him tomorrow?"

"You kidding? Not even someone stronger than a locomotive could keep me away. I've already spoken with the charge nurse. Neither Yogi nor I will leave his side until he's completely asleep. Then, Yogi will have to make an exit, but I'll be with him the whole time. They don't let me touch a scalpel, so I'll be there mostly for moral support, but I'll be there."

She leaned against me. "It doesn't matter to me that you won't be doing the actual cutting. I'll just feel better knowing you're there."

Though I only had one additional admission for the entire night, I still couldn't relax. I paced the halls, read everything I could about neuroblastoma and new clinical trials, and I did about three hundred push-ups next to the bed in the call room. Nothing succeeded in helping me to relax. Finally, when I saw the sun beginning to break through the window, it became apparent that the opportunity to sleep had passed. I grabbed a clean pair of scrubs and my toiletry kit and headed to the shower. I had accomplished nothing other than spending the whole night worrying. Maybe a blast of cold water would succeed in jump-starting my brain.

CHAPTER 16

AS PROMISED, Diane showed up at six thirty—hair combed, makeup reapplied, cappuccino in hand. She took one look at me, however, and her face dropped. "Now who's the one who looks like shit? Did you think that a shower would disguise those bloodshot eyes? Don't tell me we got another dozen admissions?" She pushed the cup of steaming liquid into my hand. "If this doesn't succeed in spoiling you, nothing will. I made a special trip by DeAngelo's Coffee on Melrose. They boast that all their coffee is brewed using an authentic Italian process. Seemed like a pretty good bet that this would supercharge your taste buds."

Despite having had a horrible night, her comment made me smile so broadly I almost burned my tongue taking the first sip. I looked at her, and I knew that, though bloodshot, my eyes were sparkling over the brim of the cup. "You nailed that one. I've recently become a connoisseur of all things Italian, and you're right: they do supercharge my taste buds… and more."

She let my comment hang in the air a moment and seemed to consider digging a little deeper, but perhaps was too distracted by my sleep-deprived appearance and the apprehensions she had about how much work was ahead of us. "So what happened? Did we get killed again last night? If you got more than eight admissions, we'll have to close the ward until we have a few discharges. We must be filled to capacity. Do we even have any empty beds?"

I let her stew a minute longer, then couldn't stand it anymore. I didn't want her to self-combust before the day even began. "Last night wasn't so bad. We only got two admissions, and I was able to finish all the work you signed out to me. I'm just tired because I fell victim to a major episode of insomnia last night. I couldn't close my eyes."

I could see Diane's intuition kick in; she immediately understood. "You're worried about Christopher, aren't you? I should have realized. If I had, I would have brought you a double."

I bumped her shoulder with mine. "You're already a star just for having gone out of your way to bring me this." I raised my cup. "Thanks." I took another sip, centered my resolve, then looked at Diane with renewed determination. "We still have to get to work, though. Between the two of us, there are twenty-eight patients on our service, and I want to make sure they're all tucked in before two this afternoon. That's when Christopher goes to surgery, and I promised him I'd be there."

Diane smiled at me warmly. "Come on, Zack, you'll be there whether your work's done or not. Have you forgotten who your wingman is? Or, in this case, your wingwoman? You'll be in that operating room even if a bomb goes off out here. Besides," she said with a smile, "doesn't Peggy follow you on call? You know how willing she is to help out in a pinch." She looked momentarily perplexed. "Oh, wait, I'm confused. We're talking about Peggy. She's the one whose panties always leave her in a pinch. Oh well, you still have one solid person on your wing. I'll get you there come hell or high water."

I threw my arm around her shoulder as we walked back toward the nurses' station. "Well, comrade, let's have at it, then. The enemy awaits."

"Who's doing the surgery, anyway?"

"Dr. Alfredo, the pediatric surgeon, is primary, which is a huge consolation because he's brilliant, a great technician, and a nice guy to boot. He'll be assisted by one of the surgeons who mostly works with adults. I heard it's going to be Dr. Klein." I made a sour face. "That's always a pleasant experience."

Diane laughed. "Oh yeah. He's a prince." She came to a standstill, brought her fist to her chin, and feigned looking pensive. "Let's see, spend an hour in the operating room with Dr. Klein or stick needles in my eyes? Hmm. That's a tough call. I'd have to ponder that one." She laughed again, and we kept walking. "You're convinced you want to be in there with him?"

I smiled but rolled my eyes. "I'm doing this for Christopher. But have the needles ready, just in case. I might change my mind."

Thankfully, the morning went by without incident. All the patients were responding reasonably well to their therapies, and there were no unanticipated surprises. Diane was at my side at least every hour asking what she could do to help me finish up. Despite still being dead tired, I somehow managed to keep working relatively efficiently. That was one of the advantages to stress: the adrenaline worked as a stimulant.

By one thirty, I had managed to eat a plain bagel and drink another cup of coffee and was making my way to Christopher's room. When I arrived, the transport attendants were already loading him onto a gurney. His parents stood vigilantly by his side, voicing words of encouragement to their son but clinging to one another for dear life. Yogi was tucked in next to Christopher on the gurney as well. I laughed silently when I saw that Yogi was wearing a red cape too. I looked over at his mom and gave her a thumbs-up. Then I stood over Christopher and ran my hand over his head. "Looks like my favorite team of superheroes is ready for a ride." I then directed my comments to the attendants. "Guess I'd better warn you guys. These two travel at the speed of light. You'd better hold on tight."

One of the attendants, who I recognized and knew had a reputation for being good with kids, jumped immediately at the prompting. "That's what I've heard. I can't believe how lucky I am to be able to take a ride with Superman. Now I don't have to be the least afraid of running into any bad guys. Anyone gives us any trouble," he said, as he touched Christopher lightly on the arm, "they're toast! Thanks for keeping the hospital safe, Superman."

Despite feeling completely demolished by the chemo and his failing liver, Christopher somehow managed to produce a small smile. "You're welcome, but Yogi helps too."

The attendant continued. "I guessed that the minute I saw his cape. Now I feel doubly safe. Let's roll. Bad guys be warned: Superman and Yogi are headed your way."

Christopher's voice was so soft it almost couldn't be heard. "When he's wearing the cape, his name is Superbear."

We stopped briefly in the holding area, and those of us who were continuing into the operating room donned surgical caps and shoe covers. Both his parents leaned over Christopher and covered him with kisses. They each held a hand, and his dad spoke to him gently. "You don't worry about a thing. We're going to be waiting right here the entire time. You're just going to take a little nap, and before you know it, you'll wake up and be right back in your room."

Christopher stared back at them and asked earnestly, "Can't one of you come with me?"

His parents looked at each other, but because his mom couldn't trust herself to answer without sobbing, his dad again spoke up. "We want to, son, but the doctors said the room is super tiny. There just wouldn't be enough space for all of us. And besides, Dr. Zack and Yogi are going to be there with you. They promised to help take care of you and report back the minute the other doctors are finished with you. Besides, we'll use the time to help prepare a special surprise that will be waiting for you the second you wake up." I knew that Christopher's dad was scrambling to think of an explanation that would make their absence in the operating room acceptable to him, but what he said seemed to work. Christopher's expression visibly relaxed.

"Is Dr. Zack going to be there too?"

I moved over, gently took Christopher's hand out of his mother's clutch, and squeezed it. "The whole time. What did I say about the three of us being a team? I'm not going to leave your side for a second, and Yogi is going to be guarding you even more carefully than me. We've got you covered, champ." I looked up at the clock, noted the time, and also observed that the attendants were eager to get him into the room. "You ready?"

His voice was unconvinced but firm. "I guess so."

Christopher's parents gave him a few dozen more kisses, then hesitantly relinquished their hold on the gurney. When they were sure Christopher could no longer see their faces, tears began to cascade freely. As we pushed him toward the door of the operating room, I looked over my shoulder one last time. They stood arm and arm, waving as their son was wheeled away from them. It was fortunate they had one another to lean on, because I was certain neither of them could have stood independently. Looking at them made me realize I now truly understood what it meant to be brokenhearted.

We were within a few feet of the operating room when we were met by one of the nurses assigned to the case. She had a cheerful demeanor but was all business. "Good afternoon. You must be Christopher. I'm Maggie, and I'm going to be the nurse taking care of you. Guess today is my lucky day. They didn't tell me I was going to be taking care of Superman." She let her eyes take a survey of the gurney. "Oh dear, it looks like we have one too many passengers. Mr. Bear is going to have to disembark here." She reached over to pull Yogi out of Christopher's arms, but I gently blocked her hand.

"Excuse me. I'm Dr. Sheldon. Might I have a quick word with you a little out of supersonic hearing range?"

She looked indignant but followed me a few yards down the corridor anyway.

"Thanks, Maggie. Listen, I know that having his teddy bear with him breaks standard protocols, but he'll only be holding it until the anesthesiologist starts to put him to sleep. The minute he's out, I'll personally take responsibility for being sure the bear is completely out of the room." I found it difficult to keep the emotion completely out of my voice. "The past month has been really rough on this little guy, and having his bear with him is a huge asset in helping him to cope."

Maggie looked sympathetic but was completely unmoved. "I'm sorry, Doctor. I'm sure he's really attached to that bear, but an operating room is a sterile environment, and the bear is restricted from entering it. I'm sure you understand that I can't make exceptions."

I tried to suppress my anger but the culmination of sleep deprivation and cumulative worry made it exceedingly difficult. "I'm sorry too, Maggie, but I'm his doctor, and I'm saying that we are going to make an exception. One look at them, and it's clearly evident that the little boy is no more sterile than the bear is. They're inseparable. Taking the bear out of his arms now, before they even start the surgical prep, is not only medically unnecessary, but at this stage would be traumatic for him. I'm sure you can appreciate my position."

She folded her arms across her chest. "I don't care whose doctor you are. No one is above policy. It's out of my hands."

I stared at her and miraculously refrained from yelling. "It surprises me that someone with so little compassion ever decides to go into medicine." I looked at her smugly. "You're right about one thing, though. It is out of your hands. I've already confirmed it with Louise Whiting, the executive nurse who oversees the entire division of surgery. She assured me that as long as the teddy bear was removed from the room before any of the sterile drapes were placed, there would be absolutely no problem. Now, we can either conduct ourselves as feeling human beings and proceed with trying to save this little boy's life, or you can make the call to your supervisor and get confirmation that what I've been trying to tell you is accurate."

She pursed her lips but walked away without any additional argument. She turned to a guy whose name tag said Moses and stomped toward the door. "I'll alert anesthesia that we're ready to proceed."

Moses was getting ready to scrub in preparation for assisting with the surgery. Because the sink was near where Maggie and I had been speaking, he'd overheard our entire conversation. As I walked near him, he offered me a bright smile but kept his voice a whisper. "Way to go, Dr. Sheldon. I've been a scrub nurse at this hospital for eight years and am intimately familiar with surgical protocol. There is absolutely no risk in having that teddy bear in there prior to hanging the drapes and opening the sterile packs of instruments. Thanks for standing up for him." He glanced over his shoulder to look at Christopher lying on the gurney. "People can get so caught up in following rules they forget we're here to tend to the needs of the patient. Looks like that little guy could use a break."

I smiled back. "Thanks, Moses. I appreciate the support, and you're absolutely correct. No one deserves a little extra consideration and caring more than a five-year-old who's already been through hell. It's the least we can do."

At that point, Maggie came back, followed closely by Dr. Zoryan, the pediatric anesthesiologist. He approached the gurney and smiled warmly at Christopher. "Hey, little man, I'm Dr. Z, and I'm the guy lucky enough to be able to help take care of you while you're down here dreaming. I can't tell you how happy I am to be able to meet you. When Dr. Sheldon told me that he was going to be bringing the man of steel and Superbear down, I didn't believe him, but sure enough, both of you are here. How are you feeling?"

Christopher clutched Yogi even tighter. His voice was so tentative Dr. Zoryan had to lean in to hear him. "I'm scared."

Dr. Zoryan ran his hand gently over Christopher's head. "There's nothing for you to worry about. All you have to do is to count to five. The rest is up to me. Can you do that?"

Christopher looked a little skeptical. "That's all I have to do?"

"Yep. And if you'd like, Superbear can count with you. It will take me just a second to"—he looked at me and shrugged—"get the anti-kryptonite medicine ready." He smiled. "But in the meantime, you're probably going to start feeling a little bit sleepy." He injected a sedative into the tubing of Christopher's IV. "I'll tell you when to start counting."

Maggie and the transport technician pushed the gurney into the actual surgical suite, and all three of us moved Christopher effortlessly from it onto the operating table. The technician wheeled the gurney out of the room, and Maggie placed monitor leads on Christopher's chest, then covered him with a warm blanket. Dr. Zoryan secured his own surgical mask, sat down at the head of the operating table, brought a mask up near Christopher's face, and adjusted some dials attached to the tubes leading to the tanks of anesthetic gas. Christopher was already almost asleep. He gently placed the mask over Christopher's face and nose and quietly whispered, "Okay, Superman, you and Superbear can start counting."

"One." Christopher was out. Within seconds, Dr. Zoryan removed the mask, intubated Christopher quickly, made a few more adjustments to the dials, then taped the endotracheal tube into place.

Without looking away from the myriad of monitors he said, "Okay, team, it's showtime. Everyone make this their best performance."

In one smooth motion, I pulled Yogi out of Christopher's embrace, carried him out of the room and put him on the gurney Christopher had been wheeled down on. It took incredible restraint not to give Maggie a smug smirk, but now the priority was Christopher. She moved in and began to apply surgical antiseptic to Christopher's side, and Moses unwrapped the surgical instruments and began to organize them on the tray.

At that moment, Dr. Alfredo came in, followed closely by Dr. Klein and Justin, a surgical resident I recognized as being one of the second years. Dr. Alfredo offered everyone a warm greeting and thanked them for their participation. Dr. Klein, on the other hand, eyed me suspiciously. "Dr. Sheldon. I didn't anticipate having nonsurgical staff in attendance. To what do we owe this dubious honor?" His voice was thick with sarcasm.

Before I had an opportunity to answer, Dr. Alfredo came to my rescue. "Zack is here as my guest. He has been following this patient since the time of admission. I thought it would be very educational for him to observe this operation. He and his team have been trying diligently to eradicate this tumor. He should be able to see firsthand what it looks like. Besides, I admire how committed he is to participating in the overall care of his patients."

Without really acknowledging Dr. Klein, I gave Dr. Alfredo an appreciative nod.

For his part, Dr. Klein gave no indication of being either convinced or impressed, but he didn't argue. Instead, he shrugged a little disdainfully. "Fair enough. At the very least, having an exposure to medicine practiced in its unadulterated form may be beneficial. Without question, surgery is the purest form of the art of medicine. Frankly, I'm not even sure there's a close second." He gave me a challenging glare and raised an eyebrow, hopeful, I was sure, that I would dare to contradict him.

Instead, I averted my eyes to look at Christopher, and again, Dr. Alfredo's voice filled the uncomfortable silence with soothing benevolence. "We all do our part. In order to be propelled forward, the pistons of a car work in unison, each firing independently, but none more important than the other in achieving the ultimate goal."

Moses assisted all three surgeons in securing their surgical gowns, and Maggie opened packages of surgical gloves in the appropriate sizes and dropped them on the sterile tray. By this time, Christopher had already been covered by surgical drapes. Only an eight-inch square of skin was exposed. When Dr. Alfredo had his latex gloves stretched tightly over each of his fingers, he turned and assessed the entire team. "Are we ready to proceed?"

Dr. Klein was standing next to the operating table opposite him. "I'm sorry, Carlos," he said, addressing Dr. Alfredo. "This is going to be a long procedure, and I sprained my ankle this weekend. I think I'm going to have to sit. Go ahead and begin but," he said as he turned to Maggie, "I'm going to need a stool."

"Right away, Doctor. There's one right here in the corner." Maggie's tone was efficient and accommodating. She'd had plenty of experience working with Dr. Klein. In addition to trying to anticipate his needs, when he said jump, the requisite response was "How high?" She brought the stool over and centered it behind him. "There you are, Doctor."

Rather than acknowledge her effort, Dr. Klein spoke to Dr. Alfredo. "Okay, Carlos, you're lead on this one. I'm just here to make sure you don't make any mistakes." He chuckled under his mask.

Dr. Alfredo simply answered, "Thank you, Maggie, we all have a big job ahead of us." With that, he placed the edge of his scalpel against Christopher's skin and made a six-inch incision.

Maggie looked at the clock and spoke to Dr. Zoryan, who was writing in the surgical log. "Official start time, 2:54."

The surgery was laborious. The tumor was large and was encroaching on numerous essential nerves and blood vessels. The surgeons worked meticulously and efficiently. Conversation was limited only to the exchange of essential information. Though caustic, Dr. Klein was talented, and Dr. Alfredo had the reputation of being one of the best pediatric surgeons on the West Coast. Christopher was undoubtedly in good hands, but watching the procedure only heightened my anxiety. It was one thing to see a tumor on an MRI. It was quite another to look at it consuming the bulk of Christopher's small abdomen. My heart sank. The likelihood that he could recover from such a devastating disease seemed even more impossible.

Two hours into the operation, Maggie temporarily left the room. Moses stood next to Dr. Klein and passed instruments. The surgical resident was next to Dr. Alfredo. He was holding a suction catheter in one hand and a retractor in the other. His job was to keep the area where the surgeons were working free of blood and in clear view. I was watching from a platform eight inches off the floor. Because I was just over Dr. Alfredo's shoulder, I had an unobstructed view of the area in which they were operating. The only sound was the soft gurgle of the suction and instruments clattering on the tray. The silence was interrupted when Dr. Klein complained that he was now too far away from the table to clearly see.

In an attempt to prevent Dr. Klein from having to endure even the slightest inconvenience, Moses quickly volunteered, "Maggie just left the room, but I think I can push in your stool."

Dr. Klein briefly diverted his eyes away from the suture he was in the process of tying and looked at Moses disdainfully. "That's a proposition I never want to hear coming from someone like you." His voice was replete with contempt. "Where the hell is Maggie?"

It took everyone a second to understand the inference of his comment, and the room fell into an uncomfortable silence. Between his mask and the edge of his surgical cap, I could see Moses's forehead burn red with embarrassment. Initially, I was in a state of momentary shock, but as I recovered, I felt nauseous. A flurry of emotions overwhelmed me. Outrage, anger, self-consciousness, and fear. Once again, one of Dr. Klein's homophobic slurs had brought all my insecurities to the surface. In one respect, I was incensed that Moses would be subjected to such a demeaning comment. In another, I was hugely apprehensive that I was precariously close to being painted with the same brush. I hung my head in shame. The biggest indignity of the whole experience was my silence. Finally, probably also at a loss for an appropriate response, Dr. Alfredo interjected. "Let's all just stay focused on the patient. He deserves our full attention." Then, without looking up, he added, "And just for the record, Moses, I've always found working with you to be a pleasure. There are many children alive today who have greatly benefited from your caring and professionalism."

He withdrew a small square of gauze from the incision with a pair of tweezers, then held open his empty hand. "Mosquito forceps."

Moses put the instrument in his hand with practiced precision and echoed, "Mosquito forceps." His voice softened as he said, "And thank you."

Dr. Klein did little more than to clench his teeth. He was completely unaccustomed to being even subtly contradicted, but because he and Dr. Alfredo shared similar stature in the hospital hierarchy, he undoubtedly recognized there could potentially be consequences were he to continue his verbal assault. "Let's just see if we can wrap this up."

I too breathed a silent acknowledgment of thanks to Dr. Alfredo. I was so appreciative that he had come to Moses's defense. Always the diplomat, he probably knew he'd run the risk of having the situation escalate if he challenged Dr. Klein directly. But at the same time, he was unwilling to let such a derogatory comment pass without somehow invalidating it. At least someone in the room had the balls to speak up. I wished it had been me. In reality, though, it was impossible for me to ever imagine having the courage to stand up to a bully whose opinion of me might somehow influence my career. I felt pathetic.

Four hours after having made the initial incision, Dr. Alfredo finished closing the wound. He looked tired but optimistic. They had succeeded in removing the vast majority of the tumor, and it was in a specimen container on its way to the pathology department for more extensive study. In addition, they had been able to save Christopher's left kidney and were relatively confident its function had been mostly preserved. Finally, though the tumor had been pressing against his spine, there didn't appear to be any permanent nerve damage.

Dr. Alfredo thanked everyone individually for their exceptional efforts, starting with Dr. Klein. "Steven, you have a phenomenal set of hands. It's a real privilege to operate with you. Thank you for your help." Dr. Klein grunted an almost unintelligible response and walked out the door. When I thought about it, I admired Dr. Alfredo's ability to emphasize a person's positive attributes.

He then turned his attention to the surgical resident. "Justin, keep up the good work. You show great promise. You have the potential to be an outstanding surgeon." He smiled. "It might be a good idea for you to review which arteries in the abdomen go where, but overall, a very good job."

Justin answered. "Thanks a lot, Dr. Alfredo. I really hope to have the opportunity to do a full rotation with you. I really learned a lot from you and appreciate your teaching style. It's refreshing to be able to work on a big case and not be made to feel like an idiot." The innuendo hung in the air, but no one ventured to elaborate. Justin gave Moses an apologetic nod, then turned back to Dr. Alfredo. "Anyway, thanks again. I'm on call tonight, so I'll be checking on Christopher frequently. I'll keep you apprised of any changes in his condition."

"I'd appreciate that." Dr. Alfredo raised his voice and directed it across the room. "Moses, Maggie, as always, a stellar performance. Thank you both for your outstanding work." He then walked across the room and intentionally shook Moses's hand. "Young man, you can operate with me anytime."

Moses blushed again, but this time from welcome embarrassment. "I appreciate that, Dr. Alfredo. I consider it a real honor to work with someone who has both exemplary ability and integrity. It's a privilege. Truly, it is."

Always the gentleman, Dr. Alfredo responded, "In my experience, it's you nurses who make us surgeons look good."

Finally, Dr. Alfredo turned to me. "Zack, Christopher is going to be in the recovery room for at least five or six hours. I want to make sure that he's fully awake, that he's making good urine, and that he's able to move his legs without difficulty. Would you like to accompany me to give his parents what is, in this situation, anyway, the best possible news?" The lines on his face deepened. "While the surgery was technically a success, I wish having that tumor out significantly changed the prognosis. I'm not sure it does. It's evident from being in there that he has an extremely aggressive disease. I felt like I was watching the tumor grow even as we were trying to cut it out. Also, there's the fact that it's already spread to the liver and the lymph nodes. It's frequently humbling to witness how ineffective we are at battling Mother Nature when she chooses to show us her ugly side." He patted my shoulder. "But, for today, anyway, the parents get a little piece of good news. We accomplished what we'd hoped to, and the outcome was better than we'd anticipated. I fear most of the news they'll be getting with regard to Christopher's overall condition will be discouraging. Let's try to make today's surgery represent a bright spot, as brief as that bright spot might be."

I tried to smile, but the effort never reached my lips. "Thanks, Dr. Alfredo. I learn something from you every time I work with you. Not so much about surgery, but about compassion. And for me, anyway, I suspect that's a more important lesson."

Dr. Alfredo patted me affectionately. "I'm not so sure, Zack. I've been at this game a lot longer than you have, but I've been watching you with patients. As far as compassion goes, I feel like you're the one who has been giving me a refresher course." He started walking toward the door. "Let's go talk to his parents. Knowing exactly what to say isn't going to be easy. Straddling that line can be a real challenge. In this situation, how does a physician encourage genuine hope while at the same time not contribute to unrealistic expectations? I've been wrestling with what I was going to say to them from the moment I placed my scalpel on their son's skin." He stopped, shook his head for a second, and looked legitimately perplexed. "To tell you the truth, I'm still not exactly sure what it's going to be." He paused and patted my shoulder one more time. "What do you say to helping me wing it?"

CHAPTER 17

THE next few weeks were a blur. Comparatively speaking, Christopher's overall condition improved. Though Dr. Herbert was apprehensive about stopping his chemotherapy temporarily, the consensus was that he should be given an opportunity to at least partially recover from his surgery before proceeding. He had endured an extensive operation, and initiating chemo too soon would significantly compromise his ability to adequately heal. So, though we knew his tumor could potentially continue to proliferate, we felt we had few alternatives. The upside was that during his chemo hiatus, Christopher's energy began to slowly return, as did his appetite. We once again began to see remnants of a vitality-filled little boy. He and I worked on more puzzles, played more games, and conquered more villains. In fact, after a shift, if Sergio was working, rather than going directly to the gym, I would frequently remain in the hospital for an additional hour just to spend time with him. On weekends, Sergio and I would even haunt secondhand stores to find vintage Superman videos. The classics were Christopher's favorites.

In addition, Sergio and I were spending most of our free time together. Despite significant conflicts in our schedules, we did whatever we could to ensure we'd be able to see each other. We laughed, we joked, we challenged one another, we argued, and we relished in the process of getting to know one another. Sometimes, if he was working a number of consecutive nights in a row, just so I'd be able to see him, I would leave the back door unlocked when I went to bed. After he closed up the restaurant, he would drive over to my house, sneak in the back door, and slide into bed next to me. Even if he were to awaken me out of a sound sleep, the excitement of having him in bed with me would invariably result in quick but satisfying sex. Afterward, I would again fall unconscious. Such escapades would sometimes make it difficult for me to haul my ass out of bed in the morning, but they were well worth it. What I suffered in fatigue was compensated for by being energized by spending time with Sergio. The other metamorphosis occurring was my beginning to feel a genuine sense of happiness.

Because Sergio slept at my apartment more often than I slept in his, when I did spend the night at his place, I sometimes awakened from a deep sleep feeling slightly disoriented. It was initially bewildering to find myself in unfamiliar surroundings. Such was the situation one morning when I found myself coming slowing awake before the alarm went off. The shadows on the wall looked strange to me. I rolled to my left side, expecting to see a faint light streaming in through the curtains, but instead was confronted by the indistinct shape of a dresser covered with an array of framed pictures and a trio of glass vases. The vases were different sizes and shapes, but even in subdued light I could appreciate that each was a clear vibrant orange. As my eyes began to slowly adjust to what was just the early glow of dawn, I kept my gaze fixed on the vases. I felt my brain slowly lifting from the fog of sleep, and I was confident I would soon remember why I wasn't in my own bed. I let my fading dream swirl around the colors in the vases. Red and yellow flashes mixed delicately throughout the orange, but each vase boasted its own unique pattern. Later, I learned they had been hand-blown on the island of Murano, near Venice. I was impressed that such a simple addition to the top of a dresser could create such a beautiful focal point. It occurred to me that to an impartial observer, my bedroom probably looked like a college dorm. *Damn, I've got to do something other than work.*

The mental critique I began of my aesthetically challenged bedroom was interrupted by soft snoring. In the same instant, I immediately remembered where I was. I slowly rolled to my right side, conscious of trying not to rock the bed, and looked at Sergio. He was still fast asleep. I raised myself on an elbow to look at him more closely. In the first glimpse of morning, it was like seeing him for the first time, and I found myself taken aback again by how handsome he was. In the depth of sleep, his expression was relaxed and peaceful. His eyelashes rested on honey-colored lids, and his unshaven jaw framed a mouth worthy of a toothpaste commercial. He had a well-sculpted nose that complemented the rest of his features perfectly, and hair that, though tousled by sleep, fell over his forehead like it had been intentionally combed that way.

Damn, I thought, *how did I get to be so lucky?* I was tempted to wrap my arms around him and let myself drift back to sleep but knew I had to get to the hospital. This morning, the ever-dreaded "chief rounds" would begin promptly at seven thirty.

Chief rounds were a medical education tradition firmly ensconced in the archives of the hurdles of humiliation one had to survive to complete a residency. They consisted of compiling the entire medical team, from the department chief, to the head of the residency program, to the chief resident, to the senior resident, to the interns, and finally down to the medical students. The participants would convene in the conference room on the pediatric ward, where, for the benefit of the medical students, introductions were made, and then a list of all the patients on the ward would be given to the chief of the department, Dr. Eugene Franklin. The list was organized by room number, each specifying the last name of the patient, the gender, the age, and the diagnosis. When the formalities were over, the fun began. The team would slowly start its migration down the corridor, stopping outside each of the rooms.

When all participants had assumed the appropriate erect and attentive posture, the job of the medical student was to formally present the history of the patient hospitalized behind the designated door. One of the essential lessons of a medical education was how to present. The presentation had to be succinct and accurate, void of extraneous information, but with enough detail to give a listener who was unfamiliar with the patient rapid familiarity with the case. It had to contain a brief history as to what the condition of the patient had been at the time of admission, which presenting symptoms warranted hospitalization, and what the progression of the patient had been subsequent to being hospitalized. Relevant test results and lab values had to be summarized, any complications had to be mentioned, and the presentation had to conclude with either a definitive diagnosis or a list of possible diagnoses. Finally, based on the presumptive diagnosis, the intended plan of management had to be outlined.

The anticipation of having to present on chief rounds had driven many a medical student to the verge of vomiting. It was worse than stage fright, because in addition to having to memorize buttloads of information, you knew that at any given instant, you could be interrupted. You might be asked to clarify a piece of information, or you might be expected to launch into an extemporaneous discussion as to which other disease entities might disguise themselves by presenting with similar symptoms.

The most anxiety-provoking aspect of all of it was that you never knew what you might be asked.

And if it was bad for the medical students, it was frequently worse for the interns. Some senior physicians derived great pleasure from drilling interns with questions until, rattled with uncertainty, they would just as soon shit themselves as have to endure the condescending stare that berated them for their ignorance. As a senior resident, if I liked the intern and thought he or she was a hard worker with a good attitude, I would try to shield them from some of the abuse. I would either interject with hints, or, as diplomatically as possible, challenge the relevance of the question as it related to the care of the patient. Sometimes this strategy then resulted in me becoming the target of the inquisition. It mattered less to me, however, because I knew I had become respected for my management of patients, and I had fewer qualms about honestly saying I didn't know something.

Either way, I knew I had to be on top of all the patients before the rounds began. I could tolerate not being able to list which seven anticonvulsants would be effective in treating a specific type of epilepsy, but I couldn't tolerate not knowing the details of the care of the children under my charge. I pulled myself out of bed before the digital clock clicked over to five thirty and turned off the alarm. If I took a five-minute shower, I could be at the hospital by six, grab a cup of coffee, and would thus have an hour and a half before rounds. Hopefully, all the patients on my service would have been stable overnight. There was nothing worse than having to start chief rounds by explaining an unanticipated complication from the night before.

I caught my reflection in the mirror on the closet door as I climbed out of bed. I was still a little unaccustomed to sleeping naked. Traditionally, perhaps due to the residual modesty from adolescence, I had always worn gym shorts to bed. By this time, Sergio and I had now been sleeping together at least three or four nights a week. I remembered that a few weeks before, after having had incredible sex, I was floating in and out of that amazing postejaculation dream state. Sergio had cleaned us both off with a warm washcloth and had then lain down with his head on my shoulder. I remember him whispering that he liked that I still smelled like him as he brought his arm up to rest across my chest. Just before I succumbed to the pull of sleep, I tried to gently push him off of me, saying I wanted to pull on a pair of shorts so I could sleep.

"Are you crazy?" he asked, pushing his weight down more heavily on top of me. "You're going to sleep just like this. I don't get to sleep with you every night, so when I do, I want to be able to feel as much of you as possible." Then, to ensure I didn't resist, he dropped his hand down to my crouch and grabbed my dick. "You try to move, you lose this!" Thus began the new tradition of sleeping naked.

Seeing my reflection in the mirror did, however, result in a fleeting sense of approval. Looking at myself objectively, I saw the results of the long hours in the gym. My chest was muscular and well-defined. My pecs themselves had short blond hair that met in the center of my chest, then traveled in a trail down the center of my abdomen. I didn't even need to flex to appreciate that my biceps formed firm, roundish mounds, and my stomach was definitely beginning to look cut. It wasn't yet a six-pack, but it was flat and was developing acceptable definition. Even my hair, bleached a lighter shade of blond from my runs on the park trails, was looking pretty good. I critiqued my appearance a few moments more. *Not bad,* I thought. *Really, not too bad.* Either my self-esteem was improving enough that I could acknowledge I really was reasonably attractive, or Sergio's adulation of me had started rubbing off. Either way, I leapt into the shower with a smile on my face. Maybe love did mean seeing the world through rose-colored glasses. Was I really falling in love?

I intentionally set the shower to a temperature a little colder than I would have liked—nothing like a blast of chilled water to immediately wake me up. I poured shampoo into my palm and briskly worked lather up through my hair. That complete, I shook the shaving cream can, spread a thin layer across my face, then grabbed my razor and shaved quickly without the benefit of a mirror. *Ahh,* I thought, *hands of a surgeon.* Just by passing my fingers over my face, I could identify the places I had missed, correct them, and still maintain a fairly symmetric sideburn line. I congratulated myself for having perfected the process of an efficient shower, and after running a bar of soap through the most intimate of crevices, I rinsed thoroughly and grabbed a towel.

I tried to sneak soundlessly back into the bedroom, intent on not disturbing Sergio, but when I peeked over at the bed, I saw it was not only empty but had been neatly made. The surprise of noting meticulously folded hospital corners on the bedspread evaporated when the aroma of freshly brewed coffee and frying bacon wafted by my nose. *What the hell? How did he accomplish all that when I couldn't have been in the shower for more than four minutes?*

I reached into my gym bag, pulled out a clean pair of underwear, some socks, and my scrubs. Though it only took mere seconds to apply deodorant, rub some moisturizer into my face, get dressed, and comb my hair, by the time I was finished, Sergio was flipping two eggs, bacon, and some toast with butter onto a plate.

He only had on a burgundy terrycloth robe with its tie knotted haphazardly around his waist. Even tied, the robe did little to cover the front of his body. For an instant, his raw handsomeness caught my breath. Bronze skin, sharply defined muscles, and little wisps of dark hair peeked out from beneath the cloth. Just beneath the tie, where the edges of the robe fell open, his dick was also welcoming the morning. When he heard my approach, he looked up and gave me his famous crooked grin. In doing so, he rotated his hips a little, and I'd be damned if the tip of his dick didn't almost graze the edge of the plate he had just put on the table for me. Again my breath caught, and for a moment I entertained the idea of skipping the eggs entirely and having him for breakfast instead.

I took a few strides to close the distance between us, pulled him into my arms, and gave him a deep kiss. When I pulled away, I was rewarded with an almost blinding sparkle from his amber-colored eyes, and my body responded to the warmth of his skin where I'd slid my hand beneath his robe to pull him into me more tightly.

With an appreciative pout, I said, "You were supposed to stay asleep. I intended to slip out without waking you."

The sparkle in his eye shifted immediately to a loving though indignant fury. "Like I'd send you off to work without something to eat." His features softened. "And without a kiss good-bye."

I pulled him more tightly against me, let my hands run more freely across his back, and then sank into a deeper kiss. When I pulled back, I dropped my hand teasingly down and gave his dick an affectionate squeeze before sitting down. "I said I didn't want to wake you, not that I didn't intend to kiss you. And," I said, letting my eyes gaze up and down his body appreciatively, "had I known that's what you'd be wearing to make breakfast, I would have given myself more time!"

Fork now in hand, I pulled him against me with my free arm and buried my face into his stomach, enjoying the warmth and the smell that was uniquely Sergio. He pushed his hands through my short hair, then pulled my head more greedily against his warm skin, forcing me to rub my cheek almost seductively against him.

Suddenly, fearful that pursing this innocent interplay even one more second could lead to a fifteen-minute diversion that would result in my being late to work, I turned my face and playfully blew a raspberry into his belly button. Then I pushed myself back into my chair and begin to shovel eggs into my mouth. By freeing my other hand from around Sergio's waist, I was able to use the toast to fully load my fork. The technique wouldn't win any etiquette awards, but it was efficient.

Before even swallowing completely, my gaze wandered back to his muscular form. He was pushing a steaming cup of coffee within my reach. I hungrily volunteered, "If you promise to wear nothing but that robe while you cook for me tonight, I'll spring for some Grade A steaks."

Despite a slight blush creeping into Sergio's cheeks, I was rewarded with his best seductive smile. "I have to work late tonight, so I won't be able to cook. That being said, however, if you want me to come by your place after I get off, I'll show up wearing only this robe and see what I can do to get you off." He punctuated the last part of the invitation by innocently pushing the edges of his robe a little farther apart and allowing the tip of his dick to rub the top of my arm as he reached for my empty plate.

I swallowed with some effort but held his gaze. "I'm gonna report you to the health department. I'm sure there are regulations about pubic hair being in such close proximity to food service."

"Hey, I served you eggs," he retorted. "It's not my fault you took more interest in my meat." He smiled smugly, dropped the dishes into the sink, and started washing them. "Besides," he said, stifling a chuckle, "the health department has already been here. They rated me 100 percent prime."

"Perfect." I pushed myself away from the table, snuck quickly up behind him to kiss the back of his neck, and whispered, "I agree with their rating." Dramatic pause. "But I'm still gonna have to taste you for myself. See if you can leave work early. I wanna have plenty of time for an extended evaluation process tonight. Now, lemme go run a toothbrush across my teeth and get out the door. There are lives to be saved."

When I got out of the bathroom, Sergio had my gym bag in one hand, my car keys in the other, and was waiting by the door of his apartment. The tie from the robe was on the floor around his feet. "Everything's packed," he said. "I wanted to save you a little time in case you thought of anything else you might wanna do before you left for work."

"Bastard." I grinned. "Forget the health department, this is a violation of the Geneva Convention. Cruel and unusual punishment. You could go to jail."

"Really?" His grin widened. "Will that require handcuffs?"

"Yes," I quipped, "but without the benefit of conjugal visits. We'll see how smug you are wearing that robe but with your hands handcuffed behind your back and with no one around to help!"

"Hmmm." He smirked, his cockiness unwavering, "Guess I'd just have to depend on one of the guards for a hand."

"Fine." I retreated, feigning defeat. I stole a quick kiss as I ran out the door. "Did I mention that all the guards were fat lesbians?"

"Now look who's being the bastard." I could still hear his laughter as he closed the door.

Damn, I thought, *this has the potential to be a great day.*

I SWIPED my identification card to open the gates of the doctor's parking lot. At that time of morning there were still lots of empty spaces, so I was able to commandeer one close to the stairs. I bounded down the two flights and again swiped my card to enter through one of the secure employee entrances. The hospital was a labyrinth of corridors, stairwells, and hallways. The pediatric ward was on the fourth floor of the north tower, so I had to navigate through the south tower and climb another two flights of stairs before even arriving at the glass-enclosed bridge that connected the two towers and allowed four lanes of traffic to pass underneath.

The sun had just crested the roof of the shopping mall that covered five acres east of the hospital, scattering spectacular colors across the carpeted floor as its light passed through the glass walls of the bridge. As I walked quickly through the beams of juxtaposed light, I couldn't help thinking Sergio would take great delight in attempting to use the display as the background for a canvas.

Though Sergio had never had formal art lessons, he really was an accomplished artist. Some of his work had been displayed in a number of local galleries, but none of the galleries were prestigious or well known. Most either doubled as coffeehouses or were small, quaint locations funded mostly by local artists who themselves were attempting to create a little name recognition. The reputations of these artists were built mostly by word of mouth, but some of them were gaining popularity. Very few people broke into the art world as instant successes. Shit, most artists were dead before anyone ever knew who they were. For Sergio, art was a passion I knew he dreamed would someday bring him both success and fame.

I pushed through the double doors that led onto the pediatric ward and walked up to the nurses' station. As was typical of our rotation, Diane had been on call the night before. She looked a little haggard as she leaned on the counter.

"Rough night?" I asked, pushing a cup of fresh coffee into her hand.

Some of the fatigue chiseled deeply into the lines of her face lifted. "Actually, we only had three admissions, but one of the kids was pretty sick." Her voice lilted with a soft laugh. "And you know, it only takes one for your night to go down the toilet. Four-year-old admitted from an outside ER. Leukemia. New diagnosis. Came in with a white count of forty-five thousand, lots of blasts, and pretty damned anemic. Had a hemoglobin of just five and a fever of 102. She was a little unstable, but we were able to draw some diagnostic labs before we gave her antibiotics and began to transfuse her up. She's already had two units of blood, five hundred milligrams of vancomycin, and is looking a ton better. Dr. Carroll is the oncologist on this week. She came in early and has already talked to the family. The kid's name"—Diane consulted her notes—"is Riley. She's going for a bone marrow biopsy and a spinal tap this morning. If we confirm the diagnosis and specific subtype of leukemia, she may start chemo as early as tomorrow. Hopefully, it will be one of the low-risk types that carries a good prognosis. Nice family."

I looked over Diane's shoulder and read her notes. Leukemia was the most common type of cancer in children. If indeed Riley had ALL, which was acute lymphocytic leukemia, her prognosis was pretty good. In my mind, I tried to recall the details of leukemia, as I was sure that it would be a hot topic for discussion during rounds.

Blood was comprised of many different cell types. Leukemia occurred when a specific type of white blood cell began to replicate out of control. This process was problematic for the body. First, these aggressive cells crowded out the production of the other cells the bone marrow should be making, and second, the white cells that were being produced weren't functional. In a nutshell, the cancer cells muscled out the mature, healthy, functioning cells.

That explained Riley's anemia. The cancerous cells her body was producing had so overwhelmed her bone marrow that she was unable to create new red blood cells. In addition, the role of mature white blood cells was to protect the body from infection. Because Riley's blood had been mostly overtaken by immature, aggressive white cells, she had an insufficient number of functioning white blood cells to protect her and was at significant risk for developing a serious infection.

"You're a star, Diane." I gave your shoulder a squeeze. "You had a shitty night, but not only were you able to wrap it up, you put it in a package and tied it with a bow."

Even under the strain of big-time sleep deprivation, she beamed at me. She understood I was both paying her a compliment and thanking her for great work. I continued, "Now, if you want to prove yourself as being truly stellar, you'll volunteer to work the next twelve hours and offer to let me go catch up on some much-needed beach time." I had to duck as she retrieved a reflex hammer from her lab coat pocket and swiped it at my head.

"Okay, okay." I grabbed her swinging arm and drew her into a hug. "Choose to stay within the ranks of the mediocre. That's your call. I just thought I'd give you the chance to rise to greatness. Seriously, though." I squeezed a little tighter so I could look over her shoulder at the list of patients she was holding. "Let me know what I can do to help you get out of here. You did a great job with Riley."

"Wow." She gave me kind of a pensive, suspicious look. "You show up bearing coffee, compliments, and with a genuine offer to help. Someone's in a good mood. Who tickled your ass with a feather?"

Keeping the mood light but being careful not to disclose even a hint of personal information, I smiled mischievously. "That's the secret; I have my own feather."

She smiled sheepishly and shook her head before refocusing on the patient list. "I don't know, based on your mood, it's either a damn big feather or you have more than one." Her cheek lifted a little on one side, and as she looked at me out of the corner of her eye, she gave me a cockeyed grin. "One of these days I'm gonna have to give myself a little peek into your closet to find out what other things you're hiding."

Her comment forced a hearty laugh from deep within my chest. I knew she intended the double entendre, but I was unwilling to take the bait. "If you come over to go rooting through my closet, it's only because you're hoping my vacuum comes with attachments for self-pleasure."

She laughed too. "If it's your vacuum, I'm sure that it was designed for self-pleasure. The question is, does it pick up dirt?"

I went from laughing to smiling smugly. "That's yet another good thing about me—there's never any dirt."

Diane reached again for her reflex hammer.

I stepped well out of the way of her blow, turned, and headed for the residents' office. "I'm gonna go print up a patient list for myself. I have to review it before chief rounds. Call me when you're ready to sign out and let me know if there's anything I can do to help you tie things up." I shot a smile over my shoulder. "That offer was and still is legit!"

As I walked away, I couldn't help but feeling a little self-conscious. Diane and I had worked together for more than two years, and in many respects had really bonded. Sharing an internship year was like surviving boot camp together. We'd been through the thick and the thin and had supported one another during some of our most harrowing times. On more than one occasion, we'd had to convince one another not to quit. I remembered during our second month of internship, when the two of us were assigned to cover the general pediatric ward together, one of the patients under our care had died. Though by every conceivable measure the death had certainly been unavoidable, neither of us could shake feeling we had somehow failed. As newly licensed doctors, we both felt a tremendous commitment to protecting our patients. By supporting one another, Diane and I had gotten through both the grieving process as well as the guilt and, ironically, had probably grown into better physicians as a consequence.

Having endured this process together, we had really gotten to know one another. When sharing a foxhole, a number of secrets get disclosed. As interns, Diane had confided in me how, the summer before, her heart had been broken when she discovered her fiancé had been sleeping with her best friend. Originally, she had committed to beginning her residency at Denver Children's in Colorado. At the last minute, however, she'd decided that staying in the same community where her ex-fiancé lived would only result in additional heartache. She was a highly recruited candidate, and when our training program ended up having an unexpected vacancy, she'd pulled up stakes and signed on. She arrived two days before we were scheduled to begin. The decision had been so last minute she hadn't even had time to arrange for housing. She packed a suitcase, checked into a hotel, and showed up the first day ready to work. No one was aware of her predicament other than our residency director, who ended up being instrumental in helping her to find an apartment. Three weeks into our internship, on her first day off, she flew back to Colorado, rented a U-Haul, and drove all her belongings back to Los Angeles. She was so upbeat none of us suspected what a difficult transition she was going through. It was only late one night, when the two of us were working together, that she tearfully shared her story with me. I pulled her into a tight hug, gently stroked her hair, and whispered to her that she was amazing, that she was wicked smart, incredibly cute, and had a sense of humor to rival mine. I told her that her fiancé must have been a huge asshole to have cheated on her and that he had lost the best thing he could ever have hoped to have. Also, I assured her as I kissed her forehead, she deserved so much more.

She'd pushed herself off my chest and looked up at me through tear-soaked eyes. An embarrassed smile crept across her face. "You're just saying that to try to convince me not to abandon your sorry ass during this godforsaken internship."

"Damn! Am I that transparent? And here I thought I was succeeding in buttering you up." I pulled her back into a tight hug. "Does this mean you'd be unwilling to pick up a few of my call nights?"

She drew her fist back and punched me playfully on the chest. "Typical man. Appealing to my vulnerable side with the singular intention of exploiting me later. First thing in the morning, I'm going to march right up to Human Resources and bring charges against you. You're contributing to a hostile work environment."

I laughed and squeezed her tighter. "When I show them the bruise on my chest, they'll know which one of us was being hostile."

After a few more moments locked in my embrace, Diane again pushed herself out of my arms, wiped her tears on the sleeve of her scrubs, and tried to push the emotion out of her voice. "Okay, now you've heard my pathetic, woeful story. What's yours, Zack? Is there a lucky girl out there who gets the privilege of resting her head on these rock-solid pecs on a regular basis?" She gave my chest another playful punch to accentuate her point. "You're always so mysterious about your personal life."

I immediately became self-conscious. Here we had just shared a very intimate moment, during which she had confided in me the details of an incredibly painful experience, and when she turned her focus on me, I suddenly felt naked. Rather than be forthcoming about who I was, I instinctively felt compelled to hide, to seek refuge behind my traditional walls. In that instant, I didn't even know what I was afraid of anymore. Hiding just became second nature. It was an indoctrinated response. I wasn't necessarily fearful that Diane would think any less of me if she knew I was gay, but every fiber of my soul nonetheless screamed it had to remain secret. That divulging it would mean being immediately ostracized. That my peers would assume my competence as both an individual as well as a doctor had been a façade, and in reality, I was somehow defective. A rational part of me acknowledged the ridiculousness of my trepidation, but an emotional part of me regressed to a pathetic little child, paralyzed by the prospect of being outed.

In an attempt to deflect the question, I took a step backward and intentionally flexed. "Do you really think they're rock solid? Our call schedule has been so hectic I haven't even had an opportunity to work out." I looked up at her and forced a smile. My intention was to give the impression that I thought we were just joking around. "Lucky thing you can't see my calves. They're a little skinny."

She looked at me, but rather than being taken in by my phony levity, her expression, though void of judgment, remained intense. She let the moment drag out a little longer, then her facial features relaxed. "You can be guarded with me if you want, Zack but you don't have to be. I'm not sure what you feel like you have to hide, but I hope you know that with me, anyway, you're safe. We've all had painful experiences in our lives. God knows you just got a firsthand glimpse into one of mine. The point is this: being friends means being able to share some of that pain. Given all of the things we've been through together, I hope you believe you can trust me. Sharing some of your pain with me might make it a lighter burden to carry." Her smile brightened. "You decide, Zack. When you're ready, you know I'm here."

It was hard for me to look directly at her. My voice caught just a bit, but I still managed to answer. "I do trust you, Diane. I guess I'm just not sure if I trust myself." I smiled and looked at her. "But if I ever succeed in getting my shit together, I guarantee, you'll be the first to know."

She continued to smile and just shook her head understandingly. "Zack, I think you already have your shit together. The problem is that you think being friends means just sharing the good stuff. Sometimes being friends also means sharing the shit, whether you have it together or not." She caught my gaze and her smile broadened. "Even if you think yours doesn't stink." She patted me on the arm. "Just know that I'm here."

That conversation had taken place more than a year before, and though I was certain Diane suspected I was gay, I had never actually admitted it to her. A bunch of times I had wanted to. A few times, I had even come close. But in the end, I always ended up rationalizing to myself that it wasn't necessary. That it was prudent to keep my professional life completely separate from my personal life. I forced myself to ignore how both ridiculous and hypocritical it was to cling to such a rigid restriction, because in every other regard, we were living in one another's back pockets. We shared laughs, we shared tears, we shared frustrations, and we shared disappointments. Hell, we'd even shared morning breath. I'd been more personal with some of my colleagues than I had been with some of my closest friends, and yet one part of my life remained carefully cordoned off. They could have their suspicions about my sexual orientation, but I'd be damned if I'd offer confirmation. Some of my gay friends thought living such a double life would be extraordinarily difficult. I'd been doing it for so long it was second nature. Sadly, I was a master at keeping people at arm's length while simultaneously having them believe we were incredibly close.

I was beginning to realize, however, that being vague about my personal life had been easier before I had begun dating Sergio. Concealing the raucous details of weekends spent with different friends was one thing, but suppressing the fact that I had someone significant in my life was a much bigger challenge. It became much more difficult to account for my free time when 90 percent of it was being spent with a single individual. In addition, I was so elated to be with Sergio that part of me wanted everyone I knew to have the opportunity to meet the guy who made my heart soar.

As I walked down the corridor toward the residents' office, I made a mental note that I would have to bring this dilemma to a better resolution. This wasn't the time, however, because thinking about the great send-off I had gotten from Sergio that morning was making my head spin, and the memory of the night before still caused my chest to feel tight. I remembered lying next to him in bed. We'd already had sex, and we were just talking lazily. Really, we were still in the process of getting to know each other.

He ran his fingers over my chest as I lay on my back staring at the ceiling. He was on his side, staring intently at my face. All his questions were punctuated by a thick Italian accent that made everything he said exponentially more endearing.

"So, what made you decide to become a doctor?"

It was a question I'd heard many times, but somehow, lying next to this handsome man, his naked body still pressed against mine, I wanted my answer to be more than just my rehearsed, canned response. I wanted it to reveal something more about who I really was.

Noticing that I hadn't immediately answered, he pushed closer into me. "I'm just asking because I was hoping to score another complete exam. I think there were a few places on my body that your tongue missed last night. I'd hate to have to report your negligence to the medical board."

My laugh shook his head on my chest. I pushed him over to his back, climbed on top, and pushed a kiss fiercely onto his lips. "I'll show you negligent." I kissed him again. "Of course, I might still get in trouble if you end up getting suffocated by kisses."

His eyes danced merrily. "How can I suffocate while you're performing mouth-to-mouth?"

"You have a point. But just to be on the safe side, I'd better keep practicing." I kissed him again.

When I pulled back, I looked at him thoughtfully, still intent on answering his question. "I suppose I became a doctor for more than one reason. Certainly, and most definitely, I wanted to help people." I raised myself on my elbows as I became a little more enthusiastic. "Especially kids. Helping kids gives me an exceptional feeling of satisfaction. They're innocent, they're resilient, and their response to kindness is genuine. It's hugely rewarding to participate in their lives when they're sick and, hopefully, to play a role in helping them to recover." I became a little more pensive. "But I also wanted to become something."

Sergio looked a little confused. "What do you mean, become something?"

I looked at him intently. We'd only been dating a couple months, but I felt amazingly close to Sergio. I felt like I was naked for the first time. Like I could let someone see who I really was and not fear being judged. My heart skipped a beat. I'd never dreamed someone as handsome as Sergio would ever be attracted to me. I had always been afraid that when someone got to know the real me, they'd immediately be turned off, that really knowing me translated into disappointment and ultimately rejection.

"You remember on our first bike ride when I told you I hadn't come out to my parents because I was afraid they'd be disappointed?"

"Yeah, I remember. In fact, as far as I know, you still haven't told them." He grinned.

I pulled the pillow out from under his head and put it over his face a second before I pulled it off. "That's not the point. Don't interrupt my explanation. Do you also remember how I described to you that I was ashamed of being gay?"

He now looked at me intently. He seemed to appreciate that I had begun to demonstrate a greater degree of self-confidence, so he listened without interruption.

"I think that to some extent, feeling ashamed of who I was also influenced my decision to become a doctor." I suppose my voice was tinged with some residual pain, because as I spoke Sergio squeezed me a little tighter. His arms around me made me feel safe and emboldened. I continued with soft but more certain conviction. "Recognizing I was gay and feeling as a consequence that I was somehow inferior made me determined to become something that could stand up against people's scrutiny. It gave me the resolve to do something admirable. If who I was as a person was insignificant, I had to become something significant. I had to become a respected professional. I thought becoming a doctor would somehow obliterate my shame." I blushed at the confession, realizing I'd never actually expressed to anyone what my subliminal motivations for becoming a doctor were. "Does that make sense? As tragic as it might seem, does it at least make sense?"

Sergio squeezed me tighter and softly kissed my eyelids, allowing my embarrassment to stay hidden behind them. His voice was low and resonated from deep within his chest when he said, "Sounds to me like you never appreciated how incredible you were before you even stepped foot into a medical school." The kisses continued. Then he drew back and searched my expression soulfully. "Do you understand that now?"

"Understand what?" Now I was the one who was a little confused.

His answer was so sincere it raised goose bumps down my back. "Being incredible has nothing to do with your being a doctor." His smile sweetened. "I'm beginning to think you're pretty damned amazing, and you've never even had to give me a prescription." His humor didn't conceal the sincerity of his voice. "Look, Zack, I have every certainty that you're on the road to becoming a great doctor, but that has nothing to do with what makes you a great person. Greatness is something you bring to your profession; it's not something your profession gives you. You're way more than just a doctor." He lifted my chin to look me directly in the eye, and then he emphasized each additional comment with an individual kiss. "You're kind, you're smart, you're genuine." He bit my chin. "You're sexy." He pulled me into a deeper kiss. "And you're gay." His smile radiated. "Sounds like just the combination I'm looking for!"

I fell forward onto Sergio's chest and pressed myself against him with more force than I might have intended. I wanted to eliminate any distance between us, wanted every possible inch of our bodies to touch. If possible, I wanted for us to feel like one.

I acknowledged that my heart was racing a little fast and felt briefly self-conscious. Sergio probably didn't have any idea how deeply his words affected me, how powerful they felt. His gentle acceptance of me, his approval, even his endorsement, felt empowering. Ultimately, I knew that developing a stronger sense of self-confidence was a journey uniquely my own; Sergio's validation of me wouldn't prove to be a missing link that, when identified, would succeed in making me feel whole. Though, as I lay on him, with my head cradled on his shoulder and with his arms wrapped tightly around me, I thought, *It sure couldn't hurt.*

I pushed myself up and extended my arms so I could look directly at him. He looked handsome, confident, assured. His dark hair fell across his forehead, his eyes were soft and welcoming, his smile genuine. I ran my fingers over his beautiful olive complexion and smiled at the irony. While I was loving being able to admire his skin, he was helping me to feel more comfortable living in mine.

The heartwarming memory didn't evaporate instantly, but it was certainly pushed to the back of my mind as I reviewed the list of patients I was responsible for. Fifteen children, fifteen different diagnoses. Chief rounds had the potential of being harrowing. Dr. Franklin, the chairman of the department, could ask anything about any one of them. My stomach felt kind of queasy. There was way too much shit to be expected to know off the top of my head. Hopefully, with such a heavy patient census, he'd choose to stick to the basics and not quiz us on minutiae. *One can only hope,* I thought dismally.

I carefully reviewed the names of all the patients on the list and then compared the list to the computer printout of labs. When I discovered an abnormality, I made certain that I understood why it had occurred and how it should be corrected. In addition, I reviewed Diane's notes from the night shift to assure myself that none of the patients' conditions had changed significantly since I'd signed out the day before. I didn't review the specifics of the patients she had admitted during the night because I knew she would be required to talk about them on chief rounds. She would sign them out to me after rounds had finished and before she was ready to go home for the afternoon. Lastly, I checked to see if any X-rays would need to be looked at. There was nothing more embarrassing than finding out during rounds that there was radiographic evidence of a new clinical finding that, as senior resident, you were unaware of.

When I got back from radiology, the team was already assembling. Dr. Franklin was shaking hands with the medical students he hadn't met and then smiled warmly at me and the two interns I was supervising, Jessica and Brian. I returned his greeting enthusiastically, but I was a little cynical. While his smile seemed genuine, I couldn't help but think it was the same smile a fox would have prior to entering a henhouse.

Diane showed up shortly thereafter, frantically giving her notes a final review. She knew part of the expectation of chief rounds was that she be familiar with even the subtle details of all her patients' conditions, even if she had just admitted some of them a few hours earlier. Though it was intended to be educational, the whole ritual accomplished little more than causing ulcers.

Diane was followed by her two interns, Shelly and Gil. Interns were on call every fourth night, so while Shelly had just arrived from home having slept, Gil had been working all night with Diane, and he showed up looking disheveled and exhausted. His eyes probably hadn't closed for more than four consecutive seconds in the past twenty-four hours.

Once all players, including the medical students assigned to the general pediatric ward service, were accounted for, the team began its procession down the hall. Moments later, the whole entourage stopped in front of the first door in the corridor. One of the four medical students, after being nudged by my intern, Jessica, launched into his well-rehearsed monologue. "Four-year-old male. Hospital day number three for treatment of right lower lobe pneumonia. Patient has responded well to IV antibiotics and has been without fever for twenty-four hours. Yesterday, he was weaned off supplemental oxygen and is now breathing room air. Plan is to switch him over to oral antibiotics and discharge him home later this afternoon, with directions to follow up with his private doctor within forty-eight hours." He made the entire presentation without taking a single breath, and when he finished he had to take a deep gasp to keep from passing out.

Dr. Franklin gave a benevolent nod of approval, but, incapable of letting an opportunity to ask a question pass, he shifted his gaze to Shelly, one of Diane's interns, and asked in a clipped voice, "Dr. Lamont. What is the oral antibiotic of choice for treatment of an uncomplicated lobar pneumonia?"

Shelly winced noticeably, but after only a moment of hesitation, she responded, albeit uncertainly, "Amoxicillin."

Dr. Franklin barely slowed his progression but acknowledged her answer with an affirmative shake of his head. "Good. Let's move on."

In front of the next door, the assigned medical student, a young woman named Jane, began speaking without prompting: "Six-year-old female. Known asthmatic admitted for respiratory distress." She consulted her notes to ensure she listed all the medications accurately and in their appropriate dosages, included them in her spiel, then concluded by saying, "She continues to require supplemental oxygen but is improving. Plan is to continue the current therapy and attempt to decrease the amount of oxygen she requires."

And so the arduous exercise continued, from one door to the next. One patient after another, the questions getting ever more complicated and more esoteric as rounds stretched into their second hour.

With just three patients to go, the team came to a stop in front of one of the final doors. Everyone's eyes were slightly glazed over in response to the barrage of information and from having been dragged through multiple inquisitions. Dr. Franklin, however, was seemingly unfazed. He looked as if he was just warming up.

The medical student dutifully made her presentation. "Five-year-old admitted with the diagnosis of orbital cellulitis. The patient didn't require surgery and is responding favorably to antibiotics." We all knew orbital cellulitis was an infection of the tissues immediately surrounding the eye; if not emergently treated, it could lead to blindness. We were surprised, though, that before the medical student had even finished her presentation, Dr. Franklin interrupted her to ask a question.

He eyed my intern, Brian, with a disapproving glare. I liked Brian. He would sometimes give the impression of being cavalier, but he was really a pretty hard worker and tried to conscientiously take care of his patients. Trouble was, he didn't always show the appropriate reverence for authority.

"Dr. Mitchell." Dr. Franklin modulated his tone as if he were asking the most obvious question in the world. "One of the complications of orbital cellulitis is thrombosis. In which sinus is the thrombosis most likely to occur?"

Everyone, including myself, froze in place. Who the fuck knew? People began to shift from one foot to the other, probably praying earnestly that should Brian fail to answer correctly, the question wouldn't be directed to them.

Brian stared pensively at the ceiling, stroked his chin, then nodded slightly, as if he had formulated the correct answer. He looked directly at Dr. Franklin, and though his voice was soft, his reply was confident. "Florence Henderson."

Silence swept over the group like a spray of ice water, and people shot each other panicked glances. Had Brian cracked under the pressure? Had he gone completely crazy?

Dr. Franklin looked at him and then, as if pleading for an explanation, looked at Dr. Mueller, the director of the residency program. Dr. Mueller was unable to offer anything more than a confused shrug.

Dr. Franklin returned his attention to Brian. "Dr. Mitchell, I didn't understand your answer."

This time, Brian shook his head even more confidently. "Florence Henderson."

Now everyone's discomfort crescendoed to an intolerable level. We averted our eyes by staring at the floor and concentrated on looking at anything other than Brian or Dr. Franklin. We anticipated that at any moment, men in white coats would show up to carry Brian away.

In an attempt to regain control over the situation, Dr. Franklin implored Brian in a very calm and patient tone, "I'm confused, Dr. Mitchell. Could you please explain your answer?"

"Well." Brian cleared his throat. "I once heard that while playing Trivial Pursuit, if you were asked a question and had no idea what the correct answer was, you had a 50 percent chance of being right if you answered Florence Henderson. I have no idea what the answer to your question is, so I figured responding 'Florence Henderson' at least gave me a 50 percent shot. Am I right?"

The silence extended for about two more seconds, then everyone fell into a fit of laughter. It was hysterical. Partly because everyone was exhausted from the intensity of the extended rounds, partly because we were relieved none of the rest of us would likely be asked the question, and partly because, though Brian had completely violated the sanctity of chief rounds, he had pulled it off without being belligerently offensive and had even succeeded in making Dr. Franklin laugh.

"You win, Dr. Mitchell. And on that note, I'll spare you from having to present the last two patients and let everyone get back to work." His smile broadened. "Oh, and Dr. Mitchell, we'll all look forward to your presentation tomorrow morning before rounds on orbital cellulitis and the dangers of cavernous sinus thrombosis." He winked. "I intend to have a front-row seat. Even in a game of Trivial Pursuit, I try to leave little to chance."

CHAPTER 18

THE phone woke me up at eight thirty on Sunday morning. Because I knew Sergio had worked the night before and was scheduled to work the brunch shift again that day, I was sure it was him calling to make plans for the evening. Trying to push the grogginess out of my voice, I reached for the receiver and whispered in a tone I hoped sounded at least a little bit sexy, "Is this my own Italian heartthrob?

"Sorry, dude." Declan's voice came booming thorough the earpiece. "Not the booty call you were hoping for. This is your conscience speaking, and it's calling to tell you that you're an asshole."

I laughed. "That's funny. My conscience sounds just like my friend Declan, which is kind of ironic because everyone knows he doesn't even have a conscience." I rolled over to look at the clock. "Besides, a good conscience would know never to call before nine in the morning on a weekend. You must have the wrong number."

Declan's tone became a little more serious. "You're right. I must have the wrong number. Maybe you can help me, though. I was trying to reach my friend Zack. This used to be his number, but it has apparently been disconnected. I haven't heard from him in more than three weeks. You wouldn't know how I might reach him, would you? Did he leave a forwarding number? Has he left the country? Has he left the planet?"

I chuckled softly. "Okay, okay. I get the message. I've been a dick. But, in my defense, the hospital has been crazy busy."

Now Declan's voice did get genuinely more stern. "That bullshit excuse might work with your other friends, but it doesn't fly with me. Your job has always been busy. It didn't used to matter, though. When you were an intern, despite the fact that you didn't sleep more than twenty hours a week, we still managed to talk to each other on a regular basis and probably never went more than about four consecutive days without seeing each other. I don't think this has anything to do with the job. I think that this has to do with your newfound fascination for Italian blow jobs."

Declan's seriousness brought me immediately awake. I sat up and held the phone more purposefully. Though he was trying to cloak his remarks with teasing, I realized his feelings were genuinely hurt, and I immediately felt awful. I hadn't been intentionally neglectful of our friendship, but now I realized the euphoria I'd been swept up in by spending time with Sergio had made me oblivious. Declan had been my best friend through thick and thin, and how had I treated him in return? The first opportunity to have a boyfriend came along, and I grabbed it without looking back. It was a sad commentary on my character. Declan was justified in expecting more from me as a friend. Besides, if things between Sergio and me didn't work out, he would be the first person I would go running to.

I didn't want the extended silence to become uncomfortable, but I was at a loss for something to say. Finally, with my chin tucked remorsefully against my chest and with the mouthpiece clutched tightly in my fingers, I said, "I'm sorry, Dec. You're absolutely right. I've been acting like a lovestruck high school girl, and I've treated you like complete shit." My apology was sincere, but I also knew I had two things going for me. Declan was ultraforgiving, and he was incapable of staying mad at me for long. I ran my hand through my hair and tried to inject a little jocularity into my voice. "Would a Cadillac margarita buy my way back into your good graces?"

Declan laughed. "Look, Zack, I'm not really trying to bust your balls, and fortunately for you, I can be bought off with a cheap shot of tequila. For the record, I'm genuinely stoked that you're hitting it off with the Italian what's-his-name. I'm just saying that pursuing a relationship shouldn't mean abandoning your friends. It would warm the cockles of my soul if you were to marry this guy, but I'd still expect to be your best friend, and I'd still want to see your ugly mug every now and then."

Now I was laughing. "Gee, Dec, I've never seen your cockles. If we get together tonight, do you promise to show them to me?"

"Why don't we start by you promising me that we'll get together tonight? We'll save the cockles exhibition for later."

"You're such a tease. But you're on. Let's definitely get together tonight. In fact, if it's cool with you, I'd like to invite Sergio. I figure it's about time my best friend met the Italian what's-his-name."

"Perfect! This doesn't get you completely off the hook, though. I still want a little one-on-one time with you too. If he's with us, you're going to be on your best behavior. And besides, I'm gonna wanna hear the unedited juicy stuff. No way you'll do any real sharing with him around."

"Okay, I promise. Let's see if we can all get together tonight, then I'll call you tomorrow when I'm leaving the hospital. We can meet at the gym to go work out together and then grab a bite afterward. Cool? If you want to know the truth, I've really missed you. Being on my best behavior is exhausting." I heard Declan's familiar chuckle on the other end of the phone and knew that once again things were right with the world. He really was amazing. The mark of an incredible friend was someone who genuinely wanted you to be happy and was willing to tolerate your shit on the journey to finding it.

"Okay, it's a date. And since we've come to this agreement and you're appropriately remorseful, I guess I'll be able to refrain from bitch-slapping you when I see you. Though God knows you deserve it for abandoning me like that. What if I'd been kidnapped by some psycho and forced to participate in some perverse sexual act against my will? Who would have come to rescue me?"

I laughed. "Come on, Dec. If you were being forced to participate in some perverse sexual act, you'd want anything other than to be rescued. Have the whole thing caught on video maybe, but rescued? Never."

"Ah, ye who thinks they know me so well. That's where you're wrong. I'm pure vanilla. The leather whips in my closet are only there should I ever have the courage to chase my real dream of running away and joining the circus. Never hurts to be prepared."

"The circus, huh? I've heard of sword swallowers, but I didn't realize they were looking to hire someone to make an orange traffic cone disappear by sitting on it naked. Yet another thing to cross off your bucket list."

By this time, we were both rocking with fits of laugher. It did feel good to once again be talking to Declan. If anyone overheard our conversations, they would think we were completely crazy. It didn't matter, though, because we thought we were hysterical together. Put the two of us in the same room, and regardless of the situation, within a few minutes, we'd be laughing uproariously about something. He really was a good friend.

After a little more verbal sparring, Declan said, "So, about tonight—I have an idea. If Sergio does agree to join us, I'll call John, we can all meet at my apartment, and then we'll drive up to these stables in Griffith Park. They offer a guided horseback ride. For twenty-five bucks each, we join a group and ride over the top of the mountain and down to a Mexican restaurant on the other side. We have dinner there, down a couple pitchers of margaritas, then ride back in the dark. I think they estimate we'll be back to the stables by eleven. It's kind of late when you consider that we all have to get up and be at work early tomorrow, but it sounds like a blast. What do you think? Seems to me you just finished saying that you owed me a Cadillac margarita."

"Sounds like I might be dragging my ass out of bed with a hangover tomorrow, but we're in. Let me call Sergio now to confirm that he's up for it. I'll call you back in a few. Do we need to make a reservation?"

"Yeah, I just called but only got a recording. They don't open until ten. Call me as soon as you've spoken to Sergio. In the meantime, I'll call John. Hope Sergio doesn't feel overwhelmed by the prospect of spending the evening with all three of us."

"Don't worry. He's not easily intimidated."

"We won't grill him too badly. Talk to you in a few."

I hung up and dialed Sergio's number. He answered on the third ring. He sounded a little sleepy. "Hello."

"Hey, you. It's me. Hope I didn't wake you."

"Hey, babe. No, I've been up for an hour. I had to get some laundry done before I went to work. Actually, I was going to call you, but I was waiting until after nine. I figured you'd be sleeping in. What's up?"

For a moment, I was speechless. He had called me "babe." It was the first time he had addressed me using a term of endearment. My head shot so far into the clouds that I had difficulty forming words. "Umm." I tried to find my tongue. It was difficult to speak through a smile that stretched across my entire face. "I was calling to see if you wanted to make plans for tonight. I just hung up the phone with Declan. I'm not sure he believes you really exist. He thinks that the studly Italian I've been talking about is just a figment of my imagination." I chuckled softly. "You're not real until he sees you in the flesh. We were talking about the possibility of him and John and you and me all getting together tonight. What do you think?"

"Let's do it. I was beginning to think you were keeping me a secret from your friends." He laughed. "Or that you were embarrassed to be seen with me." The pitch of his voice changed a little bit, but I could still tell he was joking. "I am kind of worried, though. If you've been describing me as being studly, they might be disappointed when they see me in the flesh."

"Jealous? Maybe. Shocked? More likely. But disappointed? Never. As a matter of fact, if they didn't know I was so poor, they'd probably think I was paying you to go out with me. As it is, I imagine they'll suspect that I've somehow succeeded in drugging you and am using pharmacologic brainwashing to get you to date me."

"Or, if they're really your good friends, they'll recognize how lucky I am to have the opportunity to go out with you."

My smile remained plastered in place. I was almost relieved Sergio couldn't see me. "I'm not sure how you'd say that in Italian, but in English, that translates into one of the nicest things anyone has ever said to me. I'll take the compliment. But they're my friends, they're not mentally challenged. They'll recognize that I'm the one who has really scored."

"Let's just let them be the judge. Between the two of us, I somehow suspect I'll be the one in the hot seat to prove to them that I'm good enough for you. Anyway, what did you guys have in mind? I'm up for anything."

"Hmm. Up for anything? I'll remember you said that after we ditch them and I have you all to myself." A chuckle escaped from deep within my chest. "Funny you should ask about the plan. Declan has been brainstorming. He wants us to go on a horseback ride through Griffith Park. He was a little unclear on the details, but the evening includes horses, a Mexican restaurant, and margaritas. It's either the recipe for disaster or a ton of fun. Can I tell him we're in?"

"Definitely. I've never done it, but friends of mine have. You ride over the hill to this Mexican cantina that supposedly has crappy food but great margaritas. Once you're shitfaced, the challenge is staying on top of the horse for the ride back. I've heard the trails offer killer views of the city at night. Let's do it."

"Excellent. Declan was going to call John. Once he hears from me, he'll call the stable and try to make a reservation for four people. I'm sure there's a limit to the number of people who can participate. If they're sold out, we'll just have dinner somewhere else. Either way, there are margaritas in our collective futures. What time to you expect to get off work?"

"I shouldn't have to be there past four. I'll bring a change of clothes and drive directly to your apartment after. No sense in showering if we're just going to climb onto horses. We should be able to hook up with them anytime after four thirty."

I did my utmost to force my voice to sound casual. "Okay, babe. Have a good day at work. See you a little after four." I was a little disappointed that Sergio gave no indication he'd noticed what I had called him, but the feeling dissipated the moment I heard his reply.

"Looking forward to seeing you, Zack." His voice dropped almost imperceptibly. "I always do."

Once again, my heart soared. "See you."

I briefly clicked the button on the receiver, then immediately dialed Declan's number. Without even confirming it was me, he picked up and asked, "So do we have ourselves a quorum?"

"Count us in. Zachary Sheldon and the Italian what's-his-name will officially be a part of tonight's posse."

Without missing a beat, Declan answered, "Sergio will be a welcome addition to this evening's festivities. Wish the same could be said for the asshole he's coming with."

"Wow." I tried to sound offended. "Does your best friend know you talk about him like that?"

Declan laughed. "My best friend wouldn't recognize me if I didn't. It's about nine thirty. I'll call there at ten to see if they can get us in. If they require payment, I'll put it on my card and you guys can pay me back. The website said the ride starts at six, so you all should be at my place by no later than five fifteen. If there's traffic on Los Feliz Boulevard, it could take as long as thirty minutes to get there from here."

"You've got it, Dec. If I don't hear from you, I'll assume the plan is on. Sounds like it's going to be a blast." I paused for little more than a second, then said with complete sincerity, "And, Dec, I really am sorry for being such a dick. You really do deserve better."

"Don't sweat it, Zack. No one is keeping score, but if we added up all the times I've been a dick to you, you'd still be in the black. The important thing is that we've got each other's back."

"You got that right, my man. See you a little after five." I started to hang up, then, as an afterthought, brought the phone back up to my mouth. "Oh, and Dec?"

"Yeah?"

"I know it's been awhile since you've seen me. When you meet Sergio, in case you've forgotten what I look like, I'm the good-looking one." I smiled into the phone. "I just wanted to avoid any confusion."

"Considerate of you, Zack. I'll keep that in mind. See you this afternoon."

Given that Sunday was going to be my only full day off, I had to be productive. Figuring that being on a horse for a couple hours constituted a legitimate workout, I decided to forego going to the gym and launched immediately into my errands. Sergio planned to arrive a little after four. I had six hours to clean my room, change my bed, do my laundry, complete my grocery shopping for the week, and make a run to the hardware store. I had purchased a cool set of shelves to hang on my bedroom wall three months before but didn't have the necessary molly bolts to mount them. Sergio had inspired me. His apartment looked like it had been decorated by a professional. I could at least take the initiative to make a single addition to improve the aesthetics in mine.

I jumped out of bed, grabbed a pair of khaki shorts, pulled a blue T-shirt over my head, pushed my feet into some flip-flops, and bolted out of my room to fix a bowl of instant oatmeal before starting my chores. I was on my way into the kitchen when I ran into Christian and Brent stumbling down the hall. They were both bleary-eyed, and it looked like they were attempting to walk without having fully woken up. As they neared the kitchen, I heard Christian tell Brent, "Remind me to kill you before you ever again allow me to drink a fourth mojito. I don't want to see another bottle of rum for the rest of my life."

Brent replied, "I don't know what you're complaining about; you should have taken pity on that rose bush. I'm sure it's dead already. If you were going to throw up in the flower bed, you should have at least aimed for weeds. How do you expect roses to survive a blast of vomit that's 90 percent pure alcohol?"

We all reached the kitchen at the same time, and Christian went immediately to the water dispenser while Brent reached for the bottle of Advil. I interrupted their playful bickering by asking, "So, girls, rough night? Both of you look pretty hammered." I smiled. "I hope neither one of you was the victim of date rape."

Despite what I'm sure were throbbing headaches, they both offered tentative smiles. Brent answered, "There was definitely no hanky-panky last night. Christian went to bed without brushing his teeth. I think vomit breath is the single most effective form of birth control even for straight couples. I would almost have preferred to sleep on the floor rather than share the same bed with him. Believe me, that room was void of any inappropriate touching last night."

Christian somehow managed to smile through his pain. He threw his arm around Brent's shoulders and breathed heavily into his face. "But you love me anyway."

Brent exaggerated a fake gag. "See what I deal with? Now you're witness to the treatment I endure. Morning vomit breath in the face constitutes domestic violence. You might have to testify on my behalf."

By this time, though they were both laughing and jabbing at each other, they had to hold cold dish towels on their foreheads because their laughter made their headaches worse.

I pulled my hot oatmeal out of the microwave, took a bag of frozen berries out of the freezer, and sprinkled some over it. Then I grabbed a spoon out of the drawer and started to retreat back to my room. "Don't drag me into the middle of this. The only intervention I'm willing to do for either of you is to give you the number of the local AA. I'll be in my room. I've got a bunch of chores to do. Let me know when the coffee's ready." I slapped Christian playfully on the butt.

"Chores? At this time of morning on a Sunday? What kind of efficiency bug crawled up your ass?"

I laughed. "Well, since you insist on knowing, Sergio and I are going to hook up with Declan and John this afternoon to go horseback riding through Griffith Park. It's a guided tour that starts at six in the evening. It takes us over the hill to a Mexican restaurant for dinner and margaritas, then puts our inebriated asses back into the saddle for the ride back. Sergio says he heard the nighttime ride is a blast and the views of the city are incredible."

Christian clutched his stomach. "Don't mention margaritas. The thought of horses and alcohol makes me want to hurl."

Brent took at little more enthusiastic interest in our plans. "I've heard about that ride. Friends of mine have taken it. They said it was fun." He poked Christian in the ribs. "If Pocahontas here wasn't so hungover, we would join you guys. Sadly, however, the only horse he'll be riding today is the porcelain one in the bathroom, and I'm not even sure he'll be able to stay on top of that one."

Christian tried to pretend he was ignoring Brent, but he didn't succeed in suppressing a small smile. He looked past Brent and directly at me. "So, Sergio is going to be meeting the brethren? Sounds like things are getting serious."

I knew that a pale blush had begun to spread across my face, but I tried to keep the tone of my voice confident and unflustered. "Yeah. What can I say? The guy finds me irresistible." Then, incapable of playing my emotions down, I continued with more sincerity, "Truthfully, he's pretty great. We've been seeing each other for nearly three months now, but for the past four or five weeks, we've really been spending quite a bit of time together. He's funny, he's conversant, he has a ton of interests, and is insanely talented. Also, in addition to tolerating my many insecurities and idiosyncrasies, he supports me through them." My blush deepened. "I guess it is getting kind of serious... at least, I'd like to think it is. I can't ever remember being so happy."

I turned to head back to my room but hazarded a glance over my shoulder. "And did I mention that he's got the body of death and is sexy as hell?" I smiled. "Icing on the cake, boys, icing on the cake."

MY ENTHUSIASM about the prospect for a fun evening provided the motivation to complete all my chores and errands quickly. The clock hadn't even struck three yet, and my room was clean, the shelf hung, the bed changed, my laundry done, and I had completed my grocery shopping for the week. Then I decided it would be better not to mount a horse with an empty stomach, so I went into the kitchen to make a sandwich and eat some fruit. Also, despite the fact that Sergio had already pointed out the futility of showering before going on a dusty horseback ride, I nonetheless opted for a clean meet and greet. It wasn't that I felt I needed to impress Declan and John, I just didn't want to be an unshaven, hair-plastered-to-my-head mess standing next to Sergio. Sweaty and unshaven made Sergio look sexy. It made me look homeless.

I heard Sergio's car pull up in front of our apartment and met him at the door before he had an opportunity to knock. He was just crossing to the end of the balcony when I pulled the door open. He was still wearing the clothes he had worn at work: black pants with a loose white gauze shirt. The dress code was more casual for brunch. Usually he wore a button-down tuxedo shirt with a black bow tie. He had a pair of Levi's and a plaid shirt on hangers thrown over his shoulder and was carrying cowboy boots in his hand.

"Wow," I said, looking at the clothes he was carrying as he stepped into my arms for a kiss. "Someone doesn't want to be mistaken for an amateur. I never figured that as a child you spent a lot of time on the wide-open ranges of Rome. It must have been a bitch herding cattle down the narrow streets near the Pantheon."

He laughed as he backed away from me, dropped his cowboy boots on the floor, and laid his clothes over the back of the couch. "You said we were going horseback riding. I've watched enough John Wayne movies to know how to dress. What were you intending to wear? Spandex shorts, combat boots, and a rainbow-flag cape?" He was smiling broadly as he again reached for me. With his hands free, he could now pull me into a tighter embrace.

I was laughing too. "Okay, if you think it's too much, I'll ditch the cape, but the Spandex and combat boots are a must. I don't even own a pair of cowboy boots, and besides, the Spandex shorts are plaid."

Sergio pulled back to look at me. He had a horrified expression on his face before he realized I was kidding. I put his mind at ease when I clarified, "Actually, I'm going to wear what I'm wearing." I stepped back and opened my arms so he could critique my entire outfit. "Levi's, a comfortable short-sleeved shirt, and tennis shoes. I wasn't kidding about the cowboy boots. I really don't own a pair. Also, I figured I'd tie a sweatshirt around my waist to wear on the ride back in case it gets cold." I smiled. "I might not look the part, but remember, I'm a mountain boy. I know my way around a horse."

Sergio was also smiling. "Is that the politically correct way of saying you're a horse's ass?"

I laughed and punched him in the chest. "We'll see who's laughing when you fall off your horse and I have to come rescue you. Bet you won't think you're so funny then."

Sergio again reached out, grabbed me, and pulled me against his chest. "You can rescue me anytime. In fact, I might need a little rescuing now. Do we have time? You wouldn't abandon me in my time of desperate need, would you?" He began to kiss me hungrily.

When we broke the kiss, he stared into my eyes. My breathing had accelerated, and I felt flushed. "I'd never dream of abandoning you." I looked at my watch. "But we have to be out the door in forty minutes. That only leaves time for a quick rescue effort." I pulled him toward my room. "Besides, now we'll both have to shower before we leave. I don't want the horses to think we smell like sex."

Sergio looked confused but followed me willingly. "Why do I care what the horses think we smell like?"

I was laughing. "Pheromones. I've read they can make animals crazy." I pushed him against the wall and started to unbutton his shirt. "Or, more truthfully, I don't want to be on a four-hour horseback ride with my underwear plastered to my pubes."

Sergio pulled my shirt over my head and ran his hand over my chest. "Or maybe we can just skip the horses entirely and just ride each other for four hours."

I laughed as I pushed my bedroom door closed. "That plan would get my approval in a heartbeat, but Declan would kill me."

Thirty minutes later, we sprinted, wrapped only in towels, down the corridor and into the bathroom. Though we showered together, we made a conscious effort to keep our hands just to the business of bathing. We didn't want to be late to Declan's and start the evening with him blaming us for traffic delays.

We parked in front of Declan's apartment at five after five. Ten minutes to spare. Sergio gave me a quick kiss on the cheek, and we congratulated one another for succeeding in making maximum use of time.

Before we got out of the car, Sergio looked at me inquisitively. "You aren't nervous, are you?

"About what?"

"About me meeting your friends."

"No, not really. I'm sure you guys are going to like each other. I'm really not worried about that at all. It might be a little uncomfortable in the beginning; it always is when people meet each other for the first time. I'm sure everything will be fine as soon as the ice is broken. I'm more worried about what Declan might tell you about me. We've known each other for a long time, and he'll love having the opportunity to embarrass me."

Sergio smiled. "Embarrassing you is better than grilling me. Despite what you say, these guys are your best friends, and I know they think the world of you. They're probably more protective of you than you realize. I'm the one on thin ice, here." Sergio smiled even bigger. "If I make an unfavorable impression and they don't think I'm good enough for you, they're likely to push me over a cliff."

I kissed him once more on the cheek. "The likelihood of you making an unfavorable impression is zero." I kissed him again. "I'd say that means the odds are pretty much in your favor. Don't worry about it."

I turned and was reaching for the door handle when Sergio gently caught my arm. He looked a little self-conscious as he said, "Speaking of being pushed over the cliff, before we head up the mountain, there's something I've wanted to ask you."

Rather than opening the door, I turned back to him. "What's up?"

"This is going to sound like a funny request." A little color crept into his cheeks as if he was embarrassed, but he maintained my gaze. "You remember when I told you last week that the owner of the restaurant asked me to be a shift manager?" I nodded. "Well, as a part of the promotion, I have the opportunity to get medical insurance."

"And?" I nudged him to continue.

"I was filling out the forms last night, and one of the questions was who I would authorize to make medical decisions on my behalf in the event I was unable to. In fact, they provided the paperwork to designate someone as a medical power of attorney." Then, rather than continuing to speak, Sergio looked out the front windshield as if something had suddenly grabbed his attention.

I nudged his shoulder again. "So?"

"So," he said as he turned to me, "I was wondering if I could put your name down?" He blushed again. "Don't worry. This isn't like a marriage proposal or anything, but I figure you're better qualified than anyone else. Think about it. For the past four months, we've been spending most of our time together, and you're a doctor, so you would understand all the medical stuff. Also, even if I considered putting my sister's name down, she's out of the country so much they'd probably never be able to find her." He smiled warmly. "I figure my life is the safest in your hands."

A momentary silence fell between us as we just looked at each other. Sergio must have assumed his request made me feel uncomfortable because he suddenly averted his gaze and shrugged casually. "Don't sweat it if you think that's kind of a weird thing to ask. Truthfully, I'm cool leaving the whole thing blank. I don't even have to fill that part out."

I responded by pulling him into a tight hug. For a second, my heart was so consumed by such an overwhelming feeling of warmth it was impossible to speak. Not only was I flattered he'd entrust me with such a significant decision, but it confirmed for me that I was becoming a particularly important part of his life. I kissed him affectionately on the lips. "It would be an honor." Then I pushed back to look directly at him. "But for the record, don't get too close to that cliff. I like having all of you in one piece." I playfully dropped my hand and squeezed his crotch.

He moved his mouth to the side of my head and nibbled on my ear before he softly whispered. "Don't worry. I intend to be around for a long time. In fact, if something does happen to me, don't call a mortician. Call a taxidermist. You'd be stuck with me forever."

I pushed him towards his side of the car. "Forever's good. But only if you're breathing."

WE GOT out of the car, gave each other one more affectionate kiss, then walked up to the main entry, and I pushed Declan's code into the buttons on the intercom. After a single ring, his voice came booming through the speaker. "We're headed down. You guys good to drive, or should I get my car out of the garage?"

"We're good. My backseat is empty. I can seat four comfortably. Meet us on the sidewalk."

Two minutes later, Declan and John came bounding through the door. John was wearing clothes similar to mine, but both he and Declan were wearing cowboy boots. In addition, Declan was wearing a long-sleeved button-down denim shirt and a cowboy hat. Earlier in the afternoon, I hadn't given my attire any real consideration. Now I really was embarrassed about my tennis shoes. I lifted one of my feet and compared it to everyone else's. "Guess these make me odd man out. What's up with the cowboy hat, Dec? Were you the Lone Ranger for Halloween?"

He pretended not to see me and intentionally pushed right past me. "Don't be a hater, Zack, just because you came to a horseback ride dressed like a prep school boy." He thrust his hand into Sergio's. "You must be Sergio. I'm really pleased to meet you. We've heard a lot about you. I'm Declan, and this is John." He released Sergio's hand, and John offered his. "We should have warned you. Whoever rides with Zack is responsible for dressing him. It's just like him to confuse a trail ride with a sorority party." Declan broke out into a huge grin, and we all started laughing.

I looked at Sergio. "I guess the ice is officially broken."

Declan and John piled into the backseat, and we were on our way. No sooner had the doors closed they began peppering Sergio with questions: "How long have you been in the United States? How do you like Los Angeles? How can you possibly tolerate Zack?"

As I anticipated, Sergio maintained his incredibly charming demeanor. In fact, even when they asked many of the same questions I had asked him when we initially met, rather than giving even the slightest hint of being perturbed, Sergio answered them enthusiastically and with an impressive display of humor. At one point, when one of his responses was particularly high-spirited, I couldn't resist punching him in the arm. "How come when I asked you that same question the day I met you at the pool, you growled at me?"

He looked at me with a cockeyed grin. "I was playing hard to get."

I shook my head. "If you had played any harder, I would have given up trying to talk to you and just gone back to swimming laps."

"Wouldn't have mattered. I saw the way you swam. I would have had to jump in to rescue you anyway."

"Rescue me?" Unintentionally, his reply caused me to immediately remember our conversation from earlier that afternoon and the sexual foray that it led to. "Would that have been the same rescue technique we practiced a few hours ago?" I smiled. "Wish I had known. That would have been worth drowning for." I gave him a seductive wink.

Declan made a face I could see in the rearview mirror. "Hello! Innocent passengers on board. I'm not sure what kind of rescue technique you guys are discussing, but I suspect if it had been demonstrated at the gym pool, you would have been arrested for lewd conduct. Now, can we change the subject? I'm in the backseat and don't want to get carsick."

And so the adventure began. The horseback ride over the mountain was a complete blast. Twenty-four people had made reservations, and we were broken into two groups of twelve. Our group was comprised mostly of people our age, and on such a festive occasion, everyone quickly became friends. Though all the people we rode with were more or less comfortable on the back of a horse, there were no real equestrians in our group, so the situation lent itself to a lot of good-natured teasing from the very beginning. One couple, who had only been married for a little over a month, was especially fun. They both had wicked senses of humor, and it became immediately apparent they thoroughly enjoyed teasing one another. Fortunately, their jabs were neither malicious nor insulting, and because many of their comments were entirely self-deprecating, it was impossible to be offended by anything they said. Their irreverence set the tone for the group, and soon everyone was laughing at each other. Of course, the four of us were well practiced in throwing witty barbs, so even though Sergio had only just met John and Declan, they were soon interacting like lifelong friends.

We arrived at the restaurant a little past seven thirty and were told we had an hour to eat. Eight tables had been reserved for the two groups of riders, so the four of us took one together. We ordered burritos and tacos off the menu, and shortly thereafter the first pitcher of margaritas was put down in front of us. After an hour and a half of riding horses and eating dust, we were incredibly thirsty. The first pitcher disappeared before the food even arrived, and the second pitcher was flowing freely soon thereafter.

Consuming alcohol on an empty stomach is never a good idea. The margaritas went right to our heads. They caused the hilarity of every comment to be amplified by a factor of ten. We were laughing at jokes before they were even told. At one point, we began talking about classic television shows. When the topic of our favorite *I Love Lucy* episode came up, Sergio launched into his impersonation of Lucy selling "Vitameatavegamin." Between his Italian accent and his inability to pour water into his spoon, we were rolling. Tears were streaming down our cheeks from laughing. Equally funny was the fact that Sergio couldn't successfully get beyond the famous "Hello, friends. Do you poop out at parties?" line without going into hysterics himself. Forget saying "vitameatavegamin." By the second attempt, he wasn't even able to say his own name without either stumbling or laughing.

By the time we finished dinner, I had serious doubts as to whether I would be able to get back onto my horse. The only thing that enabled me to do so was the fact that the horse was my only transportation home. It was either ride or spend the night on the restaurant porch. With both formidable effort and concentration, I put my foot in the stirrup, threw my leg over the horse, and planted my ass in the saddle. I was grateful all I had to do was point the horse in the right direction and he would follow the leader.

After an hour, we were back on the top of the mountain. Sixty minutes of being jostled back and forth on a hard leather surface had done wonders to sober us up. It was fortunate, though, because from the trail skirting the mountain peak, the view of the city was spectacular. Through the cloudless sky, we were able to see from downtown to the silhouette of Century City and beyond. Someone even commented that the faint light visible in the distant west was from the lighthouse on Catalina Island. My recollection was that Catalina only had a bell tower in its yacht club, but I appreciated the view anyway.

When we arrived back at the stable, we were all beat. A heavy meal, a ton of tequila, and having a saddle ride up your ass for an entire evening was the recipe for utter exhaustion. When we finally dismounted, we walked painfully back to the car, bowlegged. Though there continued to be a fair amount of snickering and reminiscing about our adventure, the energy on the car ride home was relatively subdued. We were all about ready to fall asleep.

I pulled up to the curve in front of Declan's apartment, and Sergio and I both got out of the car to say good-bye to Declan and John. Because Declan had gotten out on the passenger's side of the car, he hugged Sergio before me. He whispered something into Sergio's ear, and they both laughed. Then he came over to me and wrapped me in a tight embrace. He whispered in a voice only loud enough for me to hear, "Okay, I forgive you. If I had the opportunity to date a guy like Sergio, I wouldn't call you for three weeks either. Hold on to that one. He's a keeper." Then he drew back and punched me in the arm. "That doesn't mean, however, that I'm letting you out of your promise. As soon as you head out of the hospital tomorrow, you have to call me. I don't care if your ass is hungover; we're still meeting at the gym to work out."

I hugged him again. "You got it, Dec." Then I too whispered in a conspiratorial soft voice. "I really do hope things between me and Sergio work out, but either way, as far as best friends go, it's you and me forever." Then I pushed back and punched him in the arm. "And as far as the gym goes tomorrow, I'll bet you dinner that your ass is going to be dragging more than mine. Between medical school and residency, I've got sleep deprivation down to a science. I'll be as fresh as a flower."

Declan started walking up to the entry of his building. "Dude, once again, you've confused a flower with a stink weed. Either way, though, I'll see you tomorrow. And as for you, Sergio, remember what I told you: drop him like a bad habit; you're way out of his league." He winked at both of us but spoke directly to Sergio. "Careful, though. If you break his heart, John and I will personally hunt you down and kick your ass. Consider yourself warned." Everyone broke into tired grins, and Sergio threw his arm around my shoulder and kissed me on the cheek.

"Don't worry, tough guys. Zack is in good hands. I intend to take good care of him for a long time."

I again felt light-headed. I was either falling in love, or the night air suddenly held considerably less oxygen.

CHAPTER 19

SERGIO and I didn't get back to my apartment until after midnight. I dropped an Alka-Seltzer into a full liter of water, downed four Advil, took some vitamin C, brushed my teeth, set the alarm for six o'clock, and the two of us went immediately to bed. I don't think I even moved the entire night. I woke up four minutes before the alarm went off and was able to wipe a little pool of my drool off Sergio's shoulder while he was still zonked.

I turned off the alarm before it sounded, slipped out of bed, and crept noiselessly into the bathroom to take a shower. When I finished, I came back to find Sergio sitting on the side of the bed, cradling his head in his hands. Without looking up at me, he whispered in a dry crackly voice, "I'm not sure which hurts more, my head or my ass." He looked up at me but continued to keep one eye squeezed closed. "I guess my head. My ass only hurts when I try to move. My head throbs either way."

"Lucky for me." I walked over and stood next to him. "That's the part I prefer to kiss and make better." I leaned over and planted a soft kiss on the top of his head. I straightened up as I smiled down at him. "Though should the other part of your anatomy continue to cause you discomfort, my lips would be willing to offer their services down there too. They don't usually work in that neighborhood, but for you they'd make an exception."

Sergio started to chuckle and was forced to hold his head tighter. "Don't make me laugh. It makes my head hurt worse. Besides, you're cruel. You're only making that offer now because you know I'm too incapacitated to take advantage of it."

"Don't worry. For you, the offer comes without an expiration date. You can redeem it anytime you want." I kissed the top of his head again but then felt compelled to add an addendum. "Let me clarify: you can redeem it anytime you want when we're in the privacy of one of our own bedrooms. I'd just as soon you not try to collect when we're walking down a crowded street or even when we're sitting in the back of a quiet restaurant. I'm not a prude, but I do have my limits." I smiled again. "Tell you what. I'll give you a coupon. You can read the exclusions on the back."

Sergio fell back on the bed and pulled the pillow over his head. "You're torturing me. Too many words. My brain was already on the verge of exploding. Now you're filling it with redemptions and exclusions. You're trying to kill me." I could see his smile peek out from under the pillow.

"Here's what I'll do." I pulled on a clean pair of scrubs. "I'll bring you a glass of juice and some more Advil. Neither of my roommates is here. You just go back to sleep. You know where we hide the extra key. Just lock up when you leave. I'll call you tonight."

He pushed the pillow off his head just enough to look at me. "And then, through the thundering storm, I heard the voice of an angel. Bless you, my child. There is a heaven."

I laughed. "If I didn't know better, I'd think that you just called me God. Hold that thought. I'll be right back."

I went into the kitchen, got the coffeemaker going, put oatmeal into the microwave, then poured Sergio some juice. I carried the bottle of Advil back to my room, helped him sit up, put four pills into his palm, and handed him the glass of juice. He downed it in five or six quick gulps then lay back down. It took some effort for me not to run my hands over his naked body, but instead, I pulled the sheet up over him and fluffed his pillow. "There will be coffee in the pot when you get up. You just sleep. I'm going to eat breakfast and then leave without waking you." I kissed him on the lips. He tasted like orange juice. "Rest up. We'll talk later."

His response was groggy as he was already drifting back to sleep. "Thanks, babe. I love you."

For the briefest of seconds, I thought my heart had stopped. I looked down at the incredible man asleep in my bed. He was snoring softly. He might not even have been aware of what he had said. I felt my mind flood with indecision, anxiety, and self-doubts. Did he mean it? Was he just hungover? Was I starting to build unrealistic expectations?

Somehow, however, as I stood there looking at him, I was able to effortlessly push the tornado of questions out of my head. Then, with absolute sincerity, I leaned over and kissed him once more lightly on the lips. "I love you too." He emitted another soft snore without stirring. It didn't matter, though, because I realized on my way out that I had said it as much for me as I had for him.

As I skipped down the steps of my apartment, I questioned whether I was the least bit hungover. Surprisingly, I felt like a million bucks. Either I was building an impressive tolerance to alcohol, or Sergio's declaration that he loved me was an antidote for all my ills.

ON THE medical side of things, the next few weeks were relatively uneventful. I completed my rotation as resident in charge of the pediatric ward and began one of my electives: pediatric cardiology. My workdays were comparatively shorter than the ones I had grown accustomed to, but I still took call on the ward every fourth night. By continuing to maintain a presence on the ward, even though I was no longer directly responsible for helping to oversee Christopher's care, I could still closely follow his progress. In fact, if my responsibilities during my cardiology elective required I be in the hospital rather than in the outpatient clinic, I always made a special point of going to spend time with him.

He was off chemo for only two weeks immediately following his surgery. By the third week, however, the treatment protocol he was under required that he begin both high-dose chemotherapy as well as radiation to the area in his abdomen where the tumor had been. All these measures were in anticipation of readying him for a bone-marrow transplant: the only intervention that offered any possibility for survival.

When he was feeling up to it, his new favorite pastime was building with Legos. He appointed me his main contractor. Sometimes he would assist in the construction effort, but because of his fatigue, mostly he would supervise from his bed. Some of the things we built were particularly impressive. We never looked at directions. Each of our creations was the result of imaginative ingenuity. Some of our projects received such notoriety that nurses from all over the ward would come to admire the finished products. Christopher took great pride in explaining what each creation represented. One time we built what we were certain was an exact replica of the Batcave complete with computers and a bat pole. Another time we attempted to build an ogre's castle, including a drawbridge. Unfortunately, according to Christopher's specifications, it had to be taller than he was. We didn't have a sufficient number of Legos to build a base broad enough for something so tall, so the tower on the side of castle kept falling over. In the end, we decided to settle on a building a castle that could comfortably accommodate Shrek. According to Christopher, he was considerably shorter than most ogres.

Unfortunately, about six weeks after his surgery, Christopher's condition began to really deteriorate. He slept for longer periods of time and became increasing difficult to arouse. The most ominous symptoms were his breathing became more labored and his skin and the whites of his eyes turned a sallow, lifeless yellow. Evaluation of his blood work confirmed that his liver was failing. His little body just couldn't defend itself against the rapidly advancing cancer. It was destroying him despite every possible intervention.

His parents kept a constant vigil at his bedside. They neither slept nor ate. When Dr. Herbert sat down with them and explained we had exhausted all alternatives, it was as if part of them died just as the result of hearing the news. There was nothing more we could do. There were no more chances, no more hope, no more clinging to even a glimmer of optimism that an innovative new therapy might miraculously offer a cure. The only thing left for them to do was to wait, to stand helplessly back and watch a vicious cancer slowly murder their child. It was excruciating for them. Given the choice, either of them would have endured unfathomable torture in exchange for their precious boy's survival.

Though Christopher wasn't my own flesh and blood, I too shared in their tragedy. Watching his cancer slowly steal his life was one of the most painful experiences I had ever endured.

One afternoon I went to visit him and, as was the usual circumstance, I found him asleep and unresponsive to my voice. Confident he could still hear me and determined to make whatever time he had left as pleasant as possible, I sat down next to his bed and laced the fingers of one of his hands between mine. I gently ran my other hand across his little bald head, and in as animated voice as possible, whispered soft words of encouragement to him.

"Hey, Superman. What's going on, my man? What are you doing in here still sleeping? I need your help fighting the Atomic Skull. If you don't get out of bed soon, he's gonna beat me, for sure. Do you think you could open your eyes for just a second and show me a glimmer of some of your super strength?"

Incredibly, Christopher slowly pushed his eyelids open. His mom, who was sitting in a chair on the other side of the bed, lurched forward and gently grabbed his other hand. It was the first time he had opened his eyes that day. "Hey, sweetie. That's my brave little boy. I'm here. I love you. Dr. Zack came to visit you too."

He fluttered his eyes in my direction, and with incredible effort, he tried to speak. "Dr. Zack?"

I lovingly stroked his arm. "I'm here, buddy. Do you need anything? You name it, I'll make it happen."

He took as deep a breath as possible and ran his tongue arduously over his dry lips. "Will you take care of Yogi?"

His question left me feeling genuinely confused. I looked at his mom and begged an explanation. What did he mean, would I take care of Yogi?

She shrugged to indicate she didn't understand his request either and then concentrated on gently dabbing his lips with a moist sponge.

I tucked Yogi more securely under his sheet and pressed his beloved bear more firmly against him. "What do you mean, will I take care of Yogi? Yogi is right here. He hasn't left your side. He's here, helping to take care of you."

Christopher once again forced his eyes open and gazed at me earnestly. He concentrated all his strength on speaking. "I mean when I'm gone. Will you take care of Yogi when I'm gone? Promise me, Dr. Zack. Take care of him. Yogi's going to need a special friend."

Expressing his plea consumed all his strength. He closed his eyes, his breathing resumed its ragged, shallow rhythm, and his fingers became cooler to my touch.

I felt like the wind had been knocked out of me. I looked up and found his mother's gaze. Tears spilled down both our cheeks. Neither of us spoke; we were both too consumed by grief. Christopher and Yogi were inseparable. They were constant companions. By worrying that Yogi would feel abandoned, with pure and loving innocence, Christopher was acknowledging that he knew he was dying.

We remained silent; both gently caressing Christopher's arms. By now, our tears fell freely. They formed little puddles where they landed on the hospital sheet that covered him. I felt like I was being pummeled from all sides by emotions that surged through me like hurricane-force winds over the arctic tundra. I was racked by the most heart-wrenching sorrow I had ever experienced, and yet I also felt inspired by Christopher's courage. Surprisingly, I was also furious and felt betrayed. Christopher had done nothing to deserve such a horrible fate. At its very core, in the cosmic heart of the universe, unimaginable evil must exist to allow such senseless pain and tragedy to befall an innocent child.

I never said anything. I leaned over and kissed Christopher on the top of the head and then, on impulse, did the same thing to his mother. Without looking up, she wiped away some of her tears with a Kleenex and gave me a nod of genuine appreciation. In her heart, she knew our entire team would have moved heaven and earth to have arrived at a more favorable outcome. Sadly, however, that understanding wouldn't prevent her from losing her son.

She didn't shift her gaze even as she heard me quietly leave the room. She just sat and stared at Christopher, wanting to experience his every breath. She had to know there were not likely to be many more.

As I was walking away from Christopher's room, I ran into Christopher's father carrying their two-year-old son Dillon in his arms. The little boy was smiling and happy. As was our own special tradition, when Dillon saw me, he raised his hand to give me a high-five. His dad, on the other hand, was ashen gray. He looked at me, and for the benefit of Dillon, tried unsuccessfully to contain his tears. "Christopher's mom and I talked about it. We're still not certain it's the right thing to do, but we finally decided it was important to bring Dillon down to be able to say good-bye." The tears flowed more freely. "He doesn't understand cancer, he certainly doesn't understand death, but he's beginning to understand 'good-bye,' and we felt that years from now, we might regret it if we never gave him the opportunity to say it to his brother."

Dillon's animated and fun-loving expression changed to one of concern when he read the sorrow on his father's face. He lifted his little fingers to his father's face and very deliberately tried to wipe away each individual tear. "Don't cry, Daddy. Kisstofer get better. He come home to play."

Christopher's dad squeezed Dillon lovingly in his arms. "Yeah, sweetie. Christopher may come home someday. But for now, he's decided to go help Superman fight bad guys. That's why we're here today, remember? So you can tell him good-bye and wish him good luck."

Dillon pulled out of his dad's arms far enough to study his face. In a solemn voice, he whispered, "Kisstofer is very brave."

Christopher's dad squeezed him tighter. "Yes, he is, son. Yes he is."

Then, with his free arm, Christopher's dad pulled me into a hug also. "But we're all going to miss him, and we're sorry that fighting bad guys is going to take Christopher so far away."

With Dillon in his father's arms, the three of us remained locked in a firm embrace. When he released me, Christopher's dad had composed himself a little. "Okay, Dillon. Give Dr. Zack a hug and tell him thank you. He was a big help in getting Christopher ready for his trip."

Dillon reached for me with both arms. The faucet behind my eyes was again turned on. "I didn't do anything. Really, I didn't. But I can't tell you what a pleasure it's been for me to have had the chance to get to know all of you." Caught in Dillon's embrace, I was able to see past him and look at his father. Though my response to Dillon was simple, I knew his father understood the gravity and sincerity of the sentiment I was trying to express. "I'm so sorry Christopher decided not to stay." I finished returning Dillon's hug. "But I know Superman is proud of him. And I feel better knowing he's going to be flying around to protect us."

Shortly thereafter, they disappeared into Christopher's room. They later told me about an hour after they arrived, Christopher again opened his eyes briefly. He looked at his entire family purposefully and softly whispered, "I love you," and he then closed his eyes again.

Later that night, with his mom and dad by his side, Christopher drew his last breath. I was home at the time, but I could swear I felt an odd chill in the room at the very second Christopher died, like a ripple in the universe. I remembered having read somewhere in a physics book that when something precious is removed from a position in space, a vacuum is created. Though air immediately rushes in to fill the void, for all time and eternity, the space is forever altered.

I must have felt the transition when Christopher's soul left his body. I wasn't sure what the feeling meant, but I was aware that without him, the world as I knew it would never be the same.

CHAPTER 20

HAVING just one day off did little to boost my spirits. My stomach felt like I had swallowed a gallon of kerosene followed in close sequence by a lighted match. I had so many conflicting thoughts and feelings scrabbling around in my head I'd swear someone had put my brain in a blender. In one respect, I felt obligated to be stoic, set an example for the interns and medical students. Suffering losses was an inherent part of practicing medicine. It wasn't that physicians weren't entitled to feel sadness, but they were expected to shoulder the burden bravely. Appropriately sentimental but not so overwhelmed as to make them inefficient. After all, Christopher's death wasn't unanticipated. From the moment he was diagnosed, the unspoken assumption was that he wouldn't survive such an invasive cancer.

Why, then, did I feel so devastated? I didn't necessarily feel responsible. Mostly, I just felt inadequate, like I should have been more instrumental in identifying other solutions. I also felt an overwhelming sense of loss. Over the months of taking care of him, Christopher had somehow become an extension of my very being, and losing him felt intensely personal. It was as if, as a result of his death, part of me had also died. My heart ached and my head felt heavy. It felt impossible I would recover. Impossible I would ever again feel anything other than sadness. Impossible I would ever again make myself vulnerable to another patient.

If knowing what to feel was difficult, knowing how to act was equally confusing. Part of me wanted to throw myself down and sob. Realistically, however, other than being exceedingly embarrassing, sobbing would accomplish nothing except maybe identify me as too sentimental to be effective in a crisis and thus inadequate as a physician. Another part of me envisioned being able to carrying on with my responsibilities and act as if I'd suffered little more than a predicted disappointment; brave, unwavering, and dependable. Unfortunately, keeping a stiff upper lip was difficult when I felt like I was going to throw up any minute. The compromise was to spend all day in a fog. I enjoyed brief interludes of efficiency mixed with periods of trying unsuccessfully to suppress a few wayward tears.

Early in the morning, I discovered I could remain relatively unshaken as long as no one asked me how I was doing. The minute someone asked, I'd feel a huge lump develop in my throat and I'd have to vigilantly modulate my voice to keep it from cracking. Avoiding any discussion had been pretty effective until Dr. Herbert came onto the ward specifically to find me. Because I had my back turned, I didn't see her approach me from behind so was startled when I felt her hand touch my shoulder. Given my surprise, I didn't have adequate time to build the resolve required to arrest my tears. One look at the depth of compassion she held behind her eyes and mine were swimming. I brought my sleeve to my cheek to try to blot the tears before they ran down my face.

Her voice was a whisper but irrefutably direct. "May I have word with you in my office, Dr. Sheldon?" Before I had an opportunity to reply, she had turned and was already walking away. It was understood I was expected to follow.

When we got to her office, she motioned to the same chair I had sat in only six weeks before. "Have a seat, Zack." She closed the door behind us, then, rather than going to sit in the chair behind her desk, she sat down in the one next to mine. She let out a long sigh, then, before she said anything, reached over and patted my hand. "Zack, I'm not even going to ask how you're doing, because I already know the answer: shitty." She smiled at having been able to shock me, even if my reaction had been subtle. Dr. Herbert was the epitome of social decorum. She was articulate, poised, and wouldn't think of acquiescing to crudity. I didn't think she was capable of saying "shit" if she was choking on it. She smiled at me warmly. "Ordinarily, I'm not a fan of using vulgarities, but certain situations necessitate the use of a good expletive." She smiled at me again. "Don't look so surprised. I have a few more in my arsenal, and I suspect by the time we conclude this conversation, I will have used more of them.

"Look, Zack, I wish my years of experience would enable me to impart sage words of wisdom to you, but frankly, there are none. Medicine is an inexact science. It's a combination of objective data, precise measures, analytic calculations, and a lot of hope. Being a good doctor means working to master the first three but never losing sight of the fourth. You do your best to win, but the real challenge is working even harder to endure when you lose. Sadly, the failures are frequently more deeply felt than the successes." Her expression became slightly more intense. "But they all contribute to your being a better doctor. Bad things happen to wonderful people. Devastating diseases affect innocent, undeserving children. That's our reality, and fighting reality frequently means being broken by it. But, Zack, it's your willingness to fight and your willingness to care, even against insurmountable odds, that gives you the potential to be exceptional at what you do." She patted my hand again.

"If you remember, I told you at the beginning of this odyssey that you should never underestimate the power of caring. Though I don't believe any institution could have saved Christopher, I do believe that because he came here and because he had you, his death came more easily than it might have. Embrace that, Zack. I do. I believe Christopher did, and I want you to as well. Above all else, being a doctor isn't about curing disease; most importantly, it's about treating patients. You did that, and because of you, given the entirety of the situation, Christopher really did have the best possible outcome."

She stood, walked back over to the door, and put her hand on the knob. "I'm not going to kid you. Hearing that you made a significant difference in a child's life despite his dying might not make today any easier to endure, but if you take the enormity of that message to heart, it's what will enable you to survive a lifetime of being a doctor." She slowly began to open the door. "I won't keep you any longer. I know you have work to do, and besides, I don't want you to say anything right now. The experience is still all too raw. When the dust begins to settle, you know where to find me."

I stood up. I didn't trust my voice to speak. When I walked by her, however, I stopped and gave her a quick hug. "Thanks." I wanted to say more but didn't want to risk being overwhelmed by everything I was feeling. Instead, I gave her another quick hug and repeated, "Just... thanks." I walked away quickly and ducked into the public restroom, intent on washing my face. I hoped a lot of cold water and a dry paper towel would succeed in restoring my appearance to something less reminiscent of a complete emotional wreck. Instead, I spent those next few minutes crying. Ironically, I found there was a benefit to sobbing. It drained some of the painful emotion from my heart and enabled me to recalibrate my head.

By later that afternoon, I had successfully pulled myself together as well as could be expected. Diane, acting somewhat like a stealth bomber, had been circling me periodically throughout the morning. Though she was intentionally being unobtrusive, she also seemed determined to keep tabs on me. When she recognized that I needed something, she would instantaneously appear by my side. Finally, by about two o'clock, I took pity on her obsessiveness. I caught her attention and smiled. "How about I give you a break in the mother hen department, and the two of us go and get something to eat?"

She gave me a hint of a self-conscious smile. "I'm not being a mother hen. I just wanted to be sure you were doing okay." She bumped me with her shoulder. "Care for an egg salad sandwich? I laid three fresh ones this morning."

She made me laugh, and I threw my arms around her and gave her a hug. "I do appreciate you having my back. Sorry I've been so despondent today. This whole situation with Christopher threw me a greater curveball than I anticipated." I gave her a quick kiss on the top of the head. "Knowing I can depend on you is sometimes the only thing that gives me sufficient strength to endure this godforsaken job."

She hugged me back. "That would be a ditto, Zack. Besides," she said as she smiled jokingly, "there are probably dozens of men out there enduring their otherwise dismal existences just to hold on to the hope of one day being able to go to lunch with me. Fortunately for you, I just happen to be free right now. It's a pleasure for me to give you something to live for."

I suspected Diane might have a slight crush on me, but I responded in my typical fashion—by acting oblivious. "Hallelujah. The rest of them be damned. Now my life is complete." I pulled her arm through mine, and we started down the hallway, laughing. It was the first time I had laughed in a couple days.

We took the elevator to the ground level and started walking down the main hallway toward the cafeteria, still arm in arm, joking and bumping shoulders with one another. We hadn't walked more than twenty feet when we almost slammed right into Sergio. He was standing in front of the hospital directory kiosk and looked completely confused. In one hand, he was holding some directions written on a piece of paper. He was comparing what was written on it to the map of the hospital corridors. In his other hand, he was carrying a dozen red roses. When he saw us, his face broke into an exuberant smile. "I thought for sure I was going to get lost trying to find you. I knew you were having a rough day, so I wanted to surprise you by bringing you something to cheer you up. Must be my lucky day. I end up running right into you."

I froze. In fact, I'm sure the blood rushed out of my face. For my entire professional existence, I felt like my survival was dependent on keeping my work life and my private life separate. Now Sergio stood in front of me with his arms loaded with roses. The only bigger announcement I was gay would have been a Broadway marquee complete with flashing lights above my head. My tongue got temporarily lodged in the back of my throat. When I was finally able to speak, I was incapable of uttering anything more than, "What are you doing here?"

Sergio's smile was slowly wiped from his face and was replaced by an expression of utter confusion. "Like I said, I thought I'd come by to cheer you up. I thought that was what a supportive partner was supposed to do. You know, to be there when the chips were down."

His gaze wavered between mine and Diane's. She looked equally confused. Whereas before she had had her arm wrapped under mine, she now let it drop and just stared at the two of us. I was paralyzed. I stood there like a deer in the headlights. My brain refused to allow my mouth to form words. Sergio was here. The man who just a few months ago I had said I love you to for the first time. Now he was standing in front of me, and I was mortified. I wasn't ready to out myself at work. I wasn't ready for my colleagues to know I was gay. I wasn't prepared to be on the receiving end of the fallout I was certain would occur. Humiliation. Alienation. I had no desire to suffer the repercussions of being a gay physician in a homophobic hospital. In that moment, the only thing I could envision was the vitriolic contempt Dr. Klein would unleash upon me.

The flicker in Sergio's eyes began to fade. He went from looking confused to looking hurt. I still hadn't spoken, still hadn't moved. Then, beginning to feel uncomfortable by my apparent rejection, he began to get angry. "Look, I came here today because I was worried about you. I thought getting a dozen roses would make you happy. Apparently I was wrong. Sorry for the inconvenience. It won't happen again." He dropped the roses at my feet, did an immediate about-face, and walked hurriedly toward the exit.

Seeing him leaving caused the vise that held me motionless to relinquish its suffocating grip. He was already out the door when my feet finally began to move. I started to run after him. "Sergio, wait! Let me explain."

Sergio did little more than to snarl over his shoulder. "Fuck you, Zack. You don't have to explain anything. I got your message loud and clear. You don't want to see me. I get it. Rest assured, I won't bother you again. Ever!" He was down the sidewalk and through the door of the visitor's parking garage before I was able to say another word.

I dropped my head and slowly retraced my path. Diane was still standing where I had left her. Rather than looking angry, she looked sympathetic. "Zack, is there something that maybe you've been neglecting to tell me?"

Once again, my eyes welled up with tears. This time, I didn't even try to disguise them. Over the past few days, I had cried more than I had in my entire life. I stood in front of her but couldn't bring myself to look at her directly. My gaze remained fixed on the carpet at our feet. When I spoke, my voice was thick with emotion. "Do you hate me?"

Diane's response was immediate. In fact, it almost came out as a burst of laughter. "Zack, for someone who's so smart, you really are an idiot. Why would I hate you?"

I was finally able to bring my gaze up. "I don't know. For everything. For not being truthful. For disappointing you." My voice became almost inaudible. "For being gay."

Without hesitation, Diane threw her arms around me. "How could you think that? I'm not any of those things. If anything, I'm sad you didn't think you could trust me enough to tell me the truth before. We're friends, Zack. I love you. Nothing is going to change that." Her voice adopted a more joking tone. "You're gay; you're not a serial killer. Did you think my opinion of you would change? In fact, did you really think I didn't know? I mean, come on. I might not be the best judge of men; my ex-fiancé is evidence of that, but we've known each other for almost three years. We practically live in one another's back pockets. I didn't fall off the turnip truck yesterday."

Despite having a knot in my stomach the size of a small country, a hint of a smile crept across my face. "When *did* you fall off the turnip truck?'

Her voice became more serious. "Don't you dare try to change the subject again. I'm not going to offer you another convenient escape." She held my shoulders between her hands and forced me to look at her. "Tell me what's going on with you."

A few more tears appeared in the corner of my eyes. "Apparently, I'm trying desperately to completely fuck up my life."

"What do you mean?"

"Well, I'll soon be the laughing stock of the hospital, I'll probably lose everyone's respect, and the guy who I think I'm in love with is never going to speak to me again. That's a pretty good start."

This time, Diane did laugh. "Good Lord, Zack, you really are a drama queen. First of all, none of this is anyone else's business; secondly, you're not going to lose anyone's respect. Everyone I know thinks you're amazing, and no one who matters is going to give a rat's ass if they find out you're gay. And thirdly, if that guy is really worth loving, a ridiculous misunderstanding isn't going to change anything."

I looked at her pleadingly. "You're not going to tell anyone?"

For the first time since Sergio dropped the roses at my feet, Diane's expression did look hurt. "Christ, Zack. Do you really have so little regard for me or for our friendship that you think I would intentionally hurt you? I've suspected the truth for years. Has it ever affected the way I treated you?"

"Why didn't you ever say anything?"

"Come on, Zack. Don't be intentionally obtuse. I gave you a million opportunities to tell me. I just wasn't going to force the issue. I figured you'd tell me when you were ready."

My voice quivered a little. "Diane, you've got to believe that my not telling you I was gay wasn't because I didn't trust you." I tried desperately to find the words that would explain my apparent psychophrenia. I was sure I gave her the impression of having multiple contradictory personalities. "I didn't tell you because for most of my life, it wasn't something I accepted in myself. This wasn't about my lack of regard for you. Up until recently, this was about my lack of regard for me."

"Well, then, I'd say it's high time you got your head screwed on straight. Excuse the pun." Her voice became gentler. "Look, Zack. The world is a complicated place. It's woven together in an intricate, confusing pattern. Sometimes it's easy to get lost in the insignificant details. But at the end of the day, the testimony of a person's character is their integrity and their capacity to love. Who they love really says nothing about who they are. Everyone who knows you respects you for being the person you are. Being gay doesn't change anything about what's fundamentally important."

"But not everyone sees things that way. You can't look at the world through rose-colored glasses, Diane. It's filled with prejudice and homophobia. A lot of people are going to think less of me when they discover I'm gay."

"And I still resolutely believe that the only possible travesty here would be in your attempting to live your life trying to meet their expectations. They're bigots. We're not debating whether they exist. Of course they do. The only real question is whether or not you're going to allow them to set the bar for your life. Would you suggest that a black man bleach his skin because some racist finds his color objectionable? Of course not. You'd see the racist for who he was—a narrow-minded, self-loathing, ignorant fool. You would encourage the black guy to continue living his life with pride. Why won't you give yourself the same consideration?"

"You're right. Intellectually, I know you are. But sometimes there's a disparity between what I know to be true and what I feel. When you grow up with almost every element of society indoctrinating you to believe it's wrong to be gay, you don't wake up one morning and miraculously feel like embracing it. For the vast majority of my life, I've felt like being accepted required me to hide who I am. The fear I've lived with for all those years doesn't disappear just because I want it to. My denial is as much a part of me as the language I speak. It might have been something I learned, but it's the only language I know."

Diane clasped her hands on her hips. "So learn another language, Zack. People do it all the time. No one says it's going to be easy, but you can do it. Shit, Zack, if you put your mind to it, you could be fluent in four languages. Maybe even eight. Sure, you might always speak some of them with an accent; I'm not saying you won't. But you could certainly navigate through a hell of a lot of countries and feel pretty damn confident if you spoke eight languages. Isn't that a lot better than where you are now? Right now, you're making the choice to walk through life doing little more than mumbling. You're allowing the narrow-minded impressions of people you don't even know determine your value in this world. Let it go. The only person you're responsible to is yourself. If you're a good person and continue working to be an excellent doctor, nothing else really matters."

I slowly raised my head, lifted my eyebrows, and looked at her a little sheepishly. Of course she was right. I really couldn't offer a rebuttal. In fact, I was hugely relieved. Rather than being the least bit judgmental, Diane had come fiercely to my defense. "I'm not sure what to say.... *Gracias?*" I offered her an apologetic grin.

She again drew me into a tight embrace. "You really are a shithead, did you know that? In little more than three months, we're going to be done here and moving on to our respective jobs. Look how much time we wasted. We could have spent the past two years comparing notes about men." She laughed. "Speaking of men, if a hunk like that showed up to give me a dozen roses, I would have accepted them with open arms. I wouldn't even have had to know his name. With those biceps, that smile, and that sexy accent, my answer to anything he asked would have been yes."

My smile immediately faded. I absentmindedly looked in the direction where I had last seen him. "His name is Sergio Quartulli, and quite honestly, he's the most amazing man I've ever met." I pulled my gaze back and looked at Diane intently. Now that I was being honest with her, I had no conceivable reason to hold anything back. "I may very well be in love with him, and now I've completely blown it."

Diane reached up and gently stroked my arm. "It was a misunderstanding, Zack. The damage isn't irreparable."

My gaze again floated to the door where I had seen Sergio disappear. "I don't know, Diane. I've seen him angry before, but I've never seen him this upset. He went through all this effort to do something nice for me, and what thanks does he get? A coldhearted rejection. Even from my perspective, that's pretty damn unforgivable."

Diane continued to run her hand over my arm. "That's because you're always disinclined to forgive yourself, Zack. You're human. Humans are designed with imperfections, inconsistencies, and ridiculously obvious flaws. Screwing something up isn't unforgivable, it's part of being human. That's not an excuse, it's a fact. But being human doesn't absolve you of responsibility. Your job now is to try to make it right. If you try, and he still doesn't forgive you, that says something about his intolerance, not about your having made a mistake."

I looked at Diane intently while I processed what she had said. Then I threw my arm around her shoulder and gently rubbed my fist over her scalp. "Have I told you lately that you are incredible? That ex-fiancé of yours really was an idiot. Hell, if I was straight, I would marry you."

"Zack, if you were straight, I wouldn't give you any choice in the matter." We both laughed.

Though she continued to smile, her expression became more sincere. "Look, Zack. Your secret is safe with me. Though I really don't think it will matter to anyone, I believe it's important for you to be able to reveal who you are to people on your own terms. Just don't shut me out anymore. We're friends. That's not only a precious gift, but I rely on you. I wouldn't be here today if it weren't for you. From here on out, let's agree that it will be a more equal give-and-take. You shouldn't have to shoulder some of these worries alone."

"It's always been give-and-take, Diane. You know that. You've been there for me more times than I can count. In fact, I came close to telling you I was gay about a million times. My own issues prevented me from doing so, not you. But that doesn't mean I didn't depend on you to support me in every other aspect of my life. As far as residency goes, you've been my lifeline."

"Perfect. Then let me be your lifeline now. It's already after three o'clock. Give me your sign-outs now, and get your ass out of here. Go find Sergio and make things right. Grovel a little. He's Italian. Italians love groveling."

I looked at my watch. "He'll have to be at work by four, and I won't be able to talk to him there. I'm not sure how I'm going to fix this."

"Get your ass out of here anyway. Use the time to think about it. You'll figure it out."

CHAPTER 21

BY ELEVEN o'clock that night, I was leaning on the hood of Sergio's car. It was parked in the far corner of the restaurant lot. Because the majority of the patrons had long since finished their dinners and driven out, the lot was mostly empty. The only cars still remaining belonged to the employees designated to close down the restaurant. My arms were full of two dozen yellow roses. The woman from the florist shop had told me yellow was the color of forgiveness.

My stomach lurched when I heard the back door of the restaurant bang shut. I was apprehensive Sergio might do little more than just drive over me. When I looked up, I was both relieved and disappointed to see two women who I recognized as waitresses walking out. They eyed me with a curious expression. I just shrugged and said, "Courier service. They pay extra for late-night deliveries." They strutted past and got into their respective cars without saying anything directly to me, but I heard them whispering conspiratorially to one another. At that point, I didn't give a rat's ass what they thought. If it had helped to ensure Sergio would forgive me, I would have sat there naked with one of the roses between my teeth.

At a little after midnight, I heard the back door open again. When I looked up, I recognized the back of Sergio's shoulders. He was securing a padlock to an iron bar that slid between two brackets across the frame of the door. With the task completed, he dropped his head, pushed his hands into his pockets, and started walking toward his car. He didn't even look up until he was almost halfway across the parking lot. When he finally did look up, he froze midstride. I had a hard time reading his expression. Anger? Relief? Frustration?

The first few seconds were excruciating. Time ticked by in uncomfortable quiet. Finally, the discomfort of neither of us saying anything became insufferable. Better to endure a potential hostile reaction than to feel suffocated by silence. Unfortunately, however, despite having spent the entire afternoon trying to compose a perfect apology, now that Sergio was standing in front of me, I couldn't think of a single word to say.

Though I had to speak loud enough for my voice to carrying across half the parking lot, it felt like it was caught in my throat. Finally, determined to articulate something more than just a pathetic sob, I blurted out the first thing that came to mind. More accurately, I blurted out the last tangible thought that had occupied my head.

"The woman at the florist said that yellow was the color of forgiveness."

Sergio cocked his chin somewhat defiantly. "Yeah? And what did she say the color red signified?"

I dropped my head. I couldn't look him in the eye. My voice returned to an almost inaudible whisper. "Love."

"That's what I thought. In fact, that's what I intended. What I didn't predict, however, was having to throw a dozen red roses on the floor." He almost sneered.

When I didn't immediately respond, Sergio became impatient. He looked down at his feet and angrily kicked the asphalt. "Look, Zack, it's been a long day. I got your message loud and clear earlier this afternoon. Let's stop wasting one another's time." He again looked directly at me. His voice softened a little, but his expression remained hard. "I must be naïve. I kind of thought love trumped forgiveness."

Finally, I found my voice. Though tears moistened my eyes, there was now no uncertainty in my tone. "I want both."

"You want both what?"

"I love you, Sergio. I want your love and your forgiveness."

His gaze dropped back to study his feet. "You've got a funny way of showing it, Zack."

I stood up, carefully placed the bunch of roses on the hood of his car, and began to slowly walk toward him. "Sergio, you shouldn't act surprised to learn that I'm an idiot. Hollywood could make a documentary about all the stupid things I've done in my life. Had this afternoon's performance been caught on film, the audience would cringe at seeing what a complete ass I made of myself. Undoubtedly, they would have found my behavior so infuriating they probably would have gotten up and walked out of the theater. But," I said as I slowly began to close the distance between us, "if they had somehow found the patience to stay, if they had watched the movie in its entirety, in the end, they would have come to realize that my actions were the result of my own insecurities and had nothing at all to do with my feelings for you. In fact, like all great love stories, the audience would eventually have become overwhelmed with understanding and compassion. They would be willing the handsome Italian hero to give the thoughtless but well-intending, ridiculously closeted doctor another chance."

By the time I finished speaking I was standing within inches of Sergio. He still hadn't brought his head up to look directly at me. Instead, he spoke to the ground. "That's the trouble with Hollywood, Zack. It has very little to do with real life."

I was hugely apprehensive that I had completely exhausted Sergio's patience. I was afraid my neurotic behavior had finally pushed him to the point of no return and he had decided his life would be significantly more satisfying without me. My voice quivered a little when I said, "In my experience, real life is not all it's cracked up to be. You're my fantasy, Sergio. You're everything I've ever dreamed of. Trouble is, now that I've found what I've always wanted, I'm no longer sure how to live my life. My life has never been real. I've spent most of it trying to live a lie."

Our gazes finally met. "You can't live in a fantasy world, Zack." Sergio's voice softened. It wasn't impatient but instead tinged with subtle sadness. "You have to live in reality, with all its ugliness, prejudice, and homophobia. We can try to change it, but you don't get to choose. You have to live in it. I'm trying to be patient and understanding, Zack. Really, I am. I would never intentionally push you into a situation that makes you feel uncomfortable. But I won't live a lie. If you want to live a lie, you'll have to live without me."

I looked back at him. I could tell he recognized the pleading in my expression, but I also knew he must have seen my frustration. I pushed my hand through my hair and tried to calm the emotional tsunami brewing in my gut. "Sergio, if you've been trying to understand, then you'd recognize that I've been trying also. I'm not sure you appreciate how complicated this is for me. I know you think it's my choice to hide who I am, and I suppose to a great extent it is. But it's also a situation I was pushed into from an early age. I had no gay role models when I was growing up. I didn't grow up in a large urban community. Hell, I'm not even sure there was another gay man in the entire county, much less the town. The only education I got came from cruel jokes and hateful innuendos. Growing up in a small community where a young man earns respect by playing football, hunting deer, and hitting home runs, the message I got was clear: better dead than gay."

I made a conscious attempt to slow my speech. Previous experience had taught me that once these particular floodgates were opened, they weren't easily closed. "And don't think I don't know how pathetic that sounds." My voice went up in pitch. "Anyone's advice to me would be to grow up. Stop being a victim of influences you experienced as a child. The solution is always easy for someone who hasn't lived through it. Unfortunately, what well-intending people don't seem to understand is that I'm trying. A lifetime of conditioning doesn't disappear just because I will it to. Some of these feelings are so deeply engrained I sometimes can't differentiate where healthy self-esteem ends and pathologic thinking starts.

In addition, it's not as if all the negative influences have disappeared. I'm still subjected to them every day. Even as we speak, there are a number of physicians who oversee my work at the hospital who, if they knew I was gay, would love to see me fail on that basis alone. Intellectually, I know that despite the prestigious positions they hold, they're narrow-minded bigots; I still can't help having their attitudes stir my discomfort. How do I stand proudly in front of my colleagues when many of them think society is being done a disservice by even allowing gay men to work in pediatrics?"

I felt compelled to say more. I desperately wanted Sergio to understand how earnestly I was trying not only to be a man he could be proud of, but more importantly, how hard I was working to be proud of myself. In the end however, I fell silent. The week had been exhausting. The combination of losing Christopher, coming out to Diane, and arguing with Sergio made me feel like I was being crushed under a rock. I felt another tear escape my eye. "I don't want to live a lie, Sergio. I love you. That's not a lie. It's one of the most profound truths of my entire life." My head felt heavy. I didn't even have the energy to look up. Diane's words rang in my head: *Humans are designed with imperfections, inconsistencies, and ridiculously obvious flaws.* I let out a heavy sigh.

"I'm a work in progress, Sergio. Still woefully incomplete, but doing the best I can. I'm sorry that's not enough for you."

I turned to walk away. I had left my car parked on the street in front of the restaurant, so I forced my feet to move in that direction. Lifting them was an arduous task. It felt like they had been encased in cement.

Before I had taken more than three steps, I felt myself being pulled into strong arms. "Who said it's not enough?"

The feeling of again being pressed firmly against Sergio was greater than any adrenaline rush I had ever felt. The exhaustion that had consumed me just moments before evaporated like drops of water on a hot sidewalk. He turned me around, and before I knew it, my mouth was enveloped in a kiss.

When Sergio drew his head back, he looked at me intently. "I wish you could see yourself the way I do, Zack. If you did, you'd never apologize to anyone for being who you are."

I leaned my head against his shoulder. "That sounds funny coming from you, because I end up having to apologize to you on almost a daily basis."

He squeezed me tightly. "That's different. You'll still have to apologize when you're a thoughtless dick." He lifted my chin so I had to look him in the eye. "And for acting like you're ashamed to be seen with me. But you'll never have to apologize to me for being who you are."

My laugh was almost indistinguishable from a sob. "Haven't we been over this territory already? My shame is something I've been carrying since long before I met you. In fact, there have been times in my life when I felt like the burden of carrying it would surely break me. If anything, having you as a part of my life has lessened the load considerably. You might think I'm still living a lie, but actually, I'm finally getting strong enough to try to live the truth. Amazingly, though you might not appreciate it from today's pitiful exhibition, I'm less fearful of the consequences than ever before. It would be impossible for me to be ashamed to be seen with you. I would like to say that my determination for trying to get a better handle on this is for the singular purpose of feeling more comfortable living in my own skin, but that's not entirely true. Partly, I'm also doing this because of you. You make me want to be a better man. You make me want to be someone of whom you can be proud."

Sergio again tightened his squeeze around my shoulders and kissed me lightly on the cheek. "You're right, Zack. We have been over this territory before. I'm already proud of who you are. I couldn't love you if I wasn't."

I pulled back and stared into Sergio's amber eyes. Even in the faint light of the overhead security lamp, I could see them sparkle. "Fair enough. Let's call it a draw. You keep loving me, and I'll keep trying to prevent my insecurities from holding me back." I pulled Sergio's lips down to meet mine.

When we broke apart, Sergio was smiling. "I've got a better suggestion: Why don't we just concentrate on loving one another? I figure everything else will work itself out."

"Is that a suggestion that can be implemented while naked in bed?"

"Oddly enough, I believe that's exactly what the originator intended."

CHAPTER 22

THE next few weeks couldn't have played better if they'd been an orchestrated symphony. If anything, the misunderstanding between Sergio and me actually strengthened our relationship. We worried less about having to be on our best behavior in front of one another and were consistently more relaxed, just being ourselves. As was his inherent nature, Sergio continued to go to great lengths to take care of me. When I finished working a long shift, I would always come home to find dinner waiting for me. Frequently, even if he needed to be at work before I got off, he'd let himself into my apartment using the key I had given him and leave something for me to eat in the refrigerator. I felt like I was being really spoiled.

In addition, we both made more concerted efforts to be sure that we spent time with one another's friends. Certainly Declan and I eked out time to be alone together, but overall, our socializing occurred as a couple. It felt comfortable, it felt domestic, it felt right. I couldn't have been happier.

Those were among the thoughts dancing through my mind as I began to prepare to take sign-outs for another night on call. Thus far, the day had been mostly uneventful. Even though it was now kind of unusual, I had opted to sleep at home the night before because I knew I was going to be on call, and I wanted to get a good eight hours of sleep. Sergio had been working and wouldn't get off until after midnight. If I had waited for him, he would have arrived in the wee hours of the morning, I wouldn't have been able to resist molesting him, and then I would have come to work with little more than a couple hours of shut-eye. Sleeping with him always represented a huge temptation, but it would have made the prospect of having to work all night impossible. Sex was great, but not worth putting lives in jeopardy.

Most of the patients on my service were pretty stable, so I was enjoying having the luxury of being able to follow up on some of the less urgent details. I decided to go check on Emily, a five-year-old girl who had been admitted ten days before with osteomyelitis of her left femur. Osteomyelitis was an infection of the bone and required a prolonged course of IV antibiotics. The infectious disease specialist had recommended treating her for a total of fourteen days. By now she was feeling much better, so she was getting really bored. An extended hospital stay could easily result in a secondary case of cabin fever. Five-year-olds were really unaccustomed to being held captive in a hospital bed. Even though some had practiced endurance, a kid could only play so many hours of video games.

Surprisingly, though, even as I began to consider going in and trying to cheer her up, my chest tightened. Memories of Christopher came surging through my mind. His loss continued to feel raw. The world around me suddenly began to move in slow motion, and without making the conscious decision to do so, my feet came to a gradual standstill. Emily was a beautiful little girl with an engaging smile. Was I ready to begin to build another bond with a sick child? What if her condition worsened? If I became closer to her and the severity of her disease unexpectedly accelerated, would I be capable of watching her suffer? Had I lost all clinical objectivity? Had I morphed from a physician with relatively good clinical instincts into someone persistently on the verge of becoming an emotional mess?

I was about to turn around and quietly retreat in the other direction when some of Dr. Herbert's words of advice came floating through my brain: *Appreciate the power of caring, Zack. It's your willingness to fight and your willingness to care, even against insurmountable odds, that gives you the potential to be exceptional at what you do.*

Her words continued to resonate through me: *Power of caring... being exceptional.* I took a deep breath, steeled my resolve, and went into the play therapy room to grab a puzzle. I intentionally ignored the many Superman puzzles I had put together with Christopher and reached instead for a princess puzzle. What the hell, I probably had a half hour to kill; I might as well spend some of it trying to cheer Emily up. I couldn't allow

Christopher's death to forever harden my heart. It was the last thing he would have wanted, and it wasn't how I wanted to see myself. Besides, it was incredibly unlikely Emily would have a significant complication from a bone infection. Deciding to play the odds, I headed for Emily's room.

Her door was already open, but I still rapped on it with my knuckles as I entered the room, smiling. Her mother sat wearily in a chair next to her bed, flipping disinterestedly through a magazine. Emily was curled up under her bedspread with an array of dolls and stuffed animals spread out in front of her. She had a little plastic comb and was dragging it through one of the doll's matted hair. It appeared she was more likely to pull the poor doll's hair out than she was to loosen any of the tangles.

"Hey, Miss Em. I'm glad I caught you in your room. I was wondering if you could do me a favor?"

She looked at me skeptically but gave the impression that any diversion would be a welcome distraction. "What do you want?" Her voice was heavily layered with suspicion. Anytime someone from the medical team walked in, it usually meant either an exam or a painful blood draw.

"There's a seven-year-old boy down the hall," I lied. "His name is Michael. He gave me this puzzle to put together but bet me I couldn't do it." I studied the box with confused intensity. "It looks pretty hard, and I'm not too good with puzzles." I shifted my gaze to her and pasted on as helpless and as sincere expression on my face as I could. "I don't want to lose the bet, so I was hoping you could help me put it together."

She sat up in bed enthusiastically. She was too cute. Her long brown hair was pulled back from her face and secured with a Hello Kitty clip. It fell down to her shoulders in soft curls and framed a creamy white complexion accented by ocean-green eyes. "I'm good with puzzles!" she volunteered confidently.

"You are?" I beamed triumphantly. "Do you think you could help me?" Then I let the box drop to my side and tried to look dejected. "That is, if you're not too busy."

With a sweep of her hands, she knocked most of the dolls to the side of the bed. "No, I'm good with puzzles. I don't mind helping you."

I looked over at her mom and winked. Her mom's face brightened with an appreciative smile. "Great," I said, "Let me put some of these dolls onto the chair, and you scoot over so I can sit down next to you." I grabbed an armful of dolls and deposited them onto the chair. Then I dropped down on the bed next to Emily and adjusted her pillow so we could share it. When we were comfortable, I pulled her bedside table across our laps and spilled the contents of the puzzle box out in front of us.

"It's been a long time since I've done a puzzle. I don't even know where to start." I confessed.

Without hesitation, Emily shot her hands out and began manipulating the puzzle pieces. As if giving essential directions, she patiently explained, "First you have to turn all the pieces over so that you can see the pictures."

"Oh, that's a good idea. I suppose I should have thought of that. Lucky thing you're here to help me. I don't think I would ever have been able to put the puzzle together correctly if some of the pieces stayed upside down." She smiled up at me, and together we corrected the orientation of each of the pieces.

"How do you know which pieces to begin with?" I asked her, as if I were completely confused.

She accepted my ignorance as if it was to be expected and began to gently impart her strategy. "It's best to try to put together the pieces that have flat edges first, because you know those are the sides. Try to find two flat pieces that have matching colors."

When assembled, the puzzle would be a picture of a princess castle under a rainbow, and Emily reached for two pieces that were both a deep purple and snapped them together. "See, these are the purple part of the rainbow. See how they fit together?" She picked up the top of the puzzle box and directed my attention to the picture. "And see how the purple part of the rainbow is the top part of the puzzle? That's how you know they go together." She beamed at me as if she had just explained the paradigm of creating world peace.

"Wow!" I expelled an impressive sigh. "You really are an expert puzzle person. Let's see if we can put the whole thing together, and I won't tell Michael you helped me. That way, I'll win the bet for sure." I smiled warmly at Emily. "Then I'll get both of us an ice cream cone to celebrate. What do you say? Can we do it?"

Emily's eyes widened in delight. "It will be easy."

Twenty minutes later I walked out of Emily's room. The puzzle had been assembled and now covered her bedside table with an expansive rainbow. I left with the promise of returning shortly with ice cream. I laughed to myself as I headed back to the nurses' station. *That half hour might very well end up having been the most productive part of my day.*

I had no sooner gotten to within twenty feet of the nurses' station when Susan, the charge nurse, caught my eye. "I was just going to page you. Dr. Bargus called. He's sending a six-year-old boy over to be admitted with the diagnosis of painful limp."

I just rolled my eyes. We had taken to calling him "Dr. Bogus" because 90 percent of his admissions were bogus or completely unnecessary. The guy was either stupid, lazy, scared, or a combination of all three. "Painful limp? Does the kid have a fever? Has he gotten an X-ray?" I began to enumerate the steps that should have been taken to try to establish a diagnosis prior to admitting the child. Chances were, the little boy had something as simple as a sprained ankle, and rather than having to come into the hospital, he could be sent home with an Ace bandage and a bag of ice. I was about to escalate my protest when I remembered who we were talking about. With Dr. Bargus, the whole dialogue would have been pointless. He would just whine and sound increasingly concerned and helpless. I could hear it now: *I know it's unlikely, Zack, but it's better to be careful. We wouldn't want to miss a bone tumor or a septic hip.*

At that point, I'd just have to bite my tongue. I was always tempted to respond that most doctors could tell the difference between a stubbed toe and a bone tumor, but it was no use. Dr. Bargus had been on staff for the better part of a century, and he was loved by his patients. As residents, we just had to resign ourselves to the fact that his patients would be well taken care of, because if they even looked cross-eyed at him, Dr. Bargus would admit them to us to ensure any potential dangers were attended to adequately.

"Tell you what. Call him back and tell him to just send the boy to the ER. I'll see the kid down there. I suspect that, perhaps with the benefit of an X-ray, we'll establish an accurate diagnosis and be able to send him home. If the boy really needs to be admitted, I'll call you. We have a lot of empty beds, so we're safe." I smiled. "No risk of him losing his reservation."

Susan returned my smile. "I'm thinking about applying for a job in his office. Do you think he'd pay me better than I'm paid here if I just do all his work?"

I laughed. "From what I've seen lately, you're overqualified. A Boy Scout with a first-aid kit could do a better job than Dr. Bargus." We let our laughter fade. We knew we were exaggerating and were now being a little mean-spirited. The guy wasn't malicious, he was just clueless.

As I walked away, I distractedly said over my shoulder, "I'm going to check on the morning labs. I'll head down there in about thirty minutes. That should give the little boy adequate time to get checked in."

When I walked into the residents' office, I found Diane poring over a chart. She looked up at me, smiled vaguely, but kept her attention focused on the pages in front of her. "Hey, Zack, how's the Italian love life? Spicy? Or are you going a little too heavy on the garlic?" She looked up at me briefly, seeming to get great satisfaction from listening to her own witty repartee, and then directed her concentration back down.

I felt a quiver of anxiety creep down my spine. After our many recent conversations, Diane knew all about Sergio, and it wasn't as if I had anything I was trying to hide from her. I just still felt uncomfortable casually discussing my relationship while at work. Diane respected my privacy, and I knew she wouldn't broadcast her knowledge about me to anyone else, but I remained nonetheless guarded in the hospital. I couldn't help but feel it was a slippery slope. Once one person learned the personal details of my life, it could be only a matter of time before it became common knowledge. One would think I had matured beyond viewing that prospect as being so frightening, but mental evolution was slow. In many respects I hadn't grown beyond being a nervous adolescent, certain I would be the object of ridicule if everyone were to learn I was gay. I swallowed and chastised myself silently. No wonder there was so much homophobia in the world; I was a poster child for perpetuating it.

Seeming to sense my anxiety, Diane again looked up at me. "Come on, Zack, don't get your panties in a bunch. Your secret remains safe with me, but honestly, you make way too big a deal of it. No one really cares."

She might have been psychic, or, having had this discussion with me before, she could easily read my worries. "I know," I said. I relaxed just from acknowledging my discomfort to her. I went to the water cooler and filled a cup with cold water. "I feel a little silly. Old habits die hard. Little by little, I'm beginning to get less freaked out about it. In fact," I said, pasting on my most confident smile, "I'm sure in the very near future, I will think so highly of myself I won't give a shit what anyone thinks about me!"

She rolled her eyes. "Let's not go overboard. My opinion of you will always matter, and if I think you're being a shit, you'd better damn well pay attention." She laughed.

"Point taken. Let's just say I'm making progress at my own pace. Slow as a glacier, but progress." Eager to change the subject, I said, "Now, speaking of panties, what has yours in a twist? You've been glaring at that chart since I walked in. What bugs?"

"Oh." She opened the chart so that I could look over her shoulder. "I was just reviewing Baby Lash's chart. She's a three-week-old admitted a couple days ago with an elevated bilirubin. Initially, we suspected that her yellow skin was just the result of her bilirubin being only slightly above a normal range and that she'd improve with therapy. In fact, on rounds this morning, my intern said she was doing fine. But look at these values." She circled sequential numbers with her pen. "Though the baby has already been getting treatment for two days, some of these values are actually getting worse. It kind of worries me."

I evaluated the numbers she had circled and began to shake my head. "You have good cause for worry. The levels aren't skyrocketing, but they imply that the baby is at risk for having biliary atresia." Biliary atresia was when the bile ducts inside or outside the liver didn't develop normally. In babies with biliary atresia, bile flow from the liver to the gallbladder was blocked. The condition led to liver damage, which could be deadly if corrective surgery wasn't performed. I clapped Diane on the back. "Better draw some more comprehensive labs to check her liver. If they're abnormal, you'll have to put a call into the surgeon."

She looked at me with mock surprise. "Gee, you're pretty smart." Then, seeming to take pleasure in goading me, she included under her breath, "For a gay guy."

I had pretty much finished drinking my water, so I poured the rest down her back. "Bastard," she yelled as she sprang to her feet. "I was just emphasizing my point. You're a good doctor. Who cares if you're gay?"

"Hey! No one cares. And," I said, smiling, "if you believe no one cares, you'll also believe I spilled the water down your back by accident. Now, I have to get down to the ER to see one of Bogus's patients. I'm sure Bogus has already done an exhaustive workup and is depending on me only to confirm his clinical impression." I winked at her as I turned to leave. "Don't kill anyone while I'm gone."

The cup I had been drinking from bounced off the back of my head. Lucky thing it was thin plastic. I heard Diane laughing as the door closed behind me.

In an attempt to oxygenate my brain, I jogged down the four flights of stairs to the first floor of the hospital. When I was on call, the stairs were the only exercise I got. *It's too bad*, I thought. *A hospital of this size should have a staff gym. It would be great for productivity and morale.*

I walked through the ER and approached the central desk. Patty, one of my favorite nurses, was standing behind it with one phone pressed to her ear and another held against her stomach. As charge nurse, most of her job was traffic control: keep the well patients moving, keep the sick patients from dying, and keep a lid on the chaos. Not an easy job.

When she had hung up both phones, I smiled at her and asked as nonchalantly as I could, "What are you doing just kicking back? If you have nothing to do, could you at least grab me a quick cup of coffee? I take it with cream and a couple of Splendas, not sugar."

Her face read totally compliant. "Sure, it will be a pleasure to get you some coffee. You want me to mix anything else with your high colonic? Because...." She paused for emphasis. "If you expect me to get you a cup of coffee, that's how you're going to take it." She smiled at me expectantly. "I hear using lavender makes your farts smell like a French meadow."

"On second thought, maybe I'll skip the coffee. Too much caffeine makes me jittery." I held my hand out in front of me and made it shake. "Yep, thanks for your gracious offer, but I've probably had too much already." We both laughed. No doubt her humor prevented her from losing it completely.

"Listen," I said, "Dr. Bargus was sending over a six-year-old with a painful limp. Has he shown up yet?"

The question was barely out of my mouth before her phone began ringing and her beeper went off. She consulted the main triage board and whispered a response before she began speaking into the phone. "Room five, bed three." She brought the phone to her lips. "ER, Patty."

I walked into the room and found a little boy sitting on the bed. He had dark curly hair and brown eyes. His little Levi's were cuffed at the ankle, and he wore a Spider-Man T-shirt. I obviously had an affinity for attracting patients guised as superheroes. "Hey, champ." I pulled the chart out of the bedside rack and reviewed his vitals. He had no fever. "Dr.

Bargus called me and told me that you were having trouble walking." I looked at him intently. "That must be a big problem for Spider-Man. Can you still swing from a web?

I couldn't help but to chuckle softly when he answered in a solemn voice, "I'm not really Spider-Man. This is just my brother's old T-shirt."

"Oh," I replied earnestly, "my mistake. I mean, you kind of look like Spider-Man. Look at those muscles." I gently squeezed his bicep. "Okay." I again glanced at the chart and read his name. "I'll just call you Matthew, then." I rolled a stool over and sat down so I was looking at him from eye level. "So tell me, Matthew, does it really hurt when you walk?"

He nodded and answered in a soft voice, "Yeah, it hurts a lot."

"Really?" I looked at his mom and gave her a reassuring smile. "Maybe your mom can tell me how long it's been hurting."

She answered seriously, "It's only been hurting for about two days, but the pain has been getting progressively worse. Now he's pretty much refusing to bear any weight at all on his left leg."

I took his left leg gently between my hands and begin to run them up and down, palpating for any irregularity or for any obvious discomfort. "Okay, Matthew, can you tell me where your leg hurts?"

He answered cautiously, "The whole thing."

"Really? The whole thing? Hmm. That's going to make things a little tricky. Tell you what, why don't you take your pants and socks off and let me look at it."

He grimaced. "Take my pants off too?"

"And your socks." I shrugged as I pulled the curtain closed around his bed and said, as if it was the most natural thing in the world, "If your whole leg is hurting, I have to be able to see your whole leg. Don't worry. We'll keep the curtain closed, and if you're wearing Spider-Man underwear too, it will be our secret."

He hesitantly toed his shoes off, let them drop to the floor, pulled his socks off, then let his mom helped him pull down his pants.

He had barely sat back down before I realized immediately where the problem was. The bottom of his left heel was red and swollen and appeared to have something embedded in it. I positioned the exam light to direct the beam onto his foot and examined it more closely. I cocked my head at Matthew and said, "My man! It looks like you have a piece of glass stuck in your foot. Have you been walking around barefooted?"

In a state of complete disbelief, his mom walked around so she could look over my shoulder. "He does have some glass in there, Matthew," she said, looking at him incredulously, "why didn't you tell me it was your foot that hurt and that you had stepped on something?" She looked back at me apologetically. "I feel so foolish. I didn't even look at his foot." She eyed him with a hint of exasperation. "In fact, I was wondering why you hadn't been taking your socks off." She returned her gaze at me. "Initially, he wouldn't even admit his foot hurt. I just noticed he was limping. It was only when it got to be so bad he couldn't walk that he confessed his whole leg was hurting. I didn't even think to look at the bottom of his foot." She pivoted back to him. "Matthew, honey, why didn't you say something?"

Matthew looked down and tears began to spill from his eyes. "Because I knew it would hurt really bad if someone had to dig it out."

I stood up and hugged Matthew around the shoulders. "Hey, that makes sense to me. You must have thought taking it out was going to be scary." I sat back down and slouched so, despite the fact that he continued to look down, he was forced to look into my eyes. "But what if I told you I was magic and I could take it out without you feeling any pain at all?"

He brought his head up immediately, and though he gave me a hopeful glance, his voice was still filled with uncertainty when he said, "You can't really do magic."

"Sure I can." I nodded convincingly. "I've got magic medicine. The only thing I need to know is this: Are you brave enough for magic?" I clarified, "Because, as part of the magic, I'm going to make your foot feel as cold as ice for two seconds."

"Ice doesn't hurt." A little certainty crept back into his voice.

"Well, you're right. It doesn't. So, are you brave enough to give the magic medicine a try?"

His tears ceased. "You promise it's not going to hurt?"

"Hey, I'm a doctor." I smiled at him warmly. "It's against the law for me to lie."

"Okay, then," he said, nodding determinedly, "I'll be brave."

"Okay, then." I slapped his right knee. "Let me go get the magic. But, Matthew," I said, looking at him sincerely, "let's keep this a secret. I don't have enough magic to be able to use it on every little boy who comes in here. Can I trust you to keep a secret?"

His eyes became as big as saucers and he nodded. "I won't tell." I heard him confirming our plan with his mom, his voice now rich with certainty. "He's going to use magic medicine, Mom."

I went to find a nurse to elicit her help and to explain my plan to her. I was going to hang a drape so Matthew couldn't see what I was doing. Then, I would have the nurse spray his foot with ethyl chloride. Ethyl chloride was a freezing agent, and it would leave his foot numb for a period of seconds. I would use the opportunity to inject the area with an anesthetic. If I mixed lidocaine with bicarb and used a really tiny needle, I was confident that Matthew wouldn't feel a thing.

Marge, the nurse, was completely on board. I collected everything I anticipated I would need from the medicine room, grabbed a drape, then returned to Matthew's room.

When I arrived at Matthew's bedside, I instructed his mom to stand at the head of the bed next to him. Then I had him lie down with his foot extended just beyond the end of the bed. While I was positioning him, I explained that Marge was going to be my assistant and that she too had a lot of experience using magic medicine. Marge dutifully took a bow and then began helping me hang the drape between two IV poles on either side of his bed. The drape fell to Matthew's midcalf, and he was thus unable to see his foot.

"Hey, what are you guys doing?" Matthew became instantly apprehensive when the drape went up.

I looked at him over the drape and tried to appear surprised that he was asking. "This is the magic curtain. Haven't you ever seen a real magician? They always stand behind a magic curtain so no one can copy their tricks. This drape doesn't hurt, does it?

Matthew immediately looked relieved. "No, it doesn't hurt. Not even a little bit."

"Oh, good, then it's already working. Okay, are you ready for your foot to feel as cold as ice?"

Matthew squished his eyes closed and squeezed his mom's hand so tightly I could see her fingers blanch. "I'm ready."

"Then let the magic begin." I ducked behind the drape and directed Marge to begin spraying the ethyl chloride directly on the skin around the piece of embedded glass. "If the magic is working, your toes should already begin feeling really cold. Are they?" I took a peek over the drape and saw that even though Matthew kept his eyes tightly closed, he was nodding. Meanwhile, I pulled the syringe I had already filled with the anesthetic solution out of my pocket. The second Marge stopped spraying, I pushed the small needle into Matthew's numb skin and began injecting the anesthetic very slowly.

The worst part was over and Matthew hadn't so much as budged. I pushed the drape down just a few inches so he could see my face, then encouraged him to look at me. "Hey, champ, I'm almost done here. Does your foot hurt?

His eyes flew open in disbelief. "You're done? Did you get the glass out?"

"Well, it's not quite out, but I'm going to touch it and you tell me if you can feel it moving." I massaged the area around the glass with my finger to better distribute the anesthetic. "Does this hurt?"

He looked at me thoughtfully, giving the impression of being determined to answer the question correctly. "I sort of feel it, but it doesn't hurt."

"Excellent," I said, "then the magic's working. We'll have this glass out in no time."

Marge handed me a pair of forceps, and I was able to begin dislodging the glass without Matthew feeling anything. By opening the wound a little wider, I was able to grab the glass and pull it out with a gentle tug. "There you go, my friend—it's out. Now Marge is going to wash the cut a little bit. The magic show is over." I pushed the drape completely down. "What do you say? Am I pretty good magician?"

He smiled broadly though he acted as if he couldn't believe the procedure was really over. He darted his gaze between me and Marge, like any minute one of us was going to jump on him and dig the glass out with a shovel. As he became more convinced that I was really done, his smile widened even more, and he relaxed noticeably. "Yeah, you're a great magician. That magic medicine really works. I didn't feel anything." Then he looked at me and his expression became serious. "Don't worry, though. I'll keep it a secret. We won't even tell my brother, will we, Mom?"

"Not even your brother." His mom pulled him into a hug as she said it.

I stood up and addressed his mom as I began to wrap things up. "Keep the wound clean and dry for a few days. Soak it in warm soapy water a couple times a day, dry it well, then cover it with a clean dressing. It's a dirty wound, so I'm not going to close it with stitches. Fortunately, it's not very big. I'm going to leave a prescription for antibiotics with Marge. She'll give Matthew a dose before you leave, but be sure to fill the prescription today. If it gets more swollen, if the redness spreads, or if Matthew develops a fever, bring him back." I smiled at Matthew and ran my hands through his thick hair. "But I think that he's going to be fine."

I directed my parting comment directly to Matthew: "You did great, champ." I winked at him. "I think that you're even braver than Spider-Man."

I made my way back to the central desk to complete the paperwork. Patty was still juggling phones and fielding questions. When she came up for air, I waved to get her attention. She hung up the phone she had had cradled under her chin and walked over to me. "So," she kidded, "you save another life?"

"Fifth one today." I returned her teasing as I finished filling out Matthew's prescription and shoved it into Marge's in-box. "You out of here at eleven?"

"Unfortunately not. We had a couple nurses call in sick, and I have a daughter in college." She shrugged. "I'm going to end up doing a double. Won't clock out until 7:00 a.m. tomorrow." She smiled as she again reached for the ringing phone. "What can I say? No rest for the wicked. Why don't you come back down around three in the morning to keep me company? I'll buy you that cup of coffee." Her eyes danced with ominous intentions.

I pushed myself away from the desk. "I don't think so. I like to drink my coffee standing up, not bending over." I protectively covered my ass with both my hands, grimaced, then broke out into a smile. "Chances are, I'll see you at 3:00 a.m. anyway, though. I have a black cloud. When I'm on duty, it's like there's a tsunami of sick kids. I'm sure I'll be back down." I completed my note, pushed my pen back into my pocket, and waved. "So, on that note, see you around." I headed for the stairs.

The rest of the night was actually pretty easy. I had only gotten a few admissions, but they were mostly straightforward and the kids weren't too sick. As a matter of fact, I tried to suppress a little wave of optimism; if things remained quiet, I might even get some sleep. At that very moment, though, I heard the page operator's voice over the loud speaker: "Code Trauma, Code Trauma, Code Trauma." I held my breath. I knew if my beeper went off in the next few seconds, it would mean the trauma involved a child and my quiet night would hit the skids.

When after a couple minutes the beeper remained silent, I was able to breathe a sigh of relief. Maybe my night would be less than insane. Grateful for not being obligated to go to the ER, I was free to choose another activity to occupy my time. I knew a bunch of my patients had had X-rays taken that afternoon, so I decided to take advantage of the lull and run down to Radiology to review them.

It was late, and because my energy had begun to flag, I decided to take the elevator down rather than forcing myself to take the stairs. Jogging down four flights before midnight was exercise; attempting the same feat after midnight was insanity.

When the elevator door opened, I came face to face with Dr. Klein. He was flanked by his resident, Victor Maldonado, an intern and a medical student. I stepped in, nodded a greeting, the elevator door closed, and for a minute everyone stood in uncomfortable silence. We all fixed our gaze on the panel that illuminated the floor numbers as we descended. Not knowing what to say but feeling the quiet was becoming oppressive, I offhandedly commented, "I heard the code trauma announced over the hospital speaker system. You guys look pretty relaxed. Must be pretty confident in your ability to save the day." I tried to offer an unassuming smile.

Dr. Klein gave his head a disgruntled shake. "Ambulance is just rolling in. Some fairy princess from the West Village took a bullet to the chest. Probably the result of some circle jerk gone wrong. If I had my way, I'd relocate this whole hospital a little farther away from faggot central. Waste of my time to have to deal with those kind, and I resent having to operate on them. Puts my life at risk every time I have to cut into one of them. Which reminds me," he said as he scowled at Victor, "when we take this guy to the OR, be sure to double glove. No telling what kind of fucking diseases he might be carrying."

I was mortified. My cheeks burned with anger, but intimidation prevented me from voicing either my objection or my disgust. I was paralyzed by the fear that challenging him would immediately identify me as gay and that I would subsequently be the target of all his demeaning insults. That, and the label would spread through the hospital like wildfire and my reputation would suffer critical damage. Everything I had just said to Diane not six hours before suddenly rang hollow. I hadn't moved four inches closer to better accepting myself. I was just standing motionless in my life hoping desperately that one day the world would arbitrarily decide to accept me. Thankfully, I was absolved from having to face my indecision, because as soon as he finished his rant, the elevator doors opened on the ground floor and we all exited.

Despite feeling impotent, I was so furious as I walked away that I couldn't help but make a subtle parting rebuttal: "Or you might consider giving him the same compassionate care you'd give any other human being."

Dr. Klein looked at me like he'd just swallowed drain cleaner, but he didn't have an opportunity to respond—I was already practically sprinting away in the other direction.

My anger was so intense it gave me a feeling of indigestion. I was not only repulsed by Dr. Klein's hateful vitriol, I was angry at myself for being so spineless. It didn't take a gay man to protest his remarks; it just took someone who was intolerant of bigots. Arguing with him wouldn't have outed me. An open-minded straight man with an ounce of integrity and a refusal to be bullied would have challenged him without hesitation. I shook my head in frustration. In that instant, I wasn't so bothered by being gay, I was bothered by being such a pussy.

It took me about thirty minutes to go through all the pediatric X-rays I needed to look at. I just couldn't concentrate. I kept going back to Dr. Klein's tirade, and my stomach churned. This wasn't the first time he'd demonstrated the depth of his prejudice. Given an opportunity, he'd unleash his moronic opinions on anyone forced to listen.

I had just about given up on trying to make any sense of the X-rays when my beeper went off. I hoped no one needed me for anything important. I was too distracted to think. I looked at the read out on the beeper's display and recognized the number to the ER. "Shit." My first thought was that Dr. Klein had stabilized the patient and had found the time to reprimand me. Initially, my heart sank, but then I found myself thinking, *Bring it on.*

I grabbed the phone, dialed the number, and the ER receptionist picked up after only two rings. "ER, Cynthia."

I realized I was holding my breath when, after a long silence, I heard her impatiently repeat, "ER, may I help you?"

"Hey, Cynthia, it's Dr. Sheldon. Someone paged me"

"Are you on for Pediatrics?"

"Yeah, I drew the short straw tonight." I tried to inject a little humor to prevent her from thinking I was a complete idiot for taking so long to reply when she had first answered the phone.

"Dr. Simson is looking for you. Please hold. I'll transfer you to his phone." The line went quiet before I could respond.

A few seconds later I heard it ringing and was greeted with an efficient, "Dr. Simson."

"Hey, it's Zack Sheldon from Pediatrics. You were looking for me?"

"Oh yeah, hi, Zack, it's Mike. Thanks for calling back. Listen, I have a six-week-old baby boy down here brought in from home by his parents. They report having seen him turn slightly blue. They were feeding him at the time, so I initially would have guessed that he had just had a choking episode. When I examined him, however, I discovered he had a fever of 101. Neonate, fever, dusky episode." He listed three criteria I knew would result in the baby being admitted. Mike continued, "Things are pretty crazy down here, so I was hoping I might convince you to come down and do the lumbar puncture. He'll need it before we can start antibiotics."

I cursed under my breath but responded affirmatively. Any baby less than two months of age with a documented fever was sick until proven otherwise. The safest, most conservative course of action was to proactively start IV antibiotics and admit the baby to the hospital for observation. No one was willing to risk sending such a small baby home. There was just too great a chance a fever in such a small infant was an indication the baby was beginning to get seriously ill. "Okay, Mike, I'm on the first floor anyway. I'll come right over."

"Great, Zack. I owe you. Thanks a lot. I've already ordered the other lab tests. Hopefully, they'll be drawn soon. I'll talk to you more when you get here." The line went dead.

Only my concern for a sick infant pushed me in the direction of the emergency room. I dreaded going over there, certain I would run into Dr. Klein and he would use it as an opportunity to eviscerate me. With significant trepidation, I began walking. If I mustered enough mental fortitude, I might successfully dispel the notion in my brain that I had begun my own death march.

I slapped the silver pad mounted ten feet away from the doors to the ER, and they opened automatically. I saw Mike Simson on the far side of the room and knew that in order to reach him I'd have to pass by the trauma rooms. Fortunately, a cursory survey assured me that Dr. Klein wasn't in my immediate path, so I started to navigate my way through the room.

I had made it as far as the central desk when I saw a team of nurses circling the baby and making preparations to draw blood and start an IV. It would have been pointless to try to examine the baby while they were busy with him, but at the same time, I didn't want to wait where I would be so clearly visible. Why invite an altercation with Dr. Klein? There was a small room behind the desk that served as storage but also had a coffeepot that ended up being replenished hourly. I decided to discreetly creep into it. From its vantage point, I could continue to observe the baby but remain relatively hidden.

I was so confident going into the storage room would succeed in making me invisible, I was surprised that when I entered, I immediately ran into two policemen. Grateful I hadn't inadvertently run into Dr. Klein, I recovered quickly. "Good evening, gentleman. Did someone finally report that this coffee was poison?" I smiled.

"Not this time." One of them returned my grin. "Though this stuff even makes the coffee down at the station seem delicious by comparison, and it's crap." His smile widened. "We're just waiting to get some information on the shooting victim brought in earlier."

"Oh yeah, I heard about that." Of course, I didn't volunteer Dr. Klein's rendition of the evening's events. "What happened?"

"From talking to witnesses, it seems the victim had eaten dinner with a group of friends"—he referred briefly to his notepad—at a restaurant called Cables. He had apparently left his car parked in one of the back alleys and was returning to it when he was accosted. It was initially called in as having been a gay-bashing incident, but our suspicion now is that the motivation was robbery. We found the victim's wallet fifty yards away. It was empty except for an ID and a couple of pictures. Cash and credit cards were missing. We figure the victim resisted the attack and was subsequently shot in the chest."

The policeman I was talking to suddenly looked anxious. He lost his relaxed, congenial look, and began to study my face more thoroughly. His inspection of my features made me extremely uncomfortable. My mouth became immediately dry, and my tongue felt like sandpaper against its roof. Inexplicably, the way he scrutinized me made me feel he had concluded I was guilty of the crime. I tried to dodge his intense stare and couldn't resist an impulse to exonerate myself. "Why are you looking at me like that? I assure you I can't be a suspect; I've been here in the hospital since seven in the morning. I haven't left for even a second. You can ask anyone."

"It's not that, Doc. It's just… it occurred to me that you look like the guy from one of the pictures in the victim's wallet. Do you happen to know…." He again consulted the pad he had taken notes on. "Sergio Quartulli?"

My blood ran cold. The Styrofoam cup I had been holding crashed to the floor and sent coffee spilling over my shoes. My knees felt weak and threatened to buckle under my weight. The indigestion I had felt an hour before threatened an encore that this time would assuredly include violent vomiting. I backed up until I felt my shoulders touch the wall, then slid down it until I was sitting on the floor. I put my head between my knees and tried to steady my breathing. I was vaguely aware that the policeman had his hand on my back and was trying to get the attention of one of the nurses. He was standing right above me, but his voice sounded muffled, like he was talking through a tunnel from a great distance. "Can we get a little help in here?"

The room was spinning around me. When the fog began to slowly lift, I was aware that Patty was kneeling next to me, holding a cool washcloth against the back of my neck. "Hey, Zack," she was whispering softly, "just take a few slow, deep breaths. Keep your head right where it is. You'll be okay." She gently rubbed my back.

The daze was short-lived, but I still felt nauseous, and my ears continued to ring like a firecracker had gone off right next to them. I slowly lifted my head and realized no fewer than six people were staring at me intently. I recognized the two policemen, then noticed three other nurses had gathered in the doorframe, eager to assist. Patty continued to kneel by my side. She took my chin, slowly pulled it toward her so she could see my eyes, and then ran the washcloth across my forehead. I was aware she had my wrist in her other hand and was taking my pulse. Apparently convinced I would be okay, she whispered softly, "I was teasing about the colonic, Zack. It would have been okay to just drink the cup of coffee. It wasn't necessary to throw it on the ground."

I looked down and noticed that much of it had pooled on the floor and was soaking into my pant leg. At the same time, the memory of what the policeman had said came crashing back into my head like a freight train, and I felt another surge of panic.

I grabbed Patty by the arm and looked desperately into her eyes. "How is Sergio?" I forced my stomach contents back down. "Is he dead?"

My question brought a look of complete confusion to Patty's face, and she bewilderedly asked, "Who is Sergio?"

The policeman standing behind her interjected, "We believe the shooting victim we just brought in is named Sergio Quartulli."

His answer did nothing to alleviate Patty's confusion. "Do you know him?"

Now everyone's eyes were focused on me expectantly. I swallowed. This was going to be a defining moment. In many respects, it represented one of my greatest fears coming to fruition. I was going to be outed. Not only to a few trusted friends, but to the entire hospital staff. Visions of my career being flushed down the toilet came briefly to mind but were instantaneously overridden by my concern for Sergio. I wouldn't let him die on a hospital gurney, not twenty feet away from me, and deny to the world his significance in my life.

The magnitude of the realization not only shook me to the core, it also provided me with immediate clarity. Sergio needed me, and I wouldn't for one second allow my personal shame to prevent me from being there for him. In the game of life, one might choose to play his cards carefully, but at the end of the day, love trumped everything.

I stared only at Patty but answered loudly enough to be heard by everyone, "He's my partner."

Initially, my explanation did little to relieve Patty's confusion. "Your partner? Does he work here too?"

"No," I said. Surprisingly, my voice strengthened with conviction. "He's my lover."

Patty's expression registered bewilderment for just a split second, then transformed into one of complete acceptance. She kissed the top of my head. "You wait here; I'll go check on him. Kelly," she said as she motioned to one of the other nurses standing there, "you stay with him. Don't let him try to get up until I get back."

Kelly knelt next to me and immediately laced her fingers through mine. Her voice was both gentle and genuine, devoid of any judgment.

"Hang in there, Dr. Sheldon. The last thing I heard when I passed the trauma room was that he was doing okay."

I continued to sit on the floor. Ironically, I didn't feel self-conscious because I'd just announced to an entire audience that I was gay; I felt self-conscious because everyone continued to stare at me. I kept my eyes focused on the floor in front of me and felt tears begin to spill down my cheeks. I refused to accept the possibility that Sergio might be dead. My heart felt like it was being compressed within my chest by a vise. He couldn't die without knowing I was proud to be his partner. I was proud he loved me. I exhaled and heard the quiver in my breath. More importantly, I was proud to love him.

As I started to feel suffocated, another thought pushed instinctively into my head. It was a defense mechanism, a distraction to prevent me from being consumed by grief. If my brain could find another focus, if only for an instant, it might not completely implode and I would be relieved from having to consider that if I was told Sergio had been killed, I might never be able to get off the floor. I looked up and composed myself enough to say, "Dr. McClure is upstairs. Would you please call her and ask if she'd see that baby. I don't think I'm up to it."

One of the other nurses crouched in front of me and rested her hand gently on my shoulder. "She's already been called. She's on her way down."

At that very instant, Diane burst into the room and practically threw herself into my arms. She was crying harder than I was. Apparently, news traveled fast. "Zack," she sobbed. "Are you okay? Have you heard anything? How is Sergio?"

Seeing her wracked with emotion caused another wave of sadness to course through my body, and my vision again blurred with tears. I didn't trust myself to speak without crying but was somehow able to choke out a few words. "Patty went to check on him. I don't know anything yet." She threw her arms around me, held me in a tight embrace, and wept quietly onto my shoulder.

It seemed like it was quiet for the longest time. The policemen shuffled restlessly from one foot to another and occasionally barked single-word responses into their walkie-talkies. The other nurses had already busied themselves cleaning up the spilled coffee, and Kelly had released my hand when Diane had thrown herself into my arms.

The silence became even more deafening when Patty returned. She again crouched down next to me, and both Diane and I turned to face her. She began speaking slowly, her voice calm and gentle. Her demeanor didn't betray whether she intended to deliver good news or horrible news. "Sergio was shot in the upper left chest." A mournful gasp escaped my lips. "But," she said as she grabbed my hand and squeezed it to convey a sense of assurance, "Dr. Klein is confident the bullet missed any major blood vessels. They put a chest tube in his left side, and now that his lung is functioning better, Sergio is relatively stable. They're going to take him up to the operating room in a few minutes to explore the wound."

The relief that surged through me was indescribable. Not only had a weight been lifted off my chest, but I felt suddenly light-headed with optimism. For the first time since the policeman had uttered Sergio's name, I felt like I could breathe. I leapt to my feet, carrying Diane up with me. Unwilling to release me from her grip, however, Diane embraced my shoulders even more tightly. If anything, her weeping became slightly more audible. Between sobs, she whispered in my ear, "He's going to be okay, Zack, he's going to be okay."

"I have to see him." I was suddenly consumed by an overwhelming sense of urgency and began making my way toward the trauma room. Then the memory of Dr. Klein's hateful comments slammed into me. I turned to Patty and searched her expression desperately. "Who's the other in-house surgeon on tonight?"

Patty looked at me like she had been knocked over by the irrelevance of my question. "Dr. Wilber is also on tonight, but Dr. Klein is already on the case. What's the problem? He's an excellent surgeon."

The words came pouring out of me in a torrent. "Please call Dr. Wilber. Ask him to come down. Tell him it's an emergency. If you have to, tell him I would consider it a personal favor. I don't want Dr. Klein touching Sergio. Please, Patty. Call him. I'll explain later."

I ran toward the trauma room with Diane closely on my heels. On the way, she told me Dr. Simson had already gone ahead and had done the spinal tap on the six-week-old baby, so neither of our services would be needed immediately.

I walked into the room mentally prepared to have an immediate altercation with Dr. Klein, but when I arrived, he wasn't in the room. Having been primed for a fight, my adrenaline rush began to wane. I had been so fixated on readying myself for an altercation I hadn't really prepared myself to see Sergio.

The crowd around the gurney had thinned out a little, so I had no difficulty walking over and standing right next to it. Though a survey of the surrounding monitors assured me Sergio's vitals were stable, seeing him lying motionless on the bed caused another wave of emotion to surge through me, and I again felt my eyes being stung with tears.

Blood soaked the sheet underneath him. A bulky dressing was secured over his chest, and any areas not covered by bandages were covered by EKG leads. A blood-pressure cuff encircled his right bicep, and an endotracheal tube was taped to the side of his cheek. The cervical collar had been removed, however, and I could see the rest of his face clearly. If I hadn't known better, I'd have thought he was sleeping peacefully.

I grabbed his hand and held it between both of mine. Without giving it any conscious thought, I leaned over, kissed him on the cheek, and whispered in his ear, "You're going to be fine. I'm right here. I'll make sure they take good care of you. You're a fighter and too fucking stubborn to be kept down. You're going to be fine. I love you."

As I straightened up, I again became aware of tears were falling down my cheeks, but at this stage, that detail seemed trivial. Without taking my eyes off Sergio's face, I asked the nurse, "Has he been conscious?"

"When he arrived, he was weak and disoriented, but he was trying to put up a fight. We gave him some sedation.

More tears flooded my eyes. "That sounds like him." I kept his hand locked in one of mine and stroked his cheek with my other hand.

At that moment, Dr. Klein appeared from an adjacent trauma room. If he was surprised to see me, he didn't demonstrate it, and his voice maintained its traditional smugness. "Dr. Sheldon. I'm flattered by your presence here. You undoubtedly feel your clinical skills can be greatly enhanced by spending more time with surgeons, but in this instance, we won't be requiring any pediatric input. You're free to return to the monotony of the land of the little people. I'm taking this patient to the operating room."

Though I was seething with hatred, I maintained an even voice. "You're not taking this patient anywhere. I've asked Dr. Wilber to do the surgery." I turned to face him directly. "Dr. Klein, you are most assuredly a talented surgeon, but you are also a homophobic bigot, and I won't have you touching Sergio."

His cheeks turned immediately crimson with anger and the whole room fell silent. All that could be heard was the beeping of the monitors. Diane looped her arm through mine and hugged me in support. At the same time, Patty returned from the nurses' desk. She started to report that Dr. Wilber was on his way down, but when she recognized the standoff, she too fell silent.

When Dr. Klein found his voice, it came out like a scythe cutting raw flesh. "Why, you insolent little shit. I'll have you brought up on charges of insubordination. You can't talk to me that way, and as a worthless pediatric resident, you certainly have no authority to decide who performs surgery in this hospital. Now get the fuck out of my way."

I held my ground without flinching. "I'm not speaking to you as a pediatric resident. I'm speaking to you as Sergio's lover, and as the person listed on his power of attorney directive. I have the authority to make medical decisions on his behalf. That, Dr. Klein, does let me decide who performs surgery, and I refuse to allow you to touch him." I rested my hand protectively on Sergio's shoulder. "Dr. Maldonado can testify that not more than forty-five minutes ago, you stated that you resented having to operate on *our* kind, and that you thought it was a waste of your time. I will not have you waste your time operating on my partner." I glared at him. "That should be your privilege."

Now, understanding the situation more completely, Patty chimed in resolutely, "Dr. Wilber has agreed to take the case." She looked at me with understanding and compassion. "He said he'd do it as a favor to Dr. Sheldon." She paused. "I didn't have all the particulars, but when I explained what I believed to be the situation, he said he would be right down."

Dr. Klein ripped his scrub cap off his head and hissed through clinched teeth, "This is bullshit, Sheldon. Now I'm going to make it my mission to get your ass kicked out of here. You might as well kiss your career good-bye." He stormed out of the room.

Victor kind of snuck up behind me and whispered, "Good for you, Zack. The guy's an asshole. And, don't worry about Sergio. I'm still going to go to the OR with Dr. Wilber. We'll take good care of him."

Another tear trickled down my cheek.

CHAPTER 23

DR. WILBER arrived in the emergency room a few minutes later. Patty escorted him over to the edge of the nursing station, where Dr. Klein was furiously scribbling notes on Sergio's chart. From across the room, I couldn't hear their entire exchange, but I appreciated Dr. Wilber's calm, even tone even in the face of Dr. Klein's angry tirade.

Dr. Wilber was the epitome of professionalism. "Steven," he said, addressing Dr. Klein, "you'll have every opportunity to express your grievance and outrage to hospital administration. For the time being, however, we have to maintain our focus on the care of the patient. Dr. Sheldon, whom I understand is charged with making decisions on the patient's behalf, has requested that I assume"—he glanced at the name on top of Sergio's chart—"Mr. Quartulli's immediate care. I appreciate that your expert management has stabilized him for surgery, and I am thus eager to hear your assessment regarding the extent of his injuries. The sooner I'm brought up to speed, the sooner the patient goes to the operating room, and the sooner you're out of here."

Dr. Klein puffed out his cheeks but offered no additional rebuttal. He begrudgingly whipped into a review of Sergio's condition. "Single bullet hole to the upper left chest, no exit wound. Our best guess is that though extensive, the injury doesn't appear to have involved any major vessels. Regardless, he's lost a lot of blood and presented here with a collapsed left lung. He's intubated, has a chest tube in the fourth intercostal space, and has received two liters of saline and one unit of O negative blood. He currently has an acceptable blood pressure but is still relatively unstable. We see no value in getting any additional imaging studies and instead intend to take him to the operating room to explore the wound and try to control the bleeding." His expression became cynical and his tone sarcastic. "Does that bring you sufficiently up to speed? Or does Dr. Sheldon request that the information be relayed to you in the form of a fucking rainbow valentine?"

Dr. Wilber remained unfazed by Dr. Klein's vitriolic seething. "No, Steven, that's sufficient information to allow me to pick the ball up from here. Thank you for the remarkable job you did in helping to stabilize Mr. Quartulli. His compete recovery is significantly more likely as the result of your efforts." Dr. Wilber pushed himself away from the counter and started walking toward us but not before directing a final comment to Dr. Klein. "If your level of compassion was to even approximate your level of skill, you truly would be exceptional."

Dr. Klein only sneered in response. "Get off your fucking high horse, Craig. I would never allow someone's perverted lifestyle to dictate the quality of care they receive. Murderers, drug abusers, child molesters, faggots; I welcome all comers with open arms." He spread his arms wide in a mock display of greeting and plastered a contemptuous smile across his face. "Now, you'd better get cracking. I've heard tell that the fairy princess on the table over there turns back into a pumpkin at dawn."

Dr. Wilber did little more than subtly shake his head to indicate an apologetic sense of disbelief, then made his way into the trauma room, where we were waiting. He took a quick survey of the monitors, then spoke directly to me. His tone was compassionate but professional. "Let me assure you, Zack, that Dr. Klein's personal opinions are neither endorsed nor condoned by the vast majority of the medical staff here. While it's true that as physicians we are charged with improving the lives and well-being of all patients, most of us believe the value of an individual is measured by who they are, not by their race, their skin color, their religion, or especially by who they choose to love. Having known you since you started your residency here, you've impressed me as being intelligent, hardworking, compassionate, and determined to develop into an outstanding doctor. Those are the qualities that define you, and from my perspective, if you choose to share who you are with Sergio, then he's a lucky man." He gently touched my arm and gave my shoulder an encouraging squeeze. "Now, let's get him to the operating room and see what we can do to patch him back together."

Without the slightest sense of self-consciousness, I reached out and held Sergio's hand. A few wayward tears continued to cascade down my cheeks, and I maintained my focus on Sergio's pale face. The lump in my throat made my voice sound like tires driving over loose gravel. "If truth be told, between him and me, I'm the lucky one."

I straightened my shoulders, swallowed, turned to look Dr. Wilber directly in the eye, then made every effort to speak without allowing my voice to crack. "I can't thank you enough for coming down and for being willing to assume his care. I have every confidence that he's in good hands. Please do everything you can. I know it might sound selfish, but until this very moment, I didn't realize that I can't imagine my life without him."

"Believe me, Zack, I'll do everything in my power to make sure you don't have to." He turned to Patty. "I understand they're ready for us up in the operating room. Would you please coordinate immediate transfer up?" His request resulted in an instantaneous flurry of activity. A respiratory therapist gently pushed himself between me and the bed to access an ambu bag secured on a hook just above Sergio's head. He attached it to a portable oxygen tank, carefully disconnected Sergio from the ventilator, then connected the bag to Sergio's endotracheal tube and began to rhythmically squeeze oxygen into his lungs. When he confirmed with a stethoscope both lungs were being adequately filled with each compression of the ambu bag, he looked up at me with an encouraging smile. "Rest easy, Dr. Sheldon. We'll take good care of him."

I didn't trust my voice, so I just offered him an appreciative nod. I had subconsciously expected as the real significance of my relationship with Sergio became evident, I would be given a cool, isolative reception. Instead, everyone was being warm, understanding, sympathetic, and genuinely supportive.

Patty wasted no time in coordinating the nursing staff to prepare for a finely orchestrated transfer. Sergio was efficiently disconnected from the overhead monitors and connected to transport monitors secured to the foot of his bed. Pumps connected to the intravenous fluids and blood infusing into his arm were relocated to a portable pole. Within less than two minutes, Patty made a final inspection of the preparations, then confidently confirmed that Sergio was ready to be moved.

Dr. Wilber also performed a quick but thorough survey of the monitors and then turned to Victor. "Dr. Maldonado, please go on up and confirm that anesthesia is ready and the surgical nurses are prepared to prep Mr. Quartulli for surgery the second we hit the door. You can then

298 | JAKE WELLS

start scrubbing. I'm going to depend on a second good pair of hands to help me explore his chest and stop the bleeding."

Before he fled the room, Victor walked over to me and quickly threw his arm around my shoulders. "Like I said, Zack, we'll take good care of him. Don't worry." He then pulled a scrub cap out of his pocket, secured it over his head, and sprinted toward the door.

Dr. Wilber then turned to Diane. "Dr. McClure, you're going to be charged with giving Dr. Sheldon a strong shoulder to lean on while his partner is in the operating room. Are you up to the challenge?"

Diane wiped away some of the tears that had pooled in her lower lids and gave Dr. Wilber as confident a smile as possible. "Got it covered. I'm used to it. I'm the one who's had to carry his sorry ass through the last three years of training, anyway." She gave my arm a squeeze to confirm that she was joking, and I gave her a small, brief smile. Though my worry still brought me to the edge of panic, seeing my colleagues rally to my support and recognizing their genuine concern for Sergio kept me from becoming completely unglued.

The silence was broken by Patty giving an authoritative command. "Let's roll."

I released Sergio's hand as the entire team of caregivers gave each other consenting nods. I heard a sharp clank as the wheel lock on the bed was released, and then they began to glide Sergio toward the exit. Watching a patient's bed being wheeled out of the emergency room and toward the uncertainty of surgery was a scene I had observed hundreds of times before. Indeed, in countless instances, I had been one of the participants. The situation was not unfamiliar. So when I watched Sergio's pale almost lifeless profile pass in front of me on the gurney, I was surprised the loud gasp I heard had escaped from my own mouth. I was totally unprepared to deal with the sudden feelings of helplessness and worry that in that instant threatened to swallow me. Had I not been sitting on a stool, I was sure my knees would have again buckled underneath me.

Diane was quick to throw her arms around my shoulders and pull me into a tight embrace. The sensation was surreal. Though I was sitting and held securely in Diane's arms, I still felt like I was falling, as if the very earth had been pulled out from beneath me and I was catapulting through space, incapable of even partially navigating my fall. I wasn't even confident my body even existed, and yet I was somehow aware the soft sobs I heard in the now quiet room were my own.

Dr. Wilber was the last to leave. He walked over to stand in front of me. My head was down, and he gently lifted my chin until I was looking straight into his eyes. "I can't make any promises, Zack. I know you understand Sergio's condition is critical. But I promise you I'll do everything within my power to ensure the best possible outcome. That, I guarantee you." He released his grip on my chin and gave my shoulder a reassuring pat. "And, Zack, for what it's worth, it's a privilege to take care of someone so precious to you. Thank you for trusting me."

He was almost out the door before I found my voice. "Thank you, Dr. Wilber. I know Sergio is in the best hands."

The next few hours were excruciating. Without knowing exactly how I had gotten there, I found myself in the surgical waiting room. It occurred to me the last time I was there was when I had come in to report to Christopher's parents his surgery had gone well and Dr. Alfredo had successfully resected the majority of his tumor. A chill ran down my spine. Though Christopher's death still weighed heavily upon my heart, it now seemed like it had occurred a lifetime ago. I still remembered the deep lines of concern etched on his parents' faces when I first appeared to talk to them. His mom had been sitting in the very chair I now occupied, and she had leapt to her feet when she saw me approach. As I stared at the dreary beige walls, I realized I now wore the same deeply etched lines.

Diane sat next to me and kept a viselike grip on my arm. She occasionally got paged and would get up and use the phone mounted on the wall on the far side of the room to return the calls. I didn't give much consideration to who she was speaking to and only later realized she had been calling our colleagues to ensure that all the pediatric patients were taken care of in our absence. In my catatonic state, I hadn't even realized she had taken my beeper from my belt at some point and turned it off. It was only when our chief resident, Matteo, arrived and pulled me briefly into his arms that I realized the alert had gone out. He said he was sorry to hear about my friend and told me not to worry. He also told me all my shifts had been covered for the next week. In fact, despite none of my fellow residents being on call, when they got word that Sergio had been shot, four of them had left their beds in the middle of the night to come in to cover for me and Diane. They said they realized it wouldn't actually take four people to do the work of two, but when they heard who Sergio was and what he meant to me, they said they wanted to come in and do whatever they could to help.

Even in my grief-stricken state, I recognized the significance of the gesture. For years I had agonized whether I would lose their respect were they to learn the truth about me. I'd feared I would be ostracized by them and categorically shamed. Instead, they rallied behind me. They showed up in the wee hours of the morning, threw their arms around me, and insisted on staying to help maintain vigil.

I heard no malice, no disparaging remarks. In fact, all conversation centered around their support and their absolute conviction that Sergio would fully recover. Beth, who had returned from maternity leave just a few months earlier, even commented that Sergio had to get better so she'd have the opportunity to meet the guy responsible for making me so happy.

If my extreme worry hadn't resulted in me already being teary-eyed, their unconditional acceptance of me would certainly have caused me to cry.

Two and a half hours into the ordeal, I was becoming increasingly restless. I couldn't sit still anymore and began to pace back and forth. Diane watched me for as long as she could endure, then began to circle the waiting room with me.

"Zack?" she asked cautiously. "Is there anyone else you'd like me to call? Does Sergio have family? Would you like your parents here?"

If possible, even more color drained from my face. I cleared my throat and answered half her question truthfully. "Sergio's entire family is in Italy. Only one of his sisters actually lives here, but she left for Italy last week to visit their mother. I don't have any idea how to get ahold of her and even if I did, I wouldn't want to call her until Sergio's out of surgery. It would make no sense to worry her until we know more."

Diane stopped my pacing by grabbing my arm and searched my expression earnestly. We couldn't be overheard by the rest of our friends, but she nevertheless asked in little more than a whisper, "How about your parents?" Her lips quivered ever so slightly. "In the unlikely event we get less than good news, wouldn't you want them here to support you?"

Hours before, I thought I was incapable of crying any more tears. The whole experience had been so emotionally draining I was relatively certain I had already exhausted a lifetime's worth of tears. The sincerity of her question, however, proved me wrong. Tears again began to cascade down my cheeks like an untapped reservoir had been opened.

"They don't know about Sergio. They don't even know I'm gay." My response came out as a soft sob.

Diane looked momentarily confused, and though it seemed she was about to comment, in that moment, she decided not to. Instead, she again wrapped her arms around me and gave me another strong hug. "It's going to be okay, Zack. Your world is going to be a little upside down for a while, but it's all going to be okay. I can just feel it. When we're sure Sergio is out of the woods, we'll deal with everything else." She rubbed my back gently, and my quiet crying slowly began to subside. "In fact, when Sergio is up and around again, I suspect the burden you've been carrying around this whole time is going to seem monumentally lighter. All these secrets you've kept hidden away must have weighed a ton."

She was rewarded with a soft chuckle that, when I tried to steady my breathing, morphed into a hiccup. "We'll see if the burden ends up being any lighter. Dr. Klein told me he'd make it his mission to get me kicked out of the residency program. He carries a lot of clout here. What will I do then? Other training programs don't look too favorably at applicants who have been previously suspended."

Diane pushed me away from her far enough to be able to look me in the eyes. "We won't let that happen, Zack. The man might be a talented surgeon, but everyone knows he's an insufferable asshole. If there's even a suggestion of disciplinary action being brought against you, then the rest of us will walk out in protest. Let them try to run a pediatric program without any residents. It will be impossible." She drew me back into her embrace, then laughed softly. "Actually, they'll probably be left with at least one resident. Peggy will undoubtedly stay, but she and Dr. Klein deserve each other. In fact, the two of them can establish their own society. 'Dipshits Against Social Evolution.'" She drew away from me again but now was smiling. "Has a nice ring to it, don't you think?"

I could do little more than to laugh at her joke, mostly because I was speechless. The prospect of my colleagues coming so fiercely to my defense was a scenario I would never have dreamed possible. Not only had they given me every indication of accepting me, they seemed determined to support me, and if need be, even to fight for me.

I had to return to my chair to sit down. The culmination of all the thoughts going through my brain was again making me feel light-headed.

Diane sat down next to me and resumed her tight grip on my arm. "Listen, Zack. I'm here for the duration, and I doubt anyone will be going home until we hear how Sergio does in surgery, but the rest of the team is going to have to report to rounds in a few hours. Isn't there someone else who you'd like to be here?"

My mind was too numb to appreciate the magnitude of the realization but, just like breaking the surface of the water to breathe, it dawned on me I wanted Declan there. As my best friend, he knew me better than anyone. He understood the complexities of my life, and for the past five years he'd been there for me through every tumultuous event, even if the vast majority of them had been self-imposed.

I turned to Diane and answered affirmatively. "Yeah, would you please call Declan? It will help if he's here."

When she saw me nod, Diane had already gotten up to again use the phone, but when she heard his name, she came to a sudden standstill and looked at me blankly. "Who's Declan?"

A slight blush crept across my face, and I let me head drop back against the top of my chair. Once the house of cards began to fall, it collapsed in a heap. Though Diane and I had become significantly closer since the momentous day of Sergio's reveal, I still exerted a lot of energy keeping my professional and private lives separate. I would sometimes tell her about some of the experiences Sergio and I shared but only made vague reference to any of my other friends. Now, even through my exhaustion, I realized how ridiculous the façade I was trying to live behind had become.

"Declan's my best friend. We were friends way before Sergio and I even met. He'll come. He'll help hold me up."

When I looked back at Diane, it was evident that though she was trying her best not to be judgmental, she was hurt. "You've had a best friend for years that I've never heard about?"

Shit. The last thing I wanted to do was to hurt her. No, worse; she probably felt betrayed. I fixed my unfocused gaze at the ceiling. Regardless of how long I stared, however, the acoustic tiles failed to provide me with the words I needed to explain myself.

"Diane, I know I've told you this no less than fifty times, and I know it sounds clichéd, but it isn't you, it's me. Or, more accurately, it's my fucked-up self-esteem and my deeply rooted conviction that I'm seriously defective." A deep sigh escaped my lips. I knew Diane was looking at me intently, but I knew if I faced her, it would be impossible to keep talking, so I continued to direct my explanation to the ceiling. "Look, I've been hiding who I am for so long that it comes to me naturally even when I don't intend it to. Since the day you found out I was gay, I have been totally open with you. I've told you things about me and Sergio that no one else knows. It's just that you and my other friends have been separate entities for so long, it honestly didn't occur to me to try mix the groups. I didn't think my comfort zone could tolerate the two groups existing in the same space. It made me feel too vulnerable. Declan knows about my friendship with you, but only because he's been aware of my struggles for a long time. He knew about me wanting to be honest with you months before you discovered the truth. But he also understood how conflicted I was about coming out. Maybe he thought I exaggerated the risk it represented, but he nonetheless encouraged me to take the process at my own pace. He understood that I felt my professional life could be pushed onto thin ice if everyone in the hospital knew the details of my personal life."

Finally I found the courage to look at her. "I trust you, Diane. I probably always have. You've already helped me way more than you'll ever know. It's just that we met during a time in my life when I was incapable of taking more than baby steps, and introducing you to all my other friends felt like a huge leap. I just wasn't ready for it." I gave another labored sigh. "It seems especially ridiculous now, given where I'm currently sitting, but at the time, it wasn't so obvious."

I reached over and laced my fingers through hers. "I promise you can be mad at me later, but for now please just forgive me."

Diane leaned over and kissed me on the cheek. "Consider yourself fortunate that I've recently been nominated for sainthood. Now, what's Declan's number?" Rather than crossing the room to use the wall-mounted phone, Diane reached for the receiver on the phone sitting on the table next to us.

I again leaned my head back, closed my eyes, and recited Declan's number from memory. It was four thirty in the morning. After she punched the numbers, from where I was sitting, I could hear Declan's phone ringing through the receiver in Diane's hand. On the fourth ring, I heard him say a very disoriented, "Hello."

"Hey, Declan, this is Diane, Zack's friend from the hospital. Sorry to be calling you at this early hour."

There was about a three-second delay before I heard Declan's voice again. He still didn't sound fully awake, but his voice already registered alarm. "Hi, Diane. What's wrong? Is Zack okay? Did something happen to him?"

Diane's voice, though restrained, started to quiver, and her eyes again welled up with tears. "Zack's fine. In fact, he's sitting here right next to me." She paused for a few seconds to try to control her emotions. She was accustomed to keeping a cool head in emergencies, but in this situation, she wasn't speaking as a doctor, she was speaking as someone trying desperately to keep the world from coming crashing down on her good friend's head.

Before she could continue her explanation, Declan interrupted her. "I don't understand, then. Something must be wrong. Explain to me what's happening."

Diane gulped a mouthful of air and tried to continue without crying. "It's Sergio. There's been an accident." She tried to elaborate, but she seemed seconds away from breaking into sobs. "Do you think you could come to the hospital? Zack could really use the support of his best friend."

I could now clearly hear the panic in Declan's voice. "Of course I'll come. I'm on my way. What happened? How is he?"

Diane clutched the phone, but her voice refused to cooperate. I gently took it out of her hands and brought it to my mouth. "Dec?" Just saying his name caused all my fears to crash over me like an arctic wave. I made no attempt to stop crying but put inordinate effort into trying to speak without blubbering incoherently.

"Sergio was mugged, Dec." My entire body shook with grief. "The fucker who did it shot him in the chest. He's been in surgery for two hours, but we still haven't heard anything. The surgeon was optimistic going in, but Sergio lost a lot of blood. The bullet went in really close to his heart. I don't know. I just don't know." My voice dropped to a soul-wrenching whisper. "He has to survive, Dec. He just has to. He can't die without knowing how much I love him."

"He won't die, Zack. He won't." Though I knew Declan was pulling assurances out the sky, his words were nonetheless comforting. "You sit tight. I'm on my way. I'll be there. I'll be there, Zack. I'm coming now. You sit tight. You stay right where you are. I'll get directions from the lobby."

My voice regained a little strength. "Thanks, Dec. I knew I could count on you. I'll be here." I reached over and again pulled Diane against me and then let my gaze cross to the other side of the room. Beth and several other friends from the hospital were sitting in a tight circle, nodding at me encouragingly. "Diane is doing a really good job of holding me together and a few of my other friends are here as well. They've all been lifesavers." I squeezed Diane tighter. "Truly. Lifesavers. See you when you get here, Dec. Thanks." I hung up before I heard him respond, then sat back. If worry hadn't been surging through my body like a jolt of caffeine, I would have collapsed from exhaustion.

Diane kept her head on my shoulder. The rhythm of her breathing slowed, and I thought that she'd fallen asleep until I heard her quiet voice. "He's going to be okay, Zack. You'll see. Dr. Wilber will be out any minute with good news. Stay positive."

I couldn't bring myself to answer. I didn't know how I should feel. In this situation, would positive thoughts really make a difference? If so, why wouldn't positive thinking have prevented Sergio from being shot in the first place? Was he being punished? Did he somehow deserve what had happened to him? The only conclusion my sleep-deprived brain could come up with was that life was just a big crapshoot. Events in the universe occurred at random. Tsunamis struck, earthquakes happened, and assholes shot innocent people for no earthly reason. It was impossible to envision how, at such a critical junction, positive thinking might now influence the outcome of Sergio's surgery. Maybe I was feeling particularly pessimistic, but at that moment, despite every exalted hope, it seemed Sergio's ultimate fate would be determined by a metaphysical coin toss.

That realization made me feel even more sullen, and I tried to mentally prepare myself to receive heartbreaking news.

No more than fifteen minutes later, Declan came bursting into the room. His hasty departure was evidenced by his appearance. His hair stuck up from his head in every conceivable direction. He was wearing a faded pair of sweats and a baggy T-shirt, and had mismatched flip-flops on his feet. His eyes were still puffy from having just been awakened, but he raced across the room with determined purpose. I was pulled into a bone-crushing hug before I was even fully standing. Feeling his protective arms encircle me caused another wave of emotion to come slamming through me, and tears once again spilled from my eyes.

While holding my head cradled against his chest, Declan looked at Diane. "Have you heard anything? Do we know how Sergio's doing?"

Diane shook her head. There was a prolonged period of silence, then, probably in an effort to partially relieve the tension, Declan released me just long enough to give Diane a quick hug. "I'm Declan, by the way. I've heard so much about you that I feel like I already know you. Zack sings your praises all the time."

When Diane fell away from his embrace, she looked at both of us. She only smiled faintly, but her expression didn't convey any hard feelings. "And you must be the phantom friend whom I always assumed existed but was never told about specifically." She gave my arm a playful shove. "Zack apparently has a habit of keeping the good-looking secrets to himself. I'm only privy to the bad and the ugly."

I laughed a little self-consciously. "That's not entirely true. I've been telling you about Declan for years. Whenever I said that I had spent time with friends and had had a blast, he was the 'friends.' Meeting him now is just giving you the opportunity to put a face to all the stories." Then I forced a slight smile as I looked at Declan. "Though come to think about it, now that you two have finally met, I can embellish the stories with some of the juicer details."

Declan pulled me back into his arms and gave me a threatening squeeze. "Better not. You give her so much as a suggestive hint about any of my embarrassing exploits, and I start giving free tours of all the skeletons in your closet too."

"Point taken." Though we fell back into an anxious silence, Declan continued to search my expression expectantly. Finally, his solemn question broke the tomblike quiet. "What do you know so far?"

I took a deep breath and was surprised when I was able to answer without my voice quivering like the strings on a violin. "We really don't know much more than I told you. Sergio met some friends for dinner and was apparently mugged walking back to his car. The police found his wallet next to him, but it was empty of both cash and credit cards. The police assume the motive was robbery, but Sergio might have been gay bashed, then robbed as an afterthought. Either way, at some point during the altercation, the asshole or assholes who attacked him shot him in the chest. The surgeon is confident the bullet missed his heart, but his left lung collapsed, and he had a lot of internal bleeding. Sergio was in the process of getting his second blood transfusion when he was taken to the operating room. We hoped they would be able to quickly identify where the bleeding was coming from, repair the damage, and have him back to recovery long before now. It's already been more than two and a half hours, and we thus far haven't heard anything."

Explaining the seriousness of Sergio's condition caused my head to spin. I pulled myself out of Declan's embrace and slid back down into my chair. "I can't prevent myself from thinking every additional minute he's in there brings me a minute closer to losing him."

Neither Diane nor Declan responded. They saw no benefit in trying to offer what could very possibly be false hope. Instead, they sat on either side of me and each wrapped an arm around my shoulders. The silence stretched into several more minutes before I heard myself whisper, "Before I met Sergio, I'm not even sure I liked myself. I certainly didn't fully accept myself, and I've spent the majority of my life fearing people would discover who I really am. Now, if there was even a marginal chance that it would better guarantee his recovery, I'd scream the truth from a mountaintop."

Declan hugged me a little tighter. "That's the funny thing, Zack. Sergio knew the truth about you from the moment you two met. He didn't make you better; he just chose to be with someone who he recognized had great value. That's who you've always been. The thing Sergio succeeded in doing was allow you to see yourself like the rest of us have seen you for a long time."

Diane echoed Declan's sentiment by also giving me a tighter squeeze.

"I don't feel like a good person. It took him being shot to admit to the world how much he means to me."

Declan sighed. "Don't do that to yourself, Zack. Sergio knows how important he is to you. He also understands why accepting yourself has been a struggle. He didn't care if you weren't out to the whole world. He was happy you were honest with him. Facing a crisis does one of two things: it either breaks a person or it pushes them to find an inner strength they didn't know they possessed. You're just beginning to find your strength, Zack."

Another tear trickled down my cheek. "Then why do I feel broken?"

Now Diane chimed in. "You're not broken, Zack. Far from it. You're in love and you're scared. You're exactly who you should be. Now quit doing this to yourself and quit imagining the worse. You know what they say—sometimes no news is good news."

"Let's hope," I whispered to the floor. "Let's hope." The three of us again fell silent. Beth and my other friends crossed back over to our side of the waiting room and pulled up chairs to close a circle around us. The vigil continued.

About ten minutes later, Dr. Wilber appeared in the doorway. I snapped my head up and searched his facial expression as he walked slowly toward me. In my experience, a person's body language was sometimes more telling than were their actual words. My chest felt like it was immediately crushed by a wrecking ball when his expression failed to convey even a marginal degree of optimism.

My head told me I should stand to greet him, but I couldn't trust my legs to support my weight. Instead, I remained seated, and as I watched his deliberate progression through the room, I subconsciously held my breath to steel myself against the anticipation of getting horrific news.

It wasn't until he was standing in front of me and he reached up to pull his scrub cap off his head that his face brightened. "Sergio's a lucky man, Zack. I think he's going to be okay."

At first, I didn't trust my ears to have heard him correctly. The blood was pounding in them so loudly I assumed the noise had drowned out what I had convinced myself would be him delivering the news that Sergio had died in surgery. It took a few seconds for the fog in my brain to clear enough to be able to process what he had said. "You think he's going to be okay?" I didn't even recognize my own voice. It sounded more like pea gravel being shaken in a tin can.

"Yes, I'm fairly confident that though repairing the damage ended up being a trickier feat than I would have imagined, he's going to make a full recovery. Fortunately, the weapon was a small-caliber handgun. The single bullet entered his chest, deflected off a rib, then nicked his left subclavian artery just at the juncture where the left vertebral artery attaches. It's a miracle he didn't lose more blood than he did. The surgery took longer than I anticipated because there was damage to both vessels, and I wanted to guarantee both were successfully repaired. The good news is that he maintained excellent blood pressure through the entire procedure, and because of collateral circulation, I'm confident his brain always maintained good perfusion. With the exception of requiring a little downtime, I predict he should be up and around in no time. Intraoperatively, there didn't even appear to be any nerve damage, and he was already responding to commands by squeezing his fingers when he was being wheeled into recovery." By this time, Victor had appeared behind Dr. Wilber's shoulder. "In fact, thanks to Dr. Maldonado's meticulous application of subcutaneous sutures, he shouldn't even have too big a scar."

Victor offered me a sheepish smile. "Told you we'd take good care of him, Zack. Figured you'd want him to maintain those perfect pecs."

A relieved smile spread across my face as another spigot of tears opened. "That would have been my priority, Vic. Thanks for watching my back."

A collective sigh of relief rose up from the entire group, followed quickly by a few cheers.

I shook Dr. Wilber's hand so vigorously I became fearful I was putting his surgical career at risk. "I can't thank you enough, Dr. Wilber. You're a lifesaver, and for maybe the first time in my life, I mean that literally. Thank you." Another tear made its wayward journey down my cheek. "You're an incredible surgeon and an even more amazing human being. Thank you."

He pulled his hand out of my grasp and drew me into a quick hug. "It was a privilege, Zack. I'm thankful we anticipate Sergio will have a good outcome." He released me but continued to rest his hand on my shoulder. "I'm going upstairs to get a few hours' sleep. If there's any problem, the nurses can reach me in the call room. We left Sergio sedated, so he'll be pretty out of it, but if you'd like, you can visit him in recovery. Just don't stay too long. He got a lucky break, but we'd be ill-advised to push it. He needs to rest."

As he turned to walk away, Victor stepped forward to shake my hand. This time, I ignored his outstretched palm, wrapped my arms around him, and pounded him gently on the back. I whispered softly enough that no one else was able to hear, "You're more than a kickass surgeon, dude, you're fuckin' awesome. Thank you. If you hadn't been in my corner, I'm not sure I would have found the courage to stand up to Klein. You're the bomb. I hope you don't suffer any fallout."

When I released him from my embrace, Victor was smiling. "No worries, Zack. I know how to take care of myself, and besides, I'm pretty sure we both have an army of people willing to go to bat for us. At the end of the day, love, truth, and compassion triumph over bigotry." His smile broadened. "He ain't got nothing on us! We're cool."

"I'd like to think you're right, but it still took balls to be among the first to take a stand. I owe you."

"Perfect. I'll hold you to that. As soon as Sergio's out of that bed, I'll let the two of you buy me a beer."

I was still grinning as I walked back to rejoin my group of friends. Lots of hugs were shared, and I introduced Declan to the rest of the gang. Beth shook his hand and joked, "Guess it is true. The good-looking ones are always gay."

CHAPTER 24

FOUR hours later, Sergio was stable enough to be transferred to a private room. In recovery, he had opened his eyes briefly, seemed to recognize me as I pushed his hair off his forehead, but then he'd quickly fallen back to sleep. He barely even budged when they moved him from the gurney to the bed, and seeing him so unresponsive, I again had to force myself to choke down a foreboding sense of panic.

For the first several hours he was in his room, I was a sentry at his bedside. The nurse came in and out frequently, and though he never came fully awake, Sergio started to mumble when she checked his blood pressure and confirmed there was no excessive seepage from his wounds. She also observed that the drainage from his chest tube had already begun to decrease. She was encouraged that by every objective criterion, he was making impressive progress.

Though intellectually I knew her assessment was probably accurate, I also knew that deep within my heart, I wouldn't breathe a full sigh of relief until Sergio was once again up and about and propagating jubilant chaos in the lives of those he cared about. Despite being confident he was indeed stable, I still couldn't prevent myself from keeping a vigilant eye on the monitors above his bed. Even their continuous demonstration of a strong regular heart rate didn't completely curb my anxiety. I willed him to be awake, to look at me, to assure me he had not only survived his ordeal but that he'd come through it without permanent damage.

There was a small sofa in Sergio's room. Declan had fallen asleep on one end, and Diane had fallen asleep leaning against his shoulder. Looking at them caused me to appreciate how truly fortunate I was. Here were my two best friends in the world, strangers to one another, but united in their support of me. I watched them sleep and noticed how their breathing was in perfect sync. In that moment I made a pledge to myself to begin working to better integrate all the important people in my life. It was also in that moment I knew I would be able to call my parents and feel no trepidation about telling them I was gay. There would be no more secrets, particularly among the people I loved.

I pushed both of them lightly on the shoulder and coaxed them gently awake. "You guys go get some sleep. You're both exhausted. Sergio's likely to sleep most of the morning. I'll call you immediately if there's any change."

As they slowly opened their eyes, they both began to protest. "We're fine, Zack. We were just resting our eyes."

Despite my own exhaustion, I had to laugh. They both said essentially the same thing almost simultaneously. Maybe my two best friends were more alike than even I realized.

"Really! I insist. There's no way I'm going to leave here until Sergio himself kicks me out. Then, when that happens, I'm gonna want to be sure one of you is close at hand. It would be better for the two of you to go rest up. Right now we're in a waiting game. Part of the team has to conserve its energy."

Neither of them would be easily convinced. Diane was the first to protest. "I agree. But the one who should be conserving their energy is you. You just said Sergio is likely to remain asleep for the next several hours. You should go sleep now so you will be more awake when he really comes around."

Declan's agreement followed in short order. "She's absolutely correct, Zack. You haven't slept at all. I was snug in my bed until Diane called me at four thirty. I slept most of the night. I'm as fresh as a daisy. You go get some sleep in that call room I've heard so much about. Keep your phone by the bed. I'll call you if Sergio should so much as fart."

Their allegiance and concern for me was touching. Because they had both sat up, they'd left a few inches between them on the couch. I wedged myself into it and threw my arms around both their shoulders. "Dec, I don't think there's a day in your life when you've been fresh as a daisy, and if any farting occurs in here, I'll know you're the culprit. Don't blame your rancid intestinal tract on Sergio just because he can't defend himself." I squeezed them both more tightly. "I'll make you guys a deal.

We'll take shifts. But don't ask me to leave now. I just can't. You guys go get some rest but come back and check on us in a couple hours. I'll stretch out here on the couch. I'll sleep too. But this way, if Sergio wakes up, I'll be right here."

Neither of them seemed completely convinced, but they reluctantly agreed because they knew I wouldn't be dissuaded.

Declan stood and reached for Diane's hand to help pull her up. "Okay, Zack. You win. But one of us will be back in two hours, and then we'll drag your ass out of here kicking and screaming if we have to. We both know how grumpy you get when you're sleep deprived. We'll be doing Sergio a favor."

I hugged them both. "You guys are the best. I don't know what I'd do without you." I pulled back and unintentionally let the corners of my mouth slip up into a wisp of a smile. "I would say I'm forever in your debt, but I know how screwed that would leave me. For now, I'll just leave you with the irrevocable guarantee that I'll love you both forever."

Diane smiled and hugged me again. "I think I'd rather have the big-screen TV, but if love is your final offer, I guess I'll take it."

Declan then pushed me toward the couch. "Okay, Zack, but we're not going to leave until we see you lying down. You'll probably be asleep before your head hits the back cushion."

"All right already. I'm lying down. Look." I moved one of the cushions to create a pillow, lay down sideways on the couch, and drew my knees toward my chest. "Satisfied? As cozy as a baby in a manger. Now get the hell out of here so I can sleep."

They slowly walked out of the room but continued to look over their shoulders. "We'll see you in two hours," Declan said. "Don't snore."

I waited for five minutes after the door shut to make sure one of them didn't poke their head back in, then got up, pulled the chair over to the edge of Sergio's bed, then sat down and laced my fingers through his.

I awakened to the sensation of fingers being run through my hair. Because it felt good, I kept my head buried in the edge of the mattress until I remembered where I was, then lifted it with a start. Sergio's head remained cradled in his pillow, but he had turned it to face me and his free hand was resting on the top of my head. I took it and gently placed it against my cheek. I stared in his eyes intently but for a moment didn't trust myself to speak. The last thing I wanted to do was to panic him by breaking into tears. "Hey, babe." I intentionally chose the term of endearment he had referred to me by in the early weeks of our relationship. It still carried special significance because I still remembered how elated I had felt the first time he used it. "How are you feeling?"

"My chest feels like I was hit by a bus. What happened?" The words came out scratchy and hoarse, but though it obviously took a concerted effort to speak, he sounded stronger than I would have anticipated. "Why am I in a hospital bed, and why are you drooling on my sheets?"

It was impossible to contain my emotions any longer. Hearing his voice and recognizing that even in his confusion, he still had his sense of humor, I was overwhelmed. I used the back of his hand to wipe a few tears off my cheek, but the smile that suddenly found itself plastered across my face felt like the most genuine I had ever had. "You had a kind of a rough day yesterday. When you're a little better rested, I'll tell you a little about it. In the meantime, can I just say that I've never in my life been so happy to wake up next to you?"

For a brief instant it was obvious he was trying to put the pieces of the last day together in his head, but fatigue overtook him and he slowly closed his eyes. "I'm looking forward to hearing the story. If your smile is any indication, I must be great in bed." He tightened the grip on my hand, but mere seconds later he was again snoring softly and his fingers relaxed.

I, on the other hand, didn't have the slightest inclination to release his hand. I kept our fingers intertwined and used my free hand to gently stroke his arm. I whispered softly, though I knew he was already asleep, the words were more for my benefit than his, "Yeah, you're great, all right, Sergio. Greater than I ever dreamed possible. Thanks for deciding to give me another chance."

The nurse came in an hour later, and this time when she took his blood pressure, Sergio opened his eyes and kept them open. He again rolled his head over to look at me but didn't immediately try to speak. His expression indicated he was still trying to make sense of the situation. He released his free hand from my grip and reached up and felt the bandages that covered his chest. He registered brief panic, but I could see him quickly tamp down any fear he felt. He experimented with trying to take a deep breath, and though I could tell it must have been pretty uncomfortable, he seemed satisfied by proving to himself his body was at least still functioning.

It was obvious he was completely bewildered by the situation he was waking up to, but, as was typical of Sergio, he never wanted to give the impression of seeming vulnerable. "The service in this place is horrible. What does a guy have to do to get a drink of water?"

Because his comment was followed instantaneously by his unassuming smile, the nurse took no offense. Besides, she knew from our previous conversation in the wee hours of the morning that Sergio worked in a restaurant. Without missing a beat, she replied jokingly, "Maybe if you tipped better, you'd get better service. When I get back, there had better be a least a Lincoln on that tray table. Then we'll talk service." Her smile softened. "It's good to see you awake, Mr. Quartulli. How are you feeling?"

Sergio pushed his head more deeply into the pillow and let his gaze roam across the ceiling, as if trying to find the words to explain how he was feeling, then experimented with taking a few more deep breaths. "I feel like someone put a harpoon through my chest." He then looked back and forth between me and the nurse to see which one of us would confirm his suspicion.

I again grabbed his free hand and held it against my chest. "You're close. You got mugged last night, and sometime during the process, you ended up getting shot. You gave us quite a scare, but we're now absolutely certain that you'll recover completely." I intentionally tried to sound as confident and optimistic as possible.

His expression reverted to one of confusion and concern. "I don't remember anything." He again pulled his hand free from mine and rested it over his bandage. He seemed relieved that he could feel his chest expand against his fingers when he breathed. Satisfied, he turned back to me and again reached for my hand. "Are you sure I'm going to be okay? It hurts like hell."

I couldn't help letting a soft chuckle escape. "I'm sure it hurts, babe. You've only been out of surgery for about seven hours. They had to fish a bullet out of your chest. You're not made of steel, you know. You have to expect it will hurt like a son of a bitch for at least a couple of days." I drew his hand up to my lips and gave it a gentle kiss. "The important thing is that you're here to complain about it and I'm here to listen."

Sergio looked appreciatively into my eyes for several seconds. I knew he'd have a ton more questions, but for now he seemed content in the knowledge that despite being shot, he was going to be okay.

When I kissed his hand again, he seemed to suddenly become aware that the nurse was still in the room. Knowing how anxious I was about giving anyone a reason to suspect I was gay, Sergio instinctively tried to free his hand from mine. In response, I just held him tighter and pulled his hand back against my cheek.

"I'm staying right here, Sergio. Now you're stuck with me. The bullet that almost killed you ended up freeing me. No more hiding. I love you. The one thing this experience has taught me is that life is short. Too short to spend even one second denying who you are and being ashamed of whom you love. Life is a gift. Love is a gift. They should both be cherished and savored with exuberant pride." I gave his hand another squeeze and gave his fingers an additional gentle kiss. "If you're willing, I'm hoping you'd like to continue to spend this part of our lives together."

Sergio smiled and then winked at the nurse. "I'll be damned, Zack. If I didn't know better I'd say you just participated in a public display of affection. Are you sure you weren't the one who was shot?" His smile broadened, and then, with only a small grimace of pain, he pulled my hand over to his lips so he could return the kiss. "Maybe you weren't aware, Zack, but that's been my plan since the first month we met. I was just waiting for you to be brought up to speed."

I swallowed and willed the lump in my throat to disappear. "Thanks for being patient, Sergio. In case you haven't noticed, I can be a little slow sometimes."

Sergio smiled again. "You're not slow, babe. You were just running against your own clock. I always knew where the race would end. As long as we were running together, I figured we had all the time in the world."

"Yeah. All the time in the world if you promise not throw yourself in front of any more bullets."

"It's a deal. You keep a hold of my hand, and I'll try to keep myself out of trouble."

It was obvious our brief conversation had drained what little energy Sergio had, because his eyelids again began to droop. "I've gotta to rest a few minutes. Stay with me, okay, Zack?"

"Always, Sergio. Always. You can bet on it." He was asleep before the last word even escaped my lips.

The nurse checked the IV line, then gave me an affectionate pat on the shoulder. "Dr. McClure and another friend of yours came by about an hour ago. You were both asleep, so I shooed them away. I told them I'd call them when you were awake."

"Thanks, Arriana. I so appreciate it. But do me a favor. Give me another hour. They're just trying to take care of me, but if they hear that Sergio is awake and speaking, they'll try their damnedest to drag me out of here."

"Will do, Dr. Sheldon. I'll try not to let them by me for at least a couple more hours. But only if you promise me to try to get a little more sleep. As you can see, your partner is doing fine. Now you need to take care of yourself."

I loved hearing someone—who not more than six hours ago was a perfect stranger—refer to Sergio as my partner. What a difference a day made. I had spent most of our relationship fearing people would suspect we were together as more than just friends. Now, all I felt was pride. "I promise. I'll put my head back down right here." I patted the edge of the mattress. "I just want to be next to him when he wakes up again."

She smiled again. "Okay by me. Seems like you two are good together."

I smiled too, but rather than looking at her, I stared at Sergio's sleeping face. "You have no idea. We really are."

The next thing I knew I was again being awakened by someone gently tapping my shoulder. When I lifted my head, Dr. Mueller, the director of the residency program, was standing over me. "Sorry to wake you, Zack, but may I have a word with you in private? Perhaps we could step out into the corridor?"

A surge of anxiety made me catch my breath. I was sure he'd come down to fire me. Dr. Klein's grievance must have already reached the administrative heads. I had been hoping to try to institute a little damage control, but there simply hadn't been time. Besides, the die had probably already been cast—Dr. Klein was too heavy a hitter to go up against.

I felt an overwhelming sense of sadness, but ironically, was also surprised by the absence of regret. I certainly didn't want to lose my position in the residency program, but at the same time, having endured Dr. Klein's bigotry and hatefulness for the previous three years, part of me was proud of finally saying no more. Looking at Sergio asleep in the bed strengthened my resolve. He had survived and I loved him. I would never deny him again or try to disguise the significance he had in my life. Even if that meant losing my job.

As we walked toward the door, Diane's words rang in my mind: her promise that my colleagues would stand behind me. While I appreciated the sentiment, I knew the gesture would be useless. I was tremendously relieved both she and Victor liked and respected me, but I knew this situation was my own doing, and I didn't want any of them to suffer any consequence as the result of my choices.

When we got out into the corridor, Dr. Mueller checked to ensure we had plenty of privacy, then leaned against the wall and folded his arms across his chest. "Sounds like you had quite a night, Zack."

I couldn't bring myself to meet his eyes, so I stared down at the carpet in front of his feet. "Yeah, I've had my share of rough ones, but last night was definitely the worst." The silence then stretched on for several seconds, and I assumed that, like a child being reprimanded for a serious prank, he was waiting for an explanation.

I focused my thoughts on the memory of Sergio holding my hand and forced myself to continue. "I'm sorry if I embarrassed either you or the program, Dr. Mueller, and I understand why you have no recourse but to terminate me. Though I'm prepared to accept my dismissal as a necessary disciplinary action, I also need to make a statement in my defense." My voice strengthened with determination. "Dr. Klein's treatment of gay men in this hospital is unacceptable. He promotes an environment of intolerance and hate and has an attitude that I think tarnishes the reputation of this hospital as being an institution of caring, acceptance, and inclusion."

My voice then became more apologetic. "I'm sorry. Maybe I should have been more forthcoming about the fact that I myself am gay, but I seriously didn't believe it had any bearing on my ability to fulfill my obligations to the program."

Because I was looking at the floor, I was a little startled to feel Dr. Mueller touch my shoulder. When I brought my head up, I saw he was blushing, as if he was slightly embarrassed. "I'm sorry, Zack. You misunderstood the intent of my coming down here. There isn't going to be any disciplinary action brought against you. In fact, I've been in meetings all morning to try to determine what action is going to be taken against Dr. Klein. While the administration appreciates that he is a talented surgeon with an impressive history of service to this hospital, they too find his behavior objectionable. It was decided earlier today that if he chooses to maintain staff privileges here, he will have to take mandated classes in cultural diversity awareness. In addition, he will have to attend a requisite number of individual sessions with one of our staff psychologists with the express purpose of improving his social sensitivity. This is not the first time Dr. Klein's behavior has been brought to the attention of medical staff, but his recent antics have certainly been the most noteworthy. The phones of both the chief of staff and the hospital CEO were flooded with calls this morning from people who wanted to support you. You've earned yourself quite a following here, Zack."

I was speechless. In fact, I was having difficulty processing the entirety of what Dr. Mueller had said. I was so certain he had intended to reprimand me that most of the words he said after his initial apology sounded like they were being spoken in a foreign language.

For a few seconds I just stared blankly at him, and when I finally spoke, I asked what must have sounded like an idiotic question. "So I'm not being fired?"

He again patted my shoulder and smiled encouragingly. "No, Zack. You're not being fired. We have been and continue to be extremely proud to have you a part of this program. Collectively, we regret if you were ever made to feel uncomfortable, and we want to assure you that your experiences have made the entire staff even more determined to promote an environment of acceptance within the walls of this hospital. From this day forth, our 'zero tolerance for discrimination and slander' policy will be even more vigilantly enforced. We not only want you to stay here, Zack, we want you to be happy."

I felt the lump creeping back into my throat but felt confident I could answer without becoming emotional. "Thank you, Dr. Mueller." I smiled and shook his hand. "I look forward to being able to complete my training. I appreciate your understanding."

"No, Zack, I appreciate yours. We're a health-care facility. Our mission is to tend to the needs of the people within this community—to their emotional needs as well as to their physical needs. If that's our responsibility to our community, it applies doubly to our own staff. This is the last place someone should be forced to hide who they are."

Rather than releasing my hand, he covered it with his other and gave it a tighter squeeze. "On a personal note, I want to tell you how sorry I am that your partner was hurt. I've known you since you were a medical student, Zack, and have the utmost regard for you not only as a young doctor but as a friend. If there's anything I can do to make this situation easier for you, please do not hesitate to ask."

He released my hand but continued speaking. "I'd offer to give you this week off to be with your partner through the early stage of his recovery, but your fellow residents have already taken care of that. They insisted on working extra shifts to cover you. That's exceptional, Zack. I hope you recognize that. It's an accomplishment when doctors succeed in winning the admiration of their patients, but it's spectacular when they succeed in winning the admiration of their colleagues. You've earned it, Zack. More importantly, you've kept it. They were even more insistent on helping you after they learned you were gay."

Keeping the emotion out of my voice was becoming an almost impossible challenge. "I've heard every cloud has a silver lining. This one is just bigger than I ever thought possible."

EPILOGUE

Three Years Later

LEO came racing across the yard, tail up, ears back, tongue hanging out of his mouth like a big wet sponge. He was only one year old and wasn't even close to growing into his feet. Even by Alaskan malamute standards, he was going to be big. The vet suggested he'd probably tip the scale at around a hundred and fifty pounds when he reached his full adult size. As it was, he was an exuberant tornado of unbridled love. As he came to within a couple yards of me, I instinctively covered my crotch and bent my knees. I knew his intention was to change direction at the last second, but he frequently miscalculated his momentum and smashed directly into me. On more than one occasion he either had me singing soprano or had knocked me over and sent me sprawling on my ass. Of course, nothing made him happier than to succeed in getting me on the ground. Then it became his mission to cover every inch of my face with wet, sloppy kisses.

The name Leo was a compromise. My preference would have been to have given him more of a Nordic name. He was, after all, an Alaskan malamute. But Sergio wanted something that sounded more Italian. Leo satisfied both of us. It had an Italian flair, and he looked like a lion. Sergio and I had been together three and a half years and had lived together for almost three. I'd learned compromise was an imperative component of a relationship, but I was so happy it never felt like too great a sacrifice.

As I stood and watched Leo race around the yard, I found myself reflecting on the weeks surrounding Sergio's attack....

SERGIO ended up remaining in the hospital for four days after his surgery. Dr. Wilber had been amazed at how quickly he recovered, and though he'd been a little apprehensive about letting Sergio go home after such a close brush with death, he couldn't figure out any reason to keep him longer. Sergio was discharged with strict instructions to take it easy and to return immediately if he had any worrisome symptoms as all.

All my friends rallied to cover my shifts for the days Sergio was hospitalized, and by taking my final weeks of vacation early, I was able to be off a full ten days to assist Sergio during his convalescence. Though "convalescence" was an exaggeration by any definition. By his second day at home, Sergio was going stir-crazy. With the exception of having to keep his left arm immobile, he said he felt pretty good and refused to be kept down. He pulled his art supplies out and began painting, he invited Diane and Declan over and cooked dinner, and we went to the theater and saw no fewer than five movies.

By the sixth day he had taken his sling off, and by the tenth day he insisted on going back to work to resume at least some of his managerial duties. He wasn't ready to lift any heavy trays, but he told me he felt staying away from the restaurant any longer would put an unnecessary burden on his boss and coworkers. Without even fully discussing his intentions with me, he got up one morning, took two Advil, and said that he'd see me after his shift. I couldn't very well justify taking any more days off from the hospital to take care of Sergio if he had already returned to work, so I called Dr. Mueller and told him to expect me back in the trenches the following day.

He encouraged me to take all the time I needed, but I assured him the patient's energy level had already exceeded that of his caretaker, so I had no alternative. It would be patently embarrassing for the shooting victim to be back at work and for me to require additional days off.

My alarm went off at five thirty the next morning, but the butterflies in my stomach had prevented me from sleeping well. This would be my first day back at work with business as usual… except nothing was usual. The entire hospital now knew I was gay.

While Sergio had been hospitalized, my friends in the residency program had been incredibly supportive. They came to visit, they brought me food, and some of the braver ones even acknowledged the elephant in the room by teasing me a little. A bunch of us had been crowded around Sergio's bed when Corey, one of the other residents in my year, offered, "I pretty much had my suspicions a year ago when I accidently left my *Sports Illustrated* swimsuit edition in the call room. Zack followed me in the rotation, and when I went in the next morning to retrieve it, I noticed it hadn't been touched. No straight man with a pulse could resist at least flipping through the pages." Everyone laughed, partially at the joke, but mostly in relief that the topic was finally put out there. Ironically, I laughed the hardest.

"So, Corey, are you saying you figured out I was gay? Or that you were worried I was pulseless? Rumor has it that zombies can be excellent professional colleagues. The undead have been proven to be very reliable." The group offered a few more good-natured chuckles, so I continued. "Actually, I remember seeing your magazine there. I thought about looking at it, but I figured the pages would be so sticky I'd risk catching something by even touching it." That comment brought a more enthusiastic response, and any residual discomfort in the room dissipated completely.

On that first day back, I remembered feeling my breath quicken as I passed through the glass bridge connecting the two towers of the hospital. Again, I appreciated how the light reflected through the glass. So much had happened since I first considered how, with his artistic eye, Sergio would have enjoyed the colorful display the light projected across the carpet at that time of morning. I made my way up to the neonatal intensive care unit because Dr. Mueller had suggested I would be best utilized there. As I slapped the keypad to open the automatic door, I decided the best approach would be to begin the day like any other and to try to forego calling any attention to the event that had led up to my emergency absence.

When I went into the conference room just off the main unit, I was relieved to see Beth preparing for sign-outs. When she saw me come in, she immediately stood up and drew me into a hug. "Zack, it's so good to have you back. Dr. Mueller said you'd be in today. I've been thinking about you all day every day. I'm so glad Sergio is doing well." She looked wistful for just a second, then she broke out into her usual bright smile. "Now, so much for the pleasantries. We decided to celebrate your return by giving you a shitload of work. Sit down and fasten your seat belt. Today's roller-coaster ride is guaranteed to pull your head right through your asshole."

"Gee, thanks, Beth. While I appreciate your sentimental side, please don't attempt to sugarcoat anything for my benefit. Give me a realistic idea of how much fun I should expect to have today." I bumped her shoulder and offered a warm smile. "I'm not sure I'm too thrilled about a roller coaster being your idea of a welcome reception, but I do appreciate everything you guys did for me over the last few weeks. You've been awesome."

"Funny, Zack, that's what we've always thought about you." She returned the shoulder bump. "But don't think getting sentimental is going to succeed in making me feel merciful. When you see my sign-outs, you'll realize that in your absence, you were demoted to my lapdog."

I just smiled. I understood the depth of Beth's caring and appreciated that her jocularity was an attempt to defuse any discomfort. "Your lapdog? That's kind of kinky. Do I have to wear a collar?"

"In your dreams, my friend. In your dreams."

Beth's sign-outs were indeed long, but it was also apparent she'd done everything she could to get as much work done as possible. I was actually glad I was going to be busy. I figured as long as I kept my nose to the grindstone, there'd be fewer opportunities to have to answer any uncomfortable questions. I wasn't sure why I was so anxious. Thus far, everyone's treatment of me had been better than I would have ever thought possible.

When she had finished going over the last detail, I folded the papers up and put them in my pocket. I looked at Beth and smiled. "Might as well get going. The sooner I start, the sooner I'll be able to go pee on a hydrant. If I'm going to be your lapdog, I hope that you at least brought some biscuits."

"Don't get greedy. If you do a really good job, I might decide to forego the neuter."

"Wow, now that's what I call incentive."

She smiled and released a soft chuckle. "Consider it a get-well gift for Sergio. Tell him he owes me."

I laughed too. It seemed both strange and liberating to be joking about Sergio as if his being my partner was the most natural thing in the world. "I'm sure he'll be appreciative."

I walked out of the conference room and into the unit. It was a flurry of activity. I pulled Beth's list out of my pocket and began to determine which babies would require my immediate attention. Initially, the nurses did little to acknowledge my arrival other than to wave a greeting. Then, one by one, they slowly came over to where I was working and whispered personal welcomes. Some even hugged me and told me they had missed me, and that they were saddened to hear someone important to me had been so seriously hurt. Their sincerity made me feel like I had swallowed an elixir of pure happiness.

A few minutes before nine, my beeper went off. Ordinarily, the sound would have caused me to release a tirade of silent profanity in my own head, but I was feeling so positive about being back I picked up the nearest phone and dialed the extension without even an inkling of hostility.

Julie, the pediatric department secretary, picked up after only two rings. "Pediatric administration, Julie speaking. May I help you?"

"Hey, Julie, it's Zack. Someone there paged me."

"Oh yes, Dr. Sheldon. Dr. Franklin asked that you meet him in the main conference room next to his office."

"Okay, Julie. I'm on my way. Did he say what this is regarding? Is there a problem I should be aware of?"

"He didn't say, Dr. Sheldon. He just asked that you be there."

I hung up the phone and my stomach clenched ever so slightly. I couldn't imagine why the chairman of the department was asking to see me. Dr. Mueller had called multiple times during my absence. Had there been a big problem, I was sure he would have at least alluded to it. As I started down the hall, I became increasingly nervous. I hoped Dr. Mueller hadn't decided he'd forego burdening me with any bad news until I returned.

By the time I reached the corridor that led to the conference room, I was a cauldron of conflicting emotions. On one hand, I had broken into a cold sweat. What if Dr. Klein had been successful in his appeals and the administration had reconsidered? What if he had convinced them I had indeed been guilty of insubordination or that, because I had created such a public scene, they had determined I represented too great a liability to retain in the residency program? On the other hand, I was relatively calm. The uninterrupted time I had spent with Sergio had brought me to numerous realizations: First and foremost, I loved him, and even though there were no guarantees, I wanted to explore the possibility of building a life with him. Secondly, I had realized how exhausting living with so many secrets and so much shame had become, and there was no way I would go back. Carrying such a heavy burden had begun to eat away at the very fabric of my being, and I vowed I'd never again put myself in the same situation. I had always tried to fulfill my professional responsibilities with integrity. They could suspend me, but they couldn't dictate who I was.

As I neared the conference room door, I was surprised to hear the soft buzz of conversation interspersed with brief bursts of laugher coming from the other side. I had no idea what to expect. With an almost paralyzing degree of trepidation, I slowly pulled the door open and was shocked to see the majority of my colleagues mingling around the center table, which was covered with fresh croissants, a fruit plate, bagels, deli meats, juice, and a large percolator filled with coffee.

Dr. Franklin stood in the center of the room, flanked by both Dr. Mueller and Dr. Herbert. There were a few other senior physicians in the room as well as all the other interns and residents. Diane and Beth stood close to Dr. Mueller, smiling like Cheshire cats.

When I walked through the door, the room fell briefly silent, until Dr. Franklin's booming voice echoed off the walls. "Here's the guest of honor now."

I was immediately struck speechless and my cheeks burned crimson. For a brief instant, it felt as if my feet had been glued to the carpet, but then I slowly managed to kind of stumble awkwardly toward the center of the room.

Dr. Franklin draped in arm around my shoulder and gave it a brief squeeze. "Zack, you know I like nothing more than to wallow in the rapturous attention of a captive audience, but in this instance I won't belabor the point. We just wanted to welcome you back, to acknowledge that we appreciate your contributions to the program, and to emphasize that we regret if you were ever made to feel discriminated against by any personnel in this hospital. Though I concede to taking great liberties in paraphrasing the words of the famous civil rights leader Dr. Martin Luther King Junior, our intent is to judge people by the content of their character, not by either the color of their skin or whom they choose to love. Thank you for being an example of great character."

Those gathered in the room broke into applause, and I was immediately drawn into Diane and Beth's congratulatory embrace. Dr.

Mueller slapped me on the back and said with an exuberant smile, "Zack, you can wipe that terrified expression off your face. It's all good."

It was only then that I realized I had probably been holding my breath. A huge sigh of relief escaped my lips, and I broke out into an enormous grin. "You guys are too much. Thank you so much. This is unbelievable. I wasn't expecting anything. In fact, I was hoping to just sneak back into the rhythm of work as unobtrusively as possible."

Diane laughed. "Please, Zack! Obtrusive is your middle name. Your parents intended to call you 'pain in the ass,' but it wouldn't fit on the birth certificate."

Her joking immediately relieved my discomfort, and everyone, including Dr. Franklin, shared a good laugh. He turned to Diane to reply, but didn't even attempt to maintain a serious tone when he said, "Fortunately, that's a side of his character I haven't had to endure seeing."

Dr. Herbert crossed in front of me and took my hand in hers. "I believe I remember telling you bad things happen to wonderful people. I'm sorry if you ever found the working environment here to be less than hospitable, and I'm also sorry that your partner was the victim of such a vicious attack." Her facial expression warmed. "I am delighted, however, to hear he's expected to make a full recovery and that the tragedy has resulted in you expanding your circle of support. It would be a privilege for me to be included in it." She squeezed my hand tighter. "Welcome back, Zack. It's good to have you."

I was determined not to get emotional. "Thanks, Dr. H. You've already been more of a support to me than you'll ever know."

MY REMINISCING was interrupted when Leo saw Sergio come out the back door and walk up behind me. Certain Sergio had joined us specifically to engage in doggie play, Leo came running from the other side of the yard, lowered his head, and tried to run between us.

Sergio grabbed on to my shoulders in an attempt to guard us from being knocked over by a canine locomotive. Undeterred, Leo circled back and forth between our legs and continued head-butting us until we both dropped to our knees, tackled him, and began a four-fisted belly rub. He was immediately reduced to a contented mound of pliable fur and drool.

Sergio leaned over Leo and gave me a kiss on the cheek. "Everything inside is pretty much done. You'd better go shower and get dressed. I told your parents we'd eat around six. I think these late nights have begun to wear your dad down. They're not used to going to bed after midnight. He asked if we could eat a little earlier tonight."

I laughed. Mom and Dad had flown down to spend a long weekend with us. Their forays into the big city were so infrequent we tried to take advantage of every free minute. On the day they arrived, we picked them up at the airport with a picnic basket full of food and wine and drove directly to the Hollywood Bowl. They'd been mesmerized by the performance. The next day we were up early to tour the Huntington Gardens, had a light lunch in Pasadena, and then rested just briefly before we headed to downtown LA, where we had a sumptuous dinner before going to see *Phantom of the Opera* at the Ahmanson Theater.

We'd decided to make today a little more low-key. We had gotten up early and the four of us had taken Leo for a hike in Griffith Park, then we ate breakfast at a little café in Los Feliz. Though it made for a long morning, we had begun our hike from our front door. Sergio and I were currently renting a charming two-bedroom bungalow in Silver Lake. We had moved into it a year and a half before, and finding it had felt like we'd won the lottery. It had everything we were looking for: two bedrooms, two baths, a spacious kitchen, and a yard. We had barely finished unloading boxes before we initiated our quest to find a dog.

I completed my residency two months after Sergio's attack. In the time we spent together during his recovery, we resolutely decided to take our relationship to the next level and move in together. After he had been back to work for a few weeks and by every indication seemed to be nearing full recovery, I took my next full weekend off to fly up to talk to my parents. In the weeks before I made the trip, I had decided I was no longer willing to hide who I was from them. I was tempted to call them many times when Sergio lay in the hospital, but I didn't want to have the conversation with them over the phone. I was committed to telling them, but wanted to do so in person. Additionally, I was adamant that before I moved in with Sergio, everyone who participated in my life would understand his significance in my life.

I had only given my parents a day's notice that I would be flying up for the weekend. They were excited to see me but seemed apprehensive about what might have motivated me to visit them on such short notice and for only a single night's stay. I declined their offer to pick me up at the airport and instead opted to rent a car. Though I was optimistic our conversation would go well, in the unlikely event it went south, I didn't want to be dependent on them for a ride back to the airport. The distance between the airport and the small town of Echo was two hours. Having my own car would guarantee being able to escape at the time of my choosing should there be any unpleasantness.

When I pulled up in front of their house, they were out the front door before I had even set the parking brake. Their German shepherd was close at their heels, bounding over to greet me. Little wonder I was such a dog person. When I was growing up, we'd always had at least two. My parents both pulled me into a warm embrace and pounded me exuberantly on the back. Perhaps, when I had given them such short notice about my intention to visit, they expected I might show up disfigured.

Dad, in particular, had difficulty containing his curiosity, and as he reached over to take my bag, he asked, "So, to what do we owe this surprise visit?"

I was resolute that I was going to tell them and was supremely confident they'd take the news well, but I'd nonetheless had had stomach cramps from the minute I boarded the plane. Nervousness always seemed to localize to my gut. I was suddenly sorry Sergio hadn't come with me. He had wanted to, but I'd insisted it was something I needed to do alone. Now I was sorry he wasn't there for moral support.

Though I had rehearsed the speech a million times in my head, I wanted to feel more composed before I delivered it, so I pasted an unassuming smile on my face and confidently answered I had simply missed being able to come home.

Both of them searched my eyes for any evidence of deception and finding nothing obvious, let a smile of relief cross their expressions. They each wrapped an arm protectively around my shoulders and escorted me through the front door of the house I had grown up in. As usual, they were talking over each other in an attempt to bring me up to date on everything that had happened in the neighborhood. The vast majority of Echo happenings were less than newsworthy.

Mom had made lunch for us, so we sat down to sandwiches and hot homemade soup. The conversation was easy, and they related to me what my three other brothers and been up to. Ever the devoted parents, they were both proud of all of us and intermittently frustrated by what they perceived as having been the poorly thought-out decisions each of us had independently made on occasion.

As lunch was beginning to wind down, Mom looked at me inquisitively, "So, tell us about you. You'll be finishing up with your residency in little more than six weeks. Last time we spoke, you were entertaining a number of different job opportunities. Have you narrowed down your choices?"

"Actually, I think I have. I don't think I want to go directly into private practice, so I'm leaning toward working as a hospitalist at the children's hospital in Hollywood."

As he scooped another ladle of soup into his bowl, Dad inquired, "What's a hospitalist? I'm not familiar with that term."

"Rather than working in a clinic, a pediatric hospitalist only takes care of children who are sick enough to require hospitalization. That's exclusively what they do. Many community pediatricians are well adept at diagnosing aliments, but because they've been out of the trenches for so long, they feel less competent managing very sick kids in the hospital. That will be my job. When one of their patients becomes severely ill, they call whichever one of the doctors on my team is on duty, and we'll manage them in the hospital. Any kid who gets admitted will be taken care of by one of us. We'll either get patients by referral from outside pediatricians or from the emergency room." I unconsciously let a smile creep across my face. "I figure it's the perfect job for me. For the past three years, I've pretty much only taken care of really sick kids. I'm fairly good at it, the pay is excellent, and though we work twenty-four-hour shifts, I'll have way more time off than I've been getting. For the time being, it sounds like a win-win."

My mom reached across the table and squeezed my hand. "Congratulations, honey. It sounds like a wonderful opportunity, and they'll be lucky to have you."

Dad echoed her sentiments. "That's my boy. I knew people would be lining up to have you come work for them." Because he was sitting at the head of the table, I was within easy reach for him to slap me on the shoulder. "Well done, Zack. Well done indeed."

They asked me a few more questions about what I expected from my new job and how I anticipated finishing my training program. Then my mom set her spoon down, as if she'd come to a sudden realization. "Aren't your roommates finishing their training as well? Are all you guys going to continue living in the same place? Or are you going to have to look for new roommates?"

I slowly took another bite of my sandwich, then shrugged. "No, I've decided to move out."

They both looked at me hesitantly. My dad raised an eyebrow, and I was aware he was making a concerted effort not to look too suspicious. He probably assumed I had come home to ask for money to help defray the cost of moving. "Have you already found a place? Do you intend to relocate closer to your new job? You have to consider that even with a respectable paycheck, shouldering the expenses of your own place might end up being a little steep. Don't forget to budget money to pay off your student loans."

I couldn't help but smile a little. My dad was nothing if not predictable. Always looking at the practical side of things.

I took a deep breath and found myself staring down at my plate. "Not to worry, Dad. I'm actually going to move in with someone. It will be temporary, though. Once I'm in the swing of my new job, we want to find a place with a yard so we can get a dog."

I cast a quick glance up to observe their expressions. They seemed simultaneously relieved and confused. Mom was the first to chime in. "That's wonderful, Zack. It seems that you've already given this a lot of thought." She smiled as she again picked up her spoon. "You know, having a dog is a big responsibility. How will you manage if you're working twenty-four-hour shifts?"

I was so enthusiastic about the prospect of getting a dog I temporarily forgot my discomfort. "Sergio and I will share taking care of it. He's never had a dog and can't wait to get one."

They both again fell silent. My dad looked at me inquisitively, then chose his words carefully. I was pretty sure he had no idea where this conversation was going. "Sergio? That's a name we haven't heard before. Who is Sergio?"

Despite my best intentions, my lip began to quiver slightly. "Before I tell you who Sergio is, there's something else we need to discuss."

Now the silence became tomblike. Both of them sat motionless and stared at me expectantly. This wasn't how I had rehearsed this exchange in my head at all. My intention had been to somehow just casually work the topic into the conversation. Oddly enough, though, there never seemed to be an appropriate opportunity to say, "Hey, by the way, I'm gay. Please pass the ketchup." The tension in the room suddenly seemed thick.

Mom, sensing my anxiety, was the first to speak up. "What do you want to tell us, Zack? Are you in some kind of trouble?" Then, seeming to realize her question might have sounded more accusatory than she intended, she immediately rephrased it. "I mean, are you experiencing any kind of trouble?"

For what I'm sure was only a matter of seconds, time seemed to suddenly stand still. I couldn't yet bring myself to look at them directly. I knew the words I had been wanting to say were right on the tip of my tongue, but in that moment, it was impossible to say them. My lifelong fear of disappointing my mom and dad overwhelmed my entire thought process. I felt my eyes become glassy.

Again, Mom reached across the table and gently touched my hand. "Zack?"

Suddenly, images of Sergio lying in the hospital bed flooded my mind, and the memory of having been so close to losing him gave me sufficient courage to allow my mouth to start moving. "I need to tell you—" I lifted my chin to look both of them in the eye. I felt my determination finally gaining some momentum. "I need to tell you something that I've wanted to share with you for a long time." My voice cracked ever so slightly. "I need to tell you that I'm gay."

I couldn't hold their eyes anymore, but now that I had begun I wanted to get as much out as possible. "I've probably known for as long as I can remember. For most of my life, it was a secret that almost crushed me. Until recent years, it was something I was so ashamed of, I couldn't even accept myself. Then, as I slowly began to understand who I really was, I was terrified other people wouldn't accept me." I slowly brought my face back up. "But mostly, I was afraid that, as your son, I would be a disappointment to the two of you."

The words hadn't poured out of me quickly, but I had probably said all of them without taking a breath. When I finished, it felt like all the air in the room had been sucked out, and even with the adrenaline pounding through my veins, I felt exhausted.

Much to my surprise, Dad was the first one out of his chair, and he pulled me into a tight embrace. His words were choked with emotion. "Zack. You're our son. We love you. We could never be ashamed of who you are. We have always been proud of who you are and always will be. If you're gay, then we love our gay son. It's that simple. The only thing that saddens me is that you for even a single moment ever doubted that."

Mom was close to follow. She circled around the table, came over to my other side, and also threw her arms around me. Her tears flowed freely. "Your father is right, Zack. This is all so silly. You had us so worried. There's no shame in being gay. We love you for who you are. Knowing you're gay simply means we now know a little bit more about who our son is. I can't tell you how sorry we are if you felt for even one minute that we did something to contribute to your struggle."

It was no longer fear that imprisoned my voice—it was relief coupled with overwhelming emotion. Their unequivocal acceptance of me made me feel like my very soul had been liberated after a lifetime of being held captive. They had shown no hesitancy, and there had been no second-guessing, no plea for clarification. There was just acceptance.

Ironically, as I sat there with tears streaming down my face, I was struck with another emotion I'd never expected. Certainly I was relieved to finally feel truly proud of myself, but I was surprised to also feel so proud of my parents. Their acceptance of me proved to be unconditional, and I appreciated that in that moment, it contradicted all the social and religious indoctrination they had grown up with. They were the product of a generation that had zero tolerance for homosexuality. Accepting me meant making a conscious decision to choose their son over the traditional beliefs they had been raised with. My happiness soared.

When the intensity surrounding my proclamation began to ebb, we sat around the table and continued to talk. They had lots of questions about how my secret had impacted my life and wanted to know more details about who I really was. They were confused that I had dated girls in high school and I had seemed genuinely happy. In fact, they were saddened to learn how much energy I had expended in trying to give the impression of being normal.

After more than an hour of better clarifying the events of my life to them, my dad looked at me thoughtfully and said, "It sounds as if it's time for us to hear a little more about this Sergio. He's apparently someone who makes you happy."

And just like that, the tears returned. I told them about how we had met, how our relationship had grown, how he had been attacked, and how his hospitalization had resulted in my coming out to the entire hospital.

They nodded encouragingly, asked more about who he was, grieved that he had been so seriously injured, and were saddened that they hadn't been given the opportunity to support me through such a difficult ordeal.

By the conclusion of lunch, there had been a lot more hugging, and Mom and Dad had begun making plans to come down and visit the week after I finished residency. They were eager to meet Sergio, and Mom even insisted I call him that very minute so they could introduce themselves, even if only over the phone.

Three years later, here we stood. Leo was playing at our feet, and my mom and dad were in our guest room resting up before dinner. They had accepted Sergio as another son, and my dad frequently joked that Sergio would be getting a greater share of the inheritance than I would. My job was going well, and between the two of us, we had saved up enough money for a down payment on a home.

I leaned into Sergio with my back against his chest and felt him lock his arms around me. He kissed the back of my head and then let his chin drop to my shoulder.

"Why are you so quiet all of a sudden?"

"I was just thinking," I said.

"Yeah?" he said as he rubbed his bristly cheek against my neck. "About what?"

"About how lucky I am. Four years ago, part of me felt suffocated by my own life. Now here I am. Open, out, and proud. I used to feel that when I went to work in the morning and put on my white coat, I was locking myself into a closet. I don't feel that way anymore. I'm happy. Happier than I ever thought possible."

I pivoted in Sergio's arms so I could return his embrace. "I love you, Sergio." I kissed him warmly on the cheek. "Now let's go eat!"

JAKE WELLS was born a dreamer. He dreamed of distant lands, of trying to make a difference in people's lives, of falling in love, of writing a book, and of all things chocolate. Imagine how fortunate he feels to have seen most of his dreams come true. He's adventured through the far corners of the world, has a successful career practicing medicine, and shares his life with an amazing partner. Though eating chocolate continues to play a prominent role in his dreams, the icing on the cake has been writing about falling in love in a world where equality is only beginning to be embraced.

When he's not playing doctor, Jake can usually be found traipsing local hiking trails with his dogs near his West Coast home, in the kitchen trying to replicate some sumptuous dish he saw on one of the cooking channels, or sipping a glass of fine red wine with his friends.

You can contact Jake at jakezacharywells@gmail.com or via Facebook at https://www.facebook.com/jake.wells.16568.

ISLE OF WISHES

SUE BROWN

Also from DREAMSPINNER PRESS

http://www.dreamspinnerpress.com

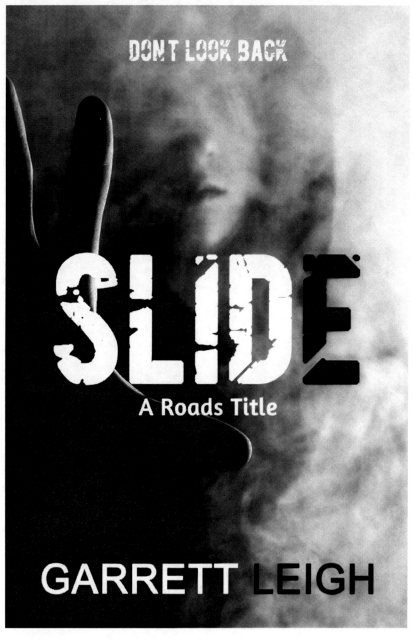

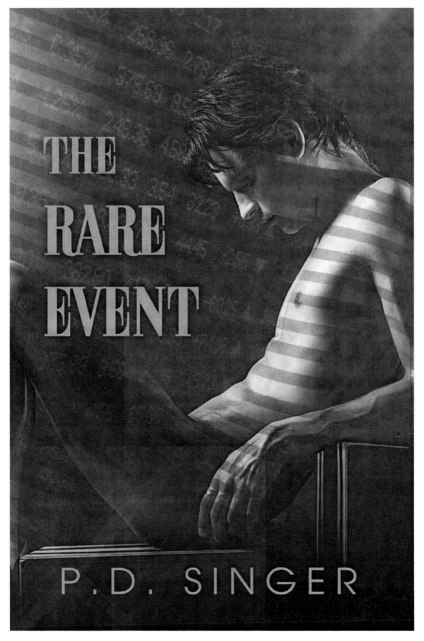

THE
RARE
EVENT

P.D. SINGER

Romance from DREAMSPINNER PRESS

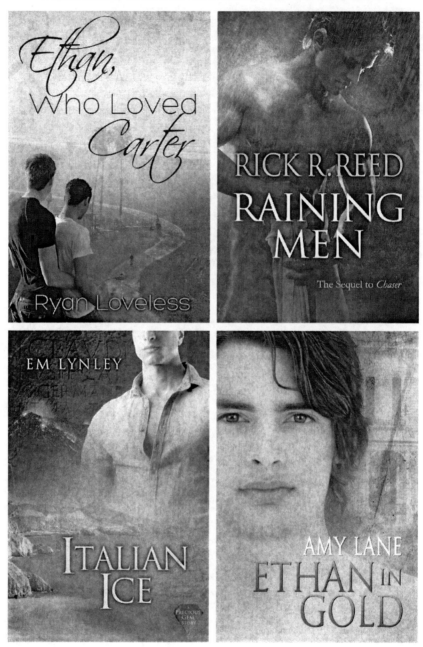

Romance from DREAMSPINNER PRESS

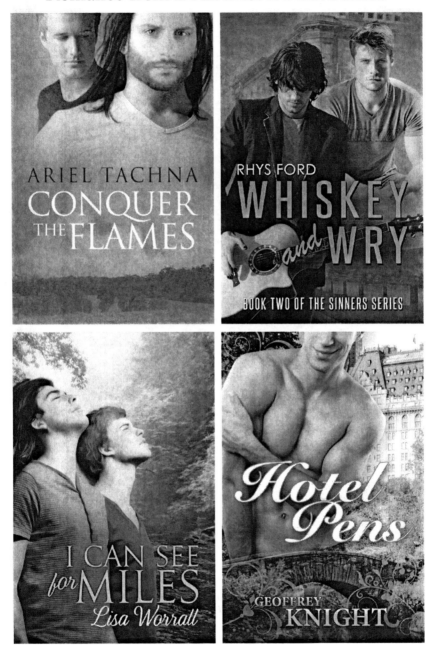

http://www.dreamspinnerpress.com

CPSIA information can be obtained at www.ICGtesting.com
Printed in the USA
LVOW12s0703040514

384258LV00007B/18/P

9 781627 982566